D0429175

SHORT STORIES
FROM
THE
NEW YORKER

19 40

SIMON AND SCHUSTER · NEW YORK

ALL RIGHTS RESERVED
INCLUDING THE RIGHT OF REPRODUCTION
IN WHOLE OR IN PART IN ANY FORM
COPYRIGHT, 1940, BY F-R PUBLISHING CORPORATION
PUBLISHED BY SIMON AND SCHUSTER, INC.
ROCKEFELLER CENTER, 1230 SIXTH AVENUE
NEW YORK, N. Y.

The editors and publishers of this collection are grateful to The Viking Press, Inc., for permission to reprint two stories from *Here Lies,* by Dorothy Parker (copyright 1930, 1933, and 1939 by Dorothy Parker), and to Messrs. Charles Scribner's Sons for permission to reprint "Only the Dead Know Brooklyn," by Thomas Wolfe (copyright 1935), and two stories from "The Earliest Dreams," by Nancy Hale (copyright 1936).

PRINTED AND BOUND IN THE UNITED STATES OF AMERICA
BY THE HADDON CRAFTSMEN, INC., CAMDEN, N. J.

CONTENTS

v

FOREWORD

The sixty-eight stories in this collection were chosen from those appearing in The New Yorker *during its first fifteen and a half years of publication—February 1925, to September, 1940. In making the selection, it was often difficult to decide where fiction began and fact left off. For the purposes of this anthology, reminiscence was ruled out—even the heightened and often fictionalized reminiscence of the Clarence Day "Father" stories, of Thurber's "My Life and Hard Times," of Joseph Mitchell's Black Ankle County stories, of Bemelmans, Mencken, and Ruth McKenney— together with the personal sorrows of day-by-day life as reported by many other writers. Parable, prophecy, fable, fantasy, satire, burlesque, parody, nonsense tales, and, with a few exceptions, stories from series were also omitted. The choice made will undoubtedly not wholly please either the writers, the public, or the individual editors of* The New Yorker, *all of whom will complain that favorites are missing. Occasionally a much reprinted story was dropped in favor of one less well-known by the same author, and some first-rate stories were not used because of duplication of theme or because, in the autumn of 1940, they seemed dated.*

THE GIRLS IN THEIR SUMMER DRESSES

❧

IRWIN SHAW

FIFTH AVENUE was shining in the sun when they left the Brevoort. The sun was warm, even though it was February, and everything looked like Sunday morning—the buses and the well-dressed people walking slowly in couples and the quiet buildings with the windows closed.

Michael held Frances' arm tightly as they walked toward Washington Square in the sunlight. They walked lightly, almost smiling, because they had slept late and had a good breakfast and it was Sunday. Michael unbuttoned his coat and let it flap around him in the mild wind.

"Look out," Frances said as they crossed Eighth Street. "You'll break your neck."

Michael laughed and Frances laughed with him.

"She's not so pretty," Frances said. "Anyway, not pretty enough to take a chance of breaking your neck."

Michael laughed again. "How did you know I was looking at her?"

Frances cocked her head to one side and smiled at her husband under the brim of her hat. "Mike, darling," she said.

"O.K.," he said. "Excuse me."

Frances patted his arm lightly and pulled him along a little faster toward Washington Square. "Let's not see anybody all day," she said. "Let's just hang around with each other. You and me. We're always up to our neck in people, drinking their Scotch or drinking our Scotch; we only see each other in bed. I want to go out with my husband all day long. I want him to talk only to me and listen only to me."

"What's to stop us?" Michael asked.

"The Stevensons. They want us to drop by around one o'clock and they'll drive us into the country."

"The cunning Stevensons," Mike said. "Transparent. They can whistle. They can go driving in the country by themselves."

"Is it a date?"

"It's a date."

Frances leaned over and kissed him on the tip of the ear.

"Darling," Michael said, "this is Fifth Avenue."

"Let me arrange a program," Frances said. "A planned Sunday in New York for a young couple with money to throw away."

"Go easy."

"First let's go to the Metropolitan Museum of Art," Frances suggested, because Michael had said during the week he wanted to go. "I haven't been there in three years and there're at least ten pictures I want to see again. Then we can take the bus down to Radio City and watch them skate. And later we'll go down to Cavanagh's and get a steak as big as a blacksmith's apron, with a bottle of wine, and after that there's a French picture at the Filmarte that everybody says—say, are you listening to me?"

"Sure," he said. He took his eyes off the hatless girl with the dark hair, cut dancer-style like a helmet, who was walking past him.

"That's the program for the day," Frances said flatly. "Or maybe you'd just rather walk up and down Fifth Avenue."

"No," Michael said. "Not at all."

"You always look at other women," Frances said. "Everywhere. Every damned place we go."

"Now, darling," Michael said, "I look at everything. God gave me eyes and I look at women and men and subway excavations and moving pictures and the little flowers of the field. I casually inspect the universe."

"You ought to see the look in your eye," Frances said, "as you casually inspect the universe on Fifth Avenue."

"I'm a happily married man." Michael pressed her elbow tenderly. "Example for the whole twentieth century—Mr. and Mrs. Mike Loomis. Hey, let's have a drink," he said, stopping.

"We just had breakfast."

"Now listen, darling," Mike said, choosing his words with care, "it's a nice day and we both felt good and there's no reason why we have to break it up. Let's have a nice Sunday."

"All right. I don't know why I started this. Let's drop it. Let's have a good time."

They joined hands consciously and walked without talking among the baby carriages and the old Italian men in their Sunday clothes and the young women with Scotties in Washington Square Park.

"At least once a year everyone should go to the Metropolitan Museum of Art," Frances said after a while, her tone a good imitation of the tone she had used at breakfast and at the beginning of their walk. "And it's nice on Sunday. There're a lot of people looking at the pictures and you get the feeling maybe Art isn't on the decline in New York City, after all—"

"I want to tell you something," Michael said very seriously. "I have not touched another woman. Not once. In all the five years."

"All right," Frances said.

"You believe that, don't you?"

"All right."

They walked between the crowded benches, under the scrubby city-park trees.

"I try not to notice it," Frances said, "but I feel rotten inside, in my stomach, when we pass a woman and you look at her and I see that look in your eye and that's the way you looked at me the first time. In Alice Maxwell's house. Standing there in the living room, next to the radio, with a green hat on and all those people."

"I remember the hat," Michael said.

"The same look," Frances said. "And it makes me feel bad. It makes me feel terrible."

"Sh-h-h, please, darling, sh-h-h."

"I think I would like a drink now," Frances said.

They walked over to a bar on Eighth Street, not saying anything, Michael automatically helping her over curbstones and guiding her past automobiles. They sat near a window in the bar and the sun streamed in and there was a small, cheerful fire in the fireplace. A little Japanese waiter came over and put down some pretzels and smiled happily at them.

"What do you order after breakfast?" Michael asked.

"Brandy, I suppose," Frances said.

"Courvoisier," Michael told the waiter. "Two Courvoisiers."

The waiter came with the glasses and they sat drinking the brandy in the sunlight. Michael finished half his and drank a little water.

"I look at women," he said. "Correct. I don't say it's wrong or right. I look at them. If I pass them on the street and I don't look at them, I'm fooling you, I'm fooling myself."

"You look at them as though you want them," Frances said, playing with her brandy glass. "Every one of them."

"In a way," Michael said, speaking softly and not to his wife, "in a way that's true. I don't do anything about it, but it's true."

"I know it. That's why I feel bad."

"Another brandy," Michael called. "Waiter, two more brandies."

He sighed and closed his eyes and rubbed them gently with his fingertips. "I love the way women look. One of the things I like best about New York is the battalions of women. When I first came to New York from Ohio that was the first thing I noticed, the million wonderful women, all over the city. I walked around with my heart in my throat."

"A kid," Frances said. "That's a kid's feeling."

"Guess again," Michael said. "Guess again. I'm older now, I'm a man getting near middle age, putting on a little fat and I still love to walk along Fifth Avenue at three o'clock on the east side of the street between Fiftieth and Fifty-seventh Streets. They're all out then, shopping, in their furs and their crazy hats, everything all concentrated from all over the world into seven blocks— the best furs, the best clothes, the handsomest women, out to spend money and feeling good about it."

The Japanese waiter put the two drinks down, smiling with great happiness.

"Everything is all right?" he asked.

"Everything is wonderful," Michael said.

"If it's just a couple of fur coats," Frances said, "and forty-five-dollar hats—"

"It's not the fur coats. Or the hats. That's just the scenery for that particular kind of woman. Understand," he said, "you don't have to listen to this."

"I want to listen."

"I like the girls in the offices. Neat, with their eyeglasses, smart, chipper, knowing what everything is about. I like the girls on Forty-fourth Street at lunchtime, the actresses, all dressed up on nothing a week. I like the salesgirls in the stores, paying attention to you first because you're a man, leaving lady customers waiting. I got all this stuff accumulated in me because I've been thinking about it for ten years and now you've asked for it and here it is."

"Go ahead," Frances said.

"When I think of New York City, I think of all the girls on parade in the city. I don't know whether it's something special with me or whether every man in the city walks around with the same feeling inside him, but I feel as though I'm at a picnic in this city. I like to sit near the women in the theatres, the famous beauties who've taken six hours to get ready and look it. And the young girls at the football games, with the red cheeks, and when the warm weather comes, the girls in their summer dresses." He finished his drink. "That's the story."

Frances finished her drink and swallowed two or three times extra. "You say you love me?"

"I love you."

"I'm pretty, too," Frances said. "As pretty as any of them."

"You're beautiful," Michael said.

"I'm good for you," Frances said, pleading. "I've made a good wife, a good housekeeper, a good friend. I'd do any damn thing for you."

"I know," Michael said. He put his hand out and grasped hers.

"You'd like to be free to—" Frances said.

"Sh-h-h."

"Tell the truth." She took her hand away from under his.

Michael flicked the edge of his glass with his finger. "O.K.," he said gently. "Sometimes I feel I would like to be free."

"Well," Frances said, "any time you say."

"Don't be foolish." Michael swung his chair around to her side of the table and patted her thigh.

She began to cry silently into her handkerchief, bent over just enough so that nobody else in the bar would notice. "Someday," she said, crying, "you're going to make a move."

Michael didn't say anything. He sat watching the bartender slowly peel a lemon.

"Aren't you?" Frances asked harshly. "Come on, tell me. Talk. Aren't you?"

"Maybe," Michael said. He moved his chair back again. "How the hell do I know?"

"You know," Frances persisted. "Don't you know?"

"Yes," Michael said after a while, "I know."

Frances stopped crying then. Two or three snuffles into the handkerchief and she put it away and her face didn't tell anything to anybody. "At least do me one favor," she said.

"Sure."

"Stop talking about how pretty this woman is or that one. Nice eyes, nice breasts, a pretty figure, good voice." She mimicked his voice. "Keep it to yourself. I'm not interested."

Michael waved to the waiter. "I'll keep it to myself," he said.

Frances flicked the corners of her eyes. "Another brandy," she told the waiter.

"Two," Michael said.

"Yes, Ma'am, yes, sir," said the waiter, backing away.

Frances regarded Michael coolly across the table. "Do you want me to call the Stevensons?" she asked. "It'll be nice in the country."

"Sure," Michael said. "Call them."

She got up from the table and walked across the room toward the telephone. Michael watched her walk, thinking what a pretty girl, what nice legs.

OVER THE RIVER AND THROUGH THE WOOD

❧

John O'Hara

MR. WINFIELD'S hat and coat and bag were in the hall of his flat, and when the man downstairs phoned to tell him the car was waiting, he was all ready. He went downstairs and said hello to Robert, the giant Negro chauffeur, and handed Robert the bag, and followed him out to the car. For the first time he knew that he and his granddaughter were not to make the trip alone, for there were two girls with Sheila, and she introduced them: "Grandfather, I'd like to have you meet my friends. This is Helen Wales, and this is Kay Farnsworth. My grandfather, Mr. Winfield." The names meant nothing to Mr. Winfield. What did mean something was that he was going to have to sit on the strapontin, or else sit outside with Robert, which was no good. Not that Robert wasn't all right, as chauffeurs go, but Robert was wearing a raccoon coat, and Mr. Winfield had no raccoon coat. So it was sit outside and freeze, or sit on the little seat inside.

Apparently it made no difference to Sheila. He got inside, and when he closed the door behind him, she said, "I wonder what's keeping Robert?"

"He's strapping my bag on that thing in the back," said Mr. Winfield. Sheila obviously was not pleased by the delay, but in a minute or two they got under way, and Mr. Winfield rather admired the way Sheila carried on her conversation with her two friends and at the same time routed and rerouted Robert so that they were out of the city in no time. To Mr. Winfield it was pleasant and a little like old times to have the direction and the driving done for you. Not that he ever drove himself any more, but when he hired a car, he always had to tell the driver just where to turn and where to go straight. Sheila knew.

9

The girls were of an age, and the people they talked about were referred to by first names only. Ted, Bob, Gwen, Jean, Mary, Liz. Listening with some care, Mr. Winfield discovered that school acquaintances and boys whom they knew slightly were mentioned by their last names.

Sitting where he was, he could not watch the girls' faces, but he formed his opinions of the Misses Wales and Farnsworth. Miss Wales supplied every other word when Sheila was talking. She was smallest of the three girls, and the peppy kind. Miss Farnsworth looked out of the window most of the time, and said hardly anything. Mr. Winfield could see more of her face, and he found himself asking, "I wonder if that child really likes anybody." Well, that was one way to be. Make the world show *you*. You could get away with it, too, if you were as attractive as Miss Farnsworth. The miles streamed by and the weather got colder, and Mr. Winfield listened and soon understood that he was not expected to contribute to the conversation.

"We stop here," said Sheila. It was Danbury, and they came to a halt in front of the old hotel. "Wouldn't you like to stop here, Grandfather?" He understood then that his daughter had told Sheila to stop here; obediently and with no dignity he got out. When he returned to the car, the three girls were finishing their cigarettes, and as he climbed back in the car, he noticed how Miss Farnsworth had been looking at him and continued to look at him, almost as though she were making a point of not helping him—although he wanted no help. He wasn't really an *old* man, an *old man*. Sixty-five.

The interior of the car was filled with cigarette smoke, and Miss Farnsworth asked Mr. Winfield if he'd mind opening a window. He opened it. Then Sheila said one window didn't make any difference; open both windows, just long enough to let the smoke get out. "My! That air feels good," said Miss Wales. Then: "But what about you, Mr. Winfield? You're in a terrible draught there." He replied, for the first use of his voice thus far, that he did not mind. And at that moment the girls thought they saw a car belonging to a boy they knew, and they were in Sheffield, just over the Massachusetts line, before Miss Farnsworth realized that the windows were open and creating a terrible draught. She realized it when the robe slipped off her leg, and she asked Mr. Winfield if he would mind closing the window. But he was unable to get the crank started; his hands were so cold there was no strength in them. "We'll be there soon," said Sheila. Nevertheless, she closed the windows, not even acknowledging Mr. Winfield's shamed apologies.

He had to be first out of the car when they arrived at the house in Lenox, and it was then that he regretted having chosen the strapontin. He started to get out of the car, but when his feet touched the ground, the hard-packed frozen cinders of the driveway flew up at him. His knees had no strength in them, and he stayed there on the ground for a second or two, trying to smile it off. Helpful Robert—almost too helpful; Mr. Winfield wasn't that old—jumped out of the car and put his hands in Mr. Winfield's armpits. The girls were frightened, but it seemed to Mr. Winfield that they kept looking toward the library window, as though they were afraid Sheila's mother would be there and blaming them for his fall. If they only knew . . .

"You go on in, Grandfather, if you're sure you're all right," said Sheila. "I have to tell Robert about the bags."

"I'm all right," said Mr. Winfield. He went in, and hung up his coat and hat in the clothes closet under the stairs. A telephone was there, and in front of the telephone a yellow card of numbers frequently called. Mr. Winfield recognized only a few of the names, but he guessed there was an altogether different crowd of people coming up here these days. Fifteen years make a difference, even in a place like Lenox. Yes, it was fifteen years since he had been up here in the summertime. These trips, these annual trips for Thanksgiving, you couldn't tell anything about the character of the place from these trips. You never saw anybody but your own family and, like today, their guests.

He went out to the darkened hall and Ula, the maid, jumped in fright. "Ugh. Oh. It's you, Mr. Winfield. You like to scare me."

"Hello, Ula. Glad to see you're still holding the fort. Where's Mrs. Day?"

"Upstairs, I think . . . Here she is now," said Ula.

His daughter came down the steps; her hand on the banister was all he could see at first. "Is that you, Father? I thought I heard the car."

"Hello, Mary," he said. At the foot of the stairs they went through the travesty of a kiss that both knew so well. He leaned forward so that his head was above her shoulder. To Ula, a good Catholic, it must have looked like the kiss of peace. *"Pax tibi,"* Mr. Winfield felt like saying, but he said, "Where have you—"

"Father! You're freezing!" Mrs. Day tried very hard to keep the vexation out of her tone.

"It was a cold ride," he said. "This time of year. We had snow flurries between Danbury and Sheffield, but the girls enjoyed it."

"You go right upstairs and have a bath, and I'll send up—what would you like? Tea? Chocolate? Coffee?"

He was amused. The obvious thing would be to offer him a drink, and it was so apparent that she was talking fast to avoid that. "I think cocoa would be fine, but you'd better have a real drink for Sheila and her friends."

"Now why do you take that tone, Father? You could have a drink if you wanted it, but you're on the wagon, aren't you?"

"Still on it. Up there with the driver."

"Well, and besides, liquor doesn't warm you up the same way something hot does. I'll send up some chocolate. I've put you in your old room, of course. You'll have to share the bathroom with one of Sheila's friends, but that's the best I could do. Sheila wasn't even sure she was coming till the very last minute."

"I'll be all right. It sounds like—I didn't bring evening clothes."

"We're not dressing."

He went upstairs. His room, the room itself, was just about the same; but the furniture was rearranged, his favorite chair not where he liked it best, but it was a good house; you could tell it was being lived in, *this year,* today, tomorrow. Little touches, ashtrays, flowers. It seemed young and white, cool with a warm breath, comfortable—and absolutely strange to him and, more especially, he to it. Whatever of the past this house had held, it was gone now. He sat in the chair and lit a cigarette. In a wave, in a lump, in a gust, the old thoughts came to him. Most of the year they were in the back of his mind, but up here Mr. Winfield held a sort of annual review of far-off, but never-out-of-sight regrets. This house, it used to be his until Mary's husband bought it. A good price, and in 1921 he certainly needed the money. He needed everything, and today he had an income from the money he got for this house, and that was about all. He remembered the day Mary's husband came to him and said, "Mr. Winfield, I hate to have to be the one to do this, but Mary—Mary doesn't—well, she thinks you weren't very nice to Mrs. Winfield. I don't know anything about it myself, of course, but that's what Mary thinks. I expected, naturally, I thought you'd come and live with us now that Mrs. Winfield has died, but—well, the point is, I know you've lost a lot of money, and also I happen to know about Mrs. Winfield's will. So I'm prepared to make you a pretty good offer, strictly legitimate based on current values, for the house in Lenox. I'll pay the delinquent taxes myself and give you a hundred and fifty thousand dollars for the house and grounds. That ought to be enough to pay off your debts and give you a fairly decent income. And, uh, I happen to have a friend who knows Mr. Harding quite well. Fact, he sees the President informally one night a week, and I know he'd be only too glad, if you were interested . . ."

He remembered that had tempted him. Harding might have fixed it so he could go to London, where Enid Walter was. But even then it was too late. Enid had gone back to London because he didn't have the guts to divorce his wife, and the reason he wouldn't divorce his wife was that he wanted to "protect" Mary, and Mary's standing, and Mary's husband's standing, and Mary's little daughter's standing; and now he was "protecting" them all over again, by selling his house so that he would not become a family charge—protecting the very same people from the embarrassment of a poor relation. "You can have the house," he told Day. "It's worth that much, but no more, and I'm grateful to you for not offering me more. About a political job, I think I might like to go to California this winter. I have some friends out there I haven't seen in years." He had known that that was exactly what Mary and her husband wanted, so he'd gone.

There was a knock on the door. It was Ula with a tray. "Why two cups, Ula?" he said.

"Oh. Di put two cups? So I did. I'm just so used to putting two cups." She had left the door open behind her, and as she arranged the things on the marble-topped table he saw Sheila and the two girls, standing and moving in the hall.

"This is your room, Farnie," said Sheila. "You're down this way, Helen. Remember what I told you, Farnie. Come on, Helen."

"Thank you, Ula," he said. She went out and closed the door, and he stood for a moment, contemplating the chocolate, then poured out a cup and drank it. It made him a little thirsty, but it was good and warming, and Mary was right; it was better than a drink. He poured out another cup and nibbled on a biscuit. He had an idea: Miss Farnsworth might like some. He admired that girl. She had spunk. He bet she knew what she wanted, or seemed to, and no matter how unimportant were the things she wanted, they were the things she wanted, and not someone else. She could damn well thank the Lord, too, that she was young enough to have a whack at whatever she wanted, and not have to wait the way he had. That girl would make up her mind about a man or a fortune or a career, and by God she would attain whatever it was. If she found, as she surely would find, that nothing ever was enough, she'd at least find it out in time; and early disillusionment carried a compensatory philosophical attitude, which in a hard girl like this one would take nothing from her charm. Mr. Winfield felt her charm, and began regarding her as the most interesting person he had met in many dull years. It would be fun to talk to her, to sound her out and see how far she had progressed toward, say, ambition or disillusionment. It would be fun to do, and it would be just plain nice of him, as former master of this house, to invite her to have a cup of cocoa with him. Good cocoa.

He made his choice between going out in the hall and knocking on her door, and knocking on her door to the bathroom. He decided on the second procedure because he didn't want anyone to see him knocking on her door. So he entered the bathroom and tapped on the door that led to her room. "In a minute," he thought he heard her say. But then he knew he must have been wrong. It sounded more like "Come in." He hated people who knocked on doors and had to be told two or three times to come in, and it would make a bad impression if he started the friendship that way.

He opened the door, and immediately he saw how right he had been in thinking she had said "In a minute." For Miss Farnsworth was standing in the middle of the room, standing there all but nude. Mr. Winfield instantly knew that this was the end of any worth-while life he had left. There was cold murder in the girl's eyes, and loathing and contempt and the promise of the thought his name forever would evoke. She spoke to him: "Get out of here, you dirty old man."

He returned to his room and his chair. Slowly he took a cigarette out of his case, and did not light it. He did everything slowly. There was all the time in the world, too much of it, for him. He knew it would be hours before he would begin to hate himself. For a while he would just sit there and plan his own terror.

THE SECRET LIFE OF
WALTER MITTY

❦

James Thurber

"WE'RE GOING THROUGH!" The Commander's voice was like thin ice breaking. He wore his full-dress uniform, with the heavily braided white cap pulled down rakishly over one cold gray eye. "We can't make it, sir. It's spoiling for a hurricane, if you ask me." "I'm not asking you, Lieutenant Berg," said the Commander. "Throw on the power lights! Rev her up to 8,500! We're going through!" The pounding of the cylinders increased: ta-pocketa-pocketa-pocketa-*pocketa-pocketa*. The Commander stared at the ice forming on the pilot window. He walked over and twisted a row of complicated dials. "Switch on No. 8 auxiliary!" he shouted. "Switch on No. 8 auxiliary!" repeated Lieutenant Berg. "Full strength in No. 3 turret!" shouted the Commander. "Full strength in No. 3 turret!" The crew, bending to their various tasks in the huge, hurtling eight-engined Navy hydroplane, looked at each other and grinned. "The Old Man'll get us through," they said to one another. "The Old Man ain't afraid of Hell!" . . .

"Not so fast! You're driving too fast!" said Mrs. Mitty. "What are you driving so fast for?"

"Hmm?" said Walter Mitty. He looked at his wife, in the seat beside him, with shocked astonishment. She seemed grossly unfamiliar, like a strange woman who had yelled at him in a crowd. "You were up to fifty-five," she said. "You know I don't like to go more than forty. You were up to fifty-five." Walter Mitty drove on toward Waterbury in silence, the roaring of the SN202 through the worst storm in twenty years of Navy flying fading in the remote, intimate airways of his mind. "You're tensed up again,"

16

said Mrs. Mitty, "It's one of your days. I wish you'd let Dr. Renshaw look you over."

Walter Mitty stopped the car in front of the building where his wife went to have her hair done. "Remember to get those overshoes while I'm having my hair done," she said. "I don't need overshoes," said Mitty. She put her mirror back into her bag. "We've been all through that," she said, getting out of the car. "You're not a young man any longer." He raced the engine a little. "Why don't you wear your gloves? Have you lost your gloves?" Walter Mitty reached in a pocket and brought out the gloves. He put them on, but after she had turned and gone into the building and he had driven on to a red light, he took them off again. "Pick it up, brother!" snapped a cop as the light changed, and Mitty hastily pulled on his gloves and lurched ahead. He drove around the streets aimlessly for a time, and then he drove past the hospital on his way to the parking lot.

. . ."It's the millionaire banker, Wellington McMillan," said the pretty nurse. "Yes?" said Walter Mitty, removing his gloves slowly. "Who has the case?" "Dr. Renshaw and Dr. Benbow, but there are two specialists here, Dr. Remington from New York and Dr. Pritchard-Mitford from London. He flew over." A door opened down a long, cool corridor and Dr. Renshaw came out. He looked distraught and haggard. "Hello, Mitty," he said. "We're having the devil's own time with McMillan, the millionaire banker and close personal friend of Roosevelt. Obstreosis of the ductal tract. Tertiary. Wish you'd take a look at him." "Glad to," said Mitty.

In the operating room there were whispered introductions: "Dr. Remington, Dr. Mitty. Dr. Pritchard-Mitford, Dr. Mitty." "I've read your book on streptothricosis," said Pritchard-Mitford, shaking hands. "A brilliant performance, sir." "Thank you," said Walter Mitty. "Didn't know you were in the States, Mitty," grumbled Remington. "Coals to Newcastle, bringing Mitford and me up here for a tertiary." "You are very kind," said Mitty. A huge, complicated machine, connected to the operating table, with many tubes and wires, began at this moment to go pocketa-pocketa-pocketa. "The new anaesthetizer is giving away!" shouted an in-

terne. "There is no one in the East who knows how to fix it!"
"Quiet, man!" said Mitty, in a low, cool voice. He sprang to the
machine, which was now going pocketa-pocketa-queep-pocketa-
queep. He began fingering delicately a row of glistening dials.
"Give me a fountain pen!" he snapped. Someone handed him a
fountain pen. He pulled a faulty piston out of the machine and
inserted the pen in its place. "That will hold for ten minutes,"
he said. "Get on with the operation." A nurse hurried over and
whispered to Renshaw, and Mitty saw the man turn pale. "Coreop-
sis has set in," said Renshaw nervously. "If you would take over,
Mitty?" Mitty looked at him and at the craven figure of Benbow,
who drank, and at the grave, uncertain faces of the two great
specialists. "If you wish," he said. They slipped a white gown on
him; he adjusted a mask and drew on thin gloves; nurses handed
him shining . . .

"Back it up, Mac! Look out for that Buick!" Walter Mitty
jammed on the brakes. "Wrong lane, Mac," said the parking-lot
attendant, looking at Mitty closely. "Gee. Yeh," muttered Mitty.
He began cautiously to back out of the lane marked "Exit
Only." "Leave her sit there," said the attendant. "I'll put her
away." Mitty got out of the car. "Hey, better leave the key." "Oh,"
said Mitty, handing the man the ignition key. The attendant
vaulted into the car, backed it up with insolent skill, and put it
where it belonged.

They're so damn cocky, thought Walter Mitty, walking along
Main Street; they think they know everything. Once he had tried
to take his chains off, outside New Milford, and he had got them
wound around the axles. A man had had to come out in a wreck-
ing car and unwind them, a young, grinning garageman. Since
then Mrs. Mitty always made him drive to a garage to have the
chains taken off. The next time, he thought, I'll wear my right
arm in a sling; they won't grin at me then. I'll have my right arm
in a sling and they'll see I couldn't possibly take the chains off
myself. He kicked at the slush on the sidewalk. "Overshoes," he
said to himself, and he began looking for a shoe store.

When he came out into the street again, with the overshoes in
a box under his arm, Walter Mitty began to wonder what the
other thing was his wife had told him to get. She had told him,

twice before they set out from their house for Waterbury. In a way he hated these weekly trips to town—he was always getting something wrong. Kleenex, he thought, Squibb's, razor blades? No. Toothpaste, toothbrush, bicarbonate, carborundum, initiative and referendum? He gave it up. But she would remember it. "Where's the what's-its-name?" she would ask. "Don't tell me you forgot the what's-its-name." A newsboy went by shouting something about the Waterbury trial.

. . ."Perhaps this will refresh your memory." The District Attorney suddenly thrust a heavy automatic at the quiet figure on the witness stand. "Have you ever seen this before?" Walter Mitty took the gun and examined it expertly. "This is my Webley-Vickers 50.80," he said calmly. An excited buzz ran around the courtroom. The Judge rapped for order. "You are a crack shot with any sort of firearms, I believe?" said the District Attorney, insinuatingly. "Objection!" shouted Mitty's attorney. "We have shown that the defendant could not have fired the shot. We have shown that he wore his right arm in a sling on the night of the fourteenth of July." Walter Mitty raised his hand briefly and the bickering attorneys were stilled. "With any known make of gun," he said evenly, "I could have killed Gregory Fitzhurst at three hundred feet *with my left hand*." Pandemonium broke loose in the courtroom. A woman's scream rose above the bedlam and suddenly a lovely, dark-haired girl was in Walter Mitty's arms. The District Attorney struck at her savagely. Without rising from his chair, Mitty let the man have it on the point of the chin. "You miserable cur!". . .

"Puppy biscuit," said Walter Mitty. He stopped walking and the buildings of Waterbury rose up out of the misty courtroom and surrounded him again. A woman who was passing laughed. "He said 'Puppy biscuit,' " she said to her companion. "That man said 'Puppy biscuit' to himself." Walter Mitty hurried on. He went into an A. & P., not the first one he came to but a smaller one farther up the street. "I want some biscuit for small, young dogs," he said to the clerk. "Any special brand, sir?" The greatest pistol shot in the world thought a moment. "It says 'Puppies Bark for It' on the box," said Walter Mitty.

His wife would be through at the hairdresser's in fifteen minutes, Mitty saw in looking at his watch, unless they had trouble drying it; sometimes they had trouble drying it. She didn't like to get to the hotel first; she would want him to be there waiting for her as usual. He found a big leather chair in the lobby, facing a window, and he put the overshoes and the puppy biscuit on the floor beside it. He picked up an old copy of *Liberty* and sank down into the chair. "Can Germany Conquer the World Through the Air?" Walter Mitty looked at the pictures of bombing planes and of ruined streets.

. . ."The cannonading has got the wind up in young Raleigh, sir," said the sergeant. Captain Mitty looked up at him through tousled hair. "Get him to bed," he said wearily, "with the others. I'll fly alone." "But you can't, sir," said the sergeant anxiously. "It takes two men to handle that bomber and the Archies are pounding hell out of the air. Von Richtman's circus is between here and Saulier." "Somebody's got to get that ammunition dump," said Mitty. "I'm going over. Spot of brandy?" He poured a drink for the sergeant and one for himself. War thundered and whined around the dugout and battered at the door. There was a rending of wood and splinters flew through the room. "A bit of a near thing," said Captain Mitty carelessly. "The box barrage is closing in," said the sergeant. "We only live once, Sergeant," said Mitty, with his faint, fleeting smile. "Or do we?" He poured another brandy and tossed it off. "I never see a man could hold his brandy like you, sir," said the sergeant. "Begging your pardon, sir." Captain Mitty stood up and strapped on his huge Webley-Vickers automatic. "It's forty kilometres through hell, sir," said the sergeant. Mitty finished one last brandy. "After all, " he said softly, "what isn't?" The pounding of the cannon increased; there was the rat-tat-tatting of machine guns, and from somewhere came the menacing pocketa-pocketa-pocketa of the new flame-throwers. Walter Mitty walked to the door of the dugout humming "Auprès de Ma Blonde." He turned and waved to the sergeant. "Cheerio!" he said. . . .

Something struck his shoulder. "I've been looking all over this hotel for you," said Mrs. Mitty. "Why do you have to hide in this old chair? How did you expect me to find you?" "Things close in," said Walter Mitty vaguely. "What?" Mrs. Mitty said. "Did you get the what's-its-name? The puppy biscuit? What's in that box?" "Overshoes," said Mitty. "Couldn't you have put them on in the store?" "I was thinking," said Walter Mitty. "Does it ever occur to you that I am sometimes thinking?" She looked at him. "I'm going to take your temperature when I get you home," she said.

They went out through the revolving doors that made a faintly derisive whistling sound when you pushed them. It was two blocks to the parking lot. At the drugstore on the corner she said, "Wait here for me. I forgot something. I won't be a minute." She was more than a minute. Walter Mitty lighted a cigarette. It began to rain, rain with sleet in it. He stood up against the wall of the drugstore, smoking. . . . He put his shoulders back and his heels together. "To hell with the handkerchief," said Walter Mitty scornfully. He took one last drag on his cigarette and snapped it away. Then, with that faint, fleeting smile playing about his lips, he faced the firing squad; erect and motionless, proud and disdainful, Walter Mitty the Undefeated, inscrutable to the last.

THE NET

❧

Robert M. Coates

WALTER HAD JUST turned the corner of Charles Street into Seventh when he saw her. She was standing a little way up the block talking to a fellow in a black overcoat and a black felt hat, and just the way they were standing—the fellow leaning back against the wall of the building there and she crowded close against him, looking up at him—was enough to let Walter know the kind of talk they were having. Almost without thinking, he stopped and stepped back a pace down Charles, out of sight around the corner.

This was the way things went, then; this was what she had left him for. He had known it, but this was the first time he had ever had sight of it, and it sent a queer feeling through him, as if more air than he could breathe had been forced into him. He was a tall man, with a pale, solemn, heavy-jawed face and a slow, slightly awkward manner of movement. He placed himself against the railing of an areaway and stood there, looking down Seventh Avenue, waiting. He knew she would have to come around the corner when she started home, and whether she was alone or the fellow was still with her, he would have a right to speak to her then. Till then he would wait. He had time.

It was growing late and the evening had been cold; there were few people walking. Down by Christopher Street there was a cluster of bright signs and illuminated buildings, but up where he was the houses were mostly dark, and the only sound was the rough, shuffling whir of the tires on pavement as the cars went flying by. Then the traffic lights changed and the cars stopped, at Charles, at Tenth, at Christopher; at Charles, a black truck crawled out across the avenue and went slowly on down the street past Walter, toward Hudson.

That was all the cross traffic there was, but for a few seconds longer the avenue was still. Then the lights went green and the headlights moved forward, sifting past each other as the cars took up their varying speeds. A moment later, Walter heard the tap of her heels on the sidewalk, coming around the corner, and she passed him.

"Hello, Ann," he said softly.

She hadn't noticed him till then; he could tell that from the way her head snapped around and the look that came over her face. Then she turned her head away. She kept on walking. "Hello, Walter," she said wearily.

He was walking along beside her. "Where you been, Ann?" he asked. "I was at your people's house and they said you'd went to the movies."

"I did."

"Yeah. The movies."

She glanced up at him, and he could see her face pinching up in the way it did when she got angry. But she didn't say anything; she just turned her face forward again, tucked her chin down in the fur collar of her coat, and walked on. He kept pace with her. "I saw you talking to that fellow back there, Ann," he went on in his slow, insistent voice. "I saw you."

"Well," she said. "So you saw me. Can't a girl meet a friend on the street?"

"Yeah. But the movies."

He knew she didn't like to be prodded like that about things, even when she was telling the truth, and he half expected her to burst out with something then and there. He could feel his chest tightening already, in that mixture of fear and excitement and stubbornness that always came over him when they got into an argument. But she just kept on walking. After a few steps she turned to him again. "You was up to the folks'?" she asked, her voice very innocent and offhand. "Who'd you see? Was Ma there?"

"Yes, your mother was there," he said. "As you doubtless know. I know what you're thinking, Ann, but I didn't think it would give you pleasure. She didn't give me no nice reception. But that don't bother me, either; that I expected. I'm not blind, and I know who it was that turned you against me and broke up our marriage. But there's an old saying, Ann, that marriages are made in heaven, and I believe it, and I believe she will get her punishment, too, for what she's done—turning a man's wife against her lawful husband. If not now, then she'll surely get it in the hereafter. But it's not her I'm worried about; I leave her to her own devices. It's you, Ann. Listen," he said. "What you don't get is, I'd take you back tomorrow. Like that. I don't care who you been with, what you done—even that fellow back there, Ann, whoever he is. I don't ask. But a fellow you got to meet on street corners, can't even show to your folks—but even him, Ann; I'd forget everything. Just so long as you'd tell me, come clean about things. But this lying and hiding. Listen, Ann—" He had thought a good deal about this meeting and had planned for it, and this was one of the things he had figured on saying, so he found himself talking faster and faster. But just then a crazy thing happened.

They were passing a series of old-fashioned houses with high-stooped entrances, and the steps running down from them made the sidewalk narrow. And there was a couple, a man and a girl, walking up the street toward them; in his excitement, Walter didn't notice them until he was upon them, and then there wasn't room for them all to pass. The man bumped him, and Walter stumbled, trying to sidestep them, but all the time his eyes were on Ann. She had walked on, never varying her pace, as if she had nothing to do with him at all, and at the sight of her tan-stockinged legs flicking briskly away beneath her black coat a kind of panic took hold of him. "I'm your husband, Ann!" he yelled suddenly. He could see both the man's and the girl's faces turned toward him, but for the moment he didn't care. He shoved past them and ran after Ann, grabbing at her arm. "I'm your husband," he repeated, his voice still loud. "Don't that mean anything to you? For better or for worse." Then he saw that she was laughing, and he let go of her arm.

It was only a little way farther on to her family's apartment house. When they reached it, she ran up the three or four steps to the entrance. Walter followed her, letting the street door swing shut behind him. They were alone in the dim vestibule. She bent her head for a moment, fumbling in her bag for the key, then she glanced up. "Well, Walter," she said. She wasn't laughing now, but she might just as well have been; he could tell from the look on her face that she was only waiting to get on upstairs to start in again. "Well, it's been a enjoyable little walk."

He could feel the air crowding into his lungs again, so hard that it made his whole chest feel hot inside. "Maybe it ain't finished yet," he said.

"Well, it is for me. I'm going up."

"I'm coming up too."

"No you won't."

"Why won't I?" Without his meaning it to, he could hear his voice getting louder. "What you got to conceal up there?"

"Oh, Walter! It ain't that and you know it. But you know what'll happen. You and Ma." He hadn't realized that he had moved closer to her, but he must have, for suddenly she stepped back a pace and stared up at him. "Walter," she said. "You been drinking?"

"I have not been drinking," he said, and he let his voice go louder still when he said it. Let her scare a little, he was thinking; at least she wasn't laughing at him any more. She was paying attention to him now. "Well, then," she said, and she began talking faster. "Listen, Walter. This kind of chasing around ain't getting us anywhere, you hiding around corners and laying for me and all that. Why don't we get together some other way, sometime? I could come up to your place sometime, even. You still got the apartment, haven't you? We could talk."

"You come up there," he said, "and maybe you wouldn't never leave it again." He hadn't meant to put it like that; what he'd meant was that if she came up, it would have to be because she wanted to stay there and be with him again, but the way it came out it sounded threatening, even to him, and she must have thought so too, for she stared at him blankly a moment. Then, suddenly, she made a kind of a dive out of the corner where he had crowded her. "Then go home then! Get out of here!" he heard her cry, and she began pushing with both hands against his chest. He grabbed her wrists and she screamed. When she screamed, his hands went directly to her throat.

He had only intended to stop her screaming, but as soon as he touched her a strange kind of strength flowed into his hands, a strength that came from somewhere inside him and that once released could not be recalled, so that he couldn't have let go if he'd tried. For a while she struggled, jerking her body this way and that and pulling at his arms with her hands. It didn't bother him. He had shoved her back against the wall, so hard that her head bumped against it and her hat tipped over sidewise. He just stiffened his legs and stood there, his hands locked hard in the flesh of her throat; he was surprised at how strongly he stood there, meeting and conquering every move she made. "Laugh now," he said once, not loud, but almost gently.

Her knee worked up somehow between them until it was pressing against his thigh, but there was no strength in it; the strength was all in him, and soon the knee slipped harmlessly down again. Then her body lashed back and forth once or twice, fast and violently, and stopped, and her eyelids, which had been tight shut, opened so that he could see through her lashes the blue of her eyes, glittering in the dim light overhead. A kind of shudder ran through her. It was some time after that before he realized that she wasn't struggling any more.

It was the strain on his arms that told him of the change. Her body was just so much weight now, almost more than he could hold, and he let her slide slowly down along the wall until she was sitting on the floor, her back propped against the corner of the vestibule. Well, I did it, he thought, I did it; and for a moment he stood looking down at her uncertainly, not knowing what he ought to do next. One leg was crooked awkwardly sidewise, he noticed, so that the skirt was pulled up above the stocking top, and he bent down and pulled the hem over the knee. Then he turned and went out the door.

At the top of the steps he stopped and looked up and down the street. At first glance it seemed there was no one in sight at all, not a soul; then he noticed a couple of people standing in front of a house farther down the block—a man and a girl, he thought, though he couldn't be sure; about all he could see was their faces, and these were no more than pale spots in the shadows where they were standing. Farther still, down almost to Hudson, he sighted two others, two men, dark against the light from a shop window on the corner. And now there was a girl clipping quickly along on the opposite sidewalk; it was amazing how silently they all moved, and how easy it was not to notice them in the darkness. He stood where he was for a while, watching them, trying to determine if there was any sign of a concerted scheme in their actions. He had a feeling that they were only moving as they did in order to set a trap for him; at a signal they might all turn and begin running to surround him.

But none of them paid any attention to him. The couple down the block just stood there, the two men walked onward, the girl hurried around the corner and disappeared. Walter went down the steps and turned up toward Seventh Avenue. Well, I did it, he thought again, and as before, the thought carried no emotion with it except relief. It had to be done, it was coming to her; that was the way his thoughts ran, and what little guilt he had was submerged in a kind of careless irresponsibility, the feeling that a drunken man has when he knows he has done something wrong, admits it, and doesn't care. The emotion was so close to that of drunkenness that even Walter recognized it. I could say I was drunk, he thought, his mind momentarily occupied with stratagems. But as soon as the idea came to him, he rejected it. I've got better reasons than that, he decided; her laughing at me, cheating on me, chasing at every corner. As he neared Fourth Street, another man, a new one, sprang up suddenly before him, a short, heavy-set fellow stepping out of the shadows and striding directly toward him.

The man passed without giving him a second glance, but after the man had gone by, Walter stopped and stepped back against a house wall, watching his progress down the street; suppose he was headed for *her* house, he was thinking, and the fear became so strong that he almost set out in pursuit of the stranger. I could ask him for a match, get him talking, lead him on past the door, he thought. As he hesitated, the man went by; he went three or four doors farther before he turned in.

Walter walked on. He didn't hurry, and when he reached the

end of the block he even stopped for a moment, glancing, as if idly, up and down before crossing the street. The night was a net, he realized, with its streets and its people walking this way and that along them; what he had to do was to find his way out without disturbing anything or anyone. The thing that worried him most now was his breathing; he discovered that it had been bothering him for some time. He would find himself breathing fast and hard, so hard that it hurt his chest, and then he would take a deep breath, so long and so deep that when he let it out he could feel the flesh of his body shrinking away from his clothes, leaving the skin damp and prickly and cool. Then the hard, quick breathing would begin again.

Like a man that's been running, he thought. That was one thing he mustn't do; without even thinking about it, he knew he mustn't run. Or talk. For a while he had had the notion of going up to his brother-in-law's place. It was just a notion, or really it was more like a picture that had come into his mind; somehow, he didn't want to go home, and suddenly he had seen himself sitting with Frank and Ethel in their warm apartment, and then he had thought how pleasant it would be, it would rest him; they'd send out for some beer even, maybe. But he saw now that it wouldn't do. He'd get to talking, and there was no way of knowing how they'd take it. At the thought, the picture in his mind changed in a way that made him go cold all over; from seeing their faces smiling at him, friendly and companionable, he had seen them go white and staring, and hard with horror as they looked at him.

It was an awful thing he had done, all right, and the funny part was that he hadn't meant to. "God sakes!" he said. For the moment he was arguing with Frank and Ethel, and he found himself talking out loud. "If I'd meant to do it, wouldn't I have planned the thing different? Me here with no more than a couple of bucks in my pocket." If it had been Friday, even, when his pay came through at the shop; then he'd have had a matter of thirty-five dollars in his hand, enough to start out with, anyway. But maybe Frank would lend him some money; he'd done as much for him on occasion.

"I swear, Frank, it's the first time I ever even laid hands on her. I never meant to harm a hair of her head." He had stopped talking out loud, but he was still arguing to himself when he remembered than Frank was Ann's brother; he had had an idea all along that his mind was running too fast for him, sort of, so that he was overlooking things. And maybe important things. This proved it. If Frank was Ann's brother, that left him out, of course; he was the last man to turn to now. It was late, too. His mind had been racing ahead, full of confidence, but now it was swarming with doubts and uncertainties: how could he expect to burst in on them now, at this hour, asking for money, without them asking questions? And even if he did get some money, where would he go? It would mean quitting his job, leaving everyone he knew, everything. "Me a man that's near forty," he thought.

It was just that Frank was the only one in the family that had ever had a decent word for him.

And the thing was, he hadn't meant to do it. All the time back there in the vestibule it had seemed like all the dozens of times in the past when he and Ann would have arguments; and she'd slump down in a chair or a sofa, so mad that she couldn't keep from crying but still trying to hide it; and he'd shout something, slam the door, and go out. And then, like as not, she'd get up, slam the door too, and go off to see one of her girl friends or something. But not now. Now she would lie where she was, in the dim hallway, until someone came in from the street or down from the apartments above, and stumbled over her.

It would happen any minute now, if it hadn't happened already, and at the thought a vast sorrow rose up slowly inside him and filled him—sorrow for himself and for Ann, but mostly for himself. "What I've got myself in for," he kept thinking. A whole group of people, men and women all talking and laughing, were coming down the steps of a house ahead of him, and he slowed his pace so as not to get tangled up with them on the sidewalk. But they just stood there, and finally he had to brush past them. As he did so, he shoved one of the men and gave the whole group such a fierce look that they must have noticed it; he was sure he saw their faces change.

"I could tell you something that would stop your giggling," he thought, and this time, when he thought of the terror he could bring to their faces, he felt an odd sort of satisfaction; it would

serve them right, he thought. When he had gone a few paces farther on, he looked back. They were all trailing off down the
street, and on an impulse he stopped and leaned against an areaway railing, watching them. It would happen any minute now,
he thought.

How long he stood there he didn't know, but it couldn't have
been long, and the thing that made him conscious of time again
was a thin knife sound like a scream or a siren; then a car's headlights turned into the street from away down at Hudson. He
watched them, and it was some seconds before he realized what
was the matter with them: the car was heading up the wrong way,
against traffic.

Only a police car would do that, he thought, and as if in con-
firmation he saw it swing in toward the curb and stop, just about
where the entrance to Ann's house would be. Well, then, the
police were coming, he thought; that was right, it was proper,
and if the old woman—he realized that one of the things he had
been worrying about was Ann's mother; he'd known she'd be
mixed up in the scene down there some way. But if the police
were there and she started her ranting and screaming—well, they'd
know how to stop her. Slowly, he pushed himself away from the
railing.

He'd go on up to Frank's, he thought, but it was only when he
started walking on up the street, toward Seventh, that he realized
how tired he was. So maybe, after all, he'd go home. "It's too
much," he thought. "It's too much to expect of a man." He was
still arguing about this question of packing up and leaving town
for good. But he was almost too tired, and too lonely, to bother
about it. Unexpectedly, as he walked, a picture came into his mind
of the couple he had bumped into when Ann and he were walking
home. Down this very block, it had been, and he could see them
again, their faces turning in surprise as he shoved past them shouting; somehow, the recollection only added to his feeling of lonely
helplessness.

If he could only talk to them, he thought, he could explain
everything; they were the only people in the world, perhaps, who
would understand. But they had gone, and the thought vanished

too, almost as soon as it had come to him. He walked on up to
Seventh and then turned north, toward the subway. Maybe he'd
go up to Frank and Ethel's after all; if there had been a reason
against going there, he had forgotten it, and anyway it wasn't
worth bothering about now. Most of all, now, he felt tired.

HOME ATMOSPHERE

Sally Benson

MILDRED KIRK came briskly into the living room. She wore a knit sweater-suit of a hard, bright blue which neither sagged nor pulled, but gave her admirable figure the wooden perfection of a model in a store window. She was smiling and as she smiled she blinked her eyes rapidly in an alert, interested way. Walking to the fireplace, she stooped down and picked up a half-smoked cigarette from the tiles and put it in a large bronze standing ash receiver.

At this movement, her husband, who had been reading the paper, looked up guiltily. "Oh," he said.

She turned toward him, still smiling. "You just forgot," she told him. "Didn't you?"

"Must have," he agreed. "Thinking of something else, I guess."

He laid his paper across his knees and sat with an expectant look on his face, as though he were waiting for something.

She sat down neatly and stared for a moment at the fireplace. A fire was laid in what seemed at first glance to be an expert manner—even lengths of shiny, dark cherry for kindling and on top of them three birch logs with curling, silvery bark, but there was no paper and no ash. Not a sign of ash.

"It's just that I think there is no reason why an open fireplace must be used as a catchall," she said. She looked around the room and her eyes softened somewhat.

"I love this room," she went on. "It really looks like *home*. Don't you think it looks like home, Willard?"

His eyes wandered slowly to the polished-maple gate-legged table, the couch facing the fireplace with the long refectory table at its back, on which stood a lamp with a blue Chinese base,

bronze bookends representing ships in full sail, a set of four ashtrays with the matchbox that went with them, and a Lalique glass
bowl filled with artificial fruit; they rested on the aggressively
bright chintz at the windows, the shades with cord fringe, the
large, expensive radio, the four Windsor chairs and the two upholstered ones; on the long dull-gold frame of the mirror hung
by a blue cord over the fireplace, and the ornaments on the
mantelpiece—two brass candlesticks holding tall, dark-blue candles, a small mahogany clock, and a green glass vase of bunched
bayberry.

Mildred Kirk moved impatiently in her chair. "Well?" she said.
"I asked you a question."

He smiled feebly at her. "Well, Mil, why shouldn't it look like
home?" he asked. "It *is* home, isn't it?"

"When I *think*, when I *think* of the place you and Billy used
to live in, it makes me shudder," she said. "How you stood being
cooped up in two rooms with a little boy, I don't see."

He frowned slightly. "Billy's a good kid."

"Of course he is," she answered, her voice conciliatory. "No
one could ask for a better little boy. I didn't mean that. I meant
this is much nicer, isn't it? Living in the country and having a real
place, a place you can move around in? Billy loves it. You just
have to look at him to see he loves it."

"Where is he, anyway?" Willard Kirk asked.

"Playing down the street with the Simpson boys. At least, that's
what Mattie says." She shook her head humorously. "Now, you
got home before I did. Why didn't *you* ask her? He is your little
boy and I'm the one who asks where he is, the minute I come in
the house."

He picked up his paper again. "Oh, I knew he was all right.
Mattie wouldn't let him go anywhere that wasn't all right."

"You seem to place a great deal of confidence in Mattie," she
said. "Not that Mattie doesn't mean well, but you couldn't exactly
say she *knows* much. And with both of us away at work all day—
well, sometimes I feel uneasy."

He threw his paper to the floor. "Now, look here," he began.
"Are you going to start *that* again?"

She looked at him and drew the corners of her mouth down as

though she were going to cry. "Really," she told him. "It's impossible to say a word to you without your flying off the handle. You should thank your lucky stars you married a woman who loves your little boy and takes an interest in him. I'd like you to hear what the people in my office say, that's all. *They* think it's wonderful that I was willing to move out here, commute and everything, just so we could have a real *home*. A home needs a firm hand, let me tell you. And it's not so easy when I'm away all day and have to leave everything to a maid."

He looked at her and decided that she was darned pretty—you had to say that for her.

"And a maid," she went on, "that's some sort of Polack and doesn't understand one thing about how a child should be brought up."

"Now, listen," he said. "Mattie's all right. Mattie's taken care of Billy since he was born and she's all right."

"But *how* has she taken care of him? How do you know how she's taken care of him? You're always away all day. You don't know what she does."

His face cleared and he began to laugh. "All you've got to do is look at him. Just look at him!"

"I don't deny," Mildred Kirk said, "that she feeds him well and looks after his clothes and all that. It's the things she tells him —all about that woman being chopped to pieces with an axe in whatever place she comes from. And about how drunk her father used to get, and her mother's black eyes."

"Oh, that stuff!" he commented impatiently. "Why, when I was a kid the best time I ever had was following an old bum who used to work at the livery stable and listening to his yarns. Stuff like that doesn't amount to anything."

She blinked her eyes rapidly for a moment and then smiled again. It had a curiously professional quality, a sort of calloused sweetness. "Anyway," she said, "someday I hope we can afford a real maid. One that looks nice. Nice and neat. You must admit that no matter what kind of uniform I buy for Mattie, she looks funny. And while she's lovely to you and all that, she isn't always so nice to me, let me tell you. But of course you wouldn't notice that."

"I never notice how Mattie looks." He picked up his paper. "Go on, get it off your chest. Just what are you getting at now? All this stuff about Mattie not being good with Billy! Go on, get it over with."

Mildred Kirk wrinkled her forehead and looked down at the floor. With the clear, light blue of her eyes hidden, she seemed prettier and younger. "Well," she said, "Mattie's sulking again."

"Her arches hurt her. She told me so."

"Arches nothing! She simply doesn't like to have people in. I merely went to the kitchen to ask her to make sandwiches and leave out glasses when she got through with the dishes and she began to sulk. Here she is alone all day, her time all her own, and I want her to do one simple little thing. Yes, she's all right with you and Billy, but she resents doing one thing for me."

"Mattie has a lot to do," Willard Kirk protested mildly. "And she's no chicken. She always gets that way. Send her out to a movie or something and she'll get over it. She loves the movies."

"I'll not cater to the whims of a feeble-minded Polack," she said indignantly. "She's going to show respect for me or I'll know the reason why. Absolutely on her own all day here alone and running things with a high hand! You've spoiled her, that's what! You cater to her far more than you do to me! I have a good notion to tell her if she isn't happy here, she can leave!"

Willard Kirk got up from his chair and walked toward his wife. "Listen, Mildred," he said, his voice flat and hard. "Mattie stays. Mattie isn't ever going to go until she walks out of here of her own free will, and she'll never do that. Why, you don't know. You just don't know, that's all. She practically raised Billy. Came all the way down from the Bronx every morning before I went to work and stayed until I got home at night. No matter what time, let me tell you! I don't care if she does sulk once in a while! So do I! So would you if you were getting old and on your feet all day and sometimes half the night. Good Lord! Can't you *see*?"

He stopped talking abruptly and went over to the window, where he stood looking out on the little suburban street, the sidewalks spotted with small pools from the recent rain. "Mattie stays," he repeated without turning around. "And that's that."

Mildred Kirk got to her feet. She pulled at her skirt, smoothing it over her firm, pretty hips. "As you say," she said. "I'm just your wife. I'm just trying to make a home for you. And a home where the people in it aren't happy all the time doesn't seem much of a home to me. No one can sulk in this house. No one! And no matter what you say, I'm going to speak to her."

He turned around and faced her angrily. "What—" he began.

She looked at him, smiling. "You don't have to worry," she said. "I told you I was just going to *speak* to her."

In the kitchen, Mattie took the small chopping bowl down from the second shelf and put a few chives and a leaf of tarragon in it. Pretty soon, she thought, she would hear Billy's step on the back porch. She gave a nervous glance at the clock. It was after dark, but he had no streets to cross. Not that she hadn't told him many times, "Look, darling. Look, like this, see, and then like that. And if no cars coming, then walk slow across."

She turned over the idea in her mind of walking to the corner to see if she could see if he were coming. But then dinner would be late, and That Woman's tongue would start up again.

The familiar events of the coming evening took shape in her head—dinner and then, an hour after, Billy's bath. Maybe let him play in the tub a while, she thought, as they were having company. Then bed and a nice talk in the dark. She frowned, thinking deeply of something especially good to tell him tonight, because she had been short with him about being late for school.

She got olive oil and lemon from the icebox and then she began to chop, slowly and deliberately. She heard the swinging door open behind her and knew That Woman stood there. She turned toward her with only slight deference.

Mildred Kirk was still smiling and her voice was clear and pleasant as she spoke. "I came to ask you a question, Mattie," she said. "A question I wanted to ask you before Billy got home."

Mattie shifted her weight from one foot to the other.

"It's this," Mildred Kirk went on. "Aren't you happy with us, Mattie?"

Mattie's expression was stunned and uncomprehending.

"Because we want you to be happy," Mildred Kirk said. "We can't have anyone around us who isn't happy here. So I thought that maybe you had too much to do. Maybe you *thought* you had too much to do. Do you, Mattie?"

"My feet sometimes," the older woman began, her face flushing a dull red.

"Exactly," Mildred Kirk agreed, nodding brightly. "So we've reached a decision. We've decided that Billy is quite big enough to bathe and undress himself. Quite big enough! And to put himself to bed. That will relieve you of that duty and you won't feel yourself so rushed when you are asked to make a few sandwiches for our friends."

Mattie swallowed painfully. "Mrs. Kirk?"

She looked at the clear blue eyes and the alert smile of the young woman and could go no farther.

"So that's settled now, isn't it, Mattie?" Mildred Kirk asked. "And any time you feel you have too much to do, simply come to me and we'll see if we can't relieve you in some way. Do you understand, Mattie?"

She stood there smiling another moment and then she turned and the swinging door closed behind her.

Mattie stared at the door and a murderous rage filled her heart. Sharp, hot pokers of fury pierced her brain and for quite a while she was not aware of anything but this fury. Then through it she heard the thump of Billy's bicycle as he wheeled it against the side of the house, and she turned back to the table and mechanically took hold of the chopping bowl. But her knees were weak and she pulled the kitchen stool toward her and sat down. The evening loomed starkly ahead of her. No bath, no talking in the dark, no stories. That Woman had taken the last moment of the day from her, the only moment now when Billy was still her baby. That Woman could do anything. Mr. Kirk had married her, hadn't he? She had got him.

As Billy's sturdy little shoes clumped up the back steps she had to put her head down in her hands a moment, trembling with fear, before she had courage to turn and face him.

"A fine hour to come home," she scolded. "A fine time."

A TOAST TO CAPTAIN JERK

❧

RUSSELL MALONEY

SATURDAY NIGHT is the night the little actors sit up late, getting drunk and boasting. Oreste's, the Italian restaurant near Eighth Avenue which is the semi-official clearing house for forty-dollar Equity minimum salary checks, was almost filled by eleven-thirty. There was a surge of words in the little smoky room, properly sustained on a column of breath, pushed forth by well-exercised, perfectly controlled diaphragms, sharply audible: *Orson definitely told me but no casting till week after next from hunger what does he think Skowhegan who else could they get for that money little bitch left my pictures three months on the Coast fake the dancing but they cut half my lines Chamberlain Brown Sardi's out of town but his secretary said they say Crosby Gaige but I can't see Zelda in one of those grass skirts from hunger.*

Only one girl in Oreste's was eating alone. She was a slender, long-boned girl, attractive in a manner that represented a definite choice. The candid wideness of her eyes was the result of spaced eyebrows and eyeshadow on the outer corners of the lids. Her hair was brushed away from her brow to make her face naked and without guile. Girls of this candid type can be becomingly greedy, and this one was eating a plate of spaghetti, winding up neat forkfuls with precise motions of her narrow brown hands, stopping now and then to drink from a tumbler of red wine. She glanced at the doorway every few minutes, raising her chin and turning her head with unconscious theatrical emphasis.

The man she was waiting for arrived a little before midnight, running lithely down the three steps that led from the street and striding straight to her table. He wore a homburg, a blue serge suit, white shirt, starched collar, plain tie, and black shoes with only a dull polish. "Mona, my dear. I'm late," he said, sitting down. He had a lean, brownish head and wide shoulders.

"That's all right," the girl said. "It must have taken you three hours to dress. You eaten?"

"Yes, yes, hours ago." The man looked over his shoulder, caught the waiter's eye, and called, "Whiskcy soda."

The waiter crossed the room and stood at the man's shoulder. "Rye whiskey or Scotch?" he said.

"Oh, for God's sake," the man said. *"Scotch."*

"The idea, Joe! Only Americans drink rye," Mona said to the waiter. "Filthy stuff, rye," she added to the man, speaking in an approximation of his own clipped accent.

"Now, Mona," the man said, "let's not—"

"Now, Tracy," she said. "Let's." Looking at him calmly, she searched her patent-leather handbag for cigarettes and matches. "Very interesting," she said, taking out a cigarette and tapping it on a scarlet thumbnail. "The clothes, I mean." She tapped the cigarette once more, and put the wrong end in her mouth. "The last time I saw you in those particular clothes, Tracy, my dear, was two summers ago, when we did 'The End of the Story.' Detective Inspector Harrod, of Scotland Yard." She lit the cigarette and flicked the match across the room. "Veddy stiff, veddy British. 'I'm afraid this is murder. No one must leave the house.' So on and so on. . . . *Joe!*" she called suddenly to the waiter. "Joe, I'd like another glass of this lovely red ink. Ink-and-soda, ch, Tracy?"

"I hoped we wouldn't get tight," Tracy said. "Tonight."

"Well, I decided we would, so shut up," she said. "As I was saying, I note with interest that we have combed our wardrobe. I know your wardrobe as well as you do, darling—do you mind? We decided against the brown tweeds, and gray jacket with flannels, and the double-breasted pin stripe, and the single-breasted herring-bone. And of course, the dinner jacket, and the tails. No, we wanted something solid and respectable, because we were mousing around in banks and steamship offices, and maybe even in the British Ambassadors office."

"The Consulate," Tracy said. "For God's sake."

"And all because we've decided that our wardrobe isn't quite complete. We want a nice little uniform, too. 'Journey's End.' Captain Stanhope."

"That's not the way to take it," Tracy said. "I'm going to do it, and you might as well make up your mind."

"My mind's made up, all right," she said. "And you're not going to do it."

"Yes."

"No. For one thing, they won't let you. With your first papers and all."

"It'll be a little irregular, perhaps," he said. "But don't tell me you don't think people are getting over. And there's Canada."

"Listen," the girl said, a note of urgency in her voice. "We won't be in it. Stay here, and you won't be in it. Why do you think you have to be in it? I bet they can have a dandy war without you."

"It's no use, Mona."

"Well, aren't actors supposed to keep on being actors in a war? In canteens and so on? They did before."

"My God, the war's *real*," the man said. "It's got nothing to do with all this we've had over here."

"And *I'm* not real. And it isn't real that we were both getting screen tests this fall, or that Gordon talked to you about that thing he's doing."

"No, not a bit real," Tracy said. "Everything I've done here is perfectly silly make-believe. You're a nice bit of make-believe, and the rest of it isn't so nice—all the cheap hotel rooms and the bit parts, and making believe that I or you or Brooks Atkinson or anybody else on earth cares a damn whether I'm any good at pretending to be Detective Inspector Harrod. Over there, it'll be real, at least."

The girl settled back in her chair. "I've lent you money for some damn silly things, but you won't get it for this," she said.

"I won't have to. I borrowed some tonight from some friends of Mother's uptown, and besides, I haven't paid my room rent for the past month. I've kept that."

"So that's what's really real, is it?" she said. "All that over there."

"It is now, for me."

"Captain Stanhope," the girl said. "Captain Jerk, the unknown fall guy. You know what I'm going to do, when this is all over?

I'm going to find where they've buried you, and put a special little epitaph over you. I'll say 'He skipped his bill at the Trafton Hotel. He was in arrears with his Equity dues. He owed Oreste twelve dollars for drinks. He behaved just as badly as everybody else in the world today.' " She sat up straight in her chair, in the smoke and the noise of laughter around her. "And if you think I'm going to apologize tomorrow for saying this, you're wrong. Because it's what I think. You're just skipping your hotel bill."

"It'll be real, at least," he said again, but there was no certainty in his face. He looked as if he might never know what was real, even if he died trying to find out.

KROY WEN

❧

Kay Boyle

THE TWO LITTLE ITALIANS looked up the tower of decks to the sight of Mr. Wurthenberger with his Panama pulled down over his eyes. Three large birds, balancing on their wings like albatrosses, and yet as black as crows, had followed them now for the past two days of quiet weather. There they were when the night came down, melting away into the tar of it, and in the morning they were riding the sky like three black crescent moons. Whether the same kind of omens were good or bad on the water as they were on land was something that the two Italians with their soft Italian faces did not know. But thoughts and menaces passed through their heads like a passing breeze, or like a feather blowing, and they never thought of any one thing for very long at a time. They had sought out the gentlest corner, and the farthest, on the lower deck of the ship, and there they had turned about upon imaginary grasses and sat down close to one another in the sun. She seemed to be making something like a red hood for her baby to wear. The baby, apparently, was going to be born in a minute or two.

The Italian woman's steel needles worked and languished in the wool. The tips of her fingers were better suited to pulling idly at the curly wool, or to lying still in the Italian's hand. They sat in the sun on their own warm soft behinds, exchanging looks at each other, with a cloud passing over their faces whenever they caught a sight of the three black birds circling after the ship. Their teeth were shining as they plucked petal after petal from the fragrant bouquets of their conversation. Garlic was part of their own breath to them, and their tongues and nostrils repined without it.

Thus could they be seen from the top deck. The black birds

were flying behind them, soiling the purity of the clear blue sky. It was no place for an artist to be, nor for a man who could feel the heart of all humanity beating against his own ribs.

"I could use those two," Mr. Wurthenberger said.

The steward had come along the deck to him, with a special tray in his hand. On it was steaming a cup of broth.

"I've brought a little cup of bouillon, Mr. Wurthenberger," said the steward. "It's quite nice and delicate, sir. I think you'll have no trouble with it."

Mr. Wurthenberger's lifted hand struck the faces of the two Italians below as if he had flashed a mirror upon them, for the sunlight had caught in the gems of his fingers and swung a blade of fire across their eyes.

"I want to go down into the steerage," was what he said.

He had taken this leisurely broad boat toward Italy to get away from art. Art and humanity were what he was escaping. Tobacco and alcohol were safe behind a resolve not to touch them again until his hand was steady as a metronome. And here was the artist soul and the love of humanity in him betraying him and dispatching the steward to find his secretary.

"There's color!" he said. "I needed a few yards of a pregnant woman. God, what atmosphere!" he said.

Out went his knees like nutcrackers and down the glittering flights he ran. As he passed through the promenade deck, his nerves played the same trick on him: he caught himself spelling backward the name of the steamer, that was lettered out on the life-preserver, so that in the tail of his eye it was read: "Kroy Wen." This had been the warning his nerves had given him when the specialist had said, "Go away. Six months, a year. You can't keep on as you've been doing. Let the movies take care of themselves."

But it would take more than a wreck of nerves to persuade him that the movies could take care of themselves. He had agreed to rest. He was taking a sea voyage. But who was to blame if art and humanity pursued him, got him by the eyes and the ears and made him act? He knew that he had a way with him, but who would have guessed it now that he had passed fifty and his teeth had turned as yellow as grains of corn? Maybe he had once been a fine-looking fellow with his belly thin and curving into his breeches, but he knew that the reputation he had in every corner of the world was gaudy enough to make a *bambino's* hood.

"Old, am I?" he thought as he stood in front of the two young Italians. They were sitting on the deck eying him gently in the sun. "These damned wops with their pretty skins!" he was thinking.

He looked at the little Italian woman shaking the gold hoops in her ears. He had begun to talk to them in his winning way. He had never owned a circus or anything like it, he answered them, but he had a great deal to say in short hard words of all the things he had done. He had even taken a star in his own hands.

"My wife is a star," was what he said to these two gentle little people.

They thought of the five sharp points and the brilliance of her.

"Your first baby you're having, is it?" he said. "Your first one, eh?"

They were sailing back to Italy for the birth of their first child. The director had no children, he said. The star had never given birth. From this their minds drifted gently to thoughts of falling stars, and of the arch of daisies which keeps the sky at night from ballooning down like a circus tent. These were usual enough thoughts for them, for the Italian had swung on a trapeze for thirteen years.

"I could use you two," the director said.

If the heavens had not wept and the wind slapped the sea so smartly, if entrails had not sought to reach for and grip the earth forever, he would have photographed them the next morning. For this reason they had sticks of greasepaint in their cabin, which they were to put on their faces once the secretary had shown them how. But the Italian woman was so sick that she felt the baby retching and dying in her. With every swell of the waters, nausea washed over her like a tide.

Mr. Wurthenberger came into their cabin in the rain. The stench of it was such that he had to disregard his resolve and light a cigar before he could bear it. There was no porthole, and even in their agony they took the little white bulbs of garlic out of a nosegay of raffia and sliced them raw upon their tough bread.

"You're a couple of kids," said the director, with a puff of sweet tobacco. "You're young, eh, to be having a baby?"

Maybe they could start taking the pictures tomorrow, said Mr. Wurthenberger, provided the rain let up.

"Noolas," he read backward as he passed the saloon. "Ssalc Dnoces."

The three black birds seemed to be carrying on in their beaks the curtain of foul weather. Even the sun was doing its best to torment him, thought Mr. Wurthenberger on the morrow. The rain was continuing to fall. He was in a temper of irritation, thinking of the lights he might have brought with him. He might have brought a lamp or two with him and it would have done his nerves less harm than fretting this way about the rain. But it was not the end of his nerves, for with the rain and the wind spanking the waters for dear life, he had to bide his time. Time he had for reflection upon his own life and all the great things he had done. He sat alone in the drawing room, not daring to call for a drink. Reflection was something that gasped for sustenance in him, like a trout ripped out of its universe into a brutal one that hammered fists of agony against its red-lipped ears. The thought and the weather had made Mr. Wurthenberger bite his nails ragged to the quick.

On the fine day that eventually dawned, he fled down to the steerage, pursued by the fear that a squall might spoil the weather. The Italian woman had fallen fast asleep after the storm. Her hand was lying in repose in the Italian acrobat's short thick hand. "She has hadda paina," her husband said.

Maybe the *bambino* was going to be born. This was a nicer scene than Mr. Wurthenberger had dared hope for. His heart began to shake in him as if he were standing upon the brink of love. Whatever it was that was going to happen, he knew he could understand it, for every human emotion was as clear to him as the day. He knew the kind of heartbreaking picture this would make and the warm source of tears that it would make spring from the apple of the eye. His hands were shaking so that he could scarcely get the camera up before the two Italians, where they were sitting in the sun.

He started taking the picture of them as she sat there asleep, leaning against the acrobat. After a while Mr. Wurthenberger said to the husband, "I tell you what, Tony. You'd better wake her up. I'm getting a picture of a woman having a child, see? She's had a couple of pains and she's feeling pretty bad, see? And maybe the baby's going to come on the boat because the weather's been rough, you see, and maybe it's going to come beforehand and not in Italy, as they'd been planning. So they're both feeling pretty bad about it, see? The doctor on the small boat they're travelling on isn't so much as a doctor, and they're both feeling pretty sick about the baby coming on the boat instead of in Italy, as they'd been looking forward to."

Mr. Wurthenberger's knees had gone soft under him with his tenderness and his love for the thing he was saying. He was stooping down before them with his hands held tight together. Beads of anguish were lying like a crown of thorns upon his head.

"Do you get it, Tony?" he was saying. "Do you get an idea of the whole thing? Now, you just wake her up a little, Tony, just gradually, you see, while I start turning the handle."

He skipped lightly back to the camera, scarcely daring to breathe, and in this way the picture went on. After a little while, the Italian woman pushed herself up until she was sitting back against the blisters of dry paint on the side of the deckhouse.

"I feel bad," she said.

She sat very still, holding her two hands under her shawl. A small white mask of agony had fallen upon her lips, but she made no sign at all. She sat close to the white blisters of paint on the side of the deckhouse and closed her eyes. Tears had begun to run slowly down the face of the Italian acrobat.

Suddenly Mr. Wurthenberger dropped the handle of the camera and walked toward them.

"You're all right, Tony," he said. When he looked at the woman, he had to hold onto himself to keep from shaking her. "She's got to register something," he said. "I'm taking a woman in childbirth, you see. She can't just sit there kind of mooning and dozing along. You're getting something in the way of cash out of this, you know. After all, you aren't doing it for the love of the thing. Now look here," he said. "She can make a few movements. She's got to bring her hands into play." He squatted patiently down before the two Italians. "Now look here," he said. "This is a big thing. This is a big human crisis, do you see?" Suddenly he was stricken by the awful futility of any kind of speech with them. He jumped to his feet. "Can't you understand? Can't you get it? Can't you get the big importance of this thing?" he cried out to them. He thought he could strike the woman for her obstinacy. She sat there in silence, stubbornly pressing the small of her back into the blistered wood.

"Open your eyes, can't you?" he said. His nerves were shaking him. He was ready to scream aloud. "Listen," he said deliberately. "You got to open your eyes, you understand?"

The Italian woman opened her eyes and looked at him.

"There," he said. "That's fine."

Nervously he skipped back to his camera against the rail.

"That's fine," he said again as he watched her through the lens. "Now hold it. That's it. Keep on looking. Now roll 'em about a bit."

The woman straightened back against the deckhouse.

"I can't," she said. Her face had no expression at all. The woman sat perfectly still. Her eyes were closed.

"Christ!" said Mr. Wurthenberger.

"Maybe it hurts her pretty bad," said the Italian in apology. He wiped his nose on the back of his hand.

Mr. Wurthenberger felt his mind revolving in his skull. He crossed the deck and crouched before them again. "Listen," he said with a cold, terrible patience. "Just let your jaw fall open and scream." He turned patiently to the little acrobat. "Does she understand me?" he said. "Just tell her to try and scream. Won't you open your mouth and scream?" he was whispering to her persuasively.

The Italian woman's head was moving from side to side.

"Maybe it hurts her," said the Italian. He didn't know what to do.

NICE GIRL

❦

SHERWOOD ANDERSON

NO ONE SAW Agnes come down the stairs. She had a way of going about unnoticed. It made her father and her brother Harry furious. Her father mentioned it sometimes but Harry didn't, which might have been because Agnes knew too much about him. Sometimes Harry just stood and looked at her. "Oh, Lord, help us," he said. Occasionally, when she came into a room where the others were, her father looked up from his book or his paper. "Well," he said in amazement, "how'd you get in here?"

"Why, I just came in," Agnes said.

She didn't like such remarks. "Just because I don't go around making a racket," she thought.

She came down the stairs from her own room and heard voices in her mother's room. So there was something in the wind. Her father was scolding. (Agnes was a slender one. She walked softly.) There was a telephone stand in the big hall near the door to her mother's room. The door was closed at the moment. It was called the "big hall" not because it was particularly magnificent but to differentiate it from the upstairs hall. That one was called the "up hall." "I left my glasses on the window ledge in the up hall." It was convenient. Most of the rooms in the house were named, often rather fantastically: "the paint room," "the cider room," "Papa's coat room." The last was from Agnes's grandfather, on her mother's side. Agnes had heard an explanation. "Oh, he always came in and threw his overcoat on the bed in there."

Agnes stopped by the telephone stand, near the door to her mother's room, and picked up the telephone book. If either her father or her mother came suddenly out there, she would be in a quite innocent-seeming position, not eavesdropping on her father and mother, just looking for a number in the book.

She stood, her eyes shining. "So, that's it." Her sister Miriam's husband, Tom Haller, wanted to get a divorce. Agnes was thrilled, even joyous. Of course, not because Miriam was in trouble. "So, she didn't tell me that *that's* why she came home from Chicago," she thought. "Tom's chucking her, eh?" and then right away her thoughts went back to Miriam. "The sly little cat—not saying a word to me." They were always thinking in the family that Miriam was open and aboveboard. "They accuse me of being sly. What about *her?*" And now both her father and her mother knew about Tom and Miriam. If it turned out that Harry also knew and that Agnes herself was the only one left out, she would be good and sore. If she had any sympathy for Miriam, it would go fast enough if she found *that* out.

Her father was furious and was tramping up and down in her mother's room. "If he comes here, I'll show him!" he shouted. Tom Haller wanted a divorce and he didn't want to pay Miriam alimony.

"By God, I'll make him pay to the last cent. I'll take his skin off inch by inch."

It would be funny to see her father trying to take Tom Haller's skin off. Alfred Wilson, the father, was a rather small man and Tom was big. As for Harry, he was a physical weakling. Harry was older than either Miriam or Agnes, and had been in the World War. He had been gassed, and there was something wrong with his lungs and he got drunk. He got drunk oftener than anyone, except Agnes, in the family knew. She knew where he kept his bottle of whiskey hidden in the house. Harry knew that she was on to a lot no one else knew. It made him a little afraid of her.

Her father kept tramping up and down in her mother's room. All the others in the house thought that Agnes was away for the afternoon. She had told them all she was going driving with Mary Culbertson and had left the house just after lunch. Then she had changed her mind and had come back. She had phoned Mary from the drugstore and had come silently into the house and had gone up to her own room. Had she been playing a hunch? She hadn't known why she suddenly decided not to go with Mary. Her father's shoes made a queer creaking noise on the floor of her mother's room.

"Alfred, where did you get those shoes?" her mother said, and "Oh, damn shoes!" her father shouted. There was talk about her father's speaking too loud. "Kate will hear you, Alfred," her mother said. Kate was the new maid, a tall red-haired country woman. She had been working in the Wilson family only two weeks. It wouldn't do to let Kate find out too much about the family too rapidly. It was no good letting a maid become too familiar, almost impertinent, the way the last one was allowed to do.

Agnes stood now by the door of her mother's room listening, the telephone book in her hand, and then her father came to the door. She saw the knob turn, but he didn't come out at once. He just stood by the door talking big. So Agnes put down the telephone book and went, softly as usual, out to the front porch. She sat there a moment and then went to the side porch. She decided she would wait there. Presently her father would go off downtown to his law office and she would go to her mother's room. She would find out if her mother wanted to go on keeping everything a secret. Miriam had left the house just before Agnes came downstairs, and Agnes knew that Miriam would go downtown and find Harry. The two would go somewhere in Harry's car. "I bet they drink together," Agnes thought. She thought that it didn't look just right, a brother and sister being so thick. Before Miriam had married Tom Haller, she and Harry were always together during the years Miriam was going away to school and coming home for summer vacations. Agnes knew at that time that Miriam used to put up with, and even encourage, Harry's drinking. Before repeal, Harry had got his liquor from a man at the filling station out on the Mud Creek Highway. Agnes had known about it. She even knew that Miriam sometimes drove out there with Harry and waited in the car while he went in. Agnes had got the filling-station man arrested and sent to jail. No one knew about it. She had written a letter to the sheriff and signed a made-up name, and it worked. The sheriff raided the place and sure enough found a lot of whiskey, and the man was tried and sent to jail, but of course Harry just began getting whiskey somewhere else.

What had most aroused Agnes the day she heard her father and mother discussing Miriam's divorce was something that happened after she went down to meet Mary Culbertson and changed her mind. She had come back into the house unnoticed and had gone to her own room, off the "up hall." Then the telegraph boy arrived on his bicycle and she saw him through the window. He rang the bell and Kate, the maid, answered it. Her father was already in her mother's room with the door closed, but he wasn't talking loud then. The new maid was such a big, red-haired, red-armed thing and she had such a harsh, untrained voice, thought Agnes. And what a nerve, too, for she came to the foot of the stairs and called. "Miriam! Miriam! Here's a telegram for you," she called. Miriam should have reprimanded her. "Such management of things to let a maid call you by your first name!" Kate often called that way to Agnes, too, but Agnes couldn't protest, because if she did, if she were the only one in the house who did, she would only make the maid sore and then she couldn't get a thing done for her. If she wanted a dress pressed in a hurry, for instance, Kate could put it off, or even get purposely careless and burn it.

After she heard Kate call, Agnes had just stayed in her room, watching and listening. The door into the hall was closed, but Agnes went and opened it a crack. Miriam came quickly out of her own room, on the other side of the hall, and went part way down the stairs. If that new maid, Kate, were well trained, as she should be, if she had been told plainly by the mother how to do things when she had first come into the house, of course she would have come quietly up the stairs to the door of Miriam's room and knocked quietly. Agnes stood inside the door of her room and, through the crack, watched Miriam going part way down the stairs to the landing where the stairs turned, and Kate coming part way up.

"I signed for it," Kate said, handing the telegram to Miriam. "I got something boiling on the stove," she said, but she stood and waited until Miriam read it. That was because she was so curious. The nerve of her, calling out Miriam's name like that, actually screaming it, "Miriam! Miriam!"

Miriam wasn't slender like Agnes and she wasn't pretty. Her mouth was too big. It was like her mother's mouth. Miriam was an intellectual and she had gone away to school, to the University of Chicago, and Agnes hadn't. Just when Agnes, who was four years older than Miriam, got out of high school, her father went and speculated, like a fool, and lost a lot of money. He got back on his feet again after three or four years, and then he offered to send Agnes away to school, but she wouldn't go. She wasn't going to be in classes where she was the oldest one.

Agnes thought she was prettier than Miriam. She knew she was. She thought it was foolish, wasting your time with books. Men didn't like bookish women. She had a mass of shining, reddish-brown hair and nice, interesting, grayish-green eyes. She spent a lot of time keeping herself looking nice. It paid. Sometimes Harry tried to kid her about it, but she knew how to tell Harry where to get off, for, once, she had seen something happen. It was with the maid, the married one, they'd had just before Kate came. Her name was Mrs. Henry and her husband had got arrested for hitting a man with a billiard cue in a tough poolroom. She was good-looking, a tall blonde, and Agnes had heard things about her. Agnes wouldn't go so far as to say there was actually something between her and Harry, but one day Harry was in the kitchen, where he never should have been, right in the middle of the afternoon. Agnes thought he was a little lit up. He was trying to get a piece of fried chicken out of the refrigerator and Mrs. Henry didn't want him to have it. Agnes had come to the kitchen door and stood looking. Mrs. Henry said that if Harry took any of the chicken there wouldn't be enough for dinner. The woman's first name was Alice. "Ah, what the hell, Alice?" Harry said, and then she started to push him away from the icebox; they were both laughing, and Harry gave her a quick push and turned her right around and slapped her on the place where a person sits down. It was a sign of something.

On the stairs that day, Kate, the new maid, was burning with curiosity. She didn't really care if something did boil over in the kitchen. If you get a telegram in a family and have a maid who is a country woman, just off the farm, she always thinks something dreadful must have happened. Country people, farmers, don't get telegrams except when someone dies. Miriam's hand trembled as she opened the envelope. She went to her room and put on her hat and coat and went downstairs and called her father out of her mother's room and said a few words to him Agnes couldn't hear, although she was in the "up hall" listening, and then Miriam went out. But afterward Agnes heard her father go back into his wife's room and heard him talking to her about the telegram. It said that Tom Haller was coming on Wednesday. It was only Monday now. He was coming to have it out with Miriam about a divorce. That was it. Agnes had got a good look at Miriam before she went out and saw how scared and upset she looked. "I'm glad she's in trouble," she thought. Then she was ashamed and thought, "No, I'm not."

She had thought something was up when Miriam first came home from Chicago, two months before. She and Mollie Wilson, her mother, were always having whispered conferences, and there was a queer strained look in Miriam's eyes. She didn't have interesting eyes like Agnes's—they were a faded kind of blue. "I'll bet she's pregnant," Agnes thought at first, but later, before she found out the truth, she had already changed her mind. (Miriam and Tom Haller had been married three years. Miriam had got him when she went to Chicago to school.) Agnes had noticed things about Miriam, and wondered why she always looked as though she had been crying and why she was letting herself get fat. But she found out that it wasn't what she thought at first. Still, it was funny that neither Miriam nor her mother told Agnes, even though the Wilsons had always been a secretive family. She thought that if it were herself—if she, rather than Miriam, had married Tom Haller —this couldn't have happened, because of the way she felt the first time she ever saw Tom, when he came to Carlsville to marry Miriam. She thought that, if it had been herself, she would have got pregnant right away, and decided that if she ever got married that would be the best way. "I'll bet I could, too," she thought.

She had a lot of thoughts, after Miriam got the telegram and before that, ever since Miriam had married Tom. Tom, who was tall and blond, had come from Chicago and had married Miriam in the Wilsons' house in Carlsville. Agnes had been bridesmaid. It was quite a wedding, because Alfred Wilson was in politics. He was in the State Senate, and of course he had to invite everyone. The joke was that two of the most important men in Carlsville to invite, for political reasons, he didn't invite at all. He thought he had invited them, but he had not. Agnes had mailed the invitations, had carried them to the post office after they were addressed, and she had taken the two invitations out of the pile and torn them up. The wives of those two politicians were rarely invited anywhere by the best people, yet even so, Agnes hardly knew why she did it. She just did.

She herself, she thought, had been quite nice at the wedding. Tom Haller had come bringing another man with him, to be best man—certainly not a very interesting-looking man. He was older than Tom, a young professor of English or something, and he wore glasses and was shy. Agnes didn't like him at all and, besides, he was poor and an intellectual and nearsighted. Agnes would even bet anything that Tom had loaned his best man the money to come down to Carlsville from Chicago. Although she didn't want to say anything against Miriam, she just couldn't see what Tom and Miriam saw in each other, whereas if Miriam had taken a fancy to that English professor—he and Miriam both being so bookish—it would have made more sense. Of course she didn't say anything of that sort. She liked Tom. Once, when she was coming downstairs, the evening before the wedding—she had been upstairs in her room trying on her bridesmaid's gown and was going down to show it to her mother—she met Tom on the stairs, and he suddenly took her into his arms and kissed her. He said it was a brotherly kiss, but it wasn't. She knew better than that.

Finally, that day, after she had found out what all the other Wilsons knew, none of them having bothered to tell her, Agnes went up into her own room and sat by a window. She had a very satisfactory hour sitting up there and thinking. So the family hadn't thought it wise to tell her. Tom Haller was coming to see Miriam to talk over with her the matter of getting a divorce. Anyway, Tom couldn't get married again until he got the divorce, but, in spite of her father, Miriam would let him have it. Very likely she wouldn't even ask for alimony. Miriam was a fool. Agnes remembered again that moment on the stairs with Tom, the night before his wedding. "They are all fools," Agnes thought, and decided that if the family wanted to go on keeping things from her, she would be justified in keeping secret her own plans. She sat for a time having her own thoughts, and then got up and looked at herself in the glass. Tom Haller was to arrive in two days. "I'll go and get me a permanent tomorrow," she thought.

H*Y*M*A*N K*A*P*L*A*N, SAMARITAN

❦

Leonard Q. Ross

"THE DAY and the night, the wik following the wik, Father hoped for end of—"

"Miss Tarnova," Mr. Parkhill interrupted gently. "We say 'day and night,' not *'the* day and *the* night.' And 'week after week,' not *'the* week *following the* week.' You seem to use the definite article when it isn't necessary, and I'm afraid you—er—omit it when it is."

Olga Tarnova's eyelids fluttered in eloquent despair; she was not made for the rarefied atmosphere of higher learning. "Father said us—"

"*Told* us, Miss Tarnova."

Miss Tarnova moaned, fluttering her eyelids again. "Pardon. So Father *told* us not worry. So we try to altogather forgat."

"To forgat altogadder!" a voice interpolated. It was the voice of Hyman Kaplan, serene, polite, consummately confident.

Miss Tarnova looked at him coldly. "To altogather forgat!"

"To forgat altogadder!"

"Er—Mr. Kaplan," began Mr. Parkhill.

Miss Tarnova stamped her foot in anger. "How *I* said? *'To altogather forgat!'* What is matter?"

"Tsplit infinitif!" Mr. Kaplan cried triumphantly.

Mr. Kaplan had, by arduous concentration, memorized three phrases concerning English grammar, and he clung to them as cosmic verities: "Wronk tansel," "Dobble nagetif!," and "Tsplit infinitif!" (Mr. Parkhill had had a difficult time teaching Mr. Kaplan to say "Tsplit infinitif" instead of "Tsplit infinity." There was something about "Tsplit infinity" which had rung bells of recognition in Mr. Kaplan's soul.) Whenever the opportunity arose to use one of these three great phrases, Mr. Kaplan, ecstatic, would

56

seize it. "Tsplit infinitif!" he cried now, and the walls resounded with its majesty.

Miss Tarnova's eyes were burning. She stamped her foot again. "Article—not article—dafinite, indafinite—splitting finitive! I am the *Rossian*! I say what is in *heart*! *Nitchevo*! I stop!"

She stalked to her seat, a flame.

"Miss Tarnova, please," said Mr. Parkhill hastily. The class was buzzing with sympathy, surprise, opposition. Battle lines were forming. Mr. Parkhill hoped to stave off bloody linguistic strife. "I'm sure Mr. Kaplan meant no harm."

The passionate "Rossian" shook her black locks.

"Won't you go on?" Mr. Parkhill urged in his most pacifying tones.

Olga Tarnova cast a self-pitying glance at the heavens and, her voice dripping with *mal de monde,* murmured, "Other time, be so good. Other time."

"*Som* odder time," Mr. Kaplan said politely.

A rich Slavic oath issued from Miss Tarnova's cherry lips.

"My!" Mr. Kaplan murmured in admiration.

Mr. Parkhill quickly called on Peter Studniczka.

It was the first Recitation and Speech period of the season. Mr. Parkhill had held off the exercise as long as he could. He had introduced the beginners' grade to the sweet mysteries of Spelling, Grammar, Vocabulary, and Open Questions. Recitation and Speech practice, an ordeal greater than any of these because of its intensely personal character, its pitiless exposure of the individual to the public wrath, he had left for the last of the class routines.

Peter Studniczka walked slowly to the front of the room. He stopped at Mr. Parkhill's desk, his eyes downcast. A thread of perspiration appeared on his brow.

Mr. Parkhill nodded encouragingly. Mr. Studniczka did not meet his glance. His face was haggard, his tongue mute.

"Er—begin, Mr. Studniczka."

Mr. Studniczka took a tortured breath. He flushed. His eyes went into a stark, expressionless glaze. He opened his mouth.

"Lds gntlmns I lk Nv—"

The words died into a gurgle and then a silence.

"That was *fine*, Mr. Studniczka," said Mr. Parkhill, trying to be gay. "Go on."

Ghastly, drawn, Mr. Studniczka took another breath. His eyes, hosts to terror, were fixed somewhere between Arcturus and the top of Mrs. Yanoff's head. He opened his parched lips; his tongue clucked drily. No words came out.

Mr. Parkhill kept smiling helplessly. Mrs. Moskowitz fumbled in her purse for a handkerchief. Miss Caravello resorted to prayer.

Suddenly, from his seat in the middle of the front row, Mr. Kaplan spoke. "Jost *talk*ink," he said in a gentle voice. "Ve all your frands, your *pels*."

Mr. Studniczka's eyes searched for the speaker.

"Tseasy! An' efter all," the Samaritan whispered, "voise den Tarnova you *ken't* be!" Mr. Parkhill looked toward Olga Tarnova in alarm.

For a moment more Peter Studniczka made no sound. Then, without warning, in one single, breath-taking torrent, uninterrupted by the slightest pause or cadence, he blurted out, "Ladies gantlemans I lak Nev York is fine place good eat also work I buy two suits with pants two on one I see nice in movie pic' for have new glass for eye to look at America sure fine more good as old place not sorry come go marry good lady cook wash hev childs boy name Frank boy name Dinko also girl not care how name thank you please."

And like a tornado which had ripped into the vast silence, shattered it with one swirling gust, and roared away, leaving a stillness more ominous, more pervasive, more terrible, Peter Studniczka, unburdened of speech, stumbled blindly to his seat.

The big clock hammered the seconds. Mr. Parkhill did not stir. The eyes of the students remained rooted to the spot where, an instant ago, Peter Studniczka had played the eruptive Demosthenes. Mr. Pinsky looked dazed. Mrs. Moskowitz breathed asthmatically, her handkerchief arrested in mid-air. Miss Tarnova was so astonished that she neglected to flutter her eyelids in astonishment. Only the irrepressible Mr. Kaplan seemed to cling to rationality; he was alive with silent joy, celebrating the triumph of his ward.

"Er—" Mr. Parkhill said at last. "Corrections?"

The beginners' grade of the American Night Preparatory School for Adults sat immobile, calcified.

"*No* corrections?" Mr. Parkhill asked again, as if by sheer will he hoped to break through the impenetrable.

Miss Mitnick found her voice. "So *fast* was it—"

There was a timid chorus of assent. "Yeh," said Mr. Marschak.

"It vas movvellous!" cried Mr. Kaplan.

"Too fest," protested Fanny Gidwitz.

"Ve livink in an aitch speed!" Mr. Kaplan stormed.

"No unnistan'," growled Stanislaus Wilkomirski.

"Go to a car spacialist!" Mr. Kaplan suggested.

"Class, please!" said Mr. Parkhill. No one seemed to hear him.

"No good!" Olga Tarnova leaped into the fray. "Is all one santence!"

Mr. Kaplan's riposte was instantaneous. "*You* should be able make op soch a santence!"

Mr. Parkhill caught his breath. "Please! Ladies! Gentlemen! Let's not forget this is a classroom."

The hot voices faded; there were scowls, grumblings, threatening looks. In the back row, Peter Studniczka stared at his palms in agony.

"Are there any *definite* corrections?" asked Mr. Parkhill.

Up shot Mr. Plonsky's hand. "Even if was so fest, *I* got corraction," he said, rather smugly. "Was missing 'the' and 'a,' also 'and.' Some woibs was prasent for past and past for prasent. 'Nev York' isn't 'New York,' and 'Thank you please' isn't good in the foist place!"

It was a staggering exhibition of scholarship. The pro-Plonsky forces rallied. Mr. Kaplan's face was a cloud.

"Well," Mr. Parkhill said, fighting for time, "that is quite a list of errors. But perhaps we shouldn't be too—er—"

A clarion voice cut through the air. "It vas a movvellous spitch! Foist-class good! I vant to sayink a few voids, plizz!" Up jumped Hyman Kaplan.

"Mr. Kaplan! It isn't your—"

"Plizz, lat me talkink, Mr. Pockheel! Lat dis be mine spitch! *Plizz!*"

Mr. Parkhill frowned and shook his head, but before he could

say a word Mr. Kaplan had taken free gigantic strides to the front
of the room, a Galahad in shining armor. He buttoned his coat,
shot his cuffs, ran his hand through his hair, and cried, "Ladies an'
gantleman an' Mr. Pockheel! Vat's de minnink Jostice?"

A hush fell upon the battalions.

"*Jostice?* Vat it minns?" Mr. Kaplan's voice was mighty.

Mr. Studniczka's big hands trembled as he fumbled with his tie.

"I'll tell you," Mr. Kaplan continued. "Jostice is vun de finest,
most beauriful emotions fromm human beinks! It's nawble, sveet,
good. It's liftink op humanity!" (Mr. Kaplan, indeed, seemed to
be lifting up with the very words; he spoke from raised heels, for
emphasis.) "Do enimals have Jostice? No. Do sevages havink? No.
Den who got?" Mr. Kaplan paused for the veriest fraction of a
moment, his eyes blazing. "Tsivilized pipple!"

"*Mr. Kaplan!*" Mr. Parkhill felt himself duty-bound to object.
But Mr. Kaplan, Jovian in wrath, had soared on.

"Vy ve all came to vunderful U. S.? Becawss here is de stritts
pasted mit gold? Ha! De stritts don't got gold. Iven de *benks* don't
got gold. Becawss ve vant to gattink reech all of a sodden? Ha! No
vun believes dis any more! Ectual, ve came to America for plain
an' tsimple rizzon. Becawss here ve got Friddom! Here ve livink
like brodders! Here ve are, like dey say, 'Vun nation, inwisible,
mit Liberty an' Jostice *free for all*!' "

The class sat transfixed.

"So now comms a fine man like Studniczka"—Mr. Studniczka
looked up in terror at the sound of his name—"an' he gats op to
make his foist spitch, to givink a semple his English our vunderful
titcher should halpink him ot. An' vat he gats?" Mr. Kaplan swept
the room with a reprimanding eye. "Sympaty? Unnisstandink?
Jostice? No, mine frands. He gats fromm *som* pipple"—Mr. Kaplan
froze the unnamed souls with an icy glance—"shop voids, smot-
elick crititzizink! Batter *ashame* should dose soitin pipple be!"
Several of them already writhed in the purgatory to which Mr.
Kaplan had consigned them.

Mr. Kaplan's voice changed. He turned to Mr. Plonsky; honey
was on his tongue. "Podden me, Plonsky. How lonk you in U. S.?"

Mr. Plonsky did not answer.

"Mine dear Plonsky, I only esk a tsimple qvastion," Mr. Kaplan smiled. The spirit of the Borgias was in that smile. "Ufcawss, if you tong-tie—"

"Ten years!" Mr. Plonsky cried defiantly.

Mr. Kaplan nodded. "Tan yiss. My! Tan yiss!" He seemed to be relaying the information to his Muse. "*Tan* yiss!" His eyes flashed. "An' still only in beginnis' cless!"

Mr. Parkhill cleared his throat.

"Studniczka, how lonk *you* in U. S.?" asked Mr. Kaplan.

The heads of the students turned to Peter Studniczka. Everything hung upon his answer. Mr. Studniczka's head was low, his cheeks flaming.

"Plizz, Studniczka." Mr. Kaplan's voice was as gentle as a sleepy child's. "You got to *halp*ink me, I should make a strong case. Like a lawyer. Vell, how lonk you in U. S.?"

Mr. Studniczka stared at his shoes. "Five year," he said.

Mr. Kaplan uttered a cry of pure rapture. "Fife yiss! Only *fife* yiss an' *also* in beginnis' cless! Studniczka, you Hau Kay! You—"

"How long *you* in America?" Mr. Plonsky cried desperately.

Mr. Kaplan drew himself up with dignity. "*I'm* comparink!" he said.

The bell rang. Without another word Mr. Kaplan marched to his seat. His smile was triumphant.

The students got up and collected their things. They argued hotly. They began to file to the door. "Good night"'s came to Mr. Parkhill in waves.

"Good night. Good night," he repeated. "Good night."

Mr. Parkhill watched them as they crowded out. It had been a deplorable evening, quite a deplorable evening. He wanted to see Mr. Kaplan alone for a moment, to warn him against future exhibitions of so disruptive a character. He felt, for some strange reason, that he wanted to thank Mr. Kaplan, too. But the students were in a thick, shuffling mass. Mr. Kaplan, his eyes aglitter with the zest of battle, was in the middle of the mob. At his heels, like a loyal dog, was Peter Studniczka. Just before they pushed their way through the door Mr. Parkhill heard Mr. Studniczka say, "Mister."

Mr. Kaplan turned his head.

"Mister," said Peter Studniczka, "you talk good."

Mr. Kaplan looked at his protégé for a moment. *"Me?"* He shook his head kindly. "No. It's to leff." He narrowed his eyes. "You know how lonk *I'm* in U. S.?"

Mr. Studniczka didn't know.

"Fifteen yiss."

"You talk good," said Mr. Studniczka stubbornly.

PRELUDE TO REUNION

❦

Oliver La Farge

THE ROOM was furnished with what the college issued: a desk, placed dead centre under the overhead light, a table, three wooden chairs, a bed, a bureau, and an empty fireplace, the brick floor of which was free of ashes and cigarette butts. One shelf of the bookcase was almost filled with textbooks, a one-volume edition of Shakespeare, and a Bible. On the table were two notebooks and a dictionary, a cup and saucer, a plate, and a small electric stove with a saucepan on it. A calendar and two pine cones had been arranged on the mantelpiece in an effort at decoration. There was a framed photograph of a middle-aged woman on the bureau, and two neckties hung from a corner of the mirror. The room looked as if its occupant had moved in that afternoon and would leave tomorrow.

The boy paced slowly, methodically, between the fireplace and the bookcase. Passing the window, he caught the smell of the night —the new, disturbing mildness of spring—and he could hear voices below on the campus. He was tall, thin, fair-haired, with too much Adam's apple and too long a nose. He was not thinking, he was stringing out the time before he should decide to take a walk.

In a few moments he would put on necktie and coat and go downstairs. As he stepped outside, he would feel a faint anticipation, a nameless, automatic stirring of hope, which he would quickly discount by a defensive reflex, a moment of pain never admitted. Then he would stroll. If he met fellows who sat in his classes, he would walk a little faster until he passed them, but sometimes even so they would remember him and nod, or say "Hello" or even "Hello, Matterson." He would say "Hello" and go on by, letting them continue their appointed ways. His own pace, too, would be a declaration that he was going somewhere.

By one route or another he would come to the Women's School.
Here his walk would be a swinging, unhesitating stride. He would
not turn his head, he would just go on through, but his eyes would
take in a wide range, the groups of girls and the pairs of girls and
fellows. Last week, the first night of the warm weather, a man who
sat next him in Biochemistry passed him with a girl. He said, "Hi,
Matterson. Sparking?" He'd answered, "Hello, Newman. Just
scouting," and Newman and the girl had laughed.

They were all just kids, really—as old as he, but nothing had
taught them seriousness, His brain could run rings around them.
He wasn't interested in their eternal play.

Beyond the School he would come out into the town, buy a
paper, and then return to his room, the room he was walking up
and down now, not thinking anything much except that it was
time, perhaps, to go out and get a paper.

A firm knock on his door brought him up sharp. He moved to
open it, then stood back and called, "Come in!"

The visitor, who entered rather self-consciously, was a well-
dressed boy of medium height, neither fair nor dark, with a
scrubbed, healthy face.

"Matterson?" he said. "I'm Bill Farraday. May I come in?"

"Hello. Sit down." His anger at himself for being so tense added
to his stiffness.

"I live in this entry, 2 B."

Matterson knew well enough, as he knew that Farraday had his
letter in hockey and was a candidate for class marshal. He nodded,
watchful.

Farraday arranged himself with an effect of relaxation for which
the chair was not well adapted. He looked around the room, said
"Nice," then broke off. The thin boy understood; it wasn't a nice
joint. Seeing that his visitor was ill at ease, he felt a shade more
comfortable.

"Looks like spring had really come, doesn't it?" Farraday said.
He became more assured at the sound of his own voice. "Here the
winter's over, and this is the first time I've been up here." Matterson listened, guarded, protecting himself. "This college is so damn
big you can't hope to know everyone, but I'd promised myself to

meet all the men in this entry. You know how it is. You get tied up in so many things and the first thing you know the ice has melted and the ball team's coming out of the cage."

Matterson said, "Yeah."

"Where do you come from? You're not from around here, are you?"

"Vermont."

"Well! Why did you pick to come here?"

"I'm going into analytical chemistry and I wanted to be under MacPherson."

"Oh. Oh yeah, sure." Farraday paused again, then took off as if from a cue. "You had a scholarship?"

"Not to start with; the first two years I worked my way. Then I got the Bernstein." He was proud of that; it was the best there was in science for undergraduates. "Now I'm hoping for the Marlin Fellowship if I can get my *magna cum* all right."

Farraday looked vaguely uncomfortable. The look passed. "Good for you. I admire a guy like you and I'm glad I came up." Again his flow of talk became smooth. His voice had a flattering frankness. "Yeah, when I get out of here I'll go to Wall Street, and I guess that twenty years from now I'll be just another bond salesman living the old country-club life, and I'll be bragging about how I used to know you. I've had it easy and you've had it tough."

The Vermonter felt an unfamiliar warmth run through him. "It's been tough sometimes," he said. He hesitated, then added with an effort, "I saw you shoot that long goal against Colmouth."

"Oh, that was just luck." Farraday was visibly pleased. He pulled out a pack of cigarettes. "Smoke?"

"No thanks."

"Oh. Do you mind—"

"Go ahead."

"Come down to my rooms sometime, won't you? Sling the bull, you know. I generally have a little beer on hand—or ginger ale."

"I like beer." Matterson considered explaining that he didn't smoke on account of the expense, then decided not to.

Farraday brightened. "That's fine. I mean it. Drop in."

"Thanks." He wanted to say more, but didn't know how.

"Say, a man like you, working your way along, and then getting fellowships and things—I'd like your slant on this endowment business."

Matterson had read the ballyhoo with a mounting sense of discomfort. The University was driving for extra endowment and the Senior Class Committee had voted a graduation gift of fifteen thousand dollars, which would mean a little over twenty dollars a member. The gift was getting a big play from the Endowment Fund's publicity bureau in going after the graduates.

"Well," he said, "I guess it's a good idea."

"Yeah, I think so, too. Our tuition fees don't cover the cost of our education. When you average it up—the men on scholarships and things—the University gives us each nearly a thousand dollars." Farraday caught himself up. "Of course," he said hastily, "that's what you expect the old place to do—help men like you who really have brains. It's part of a university's proper function." He looked around. "Got an ashtray?"

"Chuck it in the fireplace."

Farraday threw the butt, then pulled out the pack again. "I guess I'm smoking a lot right now. What with the finals coming on and all the boning to do and one thing and another, I get kind of nervous." He lit up. "This endowment business on top of the rest has me about daffy. You see, I'm in charge of this entry and we're short on our quota. I dunno how it is, some of the fellows don't seem to appreciate what the old school does for them. I guess I'm a rotten collector; it kind of burns me up to get after a man if he isn't willing." He gave a short, unreal laugh. "Yeah, I hate doing it. I've upped my share to fifty bucks, though God knows, I guess it means the sheriff will be after me, what with the old unpaid bills and all." He made the last statement with a smile, as one man speaking to another of a common problem.

Matterson just watched him, saying nothing.

"I've got you down for five bucks," Farraday said. "Of course, it's up to you. You know what you can afford, spreading it over the next two months."

Matterson continued staring at him. Out of a swirl inside himself he said quietly, without a shade of defiance in his tone, "You can put me down for ten."

"Why say, that's great. Say, that's the real spirit, Matterson.

Wait till I tell some of the other men that, the ones who've been holding out." He pulled at his cigarette, held it a moment, threw it in the fireplace. "Yeah, that's great. Well, look, I've got to get after some of the others now." He rose. "Don't forget to drop in on me sometime."

Matterson said, "Sure. Thanks."

Farraday answered heartily, "Thanks to you. Well, so long. Be seeing you."

"So long."

Matterson sat and stared at the long-awaited, casual disorder of the two cigarette stubs in the fireplace. Then he stood with his hands in his pockets. Ten dollars was catastrophic. Double what the rich boy thought him good for—pride stiffened in him, covering the pain of a warm moment betrayed. More slowly than usual, he tied his necktie, put on his coat, and went out.

A SMALL DAY

❧

ERSKINE CALDWELL

GOVERNOR GIL was standing astride the path, knocking heads off the weeds, when Walter Lane came up the hill from the spring. A wide circle of wilted weeds lay on the ground around him, and his walking stick was still swinging. It looked as if he had been waiting there for half an hour or longer.

"It's been mighty hot today," Walter said, stopping and lowering the two pails of water to the ground.

"It's a small day when the sun don't shine," Governor Gil said. "Where's the rest of your family and the girl?"

"My wife and the young ones went over to visit her folks this afternoon," Walter told him. "They'll be coming home sometime tonight after supper." He turned around and looked down the path behind. "Daisy's coming up the path any minute now. She's down at the spring filling a bucket."

Governor Gil looked down the path, but Daisy was not within sight. It was almost a hundred yards from the crown of the slope down to the bottom of the hill, where the spring was.

"I reckon I can wait here," he said, taking a new grip on his walking stick and bending forward to reach the weeds farthest away. "It's a small day when I can't afford to spend a little time waiting."

Walter watched the heads tumble off the stalks of weeds. Governor Gil went about it as if he were determined not to let a weed in the whole county go to seed that year. Every once in a while he shifted his position a little, stamping down the wilted weeds and reaching for new ones to whack at. Sometimes he started out in the morning, after breakfast, on horseback to see how his cotton and cane crops were growing, but before he got out of sight of home he always got off his horse and started whacking away at the weeds with his walking stick. He hated weeds worse than he did boll weevils or screwworms. However, for some reason or other, he never paid any attention to the weeds that grew in the yard around his house; they were so rank there that sometimes his hunting dogs got lost in the growth and had to backtrack their way out.

"Did you want to see me, Governor Gil, or was it Daisy you asked about?" Walter said, wondering.

Instead of answering, Governor Gil stopped a moment and glanced down the path. He nodded his head in that direction, and returned to swinging his stick at the weeds.

Governor Gil Counts had once, for a term, been governor of the state, about twenty-five or thirty years before, and the title suited him so well that nobody ever thought of calling him anything else. He ran his farm with the help of Walter Lane and several other tenants, and never left it. He had not been out of the county since the day he came home from the governor's office, and he had said he would never leave home again. He lived a quarter of a mile up the road in a big three-story mansion, from which the white paint had peeled while he was serving his term in office. The once-white three-story columns rising from the front porch were now as dark and rough as the bark on a pine tree.

"There's no sense in standing out here in the sun," Walter said. "Come on to my house and take a seat in the porch shade, Governor Gil. Daisy'll be along to the house just about as soon as she'll get here."

"This'll do," he said, stopping and looking down the path. "I haven't got time to sit down now."

He went past Walter and started down the path toward the spring. Walter left his pails and followed behind. Heads of weeds tumbled right and left of them.

At the crown of the slope they saw Daisy coming up. She was carrying a pail of water in one hand and fanning herself with a willow branch.

"I may as well tell you now, Walter," Governor Gil said, stopping. "It's time for your girl to marry. It's dangerous business to put it off after they get a certain age."

Walter took a half a dozen steps around Governor Gil and stopped where he could see his face.

"Who ought she to marry?" Walter said.

Governor Gil let go at some weeds around his knees, whacking his stick at them just under the seed pods. The heads flew in all directions.

"I've arranged for that," he said. "I sent my lawyer a letter today telling him to get a licence. It'll be here in a few days."

Walter looked again at Governor Gil, and then down the path. Daisy had come over the crown of the slope.

"That might be all right," Walter said, "but I don't know if she'll be tamed. Right now she's just about as wild as they come. Of course, now, I'm not raising any serious objections. I'm just going over in my mind the drawbacks a man might run into."

"A year from now there might be plenty of drawbacks," Governor Gil said. "Right this minute drawbacks don't count, because she's reached the marrying age, and nothing else matters. If I had a daughter, Walter, I'd want to do the right thing by her. I'd want her to marry before drawbacks had a chance to spoil her. I'm ready to marry her without an argument."

"You damned old fool," Daisy said, dropping her pail, "what put that into your head?"

Governor Gil had drawn back to let go at a clump of weeds swaying in the breeze beside the path, but he never finished the stroke. His stick fell back against his knees and the clump of weeds continued to sway in the wind.

"Now, that's what I was thinking about," Walter said. "I had an idea she wouldn't be willing to be tamed just yet."

"Why, I've been counting on this for a pretty long time," Governor Gil said excitedly. "I've just been biding my time all this while when you were growing up, Daisy. I've had my eyes on you for about three years now, just waiting for you to grow up."

"You damned old fool," Daisy said, stooping down for her pail and starting around them in the path.

Walter did not try to stop her. He looked at Governor Gil to see what he had to say now.

They watched her for a moment.

"She'll tame," Governor Gil said, nodding his head at Walter and following her up the path to the house.

When they got to the back door, Daisy put the pail on the shelf and sat down on the doorstep. She sat and looked at them with her knees drawn up under her elbows and her chin cupped in her hands.

"Maybe if you could just wait—" Walter began.

He was waved aside by a sweep of the walking stick.

"I'm going to have the handseling tonight," Governor Gil said, nodding his head at Daisy and flourishing the stick in the air. "The marrying can wait, but the handseling can't. The licence will be along from my lawyer in a day or two, and that's just a matter of formality, anyway."

Walter looked at Daisy, but she only stared more sullenly at them.

"I reckon we ought to wait till my wife gets back from visiting her folks," Walter said. "She ought to have a little say-so. For one thing, she'll have to make Daisy some clothes first, because Daisy hasn't got much to wear except what she's got on, and that's so little it wouldn't be decent if we weren't homefolks. Just about all she's got to her name is that little slimsy gingham jumper she's wearing. My wife will want to make her a petticoat, if nothing else. It would be a sin and a shame for her to get married like she is now. If she had something to wear under what she's got on, it might be different, but I won't be in favor of sending her out to get married in just a slimsy jumper between her and the outside world."

Governor Gil shook his walking stick in the air as if to wave away any possible objection Walter might mention.

"That's all right for the marriage," he said, "but that won't be for a few days yet. Your wife will have plenty of time to make up a petticoat for her if she wants to. But she won't even have to do that, because I'll buy her whatever she'll need after the marriage. And what she'll need for the handseling won't be worth mentioning."

He stopped and turned around to look at the sun. It was already setting behind the pine grove in the west.

"Had your supper yet?" he asked, looking at Walter and nodding at Daisy.

"Not yet," Walter said. "We didn't stop work in the cotton until about half an hour ago, and the first thing that needed doing was carrying up the water from the spring. Daisy, you go in the kitchen and start getting something ready to eat. Maybe Governor Gil will stay and eat with us tonight."

"No," he said, waving his stick at Daisy, "don't do that, Daisy. You just come up to my house and get your meal there tonight. There's no sense in you getting all worn out over a hot stove now. There's plenty to eat up there."

He turned to Walter.

"If your wife won't be home till late tonight, you just come up to my house and go around to the kitchen, and the help will set you out a good meal, Walter."

He started walking across the yard toward the road. When he got to the corner of the house, he stopped and found that neither Daisy nor her father had made a move to follow him.

"What's the matter?" he said impatiently.

"Well, now," Walter said, "I can make Daisy go up to your house, Governor Gil, but I can't be held responsible for what she does after she gets there. I wish you would wait till my wife came back tonight before you took Daisy off, but if your mind is made up not to wait, then all I can say is you'll have to charge her yourself after she gets there."

"She won't need any charging," Governor Gil said. "I've yet to know the wildest one of them that wouldn't tame when the time comes to handsel."

He turned around and started walking toward the road that led to his house, a quarter of a mile away.

Walter looked down at the doorstep, where Daisy still sat sullen and motionless.

"You ought to be tickled to death to have the chance to marry Governor Gil," he told her. "Who else is there in the county who'll treat you nice and give you all you want? I'll bet there's many a girl who'd jump at the chance to marry him."

"The damned old fool," Daisy said.

"Well, you'd better," he told her. "I'll bet your mother will make you, if I can't. She's no fool, either. She knows how well off you'll be, not having to go hungry for something to eat, and having enough clothes to cover your nakedness, neither one of which you've got now, or ever will have, if you don't go on up there like you ought to."

Walter sat down on the bottom step and waited for Daisy to say something. The sun had set, and it would be getting dark soon. If she did not go right away, Governor Gil might get mad and change his mind.

Presently he turned around and looked up at her.

"What's the matter with you, Daisy? You won't even say anything. What's got into you, anyway?"

"What does he want me to go up there tonight for?" she asked. "He said the licence wouldn't be here for two or three days."

"That's just Governor Gil's way, Daisy. He makes up his mind to do something, and nothing stops him once it's made up. He wants to marry you, and he wants to right now. There's no sense in putting it off, anyway. The best thing for you to do is to start right in before he changes his mind. If you don't, you'll live to be sorry, because tomorrow you'll have to go right back to the field again—tomorrow and every day as long as cotton grows."

Daisy got up without saying anything and went into the house. She was in her room for ten or fifteen minutes, and when she came to the door, it was dark outside. She could barely see her father sitting on the steps at her feet.

"Now, that's what I call sense," Walter said. "I thought you'd change your mind after you got to thinking about all these hot days in the sun out there in the cotton."

She went down the steps past him and crossed the yard without a word. She started up the road in the direction of Governor Gil's mansion.

After she had gone, Walter began to wonder what his wife would say when she came home. He was certain she would be glad to hear that Governor Gil wanted to marry Daisy, but he was not so sure of what she would say when he told her that the marriage licence would not come for another two or three days. He decided it would be best not to say anything about that part to her. Just as long as she knew Governor Gil had come to the house to ask Daisy to marry him, she would be satisfied.

It was pitch dark when he got up and went into the kitchen, made a light, and looked around for something to eat. He found some bread left over from dinner, and he did not have to build a fire in the cook stove after all. He sat down at the kitchen table and ate his fill of bread and sorghum.

After he had finished, he blew out the light and went to the front porch to sit and wait for his wife to come home.

Up the road he could see lights in Governor Gil's house. There was a light in the kitchen, as usual, and one in the front part of the house, too. Upstairs two or three rooms were lighted for the first time since he could remember.

Just when he was expecting his wife and children to get there any moment, he heard somebody running down the road. He got up and listened as the sound came closer. It was somebody running fast, because the sound came closer every second.

He ran out to the road to see who it was. At first he thought it might be Daisy, but he soon knew it wasn't, because a boy called out to him.

"Mr. Walter! Mr. Walter!"

"Who's that?" he shouted back.

A Negro houseboy stopped, panting, in the road beside him.

"What's the matter, Lawson?"

"Mr. Walter, Governor said to tell you if you ever raise another hellcat like Miss Daisy, he'll chop your head off. Now, Mr. Walter, I didn't say it! Please, sir, don't think I said it! It was Governor who told me to tell you that! You know I wouldn't say that myself, don't you, Mr. Walter?"

"What's the matter up there, Lawson?" Walter asked the boy.

"I don't know exactly, Mr. Walter, except that Governor started yelling upstairs a while ago, and he hasn't stopped yet. He told me to telephone for the doctor and the lawyer to come in a hurry. He hardly stopped yelling long enough to tell me, either. Soon as I telephoned for them, he told me to run down here as fast as I could and tell you what I told you."

"Was Miss Daisy up there then?" Walter asked.

"I reckon it was Miss Daisy who made him yell," Lawson said hesitatingly.

"Why?"

"I don't know if Governor wants me to tell you," Lawson said. "He only told me to tell you what I already told you, Mr. Walter."

"You'd better tell me, Lawson. What was it?"

"Miss Daisy flew into him and pretty near beat the daylights out of him. Governor was yelling and nursing his hurt so much he didn't have time to say much else."

Walter started back to the porch to sit down and wait for his wife to come home. He could not keep from laughing a little, but he tried to hold himself back so he could laugh all the more with his wife when she got there.

Lawson was still standing outside the yard. He turned around to tell the boy to go on back.

"What else did Governor Gil say, Lawson?" he asked him.

"I didn't hear him say much else, except Governor said it'll be a mighty small day when he tries to handsel a hellcat like Miss Daisy again."

Walter went to the porch and sat down. He leaned back and started to laugh. He could not wait for his wife any longer. He leaned back and laughed until he slid out of the chair.

MIDSUMMER

❧

Nancy Hale

THEY WOULD ride through the hot, dim woods that sultry, ominous August. From the hard ground, littered with spots of sifted sun, on the hills their horses would carry them in a minute to the hollows. There was something terrible about the hollows, deep-bottomed with decaying leaves, smelling of dead water and dark leafage and insufferable heat. The sound of the horses' feet was like a confused heartbeat on the swampy ground. They both felt it. They used to get off their horses, without having said a word, and helplessly submerge themselves in each other's arms, while the sweat ran down their backs under their shirts. They never talked there. They stood swaying together with their booted feet deep in the mulch, holding each other, hot and mystified in this green gloom. From far away in the upper meadows they could always hear the cicada reaching an unbearable, sharpened crescendo.

After a while the queer possession would grow too much for them, and, dizzy and faint, they would mount the horses again. The path carried them up to a long field where they would kick their horses and gallop wildly. The meadow grasses were dusty gold in all this heat, and when they galloped a hot wind pressed by them and all the million flies flew away from the horses' necks. Streaming and throbbing, they would pull up at the end of the field, and could laugh and begin to talk again. Dan would pull the squashed package of Camels out of the pocket of his wet blue shirt and they would each light one, with their horses' wet sides pressed together, and ride along at a walk. Then it would be time for Dan to go back to the stables to give his next lesson.

The country-club stable yard was bright and normal, hot as

thunder as they rode in, with the water in the trough near boiling
and the brown horses looking out of the boxes into the sunlight.
Dan put the horses away in the dark strawy stalls, and then he
would walk back to Victoria, standing at the precise point where
she had got off her horse. He would walk toward her in his blue
shirt and brick-red breeches, his black hair mounting damp and
thick from his red forehead, and his eyes as blue as an alcohol
flame, lighting another of his Camels. He would offer her one.
Then they would walk over to the stable yard well and he would
pull up a bucket of cold water. He would say, "Will you have
some water, Miss?" and hand her some in the glass that stood on
the well's edge. She looked at his shoulders and his big red throat
as she drank, and pushed damp ends of hair away from her face.
Then he would have a drink.

When Dan rode out of the yard again, with some group of
children perched on the high horses following him, she would
wave at him as he turned the corner into the road, and he would
make a little bow from the neck, the bow of an Irish groom. Then
he and the children would trot noisily down the macadam, Dan
riding so beautifully and carelessly, half-around in his saddle, with
one hand on the horse's rump, telling the children to keep their
heels down. Victoria would climb into her big green roadster and
drive out of the stable yard as fast as she dared, skidding the
corner and going up the road in the other direction with the ball
of her foot jammed down on the accelerator.

Victoria Jesse was sixteen that sultry summer. She lived on
White Hill in her parents' Italian villa with the blue tile roof,
so gruesomely out of place in the New England landscape. Her
parents were in France, but the servants and old Nana were in the
house and the garden was kept up by the disagreeable gardener,
always on his knees by the rose bushes, which dropped thick petals
on the turf. The water in the cement swimming pool was soup-
warm and dappled with tiny leaves from the privet bushes around.
The tennis court was as hard and white as marble, and the white
iron benches drawn up around its edge were so hot all day that
they could not be sat upon. The Venetian blinds in the house
were kept drawn, and the rooms were dim and still, with faint

sweat upon the silver candlesticks and the pale marble of the hall floor.

Victoria was sixteen, and sometimes, at the end of the afternoon, when she sat in a rattan chair on the shadowed lawn, when the grass grew cooler and a breeze sprang up and the exhausted birds began to sing, she thought she would go wild with the things that were happening inside her. She wanted to stand on the edge of the pool and stretch upward until she grew taller and taller, and then dive violently into the water and never come up. She wanted to climb the huge pine tree on the lawn, throw herself upward to the top by some passionate propulsion, and stretch her arms wildly to the sky. But she could only sit around interminably in chairs on the lawn in the heat and quiet, beating with hate and awareness and bewilderment and violence, all incomprehensible to her and pulling her apart.

She could only drive her car as fast as it would go, wrenching it around corners, devouring the ribbon of road with it, driving for hours with the unformed hope of adventure; she could only be cross with Nana and so passionately disagreeable to her old playmates on White Hill that she was not asked to play tennis or picnic, which gave her a melancholy satisfaction. She took a dizzy pleasure in going to the dances at the club with nothing on under her dress and a belt pulled tight around her waist, and dancing with the fuzzy, pink-faced boys of her age, pulsating in all her muscles to the jazz music, and then suddenly walking out and leaving as she had come, alone in her roadster, streaming along the white moonlit roads in the middle of the night, until she was so tired that she had to go home and fall into tossing sleep on the slippery white sheet of her bed.

She could not imagine what was happening to her; she had never imagined such violent sensations as beat at her; inside she was like the summer itself—sultry and fiery, and racked by instantaneous thunderstorms. At the end of the day the air relaxed into moist, nostalgic evening, but she had no relaxing, only a higher tension in the poignant secretness of night. She thought, with defiance, that she must be going crazy.

She had grown thin from her own fire and the unrelenting fire of the weather. She was white, and her green eyes burned unhappily in her pointed face; her bright, thick hair seemed thicker from being always a little damp.

Superimposed on all this ferment was the incessant preoccupation with Dan. She began to take riding lessons in June, to work off a little of this torturing energy, since she wanted to be away from the infuriating "younger crowd," and felt it might satisfy her to ride as violently as she drove a car. Dan took her out, and within half an hour, with this tropical immediacy with which she was feeling everything, she uncomprehendingly desired him and wanted to touch him, and could not take her eyes off him. She gave herself no time to be frightened at such unprecedented emotion. She got off her horse to get a drink at a deserted well in the middle of a field, and he got off to help her. With some kind of instinctive simplicity, she went and stood against him, facing him, touching him, waiting for him to do something. He acted; he put one arm around her, holding the horses' reins with the other hand, and leaned and kissed her hard. For a moment she had the first relief she had had in weeks, and from that moment she wanted him more and more to touch her and to kiss her. After his first reaction, Dan became very stilted, with a recollection of his "place" and his job, but by this time the turmoil inside her had concentrated itself on him, and she would not allow him to remount his horse or help her mount hers; she threw her arms around him with a wild relief.

He had no sophistry to combat her abandon and no way to reason or cope with her obvious passion. He had a conscientious feeling that he had no right to let her have her way, that it would be much better if he somehow put a stop to things, and he saw how young and bewildered she was. But he had never seen anybody as strange and as beautiful as she was, or had the sense of being so dangerously loved, and he saw her lack of reserve and her lack of coyness, and the vulnerability of her youth, and all his vague Irish mysticism made him respond to her as something akin to his horses and the wide countryside he loved. He had the simplicity to sense her quality of being lovely and lost, and different from the fat-legged Irish maids who were his normal social lot.

He left the extent of their relationship up to her, at first because he was impressed by the difference between their stations in life, and later because he loved her, too. He was nearly as bewildered by the queer, sultry passages between them as she was; he was nearly as lost and puzzled as she was, for different reasons. He thought she was a strange little thing, and sometimes when he lay on his mussy bed in the room off the tackroom where he slept, he felt a conceit that he was so irresistible to her, and that she had started it all; but in those submerged, lush hollows where they kissed, he was as bemused and possessed as she was.

None of it was leading to anything. Nothing in the world seemed to be leading to anything. Victoria had no idea of making Dan run away with her, or of young dreams of happiness—she was conscious only that her relief was in him. She got the nearest thing to peace in those dim hollows. The rest of her life had a fabulous, dreamy aspect to her; she lived through these days minute by minute.

One evening she had a telegram from her parents. She was having strawberries for dessert, and sitting limply at the end of the table while two white candles flickered in the wind from the west window. Her fresh yellow dress clung slightly to her shoulders, and her hair felt heavy. The telegram said that they would be home the next day.

She heard the mail plane to New York muttering its way through the evening sky. She heard the servants talking and rattling the dishes out in the kitchen. As long as she might live, she could never forget the immediacy of the streaky pink strawberries and cream before her, the wan look of white wax trickling down the candles, and the little wind stirring in the short hair at the back of her neck.

She got up and opened the door that led out into the garden, and all the renewed scents of evening flowed in like sweet liquors. She walked out on the grass and the dew wet her stockings above the tops of her slippers. The vicious sweetness of the summer night was intolerable and she leaned against a lilac tree, thinking, What is going to become of me? What is all this beauty and this desire that I cannot touch or take within my hand, and what shall I do? They will try to take me back, and I will never be happy again. What shall I *do*? Oh, my God, what is the matter with me?

Why do these desires for I don't know what run through me like hot and cold? I don't want to see my mother and father. I couldn't face them, because I am not their child any more, I am nobody at all, I have become only these desperate desires that drive me wild. Why am I so lost?

Her mind went round and round and helped her no more than ever, but seemed to be submerged by the smells, the touch of bark under her fingers, and the taste of flowers on the air. As usual, her vague desperation resolved itself in a need for action, and she went out to the drive and got into her car, whose seat was wet with mist. She roared out into the road and down through the town and tore out along the country roads. The bobbing glare of the headlights showed up the leaves of the branches that hung over the road, and the white road, and the grass along the edges. Outside this, the night was immense and breathing and terrible. She could only cut a white hole through it. She had worn no hat, and the wind scraped her temples and raked her hair.

She drove for two hours as fast as she could, at the end finding herself headed for the stables and Dan. As she turned in the drive into the stable yard, she thought, How ridiculous! I must have known I was coming here. Why didn't I come at once? She stopped the car and went around to the back, where the little room off the tackroom had a light in its window.

She knocked, and Dan came and let her in. He was surprised and very much embarrassed. He was dressed in his riding things, but he had taken his boots off and his breeches fitted to his bare white legs. She came in and sat down on his narrow bed. Several moths whacked against the chimney of the oil lamp. Dan had been reading the *Rider & Driver,* and it lay on the bare floor with his boots.

"You mustn't be here, Miss," he said. "It's not the place for you to be coming."

"My family's getting back tomorrow," she said.

"Will you have a cigarette?" He held his crumpled package of Camels out to her. Their little ceremony of lighting took place, with them looking at each other over the flame, solemnly.

They sat and smoked. There had never been any real attempt at verbal communication between them, and now they said nothing at all, but sat by the oil lamp and listened to the sawing of the crickets in the marshes outside. Far away somewhere, someone was playing a harmonica.

She made no reply to his telling her that she should not be there, and he said nothing about her family's return. They both forgot. They looked at each other gravely, with concentration, and said nothing.

"What am I going to do, Dan?" she asked after a long time.

"I dunno."

"What is life all about?" she asked, not really caring about an answer.

"I dunno," he said again. "I like the horses, but I dunno, if you mean about dyin' and all." His face was beautiful and simple, cut in the sharp, lovely planes of the Irish.

She had nothing to talk to him about, really. She wanted to be with him. She felt a relief now, she was almost perfectly happy, in a dazed, numb way. They simply stared at each other for a long time. She could not take her eyes from his face. All the wild, furious bewilderment in her seemed to leave her as she looked at him, and she felt she wanted to go on looking forever. Then the lamp flickered and faded. Dan got up and turned it up. The queer magic broke like an eggshell.

There was a lot she could have begun to talk about—her family, and what he and she were going to do about seeing each other when they returned, and a dozen other thoughts in the back of her mind—but she felt no real desire to.

"I wish I could stay here with you," she said, breaking the long silence.

"Ah, you couldn't do that, Miss," he said.

He came back to the bed where she sat, and sat down stiffly beside her. She lay down and pulled him down beside her. It was the first time that they had ever lain side by side. She felt calm and peaceful.

"My little darling," he mumbled suddenly into her hair. He had his arms quietly around her.

"Oh, Dan, I love you so."

After that they did not speak. They did not move. They both lay in drowsy stillness. She was plunged into a dreamless daze, wanting nothing, in a deep well of content. He felt the same strange, unreal sense of peace. Neither of them thought at all.

Finally they slept, with their cheeks together. The lamp went out after a while, and soon pale day streaked along the floor through the little window. Victoria got up, and Dan stood up too, and they moved and stretched themselves without saying anything. He threw open the door, and the fresh smells of the morning flooded the close air. On the other side of the wall, they could hear the horses champing and moving their feet.

They went out into the stable yard. Hens were making a lot of noise and some birds flew low to the ground. The green car stood there in the early mist, bulky and practical. Victoria got in and closed the door. It made a heavy, solid sound. Dan stood beside the car and they looked at each other for a moment, vaguely. Then she drove slowly out of the yard. He walked back to his room, still in his bare feet, with the breeches-ends about his calves. Victoria drove home along the country roads as it grew lighter, and threw herself into bed and was instantly asleep.

She did not wake until eleven, and then Mr. and Mrs. Jesse had returned and were waiting to have it out with her. They had had four letters from fellow-townsmen informing them that their daughter was carrying on with the riding instructor at the club, a common Irishman. The Jesses were the richest people in the town, and before Victoria was even awake they had arranged that Dan should be discharged immediately, with wages in advance. The club steward was having him packed off on the noon train. They had done everything they could. Now there was nothing left but the talk with Victoria.

They sat in the dim library, and she came in to them. The heat was already at its height. They talked and talked. They told her how common such an affair was, over and over. They tried to find out just how much she had actually done. They were furious and hurt and outraged.

Nothing they said made any impression on Victoria. She heard their voices far, far away, and she got a sort of detached impression of what they were saying. She sat in a big chair, languidly, while her dress wilted and clung around her, and watched the leaves outside make the light flicker between the slits of the Venetian blinds.

Finally, bewildered at her detachment, they told her that the instructor had already left, had been fired for his conduct. They told her four times before she understood what they were talking about. She looked at them vaguely and without saying anything for a few minutes, and then fainted and could not be brought to for some time.

Dr. Russell, with his little mustache and long tubes of colored pills, told them it was the logical result of the protracted heat wave. She was as thin as a bag of bones, and as white as a sheet, and gave every sign of physical and nervous exhaustion. He prescribed two tonics, and said she must stay in bed for a day or two.

She lay in bed all afternoon, trying to concentrate. She couldn't get anything straight in her head. She would remember that Dan had gone, and then she would remember that she loved Dan, but by that time she had forgotten that he had left, and it was impossible for her to assemble things to make any picture of what her life was. She was not very unhappy. She was hot and tired, and the only things she could think about without an effort were the sombre hollows where she and Dan had gone, with their curious green gloom and the smell of submerged decay. Her mind rested in those hollows, dim and steaming.

Her mother came in to see her late in the afternoon, with a plate of strawberries for her. She sat down on the edge of the bed and kissed Victoria gently.

"Darling," she said. "Poor little child. I shall never forgive myself for leaving you alone this summer. You mustn't be too unhappy. Daddy understands and I understand, and we want you to rest and be our happy little girl again. It's really our fault that you fell into the power of this dreadful man."

"He isn't a dreadful man," Victoria said, and closed her mouth tight. It was an effort to talk. She turned her face aside and pretended to go to sleep. After a while her mother went away, leaving the strawberries by the side of the bed. Victoria turned over and looked at them lying on the white plate.

It grew dusky in her room, and then it grew dark. The little breeze of the evening came faltering through the window. Victoria got up and went to the window and breathed the terrible sweetness of the garden at night.

In her nightgown, she climbed down the honeysuckle trellis below her window, and dropped to the grass. She had used the trellis for running away when she was small, and she stood at the foot and thought about that for a while, how impossible that that small girl was the same as herself now. She gave it up.

Barefooted, she walked along the terrace to the lilac tree where she had stood last night, and stood there again, swaying a little, remembrances and thoughts swirling in her head.

Suddenly she pulled her nightgown off over her head and threw herself down on the wet turf. The smell of it filled her nostrils. She pressed her body violently against its softness and fragrance, and ran her fingers desperately into the damp earth. Dan, Dan had gone and all her heart had gone, too. Everything had gone. If life was to be as terrible, progressively, as it had come to be at sixteen, she wished she might die now. She wished she were dead, and felt the exquisite touch of dew-soaked grass against her breast.

THE DOOR

❦

E. B. White

EVERYTHING (he kept saying) is something it isn't. And everybody is always somewhere else. Maybe it was the city, being
in the city, that made him feel how queer everything was and that
it was something else. Maybe (he kept thinking) it was the names
of the things. The names were tex and frequently koid. Or they
were flex and oid or they were duroid (sani) or flexsan (duro), but
everything was glass (but not quite glass) and the thing that you
touched (the surface, washable, crease-resistant) was rubber, only
it wasn't quite rubber and you didn't quite touch it but almost.
The wall, which was glass but thrutex, turned out on being
approached not to be a wall, it was something else, it was an opening or doorway—and the doorway (through which he saw himself
approaching) turned out to be something else, it was a wall. And
what he had eaten not having agreed with him.

He was in a washable house, but he wasn't sure. Now about
those rats, he kept saying to himself. He meant the rats that the
Professor had driven crazy by forcing them to deal with problems
which were beyond the scope of rats, the insoluble problems. He
meant the rats that had been trained to jump at the square card
with the circle in the middle, and the card (because it was something it wasn't) would give way and let the rat into a place where
the food was, but then one day it would be a trick played on the
rat, and the card would be changed, and the rat would jump but
the card wouldn't give way, and it was an impossible situation
(for a rat) and the rat would go insane and into its eyes would
come the unspeakably bright imploring look of the frustrated, and
after the convulsions were over and the frantic racing around,

then the passive stage would set in and the willingness to let anything be done to it, even if it was something else.

He didn't know which door (or wall) or opening in the house
to jump at, to get through, because one was an opening that wasn't
a door (it was a void, or koid) and the other was a wall that wasn't
an opening, it was a sanitary cupboard of the same color. He
caught a glimpse of his eyes staring into his eyes, in the thrutex,
and in them was the expression he had seen in the picture of the
rats—weary after convulsions and the frantic racing around, when
they were willing and did not mind having anything done to
them. More and more (he kept saying) I am confronted by a problem which is incapable of solution (for this time even if he chose
the right door, there would be no food behind it) and that is what
madness is, and things seeming different from what they are. He
heard, in the house where he was, in the city to which he had gone
(as toward a door which might, or might not, give way), a noise—
not a loud noise but more of a low prefabricated humming. It
came from a place in the base of the wall (or stat) where the flue
carrying the filterable air was, and not far from the Minipiano,
which was made of the same material nailbrushes are made of, and
which was under the stairs. "This, too, has been tested," she said,
pointing, but not at it, "and found viable." It wasn't a loud noise,
he kept thinking, sorry that he had seen his eyes, even though it
was through his own eyes that he had seen them.

First will come the convulsions (he said), then the exhaustion,
then the willingness to let anything be done. "And you better
believe it *will* be."

All his life he had been confronted by situations which were
incapable of being solved, and there was a deliberateness behind
all this, behind this changing of the card (or door), because they
would always wait till you had learned to jump at the certain card
(or door)—the one with the circle—and then they would change
it on you. There have been so many doors changed on me, he said,
in the last twenty years, but it is now becoming clear that it is an
impossible situation, and the question is whether to jump again,
even though they ruffle you in the rump with a blast of air—to
make you jump. He wished he wasn't standing by the Minipiano.

First they would teach you the prayers and the Psalms, and that would be the right door (the one with the circle), and the long sweet words with the holy sound, and that would be the one to jump at to get where the food was. Then one day you jumped and it didn't give way, so that all you got was the bump on the nose, and the first bewilderment, the first young bewilderment.

I don't know whether to tell her about the door they substituted or not, he said, the one with the equation on it and the picture of the amoeba reproducing itself by division. Or the one with the photostatic copy of the check for thirty-two dollars and fifty cents. But the jumping was so long ago, although the bump is . . . how those old wounds hurt! Being crazy this way wouldn't be so bad if only, if only. If only when you put your foot forward to take a step, the ground wouldn't come up to meet your foot the way it does. And the same way in the street (only I may never get back to the street unless I jump at the right door), the curb coming up to meet your foot, anticipating ever so delicately the weight of the body, which is somewhere else. "We could take your name," she said, "and send it to you." And it wouldn't be so bad if only you could read a sentence all the way through without jumping (your eye) to something else on the same page; and then (he kept thinking) there was that man out in Jersey, the one who started to chop his trees down, one by one, the man who began talking about how he would take his house to pieces, brick by brick, because he faced a problem incapable of solution, probably, so he began to hack at the trees in the yard, began to pluck with trembling fingers at the bricks in the house. Even if a house is not washable, it is worth taking down. It is not till later that the exhaustion sets in.

But it is inevitable that they will keep changing the doors on you, he said, because that is what they are for; and the thing is to get used to it and not let it unsettle the mind. But that would mean not jumping, and you can't. Nobody can not jump. There will be no not-jumping. Among rats, perhaps, but among people never. Everybody has to keep jumping at a door (the one with the circle on it) because that is the way everybody is, specially some people. You wouldn't want me, standing here, to tell you, would you, about my friend the poet (deceased) who said, "My heart has followed all my days something I cannot name"? (It had the circle on it.) And like many poets, although few so beloved, he is gone. It killed him, the jumping. First, of course, there were the preliminary bouts, the convulsions, and the calm and the willingness.

I remember the door with the picture of the girl on it (only it was spring), her arms outstretched in loveliness, her dress (it was the one with the circle on it) uncaught, beginning the slow, clear, blinding cascade—and I guess we would all like to try that door again, for it seemed like the way and for a while it was the way, the door would open and you would go through winged and exalted (like any rat) and the food would be there, the way the Professor had it arranged, everything O.K., and you had chosen the right door for the world was young. The time they changed that door on me, my nose bled for a hundred hours—how do you like that, Madam? Or would you prefer to show me further through this so strange house, or you could take my name and send it to me, for although my heart has followed all my days something I cannot name, I am tired of the jumping and I do not know which way to go, Madam, and I am not even sure that I am not tried beyond the endurance of man (rat, if you will) and have taken leave of sanity. What are you following these days, old friend, after your recovery from the last bump? What is the name, or is it something you cannot name? The rats have a name for it by this time, perhaps, but I don't know what they call it. I call it plexikoid and it comes in sheets, something like insulating board, unattainable and ugli-proof.

And there was the man out in Jersey, because I keep thinking about his terrible necessity and the passion and trouble he had gone to all those years in the indescribable abundance of a house-holder's detail, building the estate and the planting of the trees and in spring the lawn-dressing and in fall the bulbs for the spring burgeoning, and the watering of the grass on the long light evenings in summer and the gravel for the driveway (all had to be thought out, planned) and the decorative borders, probably, the perennials and the bug spray, and the building of the house from plans of the architect, first the sills, then the studs, then the full corn in the ear, the floors laid on the floor timbers, smoothed, and then the carpets upon the smooth floors and the curtains and the rods therefor. And then, almost without warning, he would be jumping at the same old door and it wouldn't give: they had changed it on him, making life no longer supportable under the elms in the elm shade, under the maples in the maple shade.

"Here you have the maximum of openness in a small room."

It was impossible to say (maybe it was the city) what made him feel the way he did, and I am not the only one either, he kept thinking—ask any doctor if I am. The doctors, they know how many there are, they even know where the trouble is only they don't like to tell you about the prefrontal lobe because that means making a hole in your skull and removing the work of centuries. It took so long coming, this lobe, so many, many years. (Is it something you read in the paper, perhaps?) And now, the strain being so great, the door having been changed by the Professor once too often . . . but it only means a whiff of ether, a few deft strokes, and the higher animal becomes a little easier in his mind and more like the lower one. From now on, you see, that's the way it will be, the ones with the small prefrontal lobes will win because the other ones are hurt too much by this incessant bumping. They can stand just so much, eh, Doctor? (And what is that, pray, that you have in your hand?) Still, you never can tell, eh, Madam?

He crossed (carefully) the room, the thick carpet under him softly, and went toward the door carefully, which was glass and he could see himself in it, and which, at his approach, opened to allow him to pass through; and beyond he half expected to find one of the old doors that he had known, perhaps the one with the circle, the one with the girl her arms outstretched in loveliness and beauty before him. But he saw instead a moving stairway, and descended in light (he kept thinking) to the street below and to the other people. As he stepped off, the ground came up slightly, to meet his foot.

TOURIST HOME

❦

BENEDICT THIELEN

WHAT I ALWAYS say is, there's no place like Miami, but I can't say as much for the rest of the Sunny South. Maybe it's the people, the way they talk—"Wheah you all gwine, honey?" that gets on your nerves after a while. Or maybe it's just that everything seems to be half asleep and kind of falling to pieces. It's hard to say. But in general, Dixie gives me a pain. Like Stevie said one day while we were driving back, "No wonder they lost the war."

The nice part about this trip was that the whole thing practically hadn't cost us a nickel. We had the breaks. Every afternoon we had picked the right ones at Hialeah. At night at the dog tracks we'd do the same. And in one place we even won a couple of bottles of champagne in a raffle. You know how it is sometimes.

We went to all the best places, too, and that's why, when Steve's wife, Agnes, come out with that bright idea of hers, you could of knocked us over with a feather. It was getting around five o'clock in the afternoon on about the second day out coming north from Miami. We were passing this place where it said "Tourist Home" when Agnes suddenly turned around from the front seat and said, "Listen, why don't we stay there tonight instead of going on?"

I looked at her and laughed—I thought she was just trying to crack wise—and Stevie said, "Now I'll tell one."

"No, honest, I mean it," she said.

Stevie slowed down to about forty-five and Agnes said, "I don't want to stay in a lousy small-town hotel. And anyway, I think it would be nice to stay out in the country one night for a change."

"You wanna listen to the birdies sing?" Stevie said.

"And besides," Agnes said, "I'd like to see what one of those old places looks like inside. Wouldn't you, Grace?"

"I certainly would," my wife said. "I'll bet there's all sorts of old furniture and stuff in there."

"So what?" Stevie said.

"It'll be a lot cheaper than staying in a regular hotel," Agnes said.

I told her we were on this trip to have a good time, not to save money, but it didn't make any difference. So in the end Stevie had to turn around and we drove back about four miles.

"Look, isn't it pretty?" Agnes said as we came up to this place. "Turn in the driveway, Stevie."

The house needed a coat of paint, like all those places down there, but aside from that it was nice enough looking, with white columns on the piazza and a lot of big trees around. When we drove in, an old coon came out, not hurrying any.

"Where's the fire, George?" Stevie called out to him, but the old coon didn't get it. He just grinned and said, "Fire, suh?" They don't know what it's all about.

"Have you any rooms for the night?" Agnes asked him in that waugh-waugh sort of English voice she gets when she's trying to put on the dog.

The coon said they had, and we got out and went in. It was a big sort of a place, with a hall and a long white stairway going up to the next floor in a curve. There were some oil paintings hanging on the wall, of people mostly, in old-fashioned costumes. At the head of the stairs there was one of a guy in a gray uniform, with a beard and a lot of medals.

"Boy, look at the zits," Stevie said when we went past him.

Both the girls turned around and gave Stevie dirty looks. I decided we better shut up. There was no use saying anything when the girls got that way.

We followed old Slow Motion down the hall to the rooms.

"Oh, isn't that lovely?" Agnes said when he had opened the doors of both rooms. "Isn't that charming?"

Stevie winked at me. "How much are they?" he said.

"Two dollars, suh," the coon said.

"Two dollars what?" Stevie asked him. "Two dollars apiece, or two dollars for both, or two dollars for—"

"Two dollars for each person, suh," the coon said.

"That's a lot of money, brother," Stevie said. "Why, in the last hotel we stopped at—"

"Can we have supper here, too?" Agnes asked.

"Yes, Ma'am, that includes supper," the coon said. "And breakfast."

When the coon went out, Agnes said, "There, I told you it would be cheap. Just imagine. Two dollars. Why—"

"There must be a hitch somewhere." Stevie looked around the room. "They can't make a proposition like this pay if they only charge two bucks for the works. Why, it stands to reason."

"Just look at this furniture, though," Agnes said. "Isn't it lovely? Didn't I say there'd probably be some beautiful furniture in this place?"

"So what?" Stevie said. "I want to see what sort of food we get in this dump before I get steamed up about the furniture."

"My God, don't you ever think about anything but food, Steve?" Agnes said.

"Well, I can't eat the furniture," Stevie said.

"Come on," I said, "let's get cleaned up and then have a little drink, shall we?" I could see we all needed one.

In our room, Grace went over to the window and then called back to me to come and see the sunset. It was pretty, all right. There were these big trees with the sky all red behind them, and it was so still out there it kind of gave you the creeps. It was certainly a change from Miami.

After a while Stevie banged on the wall and yelled at us to come over and have a drink, and we went and joined them in their room.

"Grace, just look," Agnes said, "just look at that table! Isn't that a beauty?"

The two of them stood there going on about it. It was an old-looking table, but it was made of this dark, smooth wood—mahogany, I guess—and it was shined up like a mirror.

"That certainly is pretty," I said.

"My, what enthusiasm!" Grace said. "Don't lose control of yourself."

What the hell, I was just trying to keep peace in the family, but I didn't say anything and went over to where Stevie was fixing the drinks.

"You'd think it was a museum," Stevie said, "the way they rave."

"Well, it is, practically," Agnes said.

"Why, some of these things are worth hundreds of dollars," Grace said. "That table alone."

Stevie handed her a drink and said, "You trying to kid me?"

"Of course she isn't," Agnes said. "A table like that is worth at least five hundred dollars."

Stevie looked at the table. Then he said, "Well, why don't they sell it then, instead of hanging on to it and having to run a boarding house to make a living?"

"It's probably an heirloom," Agnes said.

"Heirloom!" Stevie laughed. "They probably just don't know how much these things are worth, that's all. They don't know what it's all about, down here."

"Well, here's to us," I said, and we all took a good big drink. We felt better right away, and after we'd had some more we felt fine.

"Well, I'm ready for anything now," Stevie said. "Let's go see what sort of chow they give us."

The dining room was in the back of the house and we had the place all to ourselves.

"Now, isn't this nicer than a hotel?" Agnes said after we sat down. "It's just like being in your own home."

Stevie shook his head and said, "They must be new to the game if they think they can make a proposition like this pay." The coon came in with the soup. "Now you'll see," Stevie said.

But he was wrong about it. That was one of the best meals I ever had in my life. There was soup, and fried chicken, and sugar-cured ham, and sweet potatoes, and about three kinds of vegetables, and hot breads, and two kinds of pie for dessert.

All through the meal Stevie just kept shaking his head and saying they must be crazy, but the girls didn't pay much attention to him. They were too busy looking around the room and getting excited about the furniture and the oil paintings.

After supper the girls got up to look at the things in the room and Stevie and I sat there and smoked for a while. Then he looked at his watch and said, "My God, only eight o'clock! What'll we do now?"

"I don't suppose there's a movie anywhere," I said.

"No, and I don't suppose the Metropolitan Grand Opera House is right around the corner either," Stevie said, and gave me a look as if I was something that had just come up out of the drainpipe.

"All right," I said, "figure it out yourself."

Down at the other end of the room, the girls were giving an oil painting the once-over. After a little while Stevie said, "How about a little drink, just to cut the grease?"

I yelled to the girls that we were going up to have a drink, but they were still snooping around at the pictures and the furniture and didn't pay any attention to us. Stevie and I were just starting upstairs when he said, "What say we kill that champagne we won in the raffle? I got an awful thirst."

I had a thirst too and champagne sounded good to me, so we went and got the bottles out of the car. Coming in again, we ran across the coon and told him to bring us up some ice in a bucket on account of we were going to drink some champagne. Stevie and I laughed going up the stairs, saying this was probably the first and last time anybody in that joint had ever asked for ice for champagne.

"They'll probably have to get up the old oaken bucket that hung by the well to put it in," Stevie said.

After a time the coon came up and he had plenty of ice and he had it in a real champagne bucket, too. We didn't let on like we were surprised, but when he'd gone out, we looked at each other and Stevie said, "Say, what is this, anyhow?"

That's what I was wondering, but I couldn't figure it out any more than he could. When the girls came in, they saw the bucket and they both claimed it was genuine silver-plated. We wouldn't believe them, but finally we looked on the bottom and sure enough, it was stamped the way they are when they're real silver.

"Laugh that off," Grace said.

We killed the first bottle and then started on the second. We began to feel pretty good. I guess maybe coming on top of the rye we had before supper kind of gave the champagne a little extra authority. Anyway, it seemed to hit us. The girls kept on raving more than ever about that old table in the room and saying how all our own furniture looked like it came from the bargain basement, and Stevie sat there worrying out loud about how they could afford to run a joint like this, until finally I got sort of sick of the whole business and I said, "Listen, why don't you get the guy who runs the place and settle it? And maybe he'll sell you the whole outfit at the same time."

"Oh, they wouldn't sell this furniture," Grace said, but I could see she was crazy to take a chance on it just the same.

Stevie said, "Money talks," and leaned on the bell.

We heard the bell ringing, and after we'd rung a few times the coon came to the door and we told him we wanted to see whoever it was that ran the place. He grinned at us and said, "Ah'm sorry, suh, but Miss Sophronia done gone and retired."

"Well, you all just go and tell Miss Sophronia we want to see her," Stevie said. "Tell her it's important. Tell her we got a business proposition to make her. And step on it, see?"

"Tell her the roof's leaking and we're all drowning," I said.

The old guy staggered out, shaking his head, and Stevie called after him, "I'll ring this bell all night long till Miss Pneumonia shows up." He pressed it a couple of times to show him what he meant.

"Take it easy, Stevie," I said, because I could see that he was getting sort of sore.

"I never did like smokes," he said.

Miss Sophronia took her time about it, but finally there was a knock on the door and there she was. I guess she hadn't really gone to bed, because she had on a regular dress and her hair was up. She was an old dame with white hair, but she looked real nice, even though she wasn't smiling any. She just looked sort of blank. I was worried for a minute that Stevie would get funny with her, but he didn't. He was as smooey as all hell, telling her how sorry he was to disturb her, but we were leaving early in the morning and he had this proposition to make her and wouldn't she like to sell us that table and maybe some other things she had?

But it didn't do any good. She shook her head and said she was sorry but she wasn't interested, and was there anything else she could do for us tonight before she left?

Stevie drew out a roll of bills and said, "Now, Ah'm sure you all would consider a reasonable offer, Ma'am, wouldn't you? Say seventy-five dollars for that l'il ol' table?"

He went on like that, talking Southern, kidding her, really, although of course she didn't know she was being kidded, or if she did, she certainly didn't let on or join in the spirit of it. When he finally started peeling bills off, she just turned and went out, closing the door behind her.

Stevie pulled up his coat collar and said, "B-r-r-r," and made believe he was shivering.

Then the fireworks started. You'd think poor Stevie had done something terrible the way those two babes went for him, calling him every kind of name, saying he was disgusting and no gentleman, and a whole lot more that I couldn't follow.

By God, I thought, I'd better keep out of this, so I didn't say a word. Stevie didn't say a word either for a while. He just stood there grinning at them—because he knew it got their goat. He poured himself out another glass of champagne and then he put the glass down on the table. The girls both yelled at him at once and said for God's sake, didn't he know enough not to put a wet glass down on a table like that.

Then he got really sore. One of the girls tried to grab the glass and he pulled it out of her hand. Naturally the stuff went all over the table, and then the glass broke, too. Stevie grabbed the water tumbler from the washbasin and reached down for the bottle and filled it up. Then he picked up the bucket from the floor and set it down on the table, hard, and then he began to tell the girls what he thought of them. But by that time they weren't paying any attention to him. They grabbed up a couple of towels and started wiping off the table. When they lifted the bucket off, Stevie pulled it away from them and set it down again on the table with a bang.

Suddenly Agnes began to cry and a minute later Grace was hollering too, still trying to wipe up the table, and then I decided that the party was getting a little too rough and I grabbed Grace and said we were going to bed, and we got the hell out.

In our room I tried to calm her down, but it didn't do any good. She kept on crying, saying how awful it was to ruin a beautiful table like that and how awful Stevie was, and I don't know what all else. I told her the table could probably be fixed up as good as new, but it didn't do any good, and all the time next door I could hear them hollering at each other, until finally I heard something like a smack, and I guess Stevie must have smacked Agnes one because after that there wasn't any more noise next door. What a night, I thought, and I took some bicarbonate and an aspirin and went to bed.

Well, none of us felt so hot the next morning, but we finally had breakfast and were ready to shove off. We had to yell at the coon a couple of times to hurry him up with our baggage. When it came to paying, I asked him where the old lady was, but he said she had gone in to town and for me to pay him. I didn't know if that was true or not, but I guess it must have been because I didn't see her around anywhere. I paid him and I was fishing around for some change to give him when Stevie said no oats. If the coon was the cashier and chief cook and bottlewasher and everything else combined, there wasn't any use in our giving him a tip, and that anyway the service in the place was lousy. I hadn't thought of it just that way, but I guess he was right at that, so we didn't give him anything.

That afternoon, when it came to deciding where to stay, I said to the girls, just kidding, "Well, how about staying at some nice tourist home, girls, some nice quiet place in the country?" But they said no, they'd rather stay at a regular hotel tonight, so we stopped in the next town we came to and put up there. I couldn't hand the place much, but after supper we all went to a movie, which was better than just sitting around.

ARRANGEMENT IN BLACK AND WHITE

❦

DOROTHY PARKER

THE WOMAN WITH the pink velvet poppies wreathed round the assisted gold of her hair traversed the crowded room at an interesting gait combining a skip with a sidle, and clutched the lean arm of her host.

"Now I got you!" she said. "Now you can't get away!"

"Why, hello," said her host. "Well. How are you?"

"Oh, I'm finely," she said. "Just simply finely. Listen. I want you to do me the most terrible favor. Will you? Will you please? Pretty please?"

"What is it?" said her host.

"Listen," she said. "I want to meet Walter Williams. Honestly, I'm just simply crazy about that man. Oh, when he sings! When he sings those spirituals! Well, I said to Burton, 'It's a good thing for you Walter Williams is colored,' I said, 'or you'd have lots of reason to be jealous.' I'd really love to meet him. I'd like to tell him I've heard him sing. Will you be an angel and introduce me to him?"

"Why, certainly," said her host. "I thought you'd met him. The party's for him. Where is he, anyway?"

"He's over there by the bookcase," she said. "Let's wait till those people get through talking to him. Well, I think you're simply marvellous, giving this perfectly marvellous party for him, and having him meet all these white people, and all. Isn't he terribly grateful?"

"I hope not," said her host.

"I think it's really terribly nice," she said. "I do. I don't see why on earth it isn't perfectly all right to meet colored people. I haven't any feeling at all about it—not one single bit. Burton

—oh, he's just the other way. Well, you know, he comes from Virginia, and you know how they are."

"Did he come tonight?" said her host.

"No, he couldn't," she said. "I'm a regular grass widow tonight. I told him when I left, 'There's no telling what I'll do,' I said. He was just so tired out, he couldn't move. Isn't it a shame?"

"Ah," said her host.

"Wait till I tell him I met Walter Williams!" she said. "He'll just about die. Oh, we have more arguments about colored people. I talk to him like I don't know what, I get so excited. 'Oh, don't be so silly,' I say. But I must say for Burton, he's heaps broader-minded than lots of these Southerners. He's really awfully fond of colored people. Well, he says himself, he wouldn't have white servants. And you know, he had this old colored nurse, this regular old nigger mammy, and he just simply loves her. Why, every time he goes home, he goes out in the kitchen to see her. He does, really, to this day. All he says is, he says he hasn't got a word to say against colored people as long as they keep their place. He's always doing things for them—giving them clothes and I don't know what all. The only thing he says, he says he wouldn't sit down at the table with one for a million dollars. 'Oh,' I say to him, 'you make me sick, talking like that.' I'm just terrible to him. Aren't I terrible?"

"Oh, no, no, no," said her host. "No, no."

"I am," she said. "I know I am. Poor Burton! Now, me, I don't feel that way at all. I haven't the slightest feeling about colored people. Why, I'm just crazy about some of them. They're just like children—just as easygoing, and always singing and laughing and everything. Aren't they the happiest things you ever saw in your life? Honestly, it makes me laugh just to hear them. Oh, I like them. I really do. Well, now, listen, I have this colored laundress, I've had her for years, and I'm devoted to her. She's a real character. And I want to tell you, I think of her as my friend. That's the way I think of her. As I say to Burton, 'Well, for Heaven's sakes, we're all human beings!' Aren't we?"

"Yes," said her host. "Yes, indeed."

"Now this Walter Williams," she said. "I think a man like that's a real artist. I do. I think he deserves an awful lot of credit.

Goodness, I'm so crazy about music or anything, I don't care what color he is. I honestly think if a person's an artist, nobody ought to have any feeling at all about meeting them. That's absolutely what I say to Burton. Don't you think I'm right?"

"Yes," said her host. "Oh, yes."

"That's the way I feel," she said. "I just can't understand people being narrow-minded. Why, I absolutely think it's a privilege to meet a man like Walter Williams. Now, I do. I haven't any feeling at all. Well, my goodness, the good Lord made him, just the same as He did any of us. Didn't He?"

"Surely," said her host. "Yes, indeed."

"That's what I say," she said. "Oh, I get so furious when people are narrow minded about colored people. It's just all I can do not to say something. Of course, I do admit when you get a bad colored man, they're simply terrible. But as I say to Burton, there are some bad white people, too, in this world. Aren't there?"

"I guess there are," said her host.

"Why, I'd really be glad to have a man like Walter Williams come to my house and sing for us, some time," she said. "Of course, I couldn't ask him on account of Burton, but I wouldn't have any feeling about it at all. Oh, can't he sing! Isn't it marvellous, the way they all have music in them? It just seems to be right *in* them? Come on, let's us go on over and talk to him. Listen, what shall I do when I'm introduced? Ought I to shake hands? Or what?"

"Why, do whatever you want," said her host.

"I guess maybe I'd better," she said. "I wouldn't for the world have him think I had any feeling. I think I'd better shake hands, just the way I would with anybody else. That's just exactly what I'll do."

They reached the tall young Negro, standing by the bookcase. The host performed introductions; the Negro bowed.

"How do you do?" he said. "Isn't it a nice party?"

The woman with the pink velvet poppies extended her hand at the length of her arm and held it so, in fine determination, for all the world to see, until the Negro took it, shook it, and gave it back to her.

"Oh, how do you do, Mr. Williams," she said. "Well, how do

you do. I've just been saying, I've enjoyed your singing so awfully much. I've been to your concerts, and we have you on the phonograph and everything. Oh, I just enjoy it!"

She spoke with great distinctness, moving her lips meticulously, as if in parlance with the deaf.

"I'm so glad," he said.

"I'm just simply crazy about that 'Water Boy' thing you sing," she said. "Honestly, I can't get it out of my head. I have my husband nearly crazy, the way I go around humming it all the time. Oh, he looks just as black as the ace of—er. Well, tell me, where on earth do you ever get all those songs of yours? How do you ever get hold of them?"

"Why," he said, "there are so many different—"

"I should think you'd love singing them," she said. "It must be more fun. All those darling old spirituals—oh, I just love them! Well, what are you doing, now? Are you still keeping up your singing? Why don't you have another concert, some time?"

"I'm having one the sixteenth of this month," he said.

"Well, I'll be there," she said. "I'll be there, if I possibly can. You can count on me. Goodness, here comes a whole raft of people to talk to you. You're just a regular guest of honor! Oh, who's that girl in white? I've seen her some place."

"That's Katherine Burke," said her host.

"Good Heavens," she said, "is that Katherine Burke? Why, she looks entirely different off the stage. I thought she was much better-looking. I had no idea she was so terribly dark. Why, she looks almost like— Oh, I think she's a wonderful actress! Don't you think she's a wonderful actress, Mr. Williams? Oh, I think she's marvellous. Don't you?"

"Yes, I do," he said.

"Oh, I do, too," she said. "Just wonderful. Well, goodness, we must give someone else a chance to talk to the guest of honor. Now, don't forget, Mr. Williams, I'm going to be at that concert if I possibly can. I'll be there applauding like everything. And if I can't come, I'm going to tell everybody I know to go, anyway. Don't you forget!"

"I won't," he said. "Thank you so much."

The host took her arm and piloted her firmly into the next room.

"Oh, my dear," she said. "I nearly died! Honestly, I give you my word, I nearly passed away. Did you hear that terrible break I made? I was just going to say Katherine Burke looked almost like a nigger. I just caught myself in time. Oh, do you think he noticed?"

"I don't believe so," said her host.

"Well, thank goodness," she said, "because I wouldn't have embarrassed him for anything. Why, he's awfully nice. Just as nice as he can be. Nice manners, and everything. You know, so many colored people, you give them an inch, and they walk all over you. But he doesn't try any of that. Well, he's got more sense, I suppose. He's really nice. Don't you think so?"

"Yes," said her host.

"I liked him," she said. "I haven't any feeling at all because he's a colored man. I felt just as natural as I would with anybody. Talked to him just as naturally, and everything. But honestly, I could hardly keep a straight face. I kept thinking of Burton. Oh, wait till I tell Burton I called him 'Mister'!"

THE COURTSHIP OF MILTON BARKER

❧

Wolcott Gibbs

MILTON BARKER, the car checker, stood at the window, looking out at the freight yard. It was mid-April. A thin rain was blowing in from New York Harbor in little gusts and showers, filling the usual melancholy of the yard with further desolation. The dirt and cinders between the ties had turned to gray mud, and the smoke from a switching engine, idle in one of the leads, was flattened down by the rain and trailed off along the ground. The intricate steel towers that held the machinery for handling the car floats stood up dimly against the sky. Ben Rederson, the old switchman, went by with a lighted lantern, although it was only three o'clock in the afternoon.

"God," said Milton Barker, and rubbed the pane where his breath had clouded it.

The yardmaster looked up from the waybills he was checking.

"Some day, ain't it," he said.

"For ducks," said Milton, who was no man to slight a ritual. "Yeah."

"You got no kick coming, sitting there on your fanetta," said Milton bitterly. "Take *me*, now."

"I been out in plenty rain worse than this in my time," said the yardmaster. "Say, when I was braking on the Santa Fe . . ."

Milton yawned.

"O.K., Pop," he said. "You already told me."

There was a potbellied stove in the middle of the office and a battered kettle on top of it. Milton took the kettle down and looked inside.

"You want coffee?"

"It's a pity one of you guys couldn't wash that pot once in a while," said the yardmaster. "It's got a cake inside of it, like in a pipe."

"You drunk worse things, Pop," said Milton.

He found a tin cup and a paper bag full of sugar in one of the lockers along the wall and took them to the stove. The coffee poured black and thick. Milton carried his cup over to the window and sat down.

"How you like to be in Pom Beach, Pop?" he said, and when the yardmaster didn't answer, he found peace in the *Daily Mirror.*

After a little while a telephone bell rang.

"Get that, will you, Milty?" said the yardmaster.

"Get it yourself," said Milton, who was reading with some dismay that Miss Lupe Velez, weary of tinsel, had decided to immolate herself in a convent.

"Listen, you," said the yardmaster.

"All right, all right," said Milton, and reached over and picked up the telephone, though without removing his eyes from a photograph of Miss Velez, taken in an earlier and more secular mood. "Harbor Yard."

The telephone chattered and Milton, abandoning the paper, wrote as he listened.

"Circus train . . . Layton & Crowley . . . Five P.M. from Greenville . . . To lay over until nine A.M. . . . Yes, sir. . . . Yeah, I got it."

He hung up the receiver and looked at the yardmaster.

"Well, can you tie that?" he said.

"Circus train?" asked the yardmaster.

"Yeah. Layton & Crowley. That ain't one of the big ones, is it?"

"Nah. A mud show. Plays like Lowell and Attleboro, them places."

"Well anyway."

'Five o'clock from Greenville? That means the float ought to get here around seven. Tell the yard crew it goes up in number three on the Hill."

"O.K."

"And listen, Milty . . ."

"Yeah?"

"It ain't like the 'Follies,' see? I wouldn't be figuring on nothing if I was you."

"You ain't talking to me, Pop," said Milton, and he went out to find the yard conductor.

The circus train arrived on the float at half past six and by seven the yard engines had pulled it up on the Hill, where it was to lie until the following morning. Milton Barker, who had observed the cars sharply as they were pulled off the float, was able to report that nine of them were boxcars which presumably contained animals and stage properties, and that the tenth was a passenger coach which had its curtains drawn but must nevertheless contain the ladies and gentlemen of the cast.

"It cert'n'y *smells* like a hell of a cheap circus," he now told the yardmaster, staring up toward the Hill, where the circus train lay between two lines of empty boxcars.

"It's them elephants," said the yardmaster. "No matter what you do."

Milton nodded. The commonplace aspect of the boxcars and their outrageous fragrance had left him feeling cheated and slightly empty. He took a pair of shears out of a table drawer and began to cut the picture of Lupe Velez out of the *Mirror*. Suddenly there was a knock at the yard-office door.

"C'min!" he shouted, following the agreeable contours of the nun-to-be with the shears.

The door opened, letting in a gust of rain from the yard, and he looked up with annoyance.

"Say, how's for . . ."

He got no further because there were strangers in the doorway—two women and a man—and it was clear that they were not native to his world or even anything he could hope to classify from his previous experience.

The man, who was carrying two empty buckets, was sheathed in a purple suit. It was an opium-eater's dream of a suit, with lapels that rose vivaciously into two points that menaced its wearer's ears; the openings of the pockets ran up and down instead of crosswise and they were trimmed with braid; the trousers, which constricted him too lovingly, terminated in a pair of long, narrow suède shoes, turning up at the ends like little skis. Beneath the

upper part of these antic vestments he wore a checked vest of hell-
ish design. His face was pale and, in relation to the rest of his
body, much too large. The expression it wore was arrogant but
harassed—Monseigneur taunted by the rabble. Like his two companions, he was damp from head to foot, and in the sudden
warmth of the yard office he had begun to give off a frail steam.

The two ladies each carried a bucket. They wore dresses which
remained defiantly frilly in spite of the rain, and spoke somehow
of the indolent South. Their faces, above this girlish finery and
beneath two hats that were identical garlands of drenched flowers,
were somewhat surprising. There was a prettiness about them, but
it had a furious quality, a sort of triumphant ferocity. The ladies
indeed looked as if they had just dispatched an enemy in a manner
that had given them some dark pleasure and as if presently they
hoped to do so again. They were almost exactly alike and it seemed
reasonable to Milton to suppose that they were twins or at least
sisters.

"Was there something I could do for you?" he asked cautiously.

The three came forward and surrounded the stove.

"You the yodmaster?" asked the man in a hoarse whisper.

"No," said Milton. "Him."

"Oh," said the man. "One of the shacks told us we could get
some drinking water."

The yardmaster pointed to the washroom door.

"Hep yourself," he said. "You folks with the circus?"

"Yeah," said the man. He paused, clearly trying to think of
something to say about the circus.

"Go on, halfwit," said one of the ladies. "Get the water."

"All right, Mildred," said the man sadly. "You don't have to
holler."

She looked at him sombrely, and he picked up the four buckets
and disappeared into the washroom.

There was a silence in the yard office while the ladies steamed
and brooded in front of the stove. Suddenly the air was filled with
the smell of singeing cloth.

"*Now* what the hell?" said one of them, sniffing sharply.

"It's your skirt, Babe," said the one called Mildred. "It's on the
stove."

"Well, for God's sake," said Babe, though without any special emotion. With one accord, the ladies drew back from the stove and sat down on the edge of the table by the window. Their sultry eyes swung around the yard office and rested at last on Milton.

"You," said Mildred. "What do you do here? What's your job?"

"He's just the clerk," said Babe wearily. "Forget it."

"Well," said Mildred, "he's better than the other one. That other one is dead, if you ast me."

"Say," the yardmaster began, but he was chilled by their bleak and impersonal stare and subsided.

"Listen," said Mildred to Milton. "You know where's a drink around here?"

"I told you it's just the clerk," said Babe. "He wouldn't know. Strictly a dummy."

"Gin or whiskey," said Mildred. "I wouldn't care."

"Well," said Milton slowly, "there's no bars around here. You could ast at the lunch wagon. If they knew you."

"They know *you?*"

"Sure."

"What do they carry?" asked Babe.

"Only grappa. It's some kind of a Greek drink."

"Oh, my God," said Mildred. "Well, all right. Get two of them. Two bottles."

"Well . . ."

"It's all right. We'll give you the dough."

"It ain't that," said Milton. "It's only I oughtn't to leave the yard."

"We'll take care of the yard," said Babe. "You get the what's-this."

"You don't have to worry," said Mildred. "I'll handle any trains."

They watched him as he shrugged into a raincoat and went out the door. "Hurry back, dear," said Mildred.

Babe looked at the washroom door.

"I think that bum is drowned," she said. "Your husband. I think he fell in."

"Well, that would be O.K.," said Mildred.

When Milton came back with the grappa, Mildred and Babe were still sitting on the table, and the man was standing by the stove. The four buckets, full of water, were on the floor outside the washroom. The yardmaster was finishing a story. "So when she found out I didn't have no money, she threw my shoes out of the window, right in the hobber." He looked at them, shaking with laughter. "Right in New York Hobber. I liked to died."

"You ought to be ashamed of yourself," said Babe coldly. "An old dope like you."

"Hello, dear," said Mildred to Milton. "Did you get it?"

"Yes," he said. He took the two bottles out of the paper bag and put them on the table. The man picked one of them up and held it against the light.

"What is it?" he asked. "Mule?"

"Grappa," said Milton.

"What's this grappa?"

"You ought to know," said Mildred. "You're part Greek or something, ain't you?"

"Ah, don't be like that, Millie," said the man. "I only ast him a question."

He took the cork out and held the bottle up to his nose.

"It don't smell much."

"Well," said Milton, "a bomb don't smell either."

"Listen, you can't drink that stuff in here," said the yardmaster.

"Why not?" said Mildred.

"The superintendent is liable to show up any time," he said. "He's regularly down here every time we get a circus train."

"Ah, tell him—"

"No," said the man. "Wade a minute. Wade a minute. What would he do?"

"Plenty," said the yardmaster. "Drinking on railroad property."

"He can't do nothing to me," said Babe.

"You want to try and tell that to the railway cops?"

"Oh," said Babe. "Well, O.K."

She looked at the four buckets.

"Say, who's going to carry them things?"

"Milty," said Mildred promptly. She put her arm through his.

"Ain't you, Milty? Babe and I can each take one of the bottles and you and Stupid can carry the pails. We'll have a little drink up at the train."

"Say, I'd like to," said Milton, "but I better not leave the office, had I, Pop?"

"I don't care what you do," said the yardmaster. "I don't even care if they cut your throat."

"See," said Mildred. "He says it's O.K. Come on, Milty."

"Better leave me hold your watch," said the yardmaster.

It was raining even harder as they started across the yard toward the Hill, where the circus train lay. The floodlights on the float were enough to throw a pale gleam along the rails, but the ties were invisible, half drowned in the muddy water. Milton picked his way along them expertly, but he could hear Babe and the man with the other two pails stumbling and cursing up ahead in the darkness. Mildred came last and she too seemed to be having trouble and spoke sullenly about it.

"You need to be a duck or something," she said.

"Walk where I do," Milton told her. "Keep on the ties. I should of brung a flashlight."

"That's right," she said bitterly. "Now is when to think about it."

They were halfway up the Hill when she pulled at his sleeve.

"Let them go on ahead," she said.

"Why, what's the matter?"

"I ain't taking drinks to all that mob," she said. "There's fifty of them in that car. We wouldn't get no more than a smell. We better drink it right here."

"Listen," he said, with a daring that rather astonished him. "All them boxcars alongside your train. They're empty. How about if we go and sit in one of them for a while?"

"We-ell . . ."

"We could have a little talk," he said carelessly. "Just the two of us."

"Why, Milty," she said, and laughed unreasonably in the darkness. "All right. Whatever you say."

"Come on," he said. "Let's get going."

They reached the top of the Hill and started down the black aisle between the circus train and the empties.

"We better get far enough away from the passenger car," he said. "Some one of your friends might be coming out."

"My!" she said.

They had to walk single file between the cars. Mildred went ahead and Milton followed her with the buckets. It was very dark and the strangling smell of the animals was heavy in the air. Suddenly the night was split by hideous laughter; it was inhuman; the laughter of the demented or the damned.

"Hey," said Milton. "What's that?"

"It's only Robert Taylor," she said.

"What?"

"The hyena. We call him Robert Taylor."

"Oh."

At last he stopped before one of the boxcars. The door was open and he peered inside.

"This one looks all right," he said. "It's got some hay in it."

"You think we come far enough, dear?" she said with a giggle.

"I guess so."

"O.K. Hep me up."

He boosted her in the car and then swung in himself, leaving the buckets outside on the ground. The car had apparently contained bricks, because the floor was covered with broken fragments and little piles of straw. Mildred kicked a pile of straw together against the wall facing the open door and sat down on it with a sigh.

"My God," she said, "am I ever pooped."

He sat down beside her on the straw.

"Say, this is all right, ain't it?" he said.

"Well, it's prolly better than the rain." She picked up the bottle and pulled out the cork with her teeth.

"This had better be good," she said.

She drank in the darkness and gave a little shiver.

"You sure that Greek didn't make no mistake, Milty," she said. "Like giving you kerosene or something?"

"Let me see it," he said, and drank cautiously. "No, that's the grappa all right. It don't taste very hot, but it's got a wallop."

"I'll be right here waiting for it," she said. "Give us a cigarette, huh?"

The match lit up the interior of the boxcar and even threw a brief yellow light on the car across the way. Milton noticed that the door of that was open, and there were bars across the opening. The car seemed to contain some kind of cage. In the flare of the match Milton thought he saw vague shadows, stirring enormously.

"What's in there?"

"Some one of the animals," she said indifferently. "I wouldn't know."

"Oh."

Mildred drank again, deeply and this time without apparent displeasure.

"Maybe you was right about this stuff," she said. "I begin to feel like I might live."

"You better take it a little easy," he said. "It's stronger than you think if you ain't used to it."

"Listen, Milty," she said. "You know what happened the last guy told me that? They had to scrape him up off the floor."

"I'm only telling you," he said.

She drank again.

"No, that ain't bad stuff at all," she said gratefully. "I got to remember to get some more of that stuff sometime. What did you say its name was?"

"Grappa."

"Grappa. I like it. Hey," she said with a sharp note of inquiry in her voice. "What seems to be eating *you*?"

Milton, who had put his arm cautiously around her shoulder, withdrew it.

"Nothing," he said uneasily. "I only thought you might find it more comfortable."

"Well, for the love of God," she said. "Milty the Raper."

She laughed coarsely at this exhibition of poor taste and in the darkness Milton blushed.

"All right," she said, relenting. "Go on, put it back, Milty. I ain't sore. It's only you surprised me."

They sat for a little while in silence, in tentative embrace. Mildred's face, lighted intermittently when she drew on her cigarette, seemed relaxed and peaceful, almost amiable. Milton, his eyes more accustomed to the darkness, could see the cage in the other car quite clearly now. There really was an animal in it, a big animal, pacing soft and deadly behind the bars. He could hear the sound of its heavy breath and the creaking of the cage when it threw its weight against the bars. The cage seemed to Milton a frail and ridiculous barrier for an animal that had really made up its mind to get out.

"Say, what *is* that over there, anyway?" he asked nervously.

Mildred glanced at the cage.

"It looks like the lion," she said. "Yeah, that's what it is. Say, is he ever a crazy bastard."

"How do you mean 'crazy'?" asked Milton with anxiety.

"He gets in these crazy spells," she said. "You dassent get near him. Like the time he chewed up this fellow's arm."

"He did?"

"Like hamburger," said Mildred with satisfaction.

"He didn't ever get loose, did he?"

"Not yet. But he can give those bars hell when he gets in one of these crazy spells."

The lion had apparently noticed their voices, because he had stopped walking up and down in the cage and was standing facing the door. Milton could see his wild and luminous eyes searching the darkness. A growl, low and distant like the roll of a train on a faraway bridge, began to stir in his throat. He was rapidly developing all the symptoms of a crazy spell.

"He ain't going to bother us," said Mildred, noticing that Milton seemed tense. "He's practically a tame lion compared to some of them."

She drank again and then laid her head on Milton's shoulder.

"Listen, Milty," she said, and now unexpectedly there was pathos in her voice. "I guess you think I'm just a tramp, don't you? I guess you don't think much of a girl that would drink this grappa, laying around with a fellow in a boxcar. I guess that's what you been thinking about me, ain't it, Milty?"

"I ain't given the topic so much as a thought," said Milton gallantly, though with a wary eye on the lion.

"Shut up before I spit in your eye," said Mildred, addressing the lion, which had begun to growl in earnest. "Listen, Milty, you try being a living statue off and on for ten years, and see how you like it. When I think the number of times I been Fame leading that goddam horse. Maybe I ain't always been a plaster saint, but what the hell kind of a life is that for a girl, I ast you?"

She drank, moodily.

"Nobody is calling me no tramp," she said furiously. "That louse in Wilmington. I guess he ain't passing no more remarks about people being tramps."

"Who?" said Milton.

She must have been a volatile girl, because now she laughed merrily.

"This fellow in Wilmington," she said. "Say, that was comical! This fellow was in the act, too. He was the General—you know, sitting on the horse—when I was Fame. Well, one night we all get stiff in a bar and this fellow called Babe and me a tramp. We didn't say nothing at the time, but the next night when he's the General and I'm Fame and Babe is some kind of an angel or nimp or something laying on the ground behind the horse, she takes this big pin and sticks the horse in his backside. Well, I'm hardly out of the way before he's down off the stand and like a bat out of hell for the exit. The General can't hardly keep on a horse staying still, so he gets tossed off in one of the boxes. He busted four ribs.

"Well," she said, with another of her dark and inexplicable changes of mood, "I ain't a tramp, and I don't want to have to tell you again, Milty, that's all."

"But I didn't—"

"Let it pass," she said magnanimously.

The rumble in the lion's throat had been growing steadily stronger and now it deepened into a passable roar. He flicked his paw tentatively at the bars, which rattled ominously.

"Pipe down, you," said Mildred.

"Say, maybe we better—"

"You, too, Milty," said Mildred, speaking with some difficulty because the neck of the bottle was in her mouth. "Both of you. Pipe down."

There could be no mistake this time about the lion's roar, and he lunged heavily against the bars.

"Well, for God's sake," said Mildred disgustedly. She had been smoking a cigarette, and when the lion roared again she threw it irritably toward the cage.

"Lay down, screwball," she said.

As Milton watched with dismay, the cigarette curved through the air, between the bars, and hit the lion sharply on the nose. A little shower of sparks enveloped his head, glowed, and went out.

For a moment nothing happened, and then the lion exploded. They could see him only dimly, a black and monstrous shape, tearing at the bars, but his intentions were clear and awful. The roaring had given way to a strangled, deadly snarl, and sometimes he spit like a cat. Beneath these louder sounds Milton could hear the even more paralyzing groan and creak of the tortured bars. Mildred added her own frail voice to bedlam.

"Shut up, shut up, shut up!" she shouted. "Shut up, *shut up*, SHUT UP!"

"My God," whispered Milton, "he's breaking the damn thing down!"

She didn't hear him or, hearing, paid no attention.

"I'll fix the crazy bastard!" she cried passionately, and while he watched in agony she scrambled down out of the car and picked up one of the buckets of water.

Milton waited for no more. He vaulted down out of the car and fled desperately into the darkness. For a little while, as he ran, he could hear Mildred arguing with the lion, but presently all sound died away. It occurred to him that this might mean that the lion had got Mildred and was eating her. He thought of this gruesome possibility with horror, but there were other emotions, too.

When Milton Barker got back to the yard office, haggard, panting, mysteriously encrusted with mud and straw, the yardmaster looked at him curiously.

"Well, you cert'n'y ain't wasting no time, Milty," he said admiringly. "How'd you make out? Them babies treat you all right?"

Milton gave him a secret smile, implying many fascinating things.

"What do *you* think, Pop?" he said darkly.

Somewhere down in the yard Robert Taylor laughed his mad, derisive laughter.

HOMECOMING

❦

WILLIAM MAXWELL

IT WAS NEARLY DARK, and Jordan Smith, walking along with his eyes on the ground, came to a stretch of sidewalk where the snow had not been scraped off but was packed hard and icy. He looked up and, a trifle surprised, saw that he had come to the Farrels'. There were lights in the downstairs windows and the house was just as he had remembered it. Yet there was something wrong, something that made him stand doubtfully at the edge of the walk that had not been tended to.

He had come back to Watertown to spend Christmas with his family—with his father and mother, and his two brothers, who were both younger than he was and not quite grown. But they were not entirely the reason for his wanting to come home. Before he went away, he used to be with Tom and Ann Farrel a great deal of the time. So much, in fact, that it used to annoy his mother, and she would ask him occasionally why he didn't pack his things and go move in with the Farrels. And there was nothing that he could say; no way that he could explain to his mother that Farrel and Ann had somehow filled out his life for him and balanced it. They were the first friends that he had ever had. And the best, really. For that reason it would not do for him to go back to New York without seeing Farrel. He had never even meant to do that. But he had hoped to run into Farrel somewhere about town, coming or going. He had hoped that he wouldn't have to face Farrel in his own house now that Ann was not here. Now that Ann was dead, Jordan said to himself as he turned in and made his way up to the porch. He rang the bell twice. After a time the door opened slowly and a rather small boy looked out at him.

"Hello," Jordan said. "I've come to see your father, Timothy. Is he home?"

The boy shook his head. With a feeling which he was ashamed to recognize as relief, Jordan stepped across the sill into the front hall and the door closed behind him.

"How soon do you expect your father?" he said.

"Pretty soon."

"How soon is that?"

"I don't know." The boy seemed to be waiting stolidly until Jordan had proved himself friend or enemy.

"I expect you don't remember me. It's been three years since I left Watertown. You weren't so very old then."

Jordan had not meant to stay, but he found himself taking off his overcoat and his muffler and laying them across the newel post. The last time he had come here, Ann had met him at the door and her face had lighted up with pleasure. "It's Jordan," she had said. Even now, after three years, he could hear her voice and her pleasure at the sight of him. "Here's Jordan, Tom. He's come to say goodbye.

The front hall and the living room were both strangely still. Forgetting that he was not alone, Jordan listened a moment until the oil furnace rumbling away to itself in the basement reassured him.

"I can't stay," he said aloud to Timothy. On the hall tree was an old battered gray hat of Farrel's. Jordan started to hang his new brown one beside it, and then he changed his mind. With the hat still in his hand, he followed Timothy into the living room. There was a Christmas tree in the front window, with red balls and silver balls and tinsel and tin foil in strips hanging from it, and strand upon strand of colored lights that were not lighted. Under the tree Timothy's presents were still laid out, two days after Christmas, in the boxes they had come in: a cowboy hat, a toy revolver, a necktie and handkerchiefs, a giant flashlight, a book on scouting.

"Santa Claus must have been here," Jordan said.

Timothy did not consider, apparently, that this remark called for any answer. He waited a moment and then announced, "You're Jordan."

"That's right—Jordan Smith. But I didn't think you'd remember me."

He looked at the boy hopefully, but Timothy's face remained grave and a little pale, just as before. Jordan went over to the square, heavy, comfortable chair which was Farrel's favorite and sat down in it, and Timothy settled himself on the sofa opposite. For lack of anything better to do, Jordan took his hat and began to spin it, so that the hat went around wildly on his finger.

"You've grown, Timothy. You must have grown at least five or six inches since I saw you last."

Timothy crossed one foot over the other in embarrassment, and dug at the sofa with his heels.

"If this keeps up, we'll have to put weights in your pockets," Jordan said, and his eyes wandered past Timothy to the china greyhounds, one on either side of the mantel. "They're Staffordshire," Ann used to tell him proudly. "And if anything happened to them, I wouldn't want to go on living." Well, Jordan thought to himself—well, there they are. Nothing has happened to them. And the hat spun off the end of his finger and landed on the rug at his feet.

"Now look what I've done!" he exclaimed as he picked the hat up and placed it on Timothy's head. The hat came down well over Timothy's ears, and under the brim of it Timothy's eyes looked out at him without any eyebrows. This time Timothy was amused.

"It's too big for me," he said, smiling, and placed the hat on the sofa beside him.

"Now that it's dark outside," Jordan suggested, "why don't we light the tree?"

"Can't," Timothy said.

"Won't it light?"

Timothy shook his head.

"Get me the screwdriver, then."

A change came over Timothy. For the first time his face took on life and interest. "What do you want the screwdriver for?" he asked.

"Get me one," Jordan said confidently, "and I'll show you."

As soon as Timothy was out of the room, Jordan got up and

went over to the fireplace. The greyhounds needed dusting, but there was nothing the matter with them. Not a crack or a chip anywhere. Jordan put them down again carefully and turned, hearing a slight disturbance outside. The *Evening Herald* struck the side of the house. It was a sound that he had never heard anywhere but in Watertown. He remembered it so perfectly that he couldn't believe that he had been away. Except for Ann, he said to himself as he made his way around the Christmas tree to the front window—except for her, everything was exactly the same. He had come home. He was here in this house that he had thought so much about. And, strangely, it was no satisfaction to him whatever.

Outside, the snow had begun again. Watching the paper boy wheel his bicycle down the icy walk, Jordan wondered why he had not stayed in New York over the holidays; why it was that he had wanted so much to come home. For weeks he had been restless, uneasy, and unable to keep from thinking of home. At night he could not sleep for walking up and down these streets, meeting people that he had known, and talking to them earnestly in his mind. Now that he was here, he didn't feel the way he had expected to feel. People were awfully nice, of course, and they were pleased to see him, but it was no kind of a homecoming. Not without Farrel and Ann. Wherever he went he found himself mentioning her, without meaning to especially. And it shocked him to see that people did not care about her any more. They had grown used to her not being here. Some of them—one or two, at least—complained to him about Farrel. They liked Farrel, they said. You couldn't help liking Tom Farrel. They still enjoyed having a drink with him every now and then. And there was no question but that Ann's death was a terrible loss to him. But if she had lived, the doctor said, she would never have been well, probably. And it was a year and a half since she had been rushed to the hospital in the middle of the night, to be operated on. Tom ought to begin now to get over it. He was nursing his grief, people said.

Jordan broke off a strip of tinsel from the Christmas tree, for no particular reason, and started with it for the kitchen. At the door of the dining room he met Timothy with the screwdriver. There was a woman with him also—a tired, tall woman with gray hair that was parted in the middle, and an uncompromising look about the corners of her mouth. Jordan nodded to her.

"I'm Mrs. Ives," the woman said. "What do you want with the screwdriver?"

"I want to fix the tree," Jordan explained, realizing suddenly why it was that Farrel had taken her for a housekeeper. If Farrel had got a younger woman and a more sympathetic one, there would have been talk. "Timothy says the lights don't work, and if we have a screwdriver we can tell which one is burnt out."

"Oh," the woman said. "In that case, I guess it's all right. You come to see Mr. Farrel, didn't you?"

"Yes." Jordan could see that she was trying to make up her mind whether or not she ought to ask who he was; whether it would be polite.

"Will Mr. Farrel be home soon?" he asked.

"Sometimes he comes right home from the office, and sometimes he doesn't." She answered Jordan's question patiently, as if it had already been asked a great many times. As if it were a foolish question, and one that nobody knew the answer to. "Mostly he doesn't come home till later."

"I see." Jordan turned to Timothy, who was tugging at his sleeve. Together they dragged a straight chair across the room from the desk to the Christmas tree. Jordan balanced himself on the chair and unscrewed the first bulb. Then he looked around for the housekeeper. She was not there any longer. She had gone back to the kitchen. "I may not be able to wait," he said, and handed the little red bulb to Timothy, who was standing below him. When Jordan applied the screwdriver to the socket, nothing happened. The lights did not go on. "It wasn't that one," he said.

Timothy handed the light back to him.

"No, sir," Jordan said, looking down at him thoughtfully. "It certainly wasn't."

Nor was it the second bulb, or the third, or the fourth. All of the lights on the first strand were good, apparently. As Jordan started on the second strand, he asked in what he hoped was a casual way, "Do you like Mrs. Ives?"

"She's all right," Timothy said. And he looked down then, as if Jordan had made a mistake and would after a second realize it.

They did not speak for a time, but Jordan went on handing the bulbs to Timothy and testing the sockets with his screwdriver. When Timothy had no bulb to hold, he untwisted the wires with his hands. Quite suddenly, when Jordan came to the third bulb from the end, the whole tree blazed into light.

"It was that one!" he exclaimed, and took the new yellow bulb which Timothy held up to him. There was a moment when the lights went off again, but Jordan screwed the yellow bulb into the socket; then the lights came on and stayed on.

"How's that?" he asked.

"Fine," Timothy said, with the lights shining red and blue on his face.

Jordan stepped down from the chair and surveyed the tree from top to bottom. He could go now. There was no reason for him to stay any longer.

"When you grow up, Timothy," he said, "we'll go into the business." Then he picked his hat up from the arm of the sofa where Timothy had been sitting. "O.K?"

"O.K.," Timothy said.

"Don't forget, then."

Jordan went out into the front hall and took his scarf from the newel post. He listened for the whir and rumble of the furnace, but this time it was not enough. Now that the Christmas tree was lighted, the house was even more unnaturally quiet. Up and down the street, in other houses, people would be sitting down to dinner, but Mrs. Ives had not yet turned the dining-room light on, and the dining-room table was not even set. It seemed wrong to go away and leave a child alone here, in this soundless house. Timothy was standing in the living room, watching him, and did not appear to be upset. But when he left, Jordan thought—what would happen to Timothy *then*?

He wound the scarf round his throat and held it in place with his chin until he had worked himself into his overcoat. When he had finished and was drawing on his gloves, he said brightly, "Smith and Farrel, Fixers of Plain and Fancy Christmas Trees."

Timothy was looking right at him, but there was no telling whether the boy had heard what he said. It seemed rather as if he hadn't. "Do you have to go?" Timothy said.

"I'm afraid I do." Jordan was about to make up a long, elaborate, and convincing excuse, but there were footsteps outside on the porch, and both of them turned in time to see the door thrown open. A man stood in the doorway, with snow on his shoulders and the evening paper clasped tightly under one arm.

"Jordan," he said, "for Christ's sake!"

"Sure," Jordan said, nodding.

"But I've been looking for you all over town!"

Jordan braced himself as the man caught at him slowly with his eyes, and with his voice, and with his two hands.

"And I've been right here," Jordan said helplessly, "all the time."

ONLY THE DEAD KNOW BROOKLYN

❦

Thomas Wolfe

D ere's no guy livin' dat knows Brooklyn t'roo an' t'roo, because it'd take a guy a lifetime just to find his way aroun'
duh goddam town.

So like I say, I'm waitin' for my train t' come when I sees dis
big guy standin' deh—dis is duh foist I eveh see of him. Well, he's
lookin' wild, y'know, an' I can see dat he's had plenty, but still
he's holdin' it; he talks good an' is walkin' straight enough. So
den, dis big guy steps up to a little guy dat's standin' deh, an' says,
"How d'yuh get t' Eighteent' Avenoo an' Sixty-sevent' Street?"
he says.

"Jesus! Yuh got me, chief," duh little guy says to him. "I ain't
been heah long myself. Where is duh place?" he says. "Out in duh
Flatbush section somewhere?"

"Nah," duh big guy says. "It's out in Bensenhoist. But I was
neveh deh befoeh. How d'yuh get deh?"

"Jesus," duh little guy says, scratchin' his head, y'know—yuh
could see duh little guy didn't know his way about—"yuh got me,
chief. I never hoid of it. Do any of youse guys know where it is?"
he says to me.

"Sure," I says. "It's out in Bensenhoist. Yuh take duh Fourt'
Avenoo express, get off at Fifty-nint' Street, change to a Sea Beach
local deh, get off at Eighteent' Avenoo an' Sixty-toid, an' den walk
down foeh blocks. Dat's all yuh got to do," I says.

"G'wan!" some wise guy dat I neveh seen befoeh pipes up.
"Whatcha talkin' about?" he says—oh, he was wise, y'know. "Duh
guy is crazy! I tell yuh what yuh do," he says to duh big guy.
"Yuh change to duh West End line at Toity-sixt'," he tells him.
"Get off at Noo Utrecht an' Sixteent' Avenoo," he says. "Walk two

blocks oveh, foeh blocks up," he says, "an' you'll be right deh."
Oh, a *wise* guy, y'know.

"Oh, yeah?" I says. "Who told *you* so much?" He got me sore
because he was so wise about it. "How long you been livin' heah?"
I says.

"All my life," he says. "I was bawn in Williamsboig," he says.
"An' I can tell you t'ings about dis town you neveh hoid of,"
he says.

"Yeah?" I says.

"Yeah," he says.

"Well, den, you can tell me t'ings about dis town dat nobody
else has eveh hoid of, either. Maybe you make it all up yoehself at
night," I says, "befoeh you go to sleep—like cuttin' out papeh
dolls, or somp'n."

"Oh, yeah?" he says. "You're pretty wise, ain't yuh?"

"Oh, I don't know," I says. "Duh boids ain't usin' my head for
Lincoln's statue yet," I says. "But I'm wise enough to know a
phony when I see one."

"Yeah?" he says. "A wise guy, huh? Well, you're so wise dat
someone's goin' t'bust yuh one right on duh snoot some day,"
he says. "Dat's how wise *you* are."

Well, my train was comin', or I'da smacked him den and dere,
but when I seen duh train was comin', all I said was, "All right,
mugg! I'm sorry I can't stay to take keh of you, but I'll be seein'
yuh sometime, I hope, out in duh cemetery." So den I says to duh
big guy, who'd been standin' deh all duh time, "You come wit
me," I says. So when we gets onto duh train I says to him, "Where
yuh goin' out in Bensenhoist?" I says. "What numbeh are yuh
lookin' for?" I says. *You* know—I t'ought if he told me duh address
I might be able to help him out.

"Oh," he says, "I'm not lookin' for no one. I don't know no one
out deh."

"Then whatcha goin' out deh for?" I says.

"Oh," duh guy says, "I'm just goin' out to see duh place," he
says. "I like duh sound of duh name"—Bensenhoist, y'know—"so I
t'ought I'd go out an' have a look at it."

"Whatcha tryin' t'hand me?" I says. "Whatcha tryin' t'do—kid
me?" *You* know, I t'ought duh guy was bein' wise wit me.

"No," he says, "I'm tellin' yuh duh troot. I like to go out an' take a look at places wit nice names like dat. I like to go out an' look at all kinds of places," he says.

"How'd yuh know deh was such a place," I says, "if you neveh been deh befoeh?"

"Oh," he says, "I got a map."

"A *map*?" I says.

"Sure," he says, "I got a map dat tells me about all dese places. I take it wit me every time I come out heah," he says.

And Jesus! Wit dat, he pulls it out of his pocket, an' so help me, but he's *got* it—he's tellin' duh troot—a big map of duh whole goddam place wit all duh different pahts. Mahked out, you know— Canarsie an' East Noo Yawk an' Flatbush, Bensenhoist, Sout' Brooklyn, duh Heights, Bay Ridge, Greenpernt—duh whole goddam layout, he's got it right deh on duh map.

"You been to any of dose places?" I says.

"Sure," he says, "I been to most of 'em. I was down in Red Hook just last night," he says.

"Jesus! Red Hook!" I says. "Whatcha do down deh?"

"Oh," he says, "nuttin' much. I just walked aroun'. I went into a coupla places an' had a drink," he says, "but most of the time I just walked aroun'."

"Just walked aroun'?" I says.

"Sure," he says, "just lookin' at things, y'know."

"Where'd yuh go?" I asts him.

"Oh," he says, "I don't know duh name of duh place, but I could find it on my map," he says. "One time I was walkin' across some big fields where deh ain't no houses," he says, "but I could see ships obeh deh all lighted up. Dey was loadin'. So I walks across duh fields," he says, "to where duh ships are."

"Sure," I says, "I know where you was. You was down to duh Erie Basin."

"Yeah," he says, "I guess dat was it. Dey had some of dose big elevators an' cranes an' dey was loadin' ships, an' I could see some ships in drydock all lighted up, so I walks across duh fields to where dey are," he says.

"Den what did yuh do?" I says.

"Oh," he says, "nuttin' much. I came on back across duh fields after a while an' went into a coupla places an' had a drink."

"Didn't nuttin' happen while yuh was in dere?" I says.

"No," he says. "Nuttin' much. A coupla guys was drunk in one of duh places an' started a fight, but dey bounced 'em out," he says, "an' den one of duh guys stahted to come back again, but duh bartender gets his baseball bat out from under duh counteh, so duh guy goes on."

"Jesus!" I said. "Red Hook!"

"Sure," he says. "Dat's where it was, all right."

"Well, you keep outa deh," I says. "You stay away from deh."

"Why?" he says. "What's wrong wit it?"

"Oh," I says, "it's a good place to stay away from, dat's all. It's a good place to keep out of."

"Why?" he says. "Why is it?"

Jesus! Whatcha gonna do wit a guy as dumb as dat? I saw it wasn't no use to try to tell him nuttin', he wouldn't know what I was talkin' about, so I just says to him, "Oh, nuttin'. Yuh might get lost down deh, dat's all."

"Lost?" he says. "No, I wouldn't get lost. I got a map," he says.

A map! Red Hook! Jesus!

So den duh guy begins to ast me all kinds of nutty questions: how big was Brooklyn an' could I find my way aroun' in it, an' how long would it take a guy to know duh place.

"Listen!" I says. "You get dat idea outa yoeh head right now," I says. "You ain't neveh gonna get to know Brooklyn," I says. "Not in a hunderd yeahs. I been livin' heah all my life," I says, "an' I don't even know all deh is to know about it, so how do you expect to know duh town," I says, "when you don't even live heah?"

"Yes," he says, "but I got a map to help me find my way about."

"Map or no map," I says, "yuh ain't gonna get to know Brooklyn wit no map," I says.

"Can you swim?" he says, just like dat. Jesus! By dat time, y'know, I begun to see dat duh guy was some kind of nut. He'd had plenty to drink, of course, but he had dat crazy look in his eye I didn't like. "Can you swim?" he says.

"Sure," I says. "Can't you?"

"No," he says. "Not more'n a stroke or two. I neveh loined good."

"Well, it's easy," I says. "All yuh need is a little confidence. Duh way I loined, me older bruddeh pitched me off duh dock one day when I was eight yeahs old, cloes an' all. 'You'll swim,' he says. 'You'll swim all right—or drown.' An', believe me, I *swam!* When yuh know yuh got to, you'll do it. Duh only t'ing yuh need is confidence. An' once you've loined," I says, "you've got nuttin' else to worry about. You'll neveh forgit it. It's somp'n dat stays with yuh as long as yuh live."

"Can yuh swim good?" he says.

"Like a fish," I tells him. "I'm a regular fish in duh wateh," I says. "I loined to swim right off duh docks wit all duh odeh kids," I says.

"What would yuh do if yuh saw a man drownin'?" duh guy says.

"Do? Why, I'd jump in an' pull him out," I says. "Dat's what I'd do."

"Did yuh eveh see a man drown?" he says.

"Sure," I says. "I see two guys—bot' times at Coney Island. Dey got out too far, an' neider one could swim. Dey drowned befoeh anyone could get to 'em."

"What becomes of people after dey have drowned out heah?" he says.

"Drowned out where?" I says.

"Out heah in Brooklyn."

"I don't know watcha mean," I says. "Neveh hoid of no one drownin' heah in Brooklyn, unless you mean a swimmin' pool. Yuh can't drown in Brooklyn," I says. "Yuh gotta drown some-where else—in duh ocean, where dere's wateh."

"Drownin'," duh guy says, lookin' at his map. "Drownin'."

Jesus! I could see by den he was some kind of nut, he had dat crazy expression in his eyes when he looked at you, an' I didn't know what he might do. So we was comin' to a station, an' it wasn't my stop, but I got off anyway, an' waited for duh next train.

"Well, so long, chief," I says. "Take it easy, now."

"Drownin'," duh guy says, lookin' at his map. "Drownin'."

Jesus! I've t'ought about dat guy a t'ousand times since den an' wondered what eveh happened to 'm goin' out to look at Bensen-hoist because he liked duh name! Walkin' aroun' t'roo Red Hook by himself at night an' lookin' at his map! How many people did I see get drowned out heah in Brooklyn! How long would it take a guy wit a good map to know all deh was to know about Brooklyn!

Jesus! What a nut *he* was! I wondeh what eveh happened to 'm, anyway! I wondeh if someone knocked him on duh head, or if he's still wanderin' aroun' in duh subway in duh middle of duh night with his little map! Duh poor guy! Say, I've got to laugh, at dat, when I t'ink about him! Maybe he's found out by now dat he'll neveh live long enough to know duh whole of Brooklyn. It'd take a guy a lifetime to know Brooklyn t'roo an' t'roo. An' even den, yuh wouldn't know it all.

THE WORKS

❧

Nathan Asch

H E MET HER at a party. He had come late, and in the kitchen there was an enormous and very drunken politician, boasting how his man had been elected senator and how he had the electoral votes of his state sewed up in his pocket. A tiny woman was perched on the kitchen stool yelling, "You can't use that kind of language in front of me!" Many people were leaving. He saw this girl standing alone in the passageway between the kitchen and the living room, her eyes shining brightly, expectantly, as if she had had one or two drinks and, not being used to drinking, thought something was about to happen. Their eyes met, and he felt stirred and a little sorry for her. He said to her, "Let's get out of here."

They drove across to Virginia, holding hands, and went to the Dance Barbecue; they watched sailors and girls; they stared down at the beer rings on the table while a girl near them accused another of having stolen five dollars. They discovered that both worked for the government, she as the secretary of an important administrator, he as a statistician. They left the Barbecue still holding hands. He drove very fast along the Potomac, through Alexandria, shimmering with white walls, past the woods lining the Mount Vernon Highway. As they were coming back, the sky turned to pink, the sun rose beyond the Monument; Washington shone with rooftops, was bright green with trees. She had a lovely profile. She withdrew her hand from his, looked at him with smiling, all-encompassing eyes, and shook her head. No, she didn't want any breakfast.

That afternoon, before leaving his office, he called her up. They had dinner together that night and afterward went to a movie.

He found himself wondering how old she was and what he really thought of her. He still wondered the following evening, when he had dinner at her house. The girls she lived with were away for the night. There were silver candlesticks on the dining-room table, there was a uniformed maid, there was roast beef. She looked beautiful and young in the candlelight. She talked about her childhood: she had had a miserable, poverty-stricken time, with a mother determined her daughter would not have to suffer all her life, too. "My mother lived only to see me pass the Civil Service examination," she said. She spoke very little about the years since she had come to Washington; instead, she seemed to be under some compulsion to talk of the earlier years, of the father who had abandoned them, of her mother's illness, of the bedrooms with light housekeeping in Seattle, Portland, San Francisco, Los Angeles. She gave him coffee and brandy, and told him of a winter when she and her mother had subsisted almost solely on oranges. She had passed the examination, but while she was waiting for the appointment her mother had died, and her mother's share of the fare to Washington had been used instead for funeral expenses.

She asked him if he wanted her to play Gilbert and Sullivan, but he said no, not tonight. They sat for a long while holding hands, he thinking about his own uneventful childhood and she watching him.

Jerry, his chief in the research division, invited him to a picnic that Sunday, and he asked her did she want to come? She worried whether Jerry's wife would like her. She carried a large cardboard box from one of Washington's best caterers; she wore a ribbon around her hair, short socks, sneakers, and looked like a little girl. Jerry's wife liked her very much, insisted on sitting beside her, and the two began an intimate conversation that lasted until they got to Chesapeake Bay. Jerry's children stared at her. When he and Jerry went off to gather firewood, Jerry said, "That's a fine girl. I like her very much."

They had steaks roasted on charcoal, and *pâté-de-foie-gras* sandwiches from the caterer's box. The children ate up all the fancy cookies. Afterward he and she wandered off under a tree, and he fell asleep with his head on her lap. When he woke up it was getting dark, and when he looked up at her, her eyes were shining with tears.

The next morning, Jerry's wife called him. She said, "I like that girl. She's fine and serious." She invited the two of them to dinner. He said he was sorry, he had to go to New York. "Oh," she said, "Jerry hadn't told me." He said it wasn't on an office matter; Jerry didn't know.

Jerry said, "All right. If you want to go." The time off would be deducted from his annual leave. He went to New York, to the research foundation, his old office. Everybody was excited about the research fellowships to South America. When he asked the director if there was any chance of his being considered, he was told with a grin to keep on living off the government, out of the public trough.

He had dinner with his parents and told his mother he was going back to Washington that night. He went instead to a hotel; the next morning he took the subway to the Battery and slowly walked up Broadway. About noon he stopped in at a movie house and saw part of a feature. Twice he stopped to eat. In the evening he reached Van Cortlandt Park. He went to a drugstore and he called her up. She said, "Are you really calling from New York?" He said, "Yes. May I come to see you?" She said, "Please come."

It was too late to fly back. He arrived by train at an early morning hour, rushed the taxi through dark Washington streets. Her front door was open; by the time he reached it she appeared in the doorway, holding out her hand. When he took her in his arms she went limp all over.

She said, "We'll share everything, our thoughts and our hours. We'll become as one. We'll be so intertwined nobody will ever be able to tell us apart."

After that they seemed to be always together. He would call for her every evening and after dinner they would go for a drive, or they would return to her house and sit for hours listening to the radio. Weekends they went on picnics, they swam in hotel pools, they went cruising in Chesapeake Bay, they danced on the terrace at the edge of Rock Creek Park. She would telephone him every day at four; she had developed the habit of calling him just before he started checking the official figures for the day. She would say, "It's me." He would picture her, dark hair and very dark eyes, the receiver pressed tightly to her ear, her mouth half-open with eagerness. He would say, "Is it *really* you?" She would answer, "Yes," and hang up. His assistant would notice his smile and smile back, and he would mentally shake his head to clear it and stare down hard at the checking list.

She took him to Maryland to her administrator's house. The servants greeted her affectionately, and when the administrator came down, he quickly walked up to her, took both her hands in his, and said, underlining each word, *"How are you?"* as if he hadn't seen her only two hours before. The three of them had dinner on the veranda, did not light the lights, but sat until very late. She remained silent, peering intently in the darkness from one man to the other while they talked.

She was a close friend of several women in diplomatic circles, and he began to receive invitations to embassy garden parties. He wore striped pants to these affairs and she wore lace and a floppy hat. There was music and there was champagne, and sometimes an important official would smilingly ask her, "Can you spare him for a moment?" and would take him aside to say, "I am very much interested in the work your office is doing. I hear you are the bright young man over there."

He saw none of his old friends except Jerry and his wife. But Jerry told him one day that at the end of this job he'd probably be sent on a job to South America, that there was strong pressure being exerted to have him sent there. Apparently some of his new acquaintances were taking an active interest in his welfare. He began to think of getting married and settling in the government service, and whenever she and he would pass a real-estate development they would stop and inspect the exhibition house.

One day he told her excitedly, "You know, down at the office we've at last collected enough data to tell what is happening. I think I'll start doing my report." She said, "That's wonderful. We'll only see each other twice a week." The next day she sent him an elaborate desk set by messenger. That night he said, "When you're not with me, just forget about me. Go out and have a good time." She said, "Do you think I could?"

He sat at home in a maze of figures, trying not to think of her. The telephone rang. She said, "I'm sorry. I feel your work isn't going very well. Can I help somehow?" He said, "I'm not working. I'm just wasting my time. Let's go driving instead."

They went for a drive through Virginia, headlights scanning the receding road, tall, ghostly trees flying back on both sides. She told him again about her unhappy childhood; in a voice that seemed not meant for him alone but that filled the entire car, she described her early life on the West Coast, her mother ill—trying to manage a Seattle rooming house, trying to hide her cough, while the man from the real-estate office had said, "If you can't collect the rent, we'll get somebody who can." She had then been a little girl of ten, but her mother had been too weak to climb stairs, and she had climbed them, knocked on doors, and demanded the room rent.

Before he said good night to her, he told her, "You know I would much rather spend the time with you, but I'm trying now to write a report. No one can help me. I'll have to fight it out alone. Please try not to call when we have no date." She looked like a little girl who was being punished and said in a whisper, "I promise. I won't."

The following night she called him, in what seemed almost an official voice, and told him that an invited guest had sent last-minute regrets to a diplomatic dinner and the hostess insisted that he fill in. She said, "I know how you feel, but you can't refuse." He said, "Of course I can't refuse."

She watched him from across the table through the dinner, even seemed to follow the movement of food to his mouth. Going home in the car, she kept silent, but just before they reached her home she said, "If you want, I won't see you for a week."

He took her in his arms and kissed her, and she burst into tears. He parked the car and consoled her for a long time, but she continued to weep and continued to insist she would not see him for a week.

The following evening all the figures fitted so well together that he became deeply absorbed. When he finally rose from his table it was too late to call her. He determined to send her flowers, but in the morning he forgot. Instead he called his office to say he was not coming in, and he worked at home through the day and all night. When he had finished, he was too excited to sleep. He took a shower and went to the office. He had decided to surprise her by unexpectedly taking her out to dinner.

When he went home to dress, there was a telegram from her: "I NEVER WANT TO SEE OR HEAR FROM YOU AGAIN." He tried to call her but was told she was too ill to come to the phone. When he arrived at her house she sent word she did not want to see him. He forced his way into her room and found her in bed, looking pale and old, with rings under her eyes. He begged her to forgive him, talked to her for a long time until she relaxed and closed her eyes to sleep.

The following evening she wore a white evening gown and red roses. Everyone in the restaurant stared at her, and when he told her she was beautiful, she said, "I'm beautiful for you. I love you." They danced until the orchestra stopped playing. She sat huddled against him in the car going back and she seemed not to breathe until they reached her house.

For several nights he tried to get ahead with his report. There were almost always phone calls and letters from her, and when there weren't, he could not concentrate for thinking of her. She had become very friendly with Jerry's wife and frequently visited at Jerry's. Finally he telephoned Jerry's wife one day and said, "Please talk to her. I love her, but she gives me too much of herself. There is too much emotion. She must learn to let me alone sometime."

Jerry's wife said, "I think you ought to marry her."

He said, "I feel as if she were forcing me to at the point of a gun."

"What will probably happen," Jerry's wife said, "is that someday you will find her dead on your doorstep, a gun in her hand."

One evening a messenger brought him a thick envelope from her containing about forty pages in beautiful handwriting. The letter began, "Dearest, I can't sleep." It contained an analysis of herself, of him, and of their relationship. "We're on a turbulent stream, my darling, being pulled by a current and sucked by an undertow. We're amidst shoals and rocks, and I know you think we're about to strike at any moment and be wrecked. But, my love, I promise you, there is clear water ahead." Further along in the letter there were long paragraphs about her childhood, passages about her father. "I wish I could explain to you about my father. I remember particularly how I was always afraid that he would come home. Even now, when the bell rings and I'm not expecting anyone, I get cold at the thought that it might be he."

He put the half-read letter on his desk and went to bed. But he could not sleep. He lay a long time, then the black of night became a nightmare and he woke up cold with sweat. He rose and, still in the dark, he found the draft of the report he was working on. He held it in one hand. With the other he found her letter and threw it in the waste-basket. He dropped a lighted match after it, watched the flames consume the letter, and then he went back to bed and fell asleep.

Two weeks later, Jerry's wife called him and said, "You'd better go to see her. She is very sick." He went with a large box of flowers. When the nurse would not let him in, he felt relieved. He went to tell the florist to send her flowers daily and on the way he stopped off at a café for a drink.

The diplomatic circles forgot him and he dropped back into his old life. He went to several parties; he took a girl home. He rode up in the elevator at the bureau with Jerry's wife, and she cut him dead. Jerry spoke to him only on pressing business and never looked him in the eyes.

He began to feel bored with Washington, and he wondered whether he should resign and get a job in New York again. He heard she was going to Florida to recuperate and he telephoned to her to say goodbye. They found very little to talk about. She spoke mainly about her coming trip. She said, "Thank you for having found time to call me up."

After that he saw her only once more. Some time before he went back to New York, on a Saturday afternoon, he stopped his car at a red light on Connecticut Avenue. He saw her standing on the corner, waiting for the light to change. She was dressed in gray and she looked middle-aged. Their eyes met and with an effort he waved, and she waved back. In a moment the light turned to green and he drove away. He had gone a block or two before he thought that maybe he should have offered her a lift.

DO YOU LIKE IT HERE?

❦

JOHN O'HARA

THE DOOR WAS OPEN. The door had to be kept open during study period, so there was no knock, and Roberts was startled when a voice he knew and hated said, "Hey, Roberts. Wanted in Van Ness's office." The voice was Hughes's.

"What for?" said Roberts.

"Why don't you go and find out what for, Dopey?" said Hughes.

"Phooey on you," said Roberts.

"Phooey on *you*," said Hughes, and left.

Roberts got up from the desk. He took off his eyeshade and put on a tie and coat. He left the light burning.

Van Ness's office, which was *en suite* with his bedroom, was on the ground floor of the dormitory, and on the way down Roberts wondered what he had done. It got so after a while, after going to so many schools, that you recognized the difference between being "wanted in Somebody's office" and "Somebody wants to see you." If a master wanted to see you on some minor matter, it didn't always mean that you had to go to his office; but if it was serious, they always said, "You're wanted in Somebody's office." That meant Somebody would be in his office, waiting for you, waiting specially for you. Roberts didn't know why this difference existed, but it did, all right. Well, all he could think of was that he had been smoking in the shower room, but Van Ness never paid much attention to that. Everybody smoked in the shower room, and Van Ness never did anything about it unless he just happened to catch you.

For minor offences Van Ness would speak to you when he made his rounds of the rooms during study period. He would walk slowly down the corridor, looking in at each room to see that the proper occupant, and no one else, was there; and when he had something to bawl you out about, something unimportant, he would consult a list he carried, and he would stop in and bawl you out about it and tell you what punishment went with it. That was another detail that made the summons to the office a little scary.

Roberts knocked on Van Ness's half-open door and a voice said, "Come in."

Van Ness was sitting at his typewriter, which was on a small desk beside the large desk. He was in a swivel chair and when he saw Roberts he swung around, putting himself behind the large desk, like a damn judge.

He had his pipe in his mouth and he seemed to look over the steel rims of his spectacles. The light caught his Phi Beta Kappa key, which momentarily gleamed as though it had diamonds in it.

"Hughes said you wanted me to report here," said Roberts.

"I did," said Van Ness. He took his pipe out of his mouth and began slowly to knock the bowl empty as he repeated, "I did." He finished emptying his pipe before he again spoke. He took a long time about it, and Roberts, from his years of experience, recognized that as torture tactics. They always made you wait to scare you. It was sort of like the third degree. The horrible damn thing was that it always did scare you a little, even when you were used to it.

Van Ness leaned back in his chair and stared through his glasses at Roberts. He cleared his throat. "You can sit down," he said.

"Yes, sir," said Roberts. He sat down and again Van Ness made him wait.

"Roberts, you've been here now how long—five weeks?"

"A little over. About six."

"About six weeks," said Van Ness. "Since the seventh of January. Six weeks. Strange. Strange. Six weeks, and I really don't know a thing about you. Not much, at any rate. Roberts, tell me a little about yourself."

"How do you mean, Mister?"

"How do I mean? Well—about your life, before you decided to honor us with your presence. Where you came from, what you did, why you went to so many schools, so on."

"Well, I don't know."

"Oh, now. Now, Roberts. Don't let your natural modesty overcome the autobiographical urge. Shut the door."

Roberts got up and closed the door.

"Good," said Van Ness. "Now, proceed with this—uh—dossier. Give me the—huh—huh—*lowdown* on Roberts, Humphrey, Second Form, McAllister Memorial Hall, et cetera."

Roberts, Humphrey, sat down and felt the knot of his tie. "Well, I don't know. I was born at West Point, New York. My father was a first lieutenant then and he's a major now. My father and mother and I lived in a lot of places because he was in the Army and they transferred him. Is that the kind of stuff you want, Mister?"

"Proceed, proceed. I'll tell you when I want you to—uh—halt." Van Ness seemed to think that was funny, that "halt."

"Well, I didn't go to a regular school till I was ten. My mother got a divorce from my father and I went to school in San Francisco. I only stayed there a year because my mother got married again and we moved to Chicago, Illinois."

"Chicago, Illinois! Well, a little geography thrown in, eh, Roberts? Gratuitously. Thank you. Proceed."

"Well, so then we stayed there about two years and then we moved back East, and my stepfather is a certified public accountant and we moved around a lot."

"Peripatetic, eh, Roberts?"

"I guess so. I don't exactly know what that means." Roberts paused.

"Go on, go on."

"Well, so I just went to a lot of schools, some day and some boarding. All that's written down on my application blank here. I had to put it all down on account of my credits."

"Correct. A very imposing list it is, too, Roberts, a very imposing list. Ah, to travel as you have. Switzerland. How I've regretted not having gone to school in Switzerland. Did you like it there?"

"I was only there about three months. I liked it all right, I guess."

"And do you like it here, Roberts?"

"Sure."

"You do? You're sure of that? You wouldn't want to change anything?"

"Oh, I wouldn't say that, not about any school."

"Indeed," said Van Ness. "With your vast experience, naturally you would be quite an authority on matters educational. I suppose you have many theories as to the strength and weaknesses inherent in the modern educational systems."

"I don't know. I just—I don't know. Some schools are better than others. At least I like some better than others."

"Of course. Of course." Van Ness seemed to be thinking about something. He leaned back in his swivel chair and gazed at the ceiling. He put his hands in his pants pockets and then suddenly he leaned forward. The chair came down and Van Ness's belly was hard against the desk and his arm was stretched out on the desk, full length, fist closed.

"Roberts! Did you ever see this before? Answer me!" Van Ness's voice was hard. He opened his fist, and in it was a wristwatch.

Roberts looked down at the watch. "No, I don't think so," he said. He was glad to be able to say it truthfully.

Van Ness continued to hold out his hand, with the wristwatch lying in the palm. He held out his hand a long time, fifteen seconds at least, without saying anything. Then he turned his hand over and allowed the watch to slip onto the desk. He resumed his normal position in the chair. He picked up his pipe, slowly filled it, and lit it. He shook the match back and forth long after the flame had gone. He swung around a little in his chair and looked at the wall, away from Roberts. "As a boy I spent six years at this school. My brothers, my two brothers, went to this school. My *father* went to this school. I have a deep and abiding and lasting affection for this school. I have been a member of the faculty of this school for more than a decade. I like to think that I am part of this school, that in some small measure I have assisted in its progress. I like to think of it as more than a mere steppingstone to higher education. At this very moment there are in this school the sons of men who were my classmates. I have not been without my opportunities to take a post at this and that college or university, but I choose to remain here. Why? Why? Because I love this place. I love this place, Roberts. I cherish its traditions. I cherish its good name." He paused, and turned to Roberts. "Roberts, there is no room here for a thief!"

Roberts did not speak.

"There is no room here for a thief, I said!"

"Yes, sir."

Van Ness picked up the watch without looking at it. He held it a few inches above the desk. "This miserable watch was stolen last Friday afternoon, more than likely during the basketball game. As soon as the theft was reported to me I immediately instituted a search for it. My search was unsuccessful. Sometime Monday afternoon the watch was put here, here in my rooms. When I returned here after classes Monday afternoon, this watch was lying on my desk. Why? Because the contemptible rat who stole it knew that I had instituted the search, and like the rat he is, he turned yellow and returned the watch to me. Whoever it is, he kept an entire dormitory under a loathsome suspicion. I say to you, I do not know who stole this watch, or who returned it to my rooms. But by God, Roberts, I'm going to find out, if it's the last thing I do. If it's the last thing I do. That's all, Roberts. You may go." Van Ness sat back, almost breathless.

Roberts stood up. "I give you my word of honor, I—"

"I said you may go!" said Van Ness.

Roberts was not sure whether to leave the door open or to close it, but he did not ask. He left it open.

He went up the stairs to his room. He went in and took off his coat and tie, and sat on the bed. Over and over again, first violently, then weakly, he said it, "The bastard, the dirty bastard."

CONVERSATION PIECE

❦

Louise Bogan

MR. WILLIAMS received them. The dreadful heat outside stopped as soon as the hall door closed. Mr. Tracy knew Mr. Williams. Mrs. Tracy did not know either Mr. or Mrs. Williams. She had consented rather reluctantly to go to tea, on a hot New York afternoon, with two strangers who might bore her to death, for all she knew. However, here she and Robert were, and at least it was cool in the Williamses' front hall.

"Hello, Robert; how are you, Mrs. Tracy?" said Mr. Williams. They went into the room at the rear of the hall. The room was almost pitch-dark, owing to its situation at the back of the house with taller buildings on all sides. Two lamps were lit.

"Sybil will be here in a moment. And in a moment we'll have a cocktail. Will you have a cocktail, Mrs. Tracy?" Yes, she would have a cocktail. Mr. Williams seemed to be very nice. Then Mrs. Williams did come in as promised, and as if on cue, and greetings again went around.

"Isn't it hot?" Mrs. Williams said.

"Isn't it?" Mrs. Tracy answered. She couldn't see Mrs. Williams very clearly, the room was so dark. That sharp, appraising look invariably exchanged by two women who have never laid eyes on each other before didn't quite come off. Mrs. Tracy thought Mrs. Williams looked very nice. She had light hair and an extremely neat figure.

"What a lovely room!" exclaimed Mrs. Tracy.

"It's like living at the bottom of a well, really," said Mrs. Williams.

"That's a grand mirror," Robert remarked.

"Isn't it grand!" exclaimed Mrs. Williams. "It comes from Stun-

141

ton Fyles—that is, we are almost *sure* it comes from Stunton Fyles."
It was a large mirror that climbed the wall in scrolls almost to the
ceiling. Robert and Mrs. Williams made off across the room to
examine it more closely. Robert suddenly seemed to know all
about Stunton Fyles. An enormous house in Somersetshire that
had been cut up, after the war, and shipped to America in sections.

"Let's sit over here," said Mr. Williams to Mrs. Tracy. They sat
down on a *fauteuil* upholstered in delicate mauve brocade. Its
twin faced them from the other side of the room. That's where
Robert and Mrs. Williams would sit, thought Mrs. Tracy. She and
Robert sitting on opposite sides of the room with the host and
hostess, respectively. Very pleasant, she thought. In her own house
there was none of this charming balance. Everyone got pushed
into corners. She recognized in Mrs. Williams, although she could-
n't see her very clearly, a person who worked things out with
nicety, to a degree.

"So you've just come back to town," said Mr. Williams, at her
elbow. "Where were you?" She told him where they had been. Mr.
Williams had once been there, too. Such a beautiful view of the
mountains and the sea combined. But New Englanders did so few
things with fish. Boiled, fried, or presented in a stew. The Scandinavians, on the other hand, had taken fish and subjected it to
every culinary process known to man. Pickled, dried, preserved,
fish soup, *timbales,* pies . . . "Ah, here are the cocktails," Mr. Williams broke off to say. "Put them down here, Peter. Have one of
these, Mrs. Tracy; they're very good."

Little ships in full sail stood perfectly still in a bulb in the stems
of the cocktail glasses.

Robert and Mrs. Williams, across the room, were getting along
beautifully. Mrs. Tracy turned her gaze back to Mr. Williams.

"My friend, Knud Swenson, the pianist, has told me all about
Scandinavians and fish," Mr. Williams went on. "Do you know
Knud?" No, she didn't know him. "Grand fellow; plays Mozart
beautifully. Odd thing, for a Scandinavian to play Mozart so well,
isn't it?" She agreed. "You'd think that there'd be too much of
that heavy saga business in them, wouldn't you? Are you fond of
Mozart?" Very fond. "Do you play the piano at all?" A little. Did
Mr. Williams play the piano? Yes, Mr. Williams played. It was

unusual to find a male American who played the piano well, Mrs. Tracy had found. That was true, Mr. Williams agreed. If he hadn't gone to school in Leipzig, *he* probably never would have played the piano. Did Mrs. Tracy know Leipzig? No, she didn't.

Mr. Williams poured everyone another drink. Robert was telling Mrs. Williams about the day they went deep-sea fishing.

Mrs. Tracy felt that Mr. Williams was carrying her through the conversation with great swiftness but not very much zeal. She felt rather dull and relaxed in this cool room, after having endured August heat for three days. Mr. Williams, returning, went on about Mozart at length. Such productiveness. No one would ever hear all of Mozart, he supposed, even if he sat for hours each day with his ear against a gramophone. But the delicacy, the purity, the subtlety, the form! "Of course," Mr. Williams said, "you will agree with me that all art must have form. The theatre has its proscenium arch—"

"Jim," said Mrs. Williams, addressing her husband from the opposite *fauteuil*. "Just think, Mr. Tracy knew Bill Nixon, and he hadn't heard that Elsa had married again!"

"They were friends of my brother's. I didn't know him well," Robert said.

Mr. Williams rose to pour another drink. He frowned and shook his head, with disapprobation and concern. "If ever a woman was responsible for a man's death, Elsa is that woman," he said.

"Dear, dear!" thought Mrs. Tracy. "So Mr. Williams has his disapproving side."

"Almost immediately, she married again," Mrs. Williams went on. "What happened to the three children I can't imagine. Left in Switzerland, probably. It all happened in Switzerland, you know. They found his body in a crevasse."

"Do you know Selina Force?" Mr. Williams asked Mrs. Tracy. Yes, she knew Selina. Mr. Williams's face lit up. "Fine woman, Selina, but pretty unreliable. I used to know her when she was married to Allen Witters. Did you meet the boy she picked up last year in Tucson? I hear she wants a divorce. Do you think John will give it to her?"

"That Tucson boy is at least eight years younger than Selina," said Mrs. Williams, from across the room. "You would expect a little more sense from Selina even now, wouldn't you?" she added, in the pleasantest voice in the world.

Everyone expected more sense from Selina.

A whole shoal of mutual acquaintances, past and present, from whom one expected more sense now swam into the conversation. Cal Kimball was practically on the town; had they heard? Eunice Lynd had been making a spectacle of herself since early spring. Sara Goss (you know *Sara*) had taken up with a sailor or a steward or some such thing; and in the case of Malcolm Black, Mrs. Williams (and Mr. Williams and Mr. Tracy and Mrs. Tracy) were all certain it was suicide.

Mrs. Tracy, after the fourth cocktail, noticed the gloom in the room anew. It looked as though a thunderstorm were coming on. Perhaps it was just the tall buildings all about. She was talking in a much more animated way with Mr. Williams than at first. They were getting along famously. After the fifth cocktail she knew that she and Robert must go. It was getting late. Time had passed. Whenever her eyes became involved with details while her tongue sped merrily along under its own power, she knew that it was time to go. Her eyes went all around the room, gathering up details. They followed the graceful curve of the Regency chair legs, of the gilt rococo mirror, of the precious and chaste *fauteuil* upon which she and Mr. Williams sat. They sailed purely and calmly along with the little ship imprisoned in the stem of the cocktail glasses. As soon as Mr. Williams finished telling her every last item in the unfortunate case of Malcolm Black, she would rise; she would say "It has been delightful;" they would go. Now she sat waiting, smiling a little because, scattered on the floor in the shadows, she seemed to see the fragments of a proscenium arch, cracked right in two, and Mozart's music, splintered into pieces and lying disject: there a trill, there a scale, and there a chord. Mr. Williams, now at the most grisly point in his story, would no doubt think it queer that she smiled. Ah, but she was perhaps providing him with a minor, a very minor, topic of conversation! He could say next week, to someone seated in this room, "Are you fond of Mozart's music? Do you know that odd, grinning Mrs. Tracy?"

THE FURY

❧

Robert M. Coates

THE LITTLE GIRL'S FACE, when she looked back, was white and convulsed with terror. Mr. Flent bent his bright, his compelling gaze on her and for a moment she stood there transfixed, her eyes never leaving his.

No one else, in the darkness and the general stir as the feature picture neared its end, had noticed anything; packed in between the guardrail and the last row of seats, everyone was moving inchingly this way and that, maneuvering for the dash down the aisle when the picture was over. Even the woman whose hand the little girl was clasping hadn't noticed anything. She, too, was too busy watching the picture.

Mr. Flent remained where he was, holding the little girl's gaze tensely and surely, letting the feeling of pride and power and bright, white, imperious, vengeful majesty rise up within him.

But it never crested and overflowed as it should have done.

Without warning, the little girl's glance wavered slightly, her cheeks tucked up toward her eyes and her eyes began to pucker; she was starting to cry, but Mr. Flent had been alert for that. Instantly, his eyes lost their persuasive glitter, his face slid into its normal, noncommittal folds. His hand dropped to his side and he stepped back, drawing his raincoat more closely about him.

Someone else, pressing forward, took his place; others moved in from either side; expertly, with a minimum of disturbance, Mr. Flent let them thrust him out behind them and into the cleared space at the rear. Here he was free. There were a few girl ushers in tight-fitting tunics standing against the wall, and a dribble of people coming in through the big entrance doors. They paid no attention to him.

He kept his ears cocked for a cry, a commotion, the sound of a woman's angry voice behind him, but none came. He moved slowly—tantalizing himself now with his own slowness, dallying with the dangers he still ran—under the amber-tinted lights toward the door. Inside the hot, airless raincoat wrapped incongruously about his thin frame he felt his body grow warm and sticky. "Let them come!" he thought defiantly, and then found that he must have spoken the thought aloud, for one of the ushers turned to look at him. He twisted his wide, loose-muscled mouth into a deprecatory grin and moved a little faster. There was no pursuit.

In the street he stood a moment, dazed by the transition from darkness to mid-afternoon, too excited still to remember at first where he was. Then he saw that it was Fourteenth Street, and the street was tramping with people. "The little devil!" he thought. "The little devil. She knows what it's all about, all right!" His mouth tasted dry and there was a feeling of pressure behind his eyes. He set out walking blindly, the sights and sounds around him coming thumpingly against his consciousness yet never quite penetrating it, like seas breaking against a wall.

"Then she puts on the frightened act," he thought. Across the street was the Consolidated Gas Company building. He had been here before. On his right was a sandwich bar, its busy interior wide open to the street, the sidewalk in front of it clotted with loitering men. He stared at them as he passed, wagging his head balefully. "At that age, too," he muttered, still thinking of the little girl.

He laughed his thin, giggling laugh, and a woman glanced at him. He looked away nervously; then, a pace or two past her, he turned to stare after her. A plump piece, all right, in her thin, spotted dress sticking tight to the hips. And under that only the swelling, naked body. "And they walk the streets!" he thought, and then suddenly the heat, the noise, the little girl and the men and the glancing woman all fused to form one emotion. "Filth!" he exclaimed fiercely aloud, and stretching his arm straight out before him, he clenched his hand into a fist.

Then he opened his hand gently, tenderly, and let his arm drop slowly to his side. Abruptly, all his self-possession had returned,

and he walked now so unctuously at ease that he seemed to move
in an atmosphere of his own, from within which he looked out
shrewdly and tolerantly on the hurrying figures around him. "With
the kindest intentions in the world," he thought.

He paced onward slowly, feeling the sun, the summer air, watching the passersby present themselves casually before him and disappear. A young man and a girl walking side by side, saying things
and laughing together. Two women just entering a delicatessen
store. A man in a drugstore doorway, lighting a cigar. Another
man, leaning against an areaway railing, reading a newspaper.
There was no harm in any of them; or what harm there was he
could control, he could palliate, as if by a personal shiningness,
just by being there.

Behind him he could hear the developing roar of an "L" train.
It passed over him, rushed onward. He was on Third Avenue,
then. Or maybe it was Sixth. Anyway, he had been here before.

When he looked about him again, the Elevated structure still
filled the street beside him, but he seemed to have gotten into a
region of warehouses and factories. He had the feeling that he
must have been walking for a long time.

But the little girl, at first glance, looked almost as if she might
be the same one. Then he realized that it couldn't be, though the
light cotton dress she had on was something the same color. This
little girl seemed shorter, and chunkier. She was bouncing a ball,
solemnly and tirelessly, against the wall of a wooden, shedlike
structure, a little way down the side street from the corner on
which he stood. There was no one else about. Slowly, very slowly,
he started walking toward her.

As he approached, he could hear her counting. "Thirty-four,
thirty-five, thirty-six, thirty-seven," she said, then she dropped the
ball. She scurried to retrieve it, and began bouncing and counting
again. "One, two three, four, five, six—"

Mr. Flent had put on his kindliest smile. He knew how easy it
was to frighten these little ones. "Hello," he said.

The little girl stopped and looked up in surprise at the strange
voice, and the strange face bending over her. But she was not
frightened. "Hello," she said.

"What are you doing?" said Mr. Flent.

She looked up at him seriously, impressed by this adult interest in her game. "Practicing," she said.

"Oh, practicing," said Mr. Flent. She was delicious, really delicious. "Practicing what?" he asked, but before she could answer he went on. "And doesn't it make you thirsty?"

She considered that. "No," said the little girl.

Mr. Flent made his large eyes look wider. "Oh, doesn't it?" he said. "Well, now, you're the first little girl I ever did see that wasn't always thirsty for a nice ice-cream soda. Most little girls are always thirsty for a nice ice-cream soda."

He paused and stared down at her, smiling compellingly. Her eyes had grown large and wistful, and when she spoke her voice was a little muffled, as if it came from some well of innocence. "I like ice-cream sodas, too," she said.

"Do you now?" said Mr. Flent, and giggled roguishly. She was a cute little thing, all right. "Well, then you shall have one," and suddenly brisk and authoritative, he held out his hand for her to take. "Come along, then," he said. "We'll just skip down to the corner together and have one. A nice, big strawberry ice-cream soda. Come along," he said as she still hesitated. "If we hurry, nobody will ever know. Mamma needn't know. Nobody'll know. Maybe we'll have two," he said. "If we hurry."

"I want pineapple," she said, and put her hand in his. As they started away, however, she stopped suddenly. "Oh, where's Dixie?" she said. "I can't leave Dixie." Mr. Flent stared at her. The touch of her hand, her confidingness, had worked on him until now he was trembling almost visibly. And here she was, pulling the delaying act. Or maybe she really only needed coaxing. He couldn't be sure. The vengefulness, the fierce knowledge of the earth's iniquity, was rising in him now, and even as he looked down at her, her face and her expression seemed to fluctuate as if seen in an uneven mirror, changing from innocence to guile, from trustingness to sly coquetry—changing faster and faster, faster even than his breathing, until he almost lost sight of her features in the blur.

But he mustn't frighten her. "Whatever her game is," he thought, "I can play it; let her play her game, I'll play mine." He brought his smile to bear on her. "We haven't time," he said cajolingly. "If we want to get that nice ice-cream soda." He still held her hand tightly, but not too tightly, in his, and kept drawing her gently after him down the street.

"We must hurry," he said, and pulled a little harder, but she still hung back and he could see that she was getting frightened, so he stopped. These young ones, he thought, you must handle them delicately: young, but the youngest of them as touchy as a queen. Down the street, he saw a woman in a gray wrapper standing watching him intently. "Well," he said, and the little girl looked up obediently into his wide, bright smile. "Well. Who is Dixie?" He made his eyebrows arch very high.

"He's my dog," said the little girl, so seriously that Mr. Flent was convinced of her innocence all over again. "Your dog, is he!" he exclaimed, and—he couldn't help it—he squatted down beside her, his tight-buttoned raincoat flopping out awkwardly around him on the sidewalk, his face close to hers. He couldn't help laughing.

The little girl stared at him, a little dismayed by his sudden gesture. "He isn't really my dog," she said. "He belongs to Mr. Kramer, the delicatessen-store man. But he lets me play with him. I told him I'd be careful of him."

This was delicious. Down the street Mr. Flent could see the woman in gray talking to another woman, and both of them looking up his way, but he couldn't help it: he put his two hands on her shoulders and gave her a playful little shake, then let his hands slide affectionately down over her body. Under the thin dress he could feel the small bones, the flesh soft as wax. It made him feel young again. "Mr. Kramer's dog, then," he said, and he couldn't help laughing louder. Then he sobered suddenly and made his eyes get wide.

"But we can't bring a dog into the candy store, you know," he said, and got up to his feet and took her hand again. Down the street, the two women had started walking slowly toward him. He began speaking a little faster. "We'll have to leave him behind this time, I guess," he said, and made his eyes twinkle. "What would a doggie want with an ice-cream soda, anyway?" And he bobbed his head down at her quickly, so that his nose would have rubbed against hers if she hadn't drawn back a little. "This time," he said, with an almost loverlike cadence in his voice, "it will be just us two alone." He could see the awe and the fearful fascination growing in her eyes. "Like that?" he said, and gave her a moment to let it sink in. "Come along, then," he said, and, still holding her hand, started down the street.

But instead of obeying, she hung back. He could feel the weight of her, with her feet planted stiff on the pavement; without looking at her, he could feel her eyes, and the fear in them, fixed staring on his face. Not one thing but many things had combined to confuse her—the touch of his hands on her body, the strange bobbings up and down, the face held so close to hers, the reasonless laughter—and now the sudden tug on her arm brought them all to focus and before he had made three steps she burst out with a cry of pure terror. "No! No!" she screamed. "I won't go with you. I won't. I won't go."

Mr. Flent's first feeling was one of high rage. He had been tricked again, he had been played for a fool, and, the smile gone, he bent down again face to face with her. "You bitch!" he cried, almost beside himself. "You think you can get away with that," and seizing her about the waist he actually succeeded in heaving her up under one arm, feet kicking, arms flailing, mouth screaming; he had been ready to run with her, but when he straightened again one glance around told him he could never get away with it.

Behind him, the two women were running and yelling something. On the stoop of a house across the way a man in shirtsleeves had thrown down his newspaper and was starting down the steps. At the other end of the block, two men at the curbstone had stopped, surprised by the commotion, and had turned to look; soon they would be running. And beyond them he could see others, still moving this way and that, unconcernedly, but they were his enemies too, and soon they, too, would be running, running to rend him.

He dropped the girl, giving her a cuff as he did so that sent her sprawling. "Filth!" he screamed at her, and ran a few steps forward, then turned and ran back the way he had come. He was in a strange world, in that narrow block, and it was a world full of his enemies, but the fury had taken hold of him, and he knew that his wrath was greater than theirs, he knew that he was invincible. It was to punish such as these that he had been placed upon the earth.

He ran back past the girl, but she had crawled hastily out of his path. Shaking his fists and screaming, he charged straight at the two women: the mere impact of his madness was enough to scatter them, "Filth! Filth, all of you!" he yelled, and ran past them so close he could feel the flap of his raincoat against their skirts. They didn't touch him; they dared not, but the moment he had passed them, he heard them begin their shouting again. Like a white flash in the red haze around him he saw the face of a man just coming out of an area entrance as he passed. There was a louder shout behind him and an arm reached out for him, but he struck it aside; something whizzed past him and thumped on the sidewalk ahead of him. Then he was running free, with the bare street between him and the corner.

He reached the corner and doubled it. It was under the "L," where he had been before, and only a block or two down the street he could see the steps of a station. Behind him, he could hear the shouting feet of his pursuers, but behind that he heard another sound: the sound of an "L" train, far down the tracks, but approaching. He knew he could outwit them yet.

There were only a few people waiting on the platform. They saw him—a thin, long-nosed, dishevelled man, with a face streaming sweat and a raincoat that flapped wildly about his legs as he ran—come scrambling up the steps, pause a moment before the turnstiles, and then, as the train's approach grew louder, vault clumsily over them and come bursting out on the platform. They heard the man in the change booth give an angry shout.

Mr. Flent heard it, too. Though he did not know it, the chase had stopped at the foot of the Elevated stairs, but the shout meant only pursuit to him, and even if he had not heard it, it was doubtful if he could have stopped now. He had become an automaton; fear was all around him and he a mere running thing, escaping: all he saw was the white faces on either side of him and, down at the end of the platform, the blunt front of the "L" train, swiftly approaching. Blind to all but that, he ran toward it.

Those on the platform saw him do it, but they never knew what he was doing until it was too late. They saw him run to the edge and run off it, and then—his legs and arms still working frantically, his raincoat flattened against his scrawny back—they saw his body thump, in midair, against the front of the train. It seemed to hang there a moment, as if impaled; then his head snapped back, the face white, but the forehead bloody where it had slammed against the metal; his knees jerked upward and outward; the body began to fall.

The brakes were on, and the whole train was shrieking and shuddering under the drag of them, but it had coasted halfway into the station before it came to a halt. Long before that, the body was under the wheels.

VENETIAN PERSPECTIVE

❧

JANET FLANNER

BERTHA WENT AROUND Europe picking people up with her magnificent, carrying contralto. Mrs. Daphne's turn came in Venice, in front of the Grand Hotel, when a large, unknown lady in a red gown and green parasol, about to step into her gondola (the gondoliers were waiting for her, both looking tense and one ready with the boathook), turned and lifted her great arms toward the cerulean sky. "It's yoost a dream day," she intoned by way of introduction. The salute to nature was late Wagnerian, as was the voice. Also the pose, minus the parasol, was that of Elsa about to move off among swans. "*Ach!*" the lady added, *legato*. Her profound breasts filled, her chin drooped, she seemed to be testing her epiglottis.

She's going to sing scales, hoped Mrs. Daphne. "It's a dream day," she agreed after a moment, disappointed.

"Come riding wit' us," the *récitatif* continued. "Dot's my husband, Hans, in de boat. He has to take lots off fresh air." Not that he's getting much, with the curtains of the *felze* drawn, thought Mrs. Daphne. All she could see beneath the black hood was a pair of white-flannel trousers, then a polite straw hat. Apparently, Hans was acknowledging the only kind of introduction he ever got.

Though she didn't ride with them then, there was no evading the Bensdorps in Venice as long as there was only one Piazza San Marco. At sundown, Bertha's voice filled it like the sundown shadows. Her contralto rolled from the door of the Basilica across to the jewelry shop under the arcade at the opposite corner. The immediate pigeons rose slightly to it, as they all rose in high flight to the midday gun, then fluttered down again singly to sit on her thumb. For Bertha was used to the centre of the stage, and the pigeons took their cue. "I loff birds because dey sing," she said tenderly, disentangling a squab's claws from the real-lace cuffs, the diamond bracelet, the emerald bracelet, the chain of topazes, and the petit-point handbag handle that covered her left wrist.

"Pigeons do not sing," said Hans suddenly. It was the third time Mrs. Daphne had met him, but the first time she could recall having heard him speak. He spoke English perfectly. "As a young man —I am old now, I am turned forty—I longed to go to Australia and ranch it, so I went to London to learn the language," he explained. "But I was forced to go into a bank instead."

"V'ere you made moch money," Bertha prompted softly. "If you von't sing, birdie, go 'vay."

The squab flew.

"Yes," said Hans. "Yes. Where I made money."

No one spoke. In the presence of male suffering, Mrs. Daphne had learned, during her husband's final illness, to sit silent indefinitely.

"Und dot's v'y Hans loffs de open spaces so moch," yawned Bertha. "It vas dot Australia v'ich laid her spell on him."

"And on which he has never yet laid his eyes, I wager," said Mrs. Daphne to herself. Apparently, the Bensdorps had seen everything else, though. They had just come from Fulda and Goslar, with their pretty, confining baroque. Valley villages without view in the Vosges, squeezed in between overhanging mountain tops. Italian walled towns where one couldn't see out, Mediterranean islands where one couldn't get off. Majorca, Brioni. Brioni, Bertha especially recommended. Not a wild spot on it that she could remember, outside of the stone quarries; an island as nice as a polo lawn.

"Hans has got claustrophobia, dot's v'y ve eat outside," Bertha went on as they arrived at the restaurant, where they were dining. It was in a hedged garden on a narrow canal that smelled of August. Overhead, where the vines gaped, the trellis had been sealed in with canvas. From where he sat, packed in between them in the corner, Hans had a full view of the second violinist and the wreck of someone's lobster. Prompted, Bertha ordered three lobsters and one waltz. And *scampi*. Fried octopus. *Gnocchi bolognesi. Pollo. Polli.*

"I'd better make dem chickens two," she calculated. "Hans only likes de v'ite meats und yoost picks."

And *zucchini* in batter, raw artichokes in oil, *finocchi* and Gorgonzola, she shouted after the waiter. Soave in carafes, and Orvieto and Lacrima Cristi in bottles; that way they could take their choice, Bertha said, and leaned back in her small chair.

"Offen I haf starved enough. To eat good," she mumbled later over the leg of a chicken, dark against the jewels on her hand, "to eat good iss part off a good life. Like nature und art. Nature und art I loff so I could eat dem, too," and she cut herself some cheese. Mrs. Daphne preferred hearing about nature. The art lay in listening to Bertha. Hans set the perfect example.

Theirs had been a pure love match, a flame kindled between two lonely Nordics in a one-room front in Soho, Bertha explained, as she drank the Tears of Christ. Hans's banking *coups* began about the same time as their love. As both matured, the one room became five in a yoost darling liddle willa at Surbiton whose ten-foot back yard was to console Hans for all of Australia. When the thousands began rolling in, Bertha moved the *ménage* to a narrow Adam house in Bloomsbury, to a Mayfair service flat, to a shallow penthouse over Hyde Park, and finally to North Street and a ducky weeny Queen Anne cottage which she gave Hans for a Christmas present—it had cost him yoost a fortune. But so cute, a reg'lar liddle doll house wid liddle green doors und a simply sveet liddle bedroom dot gafe onto de street, de soot, und de sun.

"What room does he have in all this?" Mrs. Daphne asked suddenly of the fine, florid woman whose husband loved space and had it only in her.

"I have the small dressing room on the court; it used to be the bath," Hans answered, as if for once he had been addressed. In the night heat, the mass of broken food and unfulfilled memories, he looked as if he were being strangled by his life and his high collar. Without either, he would have been an easy-breathing little Baltic whose only malady was that he had once wanted to run a large ranch below the equator.

"My Hans has got de sveetest, most egspensive room in de house," Bertha intoned, "wid a genuwine Qveen Anne canopied bed like a jewel box wid fine silk curtains, thick like mist, all round it to shut out de draft und light. Not'ing is too good for my Hans."

No one disputed her. She took up her husband's hand and kissed it. He made no move. Mrs. Daphne couldn't discover if Bertha were intoxicated on three kinds of wine or on love and energy and possession. The second violinist passed the hat for the fourth time. The waltz again started filling the deserted garden and looping its three-time over the narrow, rhythmless canal.

As Hans paid the bill, Bertha looked over his shoulder. "It's a lot, t'ank God," she said, her eyes caressing the final sum. "It's enough to have paid half my troupe in de old days." She laughed.

"My wife used to be a great star in her own opera company," Hans said. "Weren't you?"

He woke the two gondoliers and helped them help Bertha in. Mrs. Daphne preferred to get in last and sit in the middle seat alone. From beneath the curtained hood, Bertha sang in her magnificent muddled contralto as they traced the narrow canals. Her voice was like an extra-heavy shadow on the water and the palaces of the city. She sang verses in the four European languages Mrs. Daphne was familiar with and café choruses in three or four more she couldn't place. "Your wife has sung all over the world, hasn't she?" she turned to ask Hans, as if Bertha were no longer present. In a way, she was not. She was gliding over some special lunar planet peopled by large women, memories, and the blare of unmuffled, cheap, male brass.

"I gather so," said Hans politely.

"I daresay she's even sung in Australia," Mrs. Daphne added, on the pier of the Grand Hotel. Bertha, who was only humming now, had moved inside to take possession of the lift.

"I daresay she even has," and the little banker reddened, as if a good customer had asked him to initial a bad check. "I'll never see Australia, though. Not now . . ."

Mrs. Daphne bent down to look at him from her blonde, perfumed height. "No. I suppose not. Good night." Mrs. Daphne said good night kindly, the way people say *bon voyage* or goodbye.

Without meaning to, three days later Mrs. Daphne met Bertha in the morning mob at Thomas Cook's. *"Ach,"* cried Bertha, "my Hans has left me! Wid'out a vord except in a letter. Yoost wrote he was returning home to pack und den go foreffer. Vun first class to London, yes; like I said, I pay for it all," she said to the ticket clerk. "Here, take it out; my husband's left me und I can't count," and she gave him the petit-point handbag bloated with banknotes. "I am crying all de morning," she said to Mrs. Daphne. "I haf no rouge on; my heart also feels as if it had no red in it. Make haste," she ordered the clerk.

"But it can't be ready before an hour, Madame. At Mestre."

"I'm all packed," she went on to Mrs. Daphne. Her bags lay like large, smooth dogs around her incongruously small feet. "He took de night train und t'inks he gets home first, but I beat him. I'm d'ere, vaiting, v'en he opens de door, me in my clot'-of-silfer tea-gown vit' orchids und champagne und caviar—dat's all Hans really likes; he don't like v'ite meat of chicken hardly at all—und moosic. I'te telegraphed for a string qvartette to play so I can sing to him. Und v'en he valks t'rough de pink-silk curtains, I'll be vaiting for him vit' my arms out—so!" And she stretched them magnificently in Thomas Cook's to show how they would look in London to Hans.

"Don't, Mrs. Bensdorp," said Mrs. Daphne. "Give Hans a chance —to come back later," she lied. I would lie to save any human being's life, she thought. "He'll come back—after Australia. Give him—"

"Gif him not'ing!" Bertha cried. "He has me und dot's enough," and she burst into unhappy laughter.

"But if he started last night, you can't—"

"I can," contradicted Bertha. "By aëroplane. A special plane for me I hire. Oh, I'll be afraid," she moaned. "I haff been afraid of not'ing in life—men, cruelty, vomen laughing, luff, starving, pretending, failure—none off dem! Yoost v'at's not on de eart' I fear. Space! Oh, de bigness; oh, de stretch; oh, de vildness of de sky; vot fear!" and she closed her eyes. "I could only do it for my Hans."

"Here's your bag, Madame, thank you; if you'll please count the change," said the clerk. "Your motorboat's waiting. You'll find your plane at Mestre."

"Vot are you doing, a pretty vidow voman alone in dis vorld?" Bertha asked tenderly as she kissed Mrs. Daphne on both cheeks. "Find a Hans, find one yoost like him. Vot ve big, childless vomen need is somet'ing dot needs us, to take care off, to luff; oh, to luff." Her face bloomed with tender passion. "Und v'en you find it," and the hand freed of the petit point, the jeweled bracelets, the gemmed chains, the real lace, reached out like a leash to attach a dear animal, "don't neffer let it get away."

PING-PONG

❦

St. Clair McKelway

I HAD SEEN MR. POWERS in and around the little inn for two or three days and I had the feeling that being in the Adirondacks was somehow not much of a change for him. Most people on vacation give you a distinct impression of alteration, I think. They put on sports clothes, their interests seem centred in recreation, and they take on a lightness of spirit which you feel sure they drop when they start back to the city. Mr. Powers stood out from the other men at this mountain resort because he wore, morning, afternoon, and night, a heavy, dark-grayish business suit. When he went outdoors, he put on a stiff felt hat. He seemed not to be interested in fishing or swimming or in any of the other sports. He had come to the mountains with his wife and a grown daughter, but the ladies seemed to stay in their rooms much of the time. Mr. Powers strolled about a good deal, alone. Once or twice I saw him standing still, smoking a cigar and watching the people who were in swimming, and he looked very odd indeed, in that mountain setting, with his business suit, his felt hat, and his cigar. In the evening Mr. Powers would look at the magazines in the lobby, while his wife and daughter went for a little walk by themselves, and then, when they returned, he would go along upstairs with them. He never spoke more than a few words to anybody else at the inn, as far as I could see.

Then one night, after the Powerses had gone upstairs, some of us started playing ping-pong in the lobby, and almost as soon as the balls were bouncing Mr. Powers came back downstairs and joined us. "I *thought* I heard a ping-pong game going on," he said as he came up to us. He was obviously very pleased. He watched the game eagerly, and before long was refereeing and keeping score. When he started playing himself, he proved to be better than any of the rest of us. Soon he dominated the situation completely. "The winner plays the next comer," he would say with authority. He nearly always won, and so he played more often than anybody else. He took it all pretty seriously and we found him a little obnoxious. I myself seemed to be runner-up to his championship, and when we had finally stopped playing he said to me, "I'm four games up on you now; is that correct? Well, I'll give you a chance to break even tomorrow." I said, without much spirit, that that would be fine, and he went on upstairs to bed. He had kept his coat on all the time he was playing, and during the last few games had smoked a cigar.

It is not easy to get away from people at a small place of that sort, and sure enough, I was playing ping-pong with Mr. Powers the next day, soon after lunch. We played six games, of which he won five, and as he laid down his racquet he began to talk.

"Well," he said, "I'll have to say this. You play a mighty good game for a beginner. Those hard shots of yours are pretty, all right, but you can't do much when they keep coming back at you, can you? I guess that's what wins in ping-pong—sending them all back. Nothing brilliant about my game, mind you—nothing flashy. Oh, I admit I can't send them back sizzling like you do sometimes. But I get them back, the fast ones and the slow ones. That's what wins in ping-pong all right."

It was perfectly clear that he had me cornered, that he had a great deal to say, and that he intended to say it. He had fooled me completely. I had taken him for a man shy and taciturn, and I realized now that he was one of those people who, naturally aggressive and voluble, affect the opposite characteristics in order to lure their victims on and catch them unawares. They have little or no small talk, as a rule. They forego the pleasures of ordinary conversation in order to taste the grand triumph of an uninterrupted monologue. The lobby was empty except for the two of us. There was no way out for me. I dropped into a chair and Mr. Powers, standing before me solidly on his two feet, like a public speaker, went on talking.

"Remember that last game there?" he said. "Eighteen to twelve you had me when we changed serves, didn't you? And I came from

behind and beat you twenty-one to nineteen, didn't I? Oh, I'm no
quitter, you can bank on that." He laughed gently to himself in a
way that I found peculiarly unpleasant. "You mustn't mind my
talk, though," he went on. "It's just my manner. Mrs. Powers—my
wife—gets after me about it sometimes and calls it my bragging.
Well, whatever it is, I guess it's just second nature with me. I like
to win, and I hate to lose, I'll say that. I like to win just as much
today, or almost, anyway, as I did when I was a young fellow. I say
'almost' because, well, I'll have to admit this: I'm feeling my age
this summer for the first time. I'm sixty, you know."

He looked at me expectantly and I said, "You don't look it."

"No? Well, and I didn't *feel* anywhere near that, either, not
until this summer. We lost our boy three months ago—last June—
you know. Oh, yes, that's why we're here at this quiet place, just
trying to get some rest and get our minds off our terrible loss.
Ordinarily we'd just stay in Sunnyside for my vacation—got a nice
home there and a car and all, and it's as good a place as any for a
vacation. Yes, I don't mind telling you, since we lost our boy I've
felt twenty years older, all at once. Why, until last June, do you
know how old I felt? About forty-five, I'd say—not a bit older. Oh,
it broke us all up—Mrs. Powers especially. I'm afraid she'll never
get over it. I suppose you've noticed she doesn't take part in the
social life here very much. Well, that's it—it's all because of the
boy. She and Marge—that's my daughter—were crazy about him.
His name was George. All over George all the time, the two of
them were, and he was a mighty lovable boy, too, he certainly was.
Not like me, mind you, or like Al—that's my other boy. Al's a
lawyer, you know. Steady as he can be and doing fine. Why, Al
won scholarships worth twelve hundred dollars in college. Paid
for most of his law-school tuition with them. Imagine that! Anybody'd be proud of a boy like that, wouldn't they? Oh, Al will get
on, there's no doubt about that at all. George was a lovable boy,
though, mind you. He was smart, too, in a way—brilliant, I guess
you'd call it. No scholarships, of course—not steady enough for
that. Well, he read a lot—I guess that was the trouble. It happened
all at once, just last June. We lost him last June. It was terrible—
a shock, you know."

For the first time since he had begun to talk, he paused. All the assurance went out of him when he was silent and he looked now as he had looked when I had seen him strolling about by himself —uneasy and a little bewildered.

"It was very sudden, was it?" I asked. "Some sort of breakdown?"

"Yes," he said, and his confidence seemed to be coming back. "A sort of breakdown. He just—went to pieces, I guess. That was the way it was," he went on. "You see, I had everything I wanted. Nice home, three stories and a basement, car, and all that. I've worked hard all my life and I'm ready to retire any time I want to. I'm office manager at Holcomb, Dubois & Canfield, real estate, you know. You've heard of them. I'm in charge of the whole place, you might say. And I don't figure on retiring just yet. I've got my work systematized these days so that it isn't strenuous, not really strenuous any more. I have a private secretary. I have fourteen men and six girls under me, and I guess I'm a pretty good boss, too. Five of them's been with me more than ten years. I guess I must be all right as a boss or they wouldn't have stayed with me ten years, eh? I like my work—really enjoy it. I'm thankful for that, too, believe me I am. I guess a man doesn't take these things as hard as a woman does, because of his work. I have my work to think about, I mean, and all that. Now, Mrs. Powers—my wife—she has nothing else to think about except this thing and it's hard on her, it certainly is.

"George was the youngest of the two, you know. He would have been just twenty this fall if we hadn't lost him. Of course George wasn't like Al, or like me, as I say. But George and me got along all right—oh, don't think we didn't. We used to go around quite a lot, especially after Al moved down to Cranford, in Jersey, to practice law. I used to take George to a baseball game quite often. We were out together that day, as a matter of fact—the day we lost him. I took George down to Cranford with me and we sat in the courtroom and watched Al win a law case. Al is smart in the courtroom. My! The way he got the chief witness for the prosecution all tangled up—I wish you could have seen him. But Al's like me, of course. Keen on winning, at work and at play."

He laughed softly again, and lit a cigar.

"Al's no quitter, believe me," he went on. "Al and me used to have some fast games of ping-pong, and still do. Yes, sir, I hate to admit it, but Al beats me pretty near as often as I beat him. Why, we have kept track of the games for years—for years, mind you! Ever since he began beating me now and then, and that was when he was in college—five years ago, at least, I guess. Al and me have a big chart down cellar where our ping-pong table is and we keep track of all the games we play. Sometimes I'll be ahead as much as ten games, maybe, and then Al will have a winning streak and before I know it *he*'ll be ahead two or three games. We kept it up even after he moved down to Cranford. Al comes up on Sunday now and then, and after dinner we play all afternoon, down cellar. Now, George—well, his mother used to speak up for the boy and I guess she was right. She'd be on his side when Al and me used to kid him a little in a good-natured way about his ping-pong game. She used to say that if he didn't care about the game, why should he care about winning? And of course there's a lot in that.

"That was about it—George wasn't keen to win like Al or me. I would know sometimes in the middle of a game that George had already quit. He'd quit when he got behind. Of course we had a chart for him down cellar for a while, but we stopped marking up his score on it eventually because George hardly ever won a game and, as his mother said, he didn't care anyway. We just left his chart there, and after a while we got to using it for marking up the day's games between Al and me. I mean we'd just put down a mark on George's chart for each game either of us won and keep track of how much ahead either one of us was for the day and then mark up the total won or lost on our own charts when we'd finished playing. That makes me remember—last Sunday, just before we came up here. How Al and me played a game or two, I mean, to try to cheer up a bit and how we felt bad all of a sudden, after the first game, when we went to put a mark down for me, and there we were starting to use the boy's chart. Neither of us said anything, but we started using an old piece of cardboard to mark down the games on—instead of the boy's old chart, I mean. It's little things like that that keep bringing it all back to me. I took down George's chart that night, of course, and put it up with his other things. Mrs. Powers is keeping all his things intact, you know.

"Oh, I suppose it's the way life goes—you have everything you want, a happy home, a little family, and then a thing like this tragedy comes to you. We had high hopes for George, and I always thought, and I used to tell him, that once he really knuckled down and put his mind to it he could do anything he wanted—become a lawyer, if he wanted to. I was willing to send him to college, scholarships or no scholarships, as soon as he showed that he was out to win, that he wasn't going to quit when he got half through. He hadn't done as well at high school as Al, of course, and I was frankly disappointed about the scholarships, but you can't expect the best from everybody and, as I used to tell him, he could make up for that some time in some other way. He just didn't seem to care about anything, though, the way I see it now. Why, Al took music lessons, for instance, when he was a kid and he turned out to be a fine pianist—play anything, almost, without having to have the music, and he put plenty of pep into it, too. I got the same teacher to give lessons to George at the same time—he was younger, but you're never too young to start in a thing like that—and he made no headway at all. He used to say he didn't like the piano— wanted a violin—can you imagine that? And there we had a baby grand piano right in the living room! Oh, I struggled to make him see his mistakes—without going too far, of course.

"That day I was telling you about, when George went down to Cranford with me to see Al win his law case in the courtroom, I was all steamed up about it coming back—about how Al had beaten down the chief witness for the prosecution and got him all mixed up—but George, he wasn't interested at all. That's the way he was, you know—just not interested in the things an ordinary fellow would be interested in. I remember I tried at dinner that night to make him see my point of view—that Al's case was a game, just like baseball or bowling or billiards or ping-pong, if you looked at it that way, and that it was something any man ought to be proud of getting a kick out of. I told him a man just has to put his heart into whatever he does, unless he's just going to give up and quit and be a failure. I guess I was pretty rough on him, but he'd never argue, you know—never let me have it back, as you might say. Mrs. Powers usually stuck up for him, but this time even she couldn't understand the way he just sat there and looked at his plate, without answering me, and she finally said to him, pretty sharp, 'George, why don't you answer your father? George, why don't you answer your father?' She said it twice, like that. He looked at her, but he didn't look at me, and he got up and went upstairs."

Mr. Powers was without words for a moment, and then he found them again.

"I remember," he said, "how interested Brownell was in Al's winning his case, for instance. Brownell's my neighbor down the street, and as good a billiard-player as I want to know. He has a table down in his cellar, you know, and I have a game with him once or twice a week. We're just about even—oh, maybe I have a little edge on him, but certainly not much of a one. Well, I went over to Brownell's that night after dinner and told him about Al winning his case and *he* was interested, all right. We had a few games and then sat around talking till pretty late—you see, I can't help remembering it all clearly because that was the night George did it. Hell, I suppose you've guessed what he did to himself by this time. I guess I'm talking too much and too long here anyway, but it's all been such a shock, you know. Of course, I tell myself, well, it's all in the game, it's the way things go, and then of course I have my work and things like that to keep my mind off it, so it isn't as hard on me as it is on Mrs. Powers. Well, and then, too, Mrs. Powers had the first shock of it—the first, awful shock. I mean, I was over at Brownell's pretty late, as I said, and when George did it, she—Mrs. Powers—was alone in the house, except for Marge. They were sitting downstairs when they heard the shot. He must have taken my gun out of the desk in my den on his way upstairs after he left the dinner table, because they hadn't heard him come downstairs after that. He sat up there in his room all that time, all the time I was down at Brownell's, before he did it. It was about time for me to come home—I always get to bed by eleven— and I was just getting ready to leave Brownell's when the people next door called up and told me what had happened. So of course it was all over by the time I got there—I mean they had him on his bed by then, so it wasn't really as much of a shock for me as it was for Mrs. Powers."

I got rather self-consciously to my feet and murmured something about being so sorry, and said that I thought I would go for a swim before dinner.

"I'll go along," he said, stopping at the door of the hotel to take his stiff felt hat off the rack. "I certainly don't intend to keep depressing you this way with my troubles. It's the way things go, I guess. Well, what do you say to a return match after dinner? I'm eight up on you now, is that correct? We must keep track of it."

When I came out of the bathhouse, he was standing by himself under a pine tree near the side of the lake, smoking a cigar and watching the swimmers.

THE THREE VETERANS

❦

LEANE ZUGSMITH

As far back as the memory of Miss Riordan, which was three months, for she had been the attending nurse in the clinic for that long, the three old women regularly appeared twice a week. Only when they managed to sit together on the bench, with their old, high-veined legs stiff ahead of them, was she able to distinguish one from the other. Otherwise, Mrs. Farrell could be mistaken for Mrs. Gaffney, or either of the two for Mrs. Betz. Each showed gaps in her front teeth when she broke into her cackle; each had yellow-gray hair wisping from beneath a moldy hat; each wore stained, shapeless outer garments; and each had the same kind of bad leg.

Outside the dispensary, the three old women did not lay eyes on one another from one clinic day to the next, but inside they formed a sisterhood. Together, they would question newcomers and advise them on their ills, but once The Doctor was in the room, they would remain respectfully silent unless he made one of his lame jokes or scolded them. Promptly then, they would cackle. Anything The Doctor said was a signal for their ingratiating brays of laughter.

The first three to enter Room 4 this morning, they sat together on the long bench, eyes alert on the door as Miss Riordan called to the patients outside, "Number 6 and 7 for Room 4."

When the pale young woman with the fretful infant came in, relinquishing her numbered green ticket for Room 4, and sat opposite them, Mrs. Betz crooked her soiled finger. "Gutsie-goo," she said to the baby. Then she addressed the mother. "Something wrong with it?" Mrs. Farrell and Mrs. Gaffney turned professional eyes on the child.

"She had an infected arm, and now she don't eat." The young woman jogged the whimpering infant with her knee.

"Only your first?" asked Mrs. Farrell, who had borne nine.

"Yes," said the young mother.

The three old women smiled knowingly at one another. Mrs. Gaffney flapped her hand down from the wrist. "Sure, you're always worrying your poor head off about the first. Isn't it the truth?" Mrs. Farrell and Mrs. Betz vigorously nodded their heads, and their moldy hats gave off a little puff of dust.

"When it don't eat, you want to pull out ten hairs from the right side of your head and braid them and twist them around its little toe," said Mrs. Betz.

"Give it honey and tea," said Mrs. Gaffney.

"It's always that way with the first of them," said Mrs. Farrell. "You'll be wanting to—"

"Who's in attendance around here? You or me?" It was The Doctor, his voice harsh, his face red.

Mrs. Gaffney and Mrs. Betz nudged Mrs. Farrell, who left her mouth open to giggle quickly with them.

"Just let me know when you want to take my job," he said, and stalked to the end of the room to visit the patients behind the screens.

The old women held their forefingers against their simpering lips. Now they would not even look at the ailing baby.

"Anyone else for Room 4?" called Miss Riordan, out in the corridor.

The eyes of the three old women frogged at the sight of the beautiful peroxide-blonde lady in a beautiful imitation-fur jacket. Everything about her seemed sweet and ripe as she handed over her green ticket and sat on the bench beside them. The three old women watched her pull down her silk stocking; she had only a little two-inch scratch on her fine, shapely leg and her skin was whiter than milk.

But Mrs. Gaffney could no longer stare at her, for now The Doctor was pressing his finger into her highest vein and she must keep her eyes submissive on his face. He whispered to the nurse and then, without looking into Mrs. Gaffney's submissive eyes, said, "You better quit staying out dancing all night, or that'll never get right."

The three old women cackled with delight. Mrs. Betz kept a meek smile on her face as The Doctor examined her leg. When he came to Mrs. Farrell, he wrinkled up his nose. "Suppose you wash your leg off yourself," he said. "Give the poor nurse a break. Just rub it up and down with *soap* and *water*. Ever heard of it?"

This time the brays of laughter from the three old women were wilder than ever. Seeing him turn to the baby, all three of the old women tried to retard Miss Riordan's manipulations of their leg wrappings so that they could remain to watch The Doctor and the beautiful peroxide-blonde lady in the beautiful imitation-fur jacket. Mrs. Gaffney elbowed Mrs. Betz as The Doctor stood before the lady.

"What's wrong with you?" he said.

She smiled invitingly up at him. "I tripped on the stairs—my landlord doesn't know enough to have safe stairs in his house—and it's been bothering me." She pointed a tapering white finger at the abrasion.

He looked at it carefully before whispering his orders to Miss Riordan. Mrs. Gaffney started to edge out of her seat, disappointed, when the beautiful lady said, "Is it serious, Doctor?"

"It hurt you, didn't it?" he said, sarcastically.

At the familiar tone, Mrs. Gaffney, Mrs. Farrell, and Mrs. Betz chuckled, but softly for fear of being sent away, now that their legs were wrapped.

"Yes," said the beautiful lady, "but I want to know what to tell my lawyer, in case—"

"Oh, your lawyer?" said The Doctor, witheringly. "I see. You want to bring suit. Well, Madam, you can tell your lawyer that anyone who's so careless as to trip on the stairs deserves more than the little scratch you have there."

The three old women lowered their heads, their soiled fingers at their mouths to curb their explosions of laughter. The beautiful lady's eyes flashed. "I don't see why you have to use that tone of voice!" she exclaimed with resentment. "Just because it's free is no reason why we can't be treated like human beings!"

The three old women waited breathlessly, their lips ready to stretch at his sally. Their waiting ears were met by silence. Their rheumy eyes saw The Doctor turn his back and regard the table of ointments and bandages. As he stood there, whistling softly, the three old women found themselves staring at one another, and not one was smiling. With gray, tired faces, they rose together. At the door, their way was blocked by the man in white whom they called The Specialist Doctor.

"Just the old friends I may want!" he cried in his ringing tones. He turned to The Doctor. "Are they varicose?"

"All three, Chief," said The Doctor.

"Are they interesting? Good enough for my Friday-night lecture?"

"I'll show you their charts," said The Doctor.

The Specialist Doctor rubbed his hands. "How would you girls like to dance in my chorus Friday night?" he boomed cheerfully.

The three old women looked at one another. The beautiful peroxide-blonde lady clack-clacked her high heels across the floor.

"No," said Mrs. Betz, heavily.

"No," said Mrs. Farrell, without looking up.

"No," said Mrs. Gaffney, plucking at the edge of her stained wrap. "Just because it's free don't mean we aren't human beings."

Then, with lowered heads and sombre faces, the three old women trudged out.

WET SATURDAY

☙

John Collier

It was July. In the sprawling house they were imprisoned by the swish and the gurgle and all the hundred sounds of rain. They were in the drawing room, behind four tall and weeping windows, in a lake of damp and faded chintz.

This house, ill-kept and unprepossessing, was necessary to Mr. Princey, who detested his wife, his daughter, and his hulking son. His life was to walk through the village, touching his hat, not smiling. His cold pleasure was to recapture snapshot memories of the infinitely remote summers of his childhood—coming into the orangery and finding his lost wooden horse, the tunnel in the box hedge and the little square of light at the end of it. But now all this was threatened—his austere pride of position in the village, his passionate attachment to the house—and all because Millicent, his cloddish daughter Millicent, had done this shocking and incredibly stupid thing. Mr. Princey turned from her in revulsion and spoke to his wife.

"They'd send her to a lunatic asylum," he said. "A criminal-lunatic asylum. We should have to move. It would be impossible."

His daughter began to shake again. "I'll kill myself," she said.

"Be quiet," said Mr. Princey. "We have very little time. No time for nonsense. I intend to deal with this." He called to his son, who stood looking out of the window. "George, come here. Listen, how far did you get with your medicine before they threw you out as hopeless?"

"You know as well as I do," said George.

"Do you know enough—did they drive enough into your head for you to be able to guess what a competent doctor could tell about such a wound?"

"Well, it's a—it's a knock or blow."

"If a tile fell from the roof? Or a piece of the coping?"

"Well, guv'nor, you see, it's like this—"

"Is it possible?"

"No."

"Why not?"

"Oh, because she hit him several times."

"I can't stand it," said Mrs. Princey.

"You have got to stand it, my dear," said her husband. "And keep that hysterical note out of your voice. It might be overheard. We are talking about the weather. If he fell down the well, George, striking his head several times?"

"I really don't know, guv'nor."

"He'd have had to hit the sides several times in thirty or forty feet, and at the correct angles. No. I'm afraid not. We must go over it all again. Millicent."

"No! No!"

"Millicent, we must go over it all again. Perhaps you have forgotten something. One tiny irrelevant detail may save or ruin us. Particularly you, Millicent. You don't *want* to be put in an asylum, do you? Or be hanged? They might hang you, Millicent. You must stop that shaking. You must keep your voice quiet. We are talking of the weather. Now."

"I can't. I . . . I . . ."

"Be quiet, child. Be quiet." He put his long, cold face very near to his daughter's. He found himself horribly revolted by her. Her features were thick, her jaw heavy, her whole figure repellently powerful. "Answer me," he said. "You were in the stable?"

"Yes."

"One moment, though. Who knew you were in love with this wretched curate?"

"No one. I've never said a—"

"Don't worry," said George. "The whole god-damned village knows. They've been sniggering about it in the Plough for three years past."

"Likely enough," said Mr. Princey. "Likely enough. What filth!" He made as if to wipe something off the backs of his hands. "Well, now, we continue. You were in the stable?"

"Yes."

"You were putting the croquet set into its box?"

"Yes."

"You heard someone crossing the yard?"

"Yes."

"It was Withers?"

"Yes."

"So you called him?"

"Yes."

"Loudly? Did you call him loudly? Could anyone have heard?"

"No, Father. I'm sure not. I didn't call him. He saw me as I went to the door. He just waved his hand and came over."

"How *can* I find out from you whether there was anyone about? Whether he *could* have been seen?"

"I'm sure not, Father. I'm quite sure."

"So you both went into the stable?"

"Yes. It was raining hard."

"What did he say?"

"He said 'Hullo, Milly.' And to excuse him coming in the back way, but he'd set out to walk over to Lyston."

"Yes."

"And he said, passing the park, he'd seen the house and suddenly thought of me, and he thought he'd just look in for a minute, just to tell me something. He said he was so happy, he wanted me to share it. He'd heard from the Bishop he was to have the vicarage. And it wasn't only that. It meant he could marry. And he began to stutter. And I thought he meant me."

"Don't tell me what you thought. Exactly what he said. Nothing else."

"Well . . . Oh dear!"

"Don't cry. It is a luxury you cannot afford. Tell me."

"He said no. He said it wasn't me. It's Ella Brangwyn-Davies. And he was sorry. And all that. Then he went to go."

"And then?"

"I went mad. He turned his back. I had the winning post of the croquet set in my hand—"

"Did you shout or scream? I mean, as you hit him?"

"No. I'm sure I didn't."

"Did he? Come on. Tell me."

"No, Father."

"And then?"

"I threw it down. I came straight into the house That's all. I wish I were dead."

"And you met none of the servants. No one will go into the stable. You see, George, he probably told people he was going to Lyston. Certainly no one knows he came here. He might have been attacked in the woods. We must consider every detail. . . . A curate, with his head battered in—"

"Don't, Father!" cried Millicent.

"Do you want to be hanged? A curate, with his head battered in, found in the woods. Who'd want to kill Withers?"

There was a tap on the door, which opened immediately. It was little Captain Smollett, who never stood on ceremony. "Who'd kill Withers?" said he. "I would, with pleasure. How d'you do, Mrs. Princey. I walked right in."

"He heard you, Father," moaned Millicent.

"My dear, we can all have our little joke," said her father. "Don't pretend to be shocked. A little theoretical curate-killing, Smollett. In these days we talk nothing but thrillers."

"Parsonicide," said Captain Smollett. "Justifiable parsonicide. Have you heard about Ella Brangwyn-Davies? I shall be laughed at."

"Why?" said Mr. Princey. "Why should you be laughed at?"

"Had a shot in that direction myself," said Smollett, with careful sang-froid. "She half said yes, too. Hadn't you heard? She told most people. Now it'll look as if I got turned down for a white rat in a dog collar."

"Too bad!" said Mr. Princey.

"Fortune of war," said the little Captain.

"Sit down," said Mr. Princey. "Mother, Millicent, console Captain Smollett with your best light conversation. George and I have something to look to. We shall be back in a minute or two, Smollett. Come, George."

It was actually five minutes before Mr. Princey and his son returned.

"Smollett," said Mr. Princey, "will you come round to the stable for a moment? There's something I want to show you."

They went into the stable yard. The buildings were now unused except as odd sheds. No one ever went there. Captain Smollett entered, George followed him, Mr. Princey came last. As he closed the door he took up a gun which stood behind it. "Smollett," said he, "we have come out to shoot a rat which George heard squeaking under that tub. Now, you must listen to me very carefully or you will be shot by accident. I mean that."

Smollett looked at him. "Very well," said he. "Go on."

"A very tragic happening has taken place this afternoon," said Mr. Princey. "It will be even more tragic unless it is smoothed over."

"Oh?" said Smollett.

"You heard me ask," said Mr. Princey, "who would kill Withers. You heard Millicent make a comment, an unguarded comment."

"Well?" said Smollett. "What of it?"

"Very little," said Mr. Princey. "Unless you heard that Withers had met a violent end this very afternoon. And that, my dear Smollett, is what you are going to hear."

"Have you killed him?" cried Smollett.

"Millicent has," said Mr. Princey.

"Hell!" said Smollett.

"It *is* hell," said Mr. Princey. "You would have remembered—and guessed."

"Maybe," said Smollett. "Yes. I suppose I should."

"Therefore," said Mr. Princey, "you constitute a problem."

"Why did she kill him?" said Smollett.

"It is one of these disgusting things," said Mr. Princey. "Pitiable, too. She deluded herself that he was in love with her."

"Oh, of course," said Smollett.

"And he told her about the Brangwyn-Davies girl."

"I see," said Smollett.

"I have no wish," said Mr. Princey, "that she should be proved either a lunatic or a murderess. I could hardly live here after that."

"I suppose not," said Smollett.

"On the other hand," said Mr. Princey, "*you* know about it."

"Yes," said Smollett. "I am wondering if I could keep my mouth shut. If I promised you—"

"I am wondering if I could believe you," said Mr. Princey.

"If I promised," said Smollett.

"If things went smoothly," said Mr. Princey. "But not if there was any sort of suspicion, any questioning. You would be afraid of being an accessory."

"I don't know," said Smollett.

"I do," said Mr. Princey. "What are we going to do?"

"I can't see anything else," said Smollett. "You'd never be fool enough to do me in. You can't get rid of two corpses."

"I regard it," said Mr. Princey, "as a better risk than the other. It could be an accident. Or you and Withers could both disappear. There are possibilities in that."

"Listen," said Smollett. "You can't—"

"Listen," said Mr. Princey. "There may be a way out. There *is* a way out, Smollett. You gave me the idea yourself."

"Did I?" said Smollett. "What?"

"You said you would kill Withers," said Mr. Princey. "You have a motive."

"I was joking," said Smollett.

"You are always joking," said Mr. Princey. "People think there must be something behind it. Listen, Smollett, I can't trust you, you must trust me. Or I will kill you now, in the next minute. I mean that. You can choose between dying and living."

"Go on," said Smollett.

"There is a sewer here," said Mr. Princey, speaking fast and forcefully. "That is where I am going to put Withers. No outsider knows he has come up here this afternoon. No one will ever look there for him unless you tell them. You must give me evidence that you have murdered Withers."

"Why?" said Smollett.

"So that I shall be dead sure that you will never open your lips on the matter," said Mr. Princey.

"What evidence?" said Smollett.

"George," said Mr. Princey, "hit him in the face, hard."

"Good God!" said Smollett.

"Again," said Mr. Princey. "Don't bruise your knuckles."

"Oh!" said Smollett.

"I'm sorry," said Mr. Princey. "There must be traces of a struggle between you and Withers. Then it will not be altogether safe for you to go to the police."

"Why won't you take my word?" said Smollett.

"I will when we've finished," said Mr. Princey. "George, get that croquet post. Take your handkerchief to it. As I told you. Smollett, you'll just grasp the end of this croquet post. I shall shoot you if you don't."

"Oh, hell," said Smollett. "All right."

"Pull two hairs out of his head, George," said Mr. Princey, "and remember what I told you to do with them. Now, Smollett, you take that bar and raise the big flagstone with the ring in it. Withers is in the next stall. You've got to drag him through and dump him in."

"I won't touch him," said Smollett.

"Stand back, George," said Mr. Princey, raising the gun.

"Wait a minute," cried Smollett. "Wait a minute." He did as he was told.

Mr. Princey wiped his brow. "Look here," said he. "Everything is perfectly safe. Remember, no one knows that Withers came here. Everyone thinks he walked over to Lyston. That's five miles of country to search. They'll never look in our sewer. Do you see how safe it is?"

"I suppose it is," said Smollett.

"Now come into the house," said Mr. Princey. "We shall never get that rat."

They went into the house. The maid was bringing tea into the drawing room. "See, my dear," said Mr. Princey to his wife, "we went to the stable to shoot a rat and we found Captain Smollett. Don't be offended, my dear fellow."

"You must have walked up the back drive," said Mrs. Princey.

"Yes. Yes. That was it," said Smollett in some confusion.

"You've cut your lip," said George, handing him a cup of tea.

"I . . . I just knocked it."

"Shall I tell Bridget to bring some iodine?" said Mrs. Princey. The maid looked up, waiting.

"Don't trouble, please," said Smollett. "It's nothing."

"Very well, Bridget," said Mrs. Princey. "That's all."

"Smollett is very kind," said Mr. Princey. "He knows all our trouble. We can rely on him. We have his word."

"Oh, have we, Captain Smollett?" cried Mrs. Princey. "You *are* good."

"Don't worry, old fellow," Mr. Princey said. "They'll never find anything."

Pretty soon Smollett took his leave. Mrs. Princey pressed his hand very hard. Tears came into her eyes. All three of them watched him go down the drive. Then Mr. Princey spoke very earnestly to his wife for a few minutes and the two of them went upstairs and spoke still more earnestly to Millicent. Soon after, the rain having ceased, Mr. Princey took a stroll round the stable yard.

He came back and went to the telephone. "Put me through to Lyston police station," said he. "Quickly . . . Hullo, is that the police station? This is Mr. Princey, of Abbott's Laxton. I'm afraid something rather terrible has happened up here. Can you send someone at once?"

SOLDIERS OF THE REPUBLIC

❦

DOROTHY PARKER

T HAT SUNDAY AFTERNOON we sat with the Swedish girl in the big café in Valencia. We had vermouth in thick goblets, each with a cube of honeycombed gray ice in it. The waiter was so proud of that ice he could hardly bear to leave the glasses on the table, and thus part from it forever. He went to his duty—all over the room they were clapping their hands and hissing to draw his attention—but he looked back over his shoulder.

It was dark outside, the quick, new dark that leaps down without dusk on the day; but, because there were no lights in the streets, it seemed as set and as old as midnight. So you wondered that all the babies were still up. There were babies everywhere in the café, babies serious without solemnity and interested in a tolerant way in their surroundings.

At the table next ours, there was a notably small one; maybe six months old. Its father, a little man in a big uniform that dragged his shoulders down, held it carefully on his knee. It was doing nothing whatever, yet he and his thin young wife, whose belly was already big again under her sleazy dress, sat watching it in a sort of ecstasy of admiration, while their coffee cooled in front of them. The baby was in Sunday white; its dress was patched so delicately that you would have thought the fabric whole had not the patches varied in their shades of whiteness. In its hair was a bow of new blue ribbon, tied with absolute balance of loops and ends. The ribbon was of no use; there was not enough hair to require restraint. The bow was sheerly an adornment, a calculated bit of dash.

"Oh, for God's sake, stop that!" I said to myself. "All right, so it's got a piece of blue ribbon on its hair. All right, so its mother

went without eating so it could look pretty when its father came
home on leave. All right, so it's her business, and none of yours.
All right, so what have you got to cry about?"

The big, dim room was crowded and lively. That morning there
had been a bombing from the air, the more horrible for broad
daylight. But nobody in the café sat tense and strained, nobody
desperately forced forgetfulness. They drank coffee or bottled
lemonade, in the pleasant, earned ease of Sunday afternoon, chatting of small, gay matters, all talking at once, all hearing and
answering.

There were many soldiers in the room, in what appeared to be
the uniforms of twenty different armies until you saw that the
variety lay in the differing ways the cloth had worn or faded. Only
a few of them had been wounded; here and there you saw one
stepping gingerly, leaning on a crutch or two canes, but so far on
toward recovery that his face had color. There were many men,
too, in civilian clothes—some of them soldiers home on leave, some
of them governmental workers, some of them anybody's guess.
There were plump, comfortable wives, active with paper fans, and
old women as quiet as their grandchildren. There were many
pretty girls and some beauties, of whom you did not remark,
"There's a charming Spanish type," but said, "What a beautiful
girl!" The women's clothes were not new, and their material was
too humble ever to have warranted skillful cutting.

"It's funny," I said to the Swedish girl, "how when nobody in a
place is best-dressed, you don't notice that everybody isn't."

"Please?" the Swedish girl said.

No one, save an occasional soldier, wore a hat. When we had
first come to Valencia, I lived in a state of puzzled pain as to why
everybody on the streets laughed at me. It was not because "West
End Avenue" was writ across my face as if left there by a customs
officer's chalked scrawl. They like Americans in Valencia, where
they have seen good ones—the doctors who left their practices and
came to help, the calm young nurses, the men of the International
Brigade. But when I walked forth, men and women courteously
laid their hands across their splitting faces and little children, too
innocent for dissembling, doubled with glee and pointed and
cried, *"Olé!"* Then, pretty late, I made my discovery, and left my

hat off; and there was laughter no longer. It was not one of those comic hats, either; it was just a hat.

The café filled to overflow, and I left our table to speak to a friend across the room. When I came back to the table, six soldiers were sitting there. They were crowded in, and I scraped past them to my chair. They looked tired and dusty and little, the way that the newly dead look little, and the first things you saw about them were the tendons in their necks. I felt like a prize sow.

They were all in conversation with the Swedish girl. She has Spanish, French, German, anything in Scandinavian, Italian, and English. When she has a moment for regret, she sighs that her Dutch is so rusty she can no longer speak it, only read it, and the same is true of her Rumanian.

They had told her, she told us, that they were at the end of forty-eight hours' leave from the trenches, and, for their holiday, they had all pooled their money for cigarettes, and something had gone wrong, and the cigarettes had never come through to them. I had a pack of American cigarettes—in Spain rubies are as nothing to them—and I brought it out, and by nods and smiles and a sort of breast stroke, made it understood that I was offering it to those six men yearning for tobacco. When they saw what I meant, each one of them rose and shook my hand. Darling of me to share my cigarettes with the men on their way back to the trenches. Little Lady Bountiful. The prize sow.

Each one lit his cigarette with a contrivance of yellow rope that stank when afire and was also used, the Swedish girl translated, for igniting grenades. Each one received what he had ordered, a glass of coffee, and each one murmured appreciatively over the tiny cornucopia of coarse sugar that accompanied it. Then they talked.

They talked through the Swedish girl, but they did to us that thing we all do when we speak our own language to one who has no knowledge of it. They looked us square in the face, and spoke slowly, and pronounced their words with elaborate movements of their lips. Then, as their stories came, they poured them at us so vehemently, so emphatically that they were sure we must understand. They were so convinced we would understand that we were ashamed for not understanding.

But the Swedish girl told us. They were all farmers and farmers' sons, from a district so poor that you try not to remember there is that kind of poverty. Their village was next that one where the old men and the sick men and the women and children had gone, on a holiday, to the bullring; and the planes had come over and dropped bombs on the bullring, and the old men and the sick men and the women and the children were more than two hundred.

They had all, the six of them, been in the war for over a year, and most of that time they had been in the trenches. Four of them were married. One had one child, two had three children, one had five. They had not had word from their families since they had left for the front. There had been no communication; two of them had learned to write from men fighting next them in the trench, but they had not dared to write home. They belonged to a union, and union men, of course, are put to death if taken. The village where their families lived had been captured, and if your wife gets a letter from a union man, who knows but they'll shoot her for the connection?

They told about how they had not heard from their families for more than a year. They did not tell it gallantly or whimsically or stoically. They told it as if— Well, look. You have been in the trenches, fighting, for a year. You have heard nothing of your wife and your children. They do not know if you are dead or alive or blinded. You do not know where they are, or if they are. You must talk to somebody. That is the way they told about it.

One of them, some six months before, had heard of his wife and his three children—they had such beautiful eyes, he said—from a brother-in-law in France. They were all alive then, he was told, and had a bowl of beans a day. But his wife had not complained of the food, he heard. What had troubled her was that she had no thread to mend the children's ragged clothes. So that troubled him, too.

"She has no thread," he kept telling us. "My wife has no thread to mend with. No thread."

We sat there, and listened to what the Swedish girl told us they were saying. Suddenly one of them looked at the clock, and then there was excitement. They jumped up, as a man, and there were calls for the waiter and rapid talk with him, and each of them shook the hand of each of us. We went through more swimming motions to explain to them that they were to take the rest of the cigarettes—fourteen cigarettes for six soldiers to take to war—and then they shook our hands again. Then all of us said *"Salud!"* as many times as could be for six of them and three of us, and then they filed out of the café, the six of them, tired and dusty and little, as men of a mighty horde are little.

Only the Swedish girl talked, after they had gone. The Swedish girl has been in Spain since the start of the war. She has nursed splintered men, and she has carried stretchers into the trenches and, heavier laden, back to the hospital. She has seen and heard too much to be knocked into silence.

Presently it was time to go, and the Swedish girl raised her hands above her head and clapped them twice together to summon the waiter. He came, but he only shook his head and his hand, and moved away.

The soldiers had paid for our drinks.

HOUSEPARTY

❧

WALTER BERNSTEIN

THE SMALL ROOM WAS CROWDED, but the boy managed to get through without spilling the drink he held in his hand.

"Hello," he said to the girl on the window seat. "Here's your drink."

The girl looked at him and then looked at her watch. "You're late," she said. "Last time you were faster."

"I couldn't help it," the boy said. "The place is filling up."

The girl accepted the glass and took a long drink. She looked up at the boy and took another drink. Then she set the glass down. "What do they put this Scotch in with—an eye dropper?" she asked.

"I'll get you some more."

"No, never mind." She turned to look out of the window.

"That's the library," the boy said.

"Your friend told me. I guess he wanted me to get the idea. He told me five times. Look," she said, "there's a clock on the other side of that tower, too, isn't there?"

"Sure," said the boy. "Four of them."

"Does it keep the same time as this one?"

"Sure."

The girl looked triumphant. "How do you know?" she asked.

"Well—" the boy said. He was a trifle uneasy. "Well, I guess it does."

"You ought to find out," the girl insisted. "You really ought to find out. That clock on the other side might be slow. If you can only see one clock at a time, how do you know it isn't slow?"

"I guess you don't know," said the boy. "You have to take their word for it."

"I'd find out if I were you," said the girl, shaking her head slowly. She took another drink. "You really ought to know." She looked out of the window, then turned back to the boy. "What do they call this place again?"

"Dartmouth," said the boy.

"That's a silly name," said the girl. She finished her drink. "Do you think you could get me another one of these with some Scotch in it?"

"Sure," said the boy. He took the glass and started through the crowd. The girl put her nose against the pane and looked out of the window.

After a while, the boy came back, holding the drink above his head so it wouldn't be spilled. He tapped the girl on the shoulder. "Hello," he said. "I'm back."

The girl looked at him. "Go away," she said. "I never heard of you."

"I'm your date," said the boy. "I'm bringing you another drink."

The girl peered at him. "So you are," she said. She took the drink and returned to the window.

"I got a little more Scotch this time," the boy said.

The girl turned around. "You're cute," she said.

The boy blushed. "Look," he said, "are you having a good time?"

"I'm having a wonderful time," the girl said. "I am having a simply wonderful time." Her eyes were very large and bright.

"I'm glad," said the boy. He sat down and took hold of her hand. The girl looked at his hand holding hers and then up at his face. She looked at his hand again and took another drink. The boy held on to her hand and leaned forward. "Do you really dance in a chorus?" he said.

"When I'm working," the girl said. "They call us chorus girls." She put her head next to his. "Who squealed?"

"Oh, no one." The boy was emphatic. "My sister told me. Remember? You know my sister. She introduced us in New York."

The girl nodded. "I know your sister." She hiccuped gently. "Little bitch."

The boy released her hand and sat up straight. Seeing his startled expression, the girl put her fingers to her mouth. "There I go again, always belching in public," she said. She leaned toward the boy. "Pardon me."

"Sure," said the boy. "Sure." He sat up very straight.

The girl was beating out a rhythm on the glass with her fingernails, watching the crowd. "How long do you have to stay in this place?" she asked.

"No special time," said the boy. "We can leave now if you want."

"Not here," said the girl. "I mean in college."

"Oh. Four years. I have one to go."

"That's a long run." She drained her glass and looked at the boy. "You're cute," she said. She put down the glass and took up his hands. "You have nice hands."

The boy gave her hands a slight squeeze. "So have you," he said, but the girl had turned away.

"You touch that glass," she was saying to a girl about to sit down, "and I'll lay you out like a rug." She retrieved the glass and held it out to the boy. "How about another drink?"

"Sure," said the boy. He took the glass and moved into the crowd. As he was pouring the liquor, another boy came over and put an arm around his shoulders.

"How're you doing?" he asked.

The boy spilled a little soda into the glass and started back toward the window.

"Fine," he called back. "Fine." He dodged someone carrying a tray. "She's a cinch," he said.

ALL THE YEARS OF HER LIFE

❦

MORLEY CALLAGHAN

THEY WERE CLOSING the drugstore, and Alfred Higgins, who had just taken off his white jacket, was putting on his coat and getting ready to go home. The little gray-haired man, Sam Carr, who owned the drugstore, was bending down behind the cash register, and when Alfred Higgins passed him, he looked up and said softly, "Just a moment, Alfred. One moment before you go."

The soft, confident, quiet way in which Sam Carr spoke made Alfred start to button his coat nervously. He felt sure his face was white. Sam Carr usually said, "Good night," brusquely, without looking up. In the six months he had been working in the drugstore Alfred had never heard his employer speak softly like that. His heart began to beat so loud it was hard for him to get his breath. "What is it, Mr. Carr?" he asked.

"Maybe you'd be good enough to take a few things out of your pocket and leave them here before you go," Sam Carr said.

"What things? What are you talking about?"

"You've got a compact and a lipstick and at least two tubes of toothpaste in your pockets, Alfred."

"What do you mean? Do you think I'm crazy?" Alfred blustered. His face got red and he knew he looked fierce with indignation. But Sam Carr, standing by the door with his blue eyes shining bright behind his glasses and his lips moving underneath his gray mustache, only nodded his head a few times, and then Alfred grew very frightened and he didn't know what to say. Slowly he raised his hand and dipped it into his pocket, and with his eyes never meeting Sam Carr's eyes, he took out a blue compact and two tubes

187

of toothpaste and a lipstick, and he laid them one by one on the counter.

"Petty thieving, eh, Alfred?" Sam Carr said. "And maybe you'd be good enough to tell me how long this has been going on."

"This is the first time I ever took anything."

"So now you think you'll tell me a lie, eh? What kind of a sap do I look like, huh? I don't know what goes on in my own store, eh? I tell you you've been doing this pretty steady," Sam Carr said as he went over and stood behind the cash register.

Ever since Alfred had left school he had been getting into trouble wherever he worked. He lived at home with his mother and his father, who was a printer. His two older brothers were married and his sister had got married last year, and it would have been all right for his parents now if Alfred had only been able to keep a job.

While Sam Carr smiled and stroked the side of his face very delicately with the tips of his fingers, Alfred began to feel that familiar terror growing in him that had been in him every time he had got into such trouble.

"I liked you," Sam Carr was saying. "I liked you and would have trusted you, and now look what I got to do." While Alfred watched with his alert, frightened blue eyes, Sam Carr drummed with his fingers on the counter. "I don't like to call a cop in point-blank," he was saying as he looked very worried. "You're a fool, and maybe I should call your father and tell him you're a fool. Maybe I should let them know I'm going to have you locked up."

"My father's not at home. He's a printer. He works nights," Alfred said.

"Who's at home?"

"My mother, I guess."

"Then we'll see what she says." Sam Carr went to the phone and dialled the number. Alfred was not so much ashamed, but there was that deep fright growing in him, and he blurted out arrogantly, like a strong, full-grown man, "Just a minute. You don't need to draw anybody else in. You don't need to tell her." He wanted to sound like a swaggering, big guy who could look after himself, yet the old, childish hope was in him, the longing that someone at home would come and help him. "Yeah, that's right, he's in trouble," Mr. Carr was saying. "Yeah, your boy works for me. You'd better come down in a hurry." And when he was finished Mr. Carr went over to the door and looked out at the street and watched the people passing in the late summer night. "I'll keep my eye out for a cop" was all he said.

Alfred knew how his mother would come rushing in; she would rush in with her eyes blazing, or maybe she would be crying, and she would push him away when he tried to talk to her, and make him feel her dreadful contempt; yet he longed that she might come before Mr. Carr saw the cop on the beat passing the door.

While they waited—and it seemed a long time—they did not speak, and when at last they heard someone tapping on the closed door, Mr. Carr, turning the latch, said crisply, "Come in, Mrs. Higgins." He looked hard-faced and stern.

Mrs. Higgins must have been going to bed when he telephoned, for her hair was tucked in loosely under her hat, and her hand at her throat held her light coat tight across her chest so her dress would not show. She came in, large and plump, with a little smile on her friendly face. Most of the store lights had been turned out and at first she did not see Alfred, who was standing in the shadow at the end of the counter. Yet as soon as she saw him she did not look as Alfred thought she would look: she smiled, her blue eyes never wavered, and with a calmness and dignity that made them forget that her clothes seemed to have been thrown on her, she put out her hand to Mr. Carr and said politely, "I'm Mrs. Higgins. I'm Alfred's mother."

Mr. Carr was a bit embarrassed by her lack of terror and her simplicity, and he hardly knew what to say to her, so she asked, "Is Alfred in trouble?"

"He is. He's been taking things from the store. I caught him red-handed. Little things like compacts and toothpaste and lipsticks. Stuff he can sell easily," the proprietor said.

As she listened Mrs. Higgins looked at Alfred sometimes and nodded her head sadly, and when Sam Carr had finished she said gravely, "Is it so, Alfred?"

"Yes."

"Why have you been doing it?"

"I been spending money, I guess."

"On what?"

"Going around with the guys, I guess," Alfred said.

Mrs. Higgins put out her hand and touched Sam Carr's arm with an understanding gentleness, and speaking as though afraid of disturbing him, she said, "If you would only listen to me before doing anything." Her simple earnestness made her shy; her humility made her falter and look away, but in a moment she was smiling gravely again, and she said with a kind of patient dignity, "What did you intend to do, Mr. Carr?"

"I was going to get a cop. That's what I ought to do."

"Yes, I suppose so. It's not for me to say, because he's my son. Yet I sometimes think a little good advice is the best thing for a boy when he's at a certain period in his life," she said.

Alfred couldn't understand his mother's quiet composure, for if they had been at home and someone had suggested that he was going to be arrested, he knew she would be in a rage and would cry out against him. Yet now she was standing there with that gentle, pleading smile on her face, saying, "I wonder if you don't think it would be better just to let him come home with me. He looks a big fellow, doesn't he? It takes some of them a long time to get any sense," and they both stared at Alfred, who shifted away with a bit of light shining for a moment on his thin face and the tiny pimples over his cheekbone.

But even while he was turning away uneasily Alfred was realizing that Mr. Carr had become aware that his mother was really a fine woman; he knew that Sam Carr was puzzled by his mother, as if he had expected her to come in and plead with him tearfully, and instead he was being made to feel a bit ashamed by her vast tolerance. While there was only the sound of the mother's soft, assured voice in the store, Mr. Carr began to nod his head encouragingly at her. Without being alarmed, while being just large and still and simple and hopeful, she was becoming dominant there in the dimly lit store. "Of course, I don't want to be harsh," Mr. Carr was saying. "I'll tell you what I'll do. I'll just fire him and let it go at that. How's that?" and he got up and shook hands with Mrs. Higgins, bowing low to her in deep respect.

There was such warmth and gratitude in the way she said, "I'll never forget your kindness," that Mr. Carr began to feel warm and genial himself.

"Sorry we had to meet this way," he said. "But I'm glad I got in touch with you. Just wanted to do the right thing, that's all," he said.

"It's better to meet like this than never, isn't it?" she said. Suddenly they clasped hands as if they liked each other, as if they had known each other a long time. "Good night, sir," she said.

"Good night, Mrs. Higgins. I'm truly sorry," he said.

The mother and son walked along the street together, and the mother was taking a long, firm stride as she looked ahead with her stern face full of worry. Alfred was afraid to speak to her, he was afraid of the silence that was between them, so he only looked ahead too, for the excitement and relief were still pretty strong in him; but in a little while, going along like that in silence made him terribly aware of the strength and the sternness in her; he began to wonder what she was thinking of as she stared ahead so grimly; she seemed to have forgotten that he walked beside her; so when they were passing under the Sixth Avenue elevated and the rumble of the train seemed to break the silence, he said in his old, blustering way, "Thank God it turned out like that. I certainly won't get in a jam like that again."

"Be quiet. Don't speak to me. You've disgraced me again and again," she said bitterly.

"That's the last time. That's all I'm saying."

"Have the decency to be quiet," she snapped. They kept on their way, looking straight ahead.

When they were at home and his mother took off her coat, Alfred saw that she was really only half-dressed, and she made him feel afraid again when she said, without even looking at him, "You're a bad lot. God forgive you. It's one thing after another and always has been. Why do you stand there stupidly? Go to bed, why don't you?" When he was going, she said, "I'm going to make myself a cup of tea. Mind, now, not a word about tonight to your father."

While Alfred was undressing in his bedroom, he heard his mother moving around the kitchen. She filled the kettle and put it on the stove. She moved a chair. And as he listened there was no shame in him, just wonder and a kind of admiration of her strength and repose. He could still see Sam Carr nodding his head encouragingly to her; he could hear her talking simply and earnestly, and as he sat on his bed he felt a pride in her strength. "She certainly was smooth," he thought. "Gee, I'd like to tell her she sounded swell."

And at last he got up and went along to the kitchen, and when he was at the door he saw his mother pouring herself a cup of tea. He watched and he didn't move. Her face, as she sat there, was a frightened, broken face utterly unlike the face of the woman who had been so assured a little while ago in the drugstore. When she reached out and lifted the kettle to pour hot water in her cup, her hand trembled and the water splashed on the stove. Leaning back in the chair, she sighed and lifted the cup to her lips, and her lips were groping loosely as if they would never reach the cup. She swallowed the hot tea eagerly, and then she straightened up in relief, though her hand holding the cup still trembled. She looked very old.

It seemed to Alfred that this was the way it had been every time he had been in trouble before, that this trembling had really been in her as she hurried out half-dressed to the drugstore. He understood why she had sat alone in the kitchen the night his young sister had kept repeating doggedly that she was getting married. Now he felt all that his mother had been thinking of as they walked along the street together a little while ago. He watched his mother, and he never spoke, but at that moment his youth seemed to be over; he knew all the years of her life by the way her hand trembled as she raised the cup to her lips. It seemed to him that this was the first time he had ever looked upon his mother.

THE EXPLORERS

JEROME WEIDMAN

IT WAS A WARM DAY, too warm for that time of year, and the lake in the park had a couple of dozen rowboats on it. The freshly painted benches had been brought out on the asphalt apron between the boathouse and the water. Here and there people sat on them, reading newspapers or straining their faces to the sun, their eyes closed, trying to catch a bit of sunburn to carry home proudly. The weather was of the sort that, had it come on a Sunday, would have permitted the newspapers to report record-breaking crowds in the park. But it was an ordinary Wednesday morning and there weren't any crowds.

Just that handful of unexciting people, spread about as though by arrangement, one to a bench. They seemed to have no interest in one another beyond a sharp glance or two when a newcomer arrived and began to hunt for a seat. Nobody chose a bench with someone on it already, even though the man or woman might be sitting all the way over at one end. Everybody wanted a bench to himself.

The boathouse was a gray imitation-stone affair, with a huge clock on it that faced the lake so that the people who had rented boats and were out on the water would know when their time was up. The benches were arranged in front of it in two rows. This left a lane down the middle, four or five feet wide, that led from the cashier's window of the boathouse to the water's edge, where the boats were tied.

The three young men came down this lane at a curious gait, walking a shade faster than the ordinary bench hunter and yet too slowly to indicate any other purpose. They were very well dressed, much better dressed than most of the people on the benches. But their coats were taken in a trifle too much at the waist and the brims of their hats snapped a bit too sharply. They advanced to the water's edge and looked at the lake.

They did it as though somebody had told them recently that a lake was a fascinating thing but they didn't believe it and had come to look for themselves. They didn't seem to be impressed. Their faces, which had started out with identical looks of faint incredulity, were soon reflecting definite contempt. After a few moments they turned their backs on the lake abruptly and lit cigarettes. All three of them. They smoked slowly, inhaling huge quantities of smoke, and sent their eyes over the people on the benches. They were quick little eyes that moved in darts. For a while they saw nothing, apparently, that merited changing the expression on their faces, which continued to reflect their uncomplimentary opinion of the lake. Then the roving eyes stopped on the last bench to the left.

A young girl, a pretty girl, was sitting in the exact centre of the bench, reading the *Times*. She, too, seemed to be much better dressed than the other people on the benches. She held the *Times*, which was folded lengthwise down the middle, in her left hand and her left elbow rested on the back of the bench. This brought her shoulders at almost right angles to the bench. Sitting like that, with her legs crossed and her right hand resting in her lap and touching the bottom of the *Times* lightly, she made a very attractive picture.

The three young men at the water's edge looked at her for a moment. Then the one in the middle nudged the other two and winked. He was carrying a copy of the *Daily News* folded under one arm. He dropped his cigarette and walked up the lane swiftly. The others followed and they all stopped next to the girl's bench. The first young man leaned toward the girl and held out his folded newspaper.

"Pardon me, Miss," he said, "but you through with that paper? I'm through with this one. I figured you give me the *Times*, I give you the *News*?"

The girl looked up quickly, startled and confused. But somehow she didn't seem to be startled or confused enough. Her elbow, for instance, which appeared to be perched so precariously on the back of the bench, didn't slip from its resting place, even though she had jumped visibly. She looked up at the young man for a moment and then swung herself forward on the bench and buried her eyes in the paper. The young man looked at his two friends. His face was expressionless.

"You think it's possible she don't read the *News?*" he said aloud. "Only the *Times?*"

"You ask me?" one of the others said. "Ask her."

"A nice girl like that reading only the *Times?*" The young man with the folded paper shook his head as though he couldn't quite believe that. "She doesn't read the *Tribune*, she doesn't read the *Mirror*, she doesn't read the *Daily Worker*—all right, a thing like that I could understand. But the *News?*" He leaned toward the girl again. "Pardon me, Miss. You got a grudge against the *News?*"

The girl's face took on a look of exaggerated disdain, but she did not raise her head from the *Times*.

"That's how life is," one of the other young men said. They all spoke alike, in loud, clear voices, as though they were accustomed to addressing slightly deaf people. "A pretty girl like that, she's got nice clothes, so three gorillas come along and bother her. She didn't have such nice clothes, she didn't look so pretty, so no three gorillas wouldn't bother her." He shook his head sorrowfully.

"It's not a question of bothering," the first young man said. "A pretty girl like that, she don't read the *News*, that's something must be looked into. You can't leave things like that without looking into it."

"You wanna look into it, Flassy?" the second young man asked.

"We *must* look into it, Lou," said Flassy.

He sat down quickly, about two feet to the right of the girl. At the same time Lou sat down at her left, the same distance away. The third young man took up his post in back of the bench, about two feet behind her, so that she was completely surrounded. For a moment, while this was happening, the girl looked genuinely frightened. Then she recovered, turned a page of the *Times* defiantly, and continued reading. She continued looking at the paper, anyway.

"We gotta study this calmly," Flassy said.

"Calmly, I don't care," said Lou, on the left. "Intelligently we gotta study it."

"All right," the one in the rear said. "But let's study it."

They talked across the girl and over her head. They leaned toward each other and peered closely at the paper she was holding. But they were scrupulously careful not to touch her or even brush her clothes. They never touched her once.

"Books maybe," Flassy said. The girl was looking at the book page of the paper. "Ask her she likes books."

"That's an idea." Lou leaned toward the girl. "You like books, Miss?"

The girl read on stonily.

"Tell her I read a book once," Flassy said. "Very good, too."

"I don't think she likes us, Flassy," Lou said.

"No, no. That's too hasty. It's only books she don't like." Flassy peered at the paper in the girl's hands. It was open at the theatrical page. "I know what she likes. She likes Ethel Barrymore. Ask her."

Lou leaned toward the girl. "There's a rumor going around you like Ethel Barrymore. You like Ethel Barrymore, Miss?"

The girl turned the page calmly. She had recovered from her original surprise.

"She don't like Ethel Barrymore," Lou said.

"John, maybe. Ask her she likes John."

"Pardon me, Miss. You like John? John Barrymore?"

No answer.

"She don't like John, either."

"Maybe because he's married. *You* ask her this time, Gus," said Lou to the man in the rear.

Gus leaned forward to look down on the girl. "You don't like John because he's married, Miss?" he asked.

Flassy nudged his arm. "Tell her we can fix that," he said.

"Miss, you don't like John because he's married, we can fix that," said Gus. "You want us to fix that?"

The girl turned a page carefully.

"Maybe we wouldn't have to fix that," Lou said. "You know John."

"That's right. The way John is, maybe by this time we won't have to fix that," said Flassy.

Gus shook his head. "I'm afraid it's not John, fellas."

"Who then? Bob?"

"Bob? Yeah, well, maybe. It could be Bob."

"Bob who? Which Bob?" asked Flassy.

Lou seemed surprised. "That's a question to ask? A pretty girl like this, a pretty girl with sucha nice clothes, which Bob would it be? Use your head."

"All right with my head. But it could be two Bobs. It could be Taylor. It could be Montgomery."

Gus shook his head at him. "Flassy," he said, "you surprise me. Honest. A girl like this you say Taylor? With a girl like this Taylor hasn't got a chance. A Chinaman's chance. This is a Montgomery girl, Flassy."

Flassy shrugged. "Maybe," he said. "I could be wrong. I was wrong once. But how I could be wrong with a girl like this, I don't know. Montgomery? Better ask her."

Lou leaned over. "Pardon me, Miss. There is an argument here. We decided with you it's a Bob. But question: Are you a Taylor or a Montgomery? Which?"

The girl turned another page and rustled the paper into comfortable reading position.

"You know what I think, fellas?" Gus said. He was looking across her shoulder at the paper.

"What?"

"I think we're getting no place very fast."

Flassy looked shocked. "I can't believe that," he said. "That's impossible. Why should you say a thing like that?"

Lou pointed at the paper. "She's reading the editorials," he said.

Flassy was impressed. "Editorials," he said. He shook his head. "I'll admit it looks bad. Editorials. My God!"

He turned to look out across the benches toward the lake. A small Negro boy of seven or eight was walking idly down the lane toward the water.

"Hey!" Flassy called. "Hey, Joe Louis!"

The small boy turned quickly.

"C'm 'ere, kid," Flassy said. He motioned toward the bench with his hand. "Something I wanna ask you."

The boy came up shyly. He seemed a little frightened, but not much. He was wearing a half-sleeved light-blue jumper that fastened to the top of his short pants with large white buttons. His knees were bare and looked startlingly thin and fragile.

"Yes, suh?" he said timidly.

"You wanna make a nickel?" Flassy asked.

"Yes, suh," the boy said eagerly.

"Find out first he's got working papers," Gus said.

"Flassy wants him only for a small job," Lou said. "For what Flassy wants him, he don't need no working papers."

"That's right," Flassy said. "What I want you for, it'll take a minute. Easiest nickel you ever made, Joe Louis."

"I don't think his name is Joe Louis," Gus said.

The girl rustled the paper as she turned a page.

"Better work fast, Flassy," Lou said. "She's getting impatient."

"A pretty girl like that," Gus said, "she's got a right to be impatient." He leaned toward the girl. "You go ahead and be impatient, Miss. You got a right."

The girl's lip curled slightly as she read through the *Times* obituaries.

"I'm working fast as I can," Flassy said. "This is a delicate situation. Has to be handled with kid gloves. I gotta work through a third party. I gotta work through Joe Louis here."

"I still don't think his name is Joe Louis," Gus said.

"Better get his right name, Flassy," said Lou. "Always get the right name."

Flassy turned back to the small boy. "What's your right name, Joe Louis?"

"Johnson," the boy said.

"Johnson?" Gus said, looking at the sky. "Johnson? Johnson? Johnson? Never heard that name before."

"The first name," Lou said. "Get the first name, Flassy."

"What's your first name, Johnson?"

"Martin, suh," the small boy said.

"Martin Johnson?"

"Yes, suh."

"That's an explorer," Flassy said. "Martin Johnson is an explorer."

"No," Gus said. "He goes to Africa with a camera. He takes pictures."

"But he goes to Africa. No?"

"Sure."

"Then he's an explorer. Anybody goes to Africa, he's an explorer."

"He's no explorer. He's married," said Gus.

"Him, too? Everybody's married. It's the new thing."

"Not Martin Johnson," Lou said. "He got killed in an airplane crash."

"That's right," said Flassy. "My God. First he was married. Now he's dead. My God."

"You gotta work fast here, Flassy."

"That's right." Flassy spoke to the small boy. "Here's what I want you to do, Johnson. You see this very pretty girl here?" He nodded toward the girl beside him, and the small boy looked at her.

"Yes, suh," he said, but the eagerness for the promised nickel was gone from his voice. It sounded troubled and his eyes began to look vaguely frightened again.

"You go up to this here pretty girl," Flassy said, "and you ask her why she don't like us. That's all. Just you say to her, 'Miss, why don't you like these three very handsome gentlemen?' For that you get a nickel. Think you can handle the job, Johnson?"

The small boy mumbled something in a scared voice and began to back away. Flassy's hand shot out and clamped down on the boy's wrist.

"Johnson," he said, "you shock me. You yellow, Johnson?"

"Flassy," Gus said, "you're color-blind. He's not yellow. He's—"

"Quiet," Flassy said. "I'm handling this."

"O.K.," Gus said. "Handle it."

Flassy turned to the boy again and pulled on his arm slowly until he was back where he had been.

"Johnson," he said, "three friends ask you to do them a favor. Three of the best friends you ever had, Johnson. A little thing they ask you to do, and they want to give you a nickel to do it. You going to turn them down, Johnson?"

The terror in the small boy's eyes spread to the rest of his face and to his body. He strained away from Flassy and tried to free his hand, but the hold on his wrist did not relax.

"He's not talking," Lou said.

"He'll talk," Flassy said. He drew the small, frightened boy to him and held him between his knees. Then he lowered his face to look into the boy's eyes. "Johnson," he said, "I am very much annoyed. I am disturbed. I am disappointed. I am all these things. But mostly I am annoyed. The way things are going, Johnson, I may even get sore. I hate to get sore, because it makes my collar wilt. It is not gentlemanly. Johnson, don't make my collar wilt. Now, once more." He held up his forefinger in front of the terrified boy. "You will go up to this very pretty young girl here and you will say, 'Miss, why don't you like these three gentlemen?' That's all. For that you will get a nickel. O.K., Johnson?"

The girl didn't raise her head from the paper, but her eyes were watching the scene. The small Negro boy's chin began to quiver. The girl bit her lip and dropped her eyes to the paper again.

"Johnson isn't talking," Gus said.

"True," Flassy said. "Johnson isn't talking." He sighed and pulled a small leather notebook from his pocket. He flipped it open and held up his hand. "Pencil," he said. Gus took out a pencil and put it into the upraised hand. Flassy lowered the pencil to the notebook. "Johnson," he said, "what are you doing in the park this time of day? Why aren't you in school?"

The small boy scowled and dug his fist into his eye.

"I—I—" he began.

"Too bad, Johnson," Flassy said. "Hooky. I thought so." He sighed again. "You know who I am, Johnson?"

"Tell him, Flassy," Lou said.

"I will," Flassy said. "I'm a truant officer, Johnson."

The small boy started to cry violently. His shoulders shook with his sobs and the tears rolled down his face like water from a dripping faucet. Flassy pushed him a little further away, but still held him clamped between his knees.

"Careful of the suit, Johnson," he said. He dug the pencil into the paper of the notebook. "Martin Johnson," he said as he wrote, "I asked you a simple favor, but you wouldn't do it." He shook his head sadly. "Too bad, Johnson. Now I must report you. What class, Johnson?"

"Two B," the boy said through his tears.

Flassy wrote.

"Teacher's name?" he asked.

"M— M— Miss Goldberg," the boy said, sobbing.

"Miss Goldberg?" Flassy said. He looked up at the other young men. "You hear that? Playing hooky from Miss Goldberg!"

"One of the nicest teachers I ever saw," Gus said.

"Playing hooky from Miss Goldberg," Lou said. "My God!"

Flassy shook his head.

"This is bad, Johnson. Bad." He started to write the name, and stopped. "You got one more chance, Johnson. You talk to this pretty girl here like I asked you, you do what I tell you, I won't report you. What do you say, Johnson?"

The small boy stopped crying for a moment and looked at the girl, sniffing. Then he was off again, blubbering wildly, his thin little body shaking, and hiding his face in the bend of his elbow.

"Tchk! Tchk! Tchk!" Flassy said, beginning to write. "I'm afraid it's curtains, Johnson. This is too—"

Suddenly the girl smacked the *Times* onto her lap angrily.

"Oh, why don't you let the boy alone!" she snapped. "You—you —you great big overgrown—"

The three young men stared at her and then at each other in pleased surprise.

"Say!" Gus said. "She's talking!"

"I told you let me handle this," Flassy said. He swung himself around to face the girl and the pressure of his knees was released. The small boy darted out and began to run. Flassy reached for him quickly, but missed. "C'm 'ere, you dirty little—"

"I'll get him," Gus said.

"Never mind," Flassy said. "We don't need him any more. Let him go. We saved a nickel. We got her talking."

The girl rustled the paper in her lap and glared at him. She was breathing quickly and her lips were pressed thin.

"A poor little kid like that," she said.

"Girlie," Flassy said, "a girl with eyes like yours, you shouldn't never—"

Lou reached over and touched Flassy's knee. He pointed to the clock on the boathouse. "Flassy," he said, "it's late. We better get going. Morris'll be waiting."

All three of them looked at the clock.

"That's right," Flassy said.

He stood up at once and the three of them walked away briskly. They buttoned their tight coats and adjusted their hats as they went, but they did not look back at the girl on the bench.

THE OLD LADY

❧

Thyra Samter Winslow

THE OLD LADY lives with her daughter and her son-in-law, and they really do everything in the world for her. Hardly a day passes that Mrs. Zwill, the Old Lady's daughter, doesn't put herself out for her mother's comfort. Often she is the first to leave a bridge party when there are still nibbles of refreshments, saying, as she smooths her lip rouge with her little finger, "I've got to hurry home! You know how Mamma is! If I don't get home she will be fussing around in the kitchen. There isn't a thing for her to do—Annie is such a good maid—and she hates to have Mamma bothering her."

Mrs. Zwill is good to her mother in other ways, too. She picks out, carefully, her mother's clothes. They aren't the things old Mrs. Schellingheim would pick out for herself, but they are in much better taste, as any of Mrs. Zwill's acquaintances will testify.

"I want Mamma to look modern," she tells them. "Why, if I let her alone she'd buy bonnets! I like her to look up-to-date. It would make me seem a thousand years old to have an old granny-looking woman for a mother. Henry's making enough money so that Mamma can dress well."

Mrs. Zwill likes to have her mother live with her. She often says so. To be sure, sometimes it is a bit embarrassing when she gets people like the Mannenbergs to come to dinner—Phil Mannenberg has such a wonderful position, and the people they go with! Even though it would be more convenient otherwise—her mother has such, well, funny table manners—Mrs. Schellingheim eats right with the family. She never has her dinner in her room the way old Mrs. Plotz does when her family has guests in. Of course, Mrs. Schellingheim makes errors in speech and even tactful joking can't make her quite lose her accent. After all, though, haven't most families got an accent in the family some place, even if sometimes it is a generation in the background?

When Mrs. Schellingheim first came to live with the Zwills a lot of funny old ladies were always coming in and staying for hours. Some of them have died since then, though, and the others gradually got to understand that, while they were welcome and all, being her mother's friends, Mrs. Zwill didn't feel that they exactly fitted in. Besides, they always talked about old times and Mrs. Schellingheim would cry after they went away.

Mrs. Schellingheim had a lot to say about the way the house was run at first, but Mrs. Zwill, though she loved her mother—and said so—had to point out that it was her home. Mrs. Schellingheim doesn't interfere a great deal now.

The thing that Mrs. Zwill can't understand is the way her mother feels about her room. When Pa Schellingheim died, five years ago, the Old Lady was perfectly willing to sell all the furniture excepting the things she had had in her own bedroom and she won't part with those things, now. It seems silly to Mrs. Zwill because it isn't as if the pieces were heirlooms. If they were she could understand. Wouldn't it be wonderful if the Zwills had antiques in the family! But these pieces are of the most hideous period of American furniture, Mrs. Zwill knows, and they were bought, as nearly as Mrs. Zwill can find out, just because Pa Schellingheim started to prosper in business. Why, they haven't even any special memories around them. The furniture is of a peculiarly hideous golden oak and the bed has machine-carved high head- and foot-boards. There is a large and elaborate dresser and one of the chairs is a rocker. If it were only "quaint" Mrs. Zwill could make quite a talking point of it. How delightful if one had a mother who fixed up her room in real last-generation style!

Mrs. Zwill knows a lot about interior decoration. She looks at the model rooms in Wanamaker's and Abraham & Straus, so she knows how rooms ought to look, and sometimes she goes into shops on Madison and Lexington Avenues to see what folks are buying. Her own overstuffed furniture is very elegant—mohair and velours in a two-color combination. Her bridge lamps, with their parchment shades, are quite smart, and she has two sets of curtains —colored organdie for summer and elaborate satin overdrapes for cold weather. A very good decorator—that little Miss Pickens, she is awfully reasonable, you must try her sometime!—came in with samples and Mrs. Zwill chose the curtains with her. Mrs. Zwill has long passed the stage where you go into a department store and buy materials and then make the curtains up at home.

So you can imagine how her mother's room gets on Mrs. Zwill's nerves! If she had her way she would buy delightful things for the Old Lady. She would get her an old-fashioned four-poster bed and a quaint chest of drawers, in maple or mahogany—maple would be sweet!—and some hooked rugs. Mrs. Zwill's own bedroom—which is, in a way, shared by Mr. Zwill—is in Circassian walnut with elegant twin-bed coverings and overdrapes of changeable taffeta—in winter. On the glass-covered dressing table there is a great profusion of toilet articles—things that are advertised in the smart magazines and that Mrs. Zwill believes enable her to keep young-looking —none of "the girls" ever guess her to be within five years of her age.

Usually, Mrs. Schellingheim's room doesn't worry Mrs. Zwill, though she is glad that Mr. Zwill can afford to give his mother-in-law her own room and bath. "A complete little suite, my dear! So much more convenient!" Still, Mrs. Zwill is rather embarrassed sometimes when she shows her apartment to new friends.

There is the kitchen with its electric refrigerator, all of the little cubes of ice so busily freezing themselves; Mr. Zwill's newest radio that can get almost any distance after midnight in cold weather, though it's so hard to get distance on the usual radio in a steel-constructed apartment building; the bookcase with some of the very best sets behind its glass doors; the grand piano with the electric player; the newest thing in smoking stands. When they get to Mrs. Schellingheim's room Mrs. Zwill always has to make explanations.

"You know how old people are," she says. "I have just begged Mamma to let me do her room over for her for Christmas but she just *clings* to her old things! It's such a big, sunny room, too—the sun comes in all morning just as if it weren't on a court at all.

When, that is, I mean, if—if anything should ever happen to Mamma, I'm going to do her room over as a guest room. I'll use either maple or some of that new enamelled furniture. Still, I want you to see the room. No, she won't mind your coming in, but you'll have to speak kind of loud—she doesn't hear very well."

A MATTER OF PRIDE

❦

CHRISTOPHER LA FARGE

ON THE EIGHTH OF APRIL, Joe Wilson realized that the next Monday was the fifteenth. He called up Eddie Frissell and made the date with him; they had fished together on the first day of the season for eight consecutive years—in fact, ever since Joe Wilson had become an officer in the bank and could take a day off now and then. During the two-hours-for-lunch period, he studied the map of Rhode Island rivers and ponds that the Fish and Game Club got out annually. It annoyed him to see that this year even more of Deer River was marked in the blue that indicated posted water. That damn syndicate had got hold of more river, he thought. But there was still the state land, even though the syndicate owned and stocked the river above and below the state's short strip. What was more, he and Eddie had always fished the whole of Deer River and they'd go right on doing so.

He was happy when he got home, and he went straight upstairs to the big bedroom and found his wife there, busy at her desk.

"Hi-yo," he said. She pushed her glasses up onto her forehead as he kissed her. "Listen, Fairlie, I don't want to get our wires crossed. I've made a date with Eddie to go fishing next Monday. It's the opening, so put that down in your book, will you?"

She looked at her engagement pad. "Oh, Joe! But that's the night we dine with the Medfords, darling."

"Damn!" he said. "I knew there'd be a snag. Have you accepted already?"

"Yes," she said, "of course."

"What do you mean 'of course'?" he said. "Why the devil can't you ask me about it, eh? Then I'd have told you to keep the fifteenth clear."

"You mean you'd have refused the Medfords' invitation?"

"Sure I'd have refused. I've fished with Eddie Frissell on the opening for nearly ten years. You know that."

"And for how many years, sweet, have the Medfords invited us to dine?"

He shrugged his shoulders and walked over to the chaise longue, threw off five of the lace-covered cushions, and sat down. "What the hell?" he said. "Call them up and say I can't make it, have to be in New York or something."

"Darling!" she said. "You're not serious?"

"Sure I am." His voice lacked conviction.

"But they might not ask us a second time. We can't refuse! It would be criminal," she said, "if only for yourself and the bank. The biggest people in Providence, the greatest power in—"

"Oh, hell," he said, "you don't have to tell me about the Medfords."

"And for Hilda next summer, with their Ellen at Matunuck. For Chester, with their Frank at day camp, and he's just ten, too. And I'm not saying a word about myself."

"All right!" he said. "When do they eat?"

"At eight-thirty."

"Suppose I'll have to dress, too," he said.

"Naturally," she said. "Black tie."

"Where do you get this 'black tie' stuff?" he asked. "It's been a tuxedo to me ever since I owned one."

"A tuxedo, then," she said, and smiled. "You look *so* well in one, Joe."

"Nuts," he said. "Eight-thirty? I suppose we can fish and get back, though it'll mean quitting early."

"That's a dear," she said. "And don't fish Deer River, darling."

"For God's sake!" he said, jumping to his feet. "Are you to tell me where to fish as well as where to eat and what to wear?"

"Ah, darling!" she said, and came over to him. "Don't be so touchy. Here you are, young, good-looking, successful—we have some money now. Everyone envies you. Don't be cross with me when I try to help you."

"But what is all this about Deer River?"

"Why, sweet, it's because Mr. Medford—I just heard it at that lunch the other day—is head of the syndicate that owns the water, and I know if you'll be willing to wait and talk to him about fishing, he'll ask you to fish there."

"I don't suck up to anyone for anything!" For a moment he felt fighting mad, but that passed, and he thought, She's a clever woman, she is. He laughed and said, "I'll be here on Monday night at eight-fifteen, dressed like a waiter, and ready to go out."

"But not Deer River, Joe?"

"I've never got into trouble yet, have I?" he said. "I'll fish where I please."

He picked up Eddie Frissell at six-thirty, and they had breakfast in Cottrellton. Then they drove out the West Highway to the Carpenter farm and turned north on the dirt road. While he drove, Joe told Eddie about his dinner date with the Medfords. He wasn't bragging, just telling of it. When they got past the State Experimental Fields, they turned into the laurels and parked the car in a place they knew. It was a fine place, hidden from anyone but a most careful searcher. They were pretty quiet then, and talked in whispers. Both of them felt the undercurrent of their excitement.

Joe got rigged first. He slung his creel over his shoulder, hung his bait box to the strap of it, and watched Eddie.

"What you using, Ed," he said, "flies?"

"Yeah, I thought I'd try them."

"You're going fancy on me," said Joe. "You'll catch nothing but trees."

"Oh, I don't know," said Eddie. "I can always change back to good old ground hackle if I don't do so good." He had a bait box too, and he fastened it to a loop on his jacket.

"Let's begin in the maples," Joe said. "Then we can see if there's anyone moving."

Eddie nodded and they walked away from the car, following a narrow trail that wound down through the laurels. They came out suddenly on a maple swamp with the river beyond.

"What makes me sore," said Eddie softly, "is that did you ever notice they don't clear a path at all opposite this state land?"

"Yes," Joe said. They made slow progress through the heavy undergrowth of the swamp and stood to breathe on the bank of the stream. The water was high, Joe saw, and browner than he'd expected. "Let's go," he said. "You won't do good with flies in this water." He put a worm on his hook, added a tiny split-shot sinker to the gut, and stepped into the water. It was flowing deep and strong and cold. The feel of it against his legs through the boots made him happy.

They had begun at the upper end of the state's maple swamp, and they fished to the lower end. Joe caught two trout, and though one of them was only six inches, he couldn't put it back, it was so deeply hooked. He cached it in moss by the bank and broke a twig near it: no use asking for trouble. Eddie caught nothing. They stood at the edge of the swamp and surveyed the still reach beyond, shining under the sun. On each of the last two maples that overhung the stream was a large, new white poster. They could see no one and hear nothing but the rush of the water.

"Well?" said Joe.

"Let's go," said Eddie. He had changed his fly to a bait hook and on it wriggled a pink worm.

They fished silently down the reach. At the pool in the bend, where the river widened before turning east, they both got fast two fine, fat trout, and after a short fight landed them. Both Joe and Eddie were so engrossed that they didn't see the man who was standing on the bank watching them until he said, "Good morning. Worm-fishing?"

"Hello," said Joe. Eddie said nothing.

"I'll have to see your licences," the man said.

"Who are you?" said Joe.

"The guardian here," said the man. "I'm deputy warden, too." He showed his badge on his waistcoat. "This land is posted." He pointed to a large sign that was nailed to a rail just at the bend.

"Oh," said Joe. "Well, I'll be damned! I certainly never noticed the poster. Thought we were on state land."

"Is that so?" said the man. "Two posters on the maples where you came from, two on this reach above you, one here. I'll see your licences, please."

They produced the licences. The man took a pencil and a black notebook from his hip pocket and copied from the licences, industriously.

At last he handed them back. "I'll take the fish now."

"What happens from all this?" asked Eddie.

"Summons," said the man. "Be about Friday, at Chog's Cove Courthouse. Five dollars and costs, usually."

"Suppose we paid you the costs and fine now?" said Eddie. "Say twenty dollars. Save us all a lot of headache."

The man smiled. "Mr. Medford, he pays me all I get," he said. "Let's have them fish, please."

Eddie nudged Joe. "Tell him," he said. Joe shook his head. They handed their fish over. "This one I caught in the maples," said Joe.

"O.K.," said the man, and he handed it back to him. Joe returned it to his creel.

"I suppose you got to tell Medford about this?" asked Joe.

"Oh, surely," said the man. "Upstream, please. One hundred feet north of the two posted maples is the stone marker for the state land. Quarter mile north of that is the north bound, where an oak has fell across into them two willows on the west bank. The oak has a poster onto it. You can't miss it. Good day." He stepped back into the blueberries and disappeared. They stood silent for a minute or two.

"Well," said Eddie. "Why in hell didn't you tell him you knew Medford?"

"Nix," said Joe. He turned and waded noisily upstream. The day was ruined. They fished the state water, but got nothing. They left and fished the open water of Otter River, but they got nothing there. There were five other men fishing it, too. By the time they started back to Providence at four o'clock, Joe remembered he'd left the undersized fish by the bank. Well, he thought, it was lucky I didn't have it on me.

When they got into town, he stayed on drinking rye at Eddie's house till eight and then rushed home and dressed in a hurry, giving Fairlie hardly a chance to say more than "Hello" to him. On the way to the Medfords' he maintained a silence that defeated her. The excellent dinner, all the good wines to drink, were a nightmare to him. His neck felt hot and he couldn't think what to do. God, what Fairlie would say when she heard! After dinner was worse, for the eight men of the party forgathered for hours in the library and smoked and drank there. All the talk was of fishing, and mostly of Deer River. When Mr. Medford got up to join the ladies, Joe rose too, and as he did so came to an immediate decision. He went over to Mr. Medford and touched his arm.

"Well, Mr. Wilson?" said Medford, smiling.

"Look here," Joe said. "I ought to have done this sooner. I want to ask you a great favor."

"Why, surely," said Medford. "What can I do?"

"It's about Deer River and fishing." Joe could see his host's face freeze up.

"Of which, of course, I'm only a part owner," said Medford.

"Yes," Joe said. "It's not what you think. I fished on your water today and I got caught."

"Oh!" Medford looked Joe up and down. Then he smiled and patted Joe on the shoulder. "Cranston's a smart guardian," he said. "But don't worry, Wilson. We all make mistakes. I'll stop the summons."

"No, that's not what I meant. I did it on purpose. The favor I want of you is just not to do anything about it."

"I'll telephone Cranston tomorrow," Medford said.

"I don't want the summons stopped," Joe said. "I'll feel better that way. I don't want it to be called off just because your wife asked my wife to dinner. Do you see?"

"Nonsense," said Medford. "Fish any time you want to. Of course I'll stop Cranston. Fellow-banker and all that sort of rubbish."

"Please," Joe said. "Let it ride as it is."

"Nonsense, my dear fellow. We're keeping the ladies on pins and needles for our brilliant society. Come along, gentlemen." Medford led the way into the long drawing room.

"Jesus!" said Joe to himself, and his neck burned hotter than ever. It seemed to him as if the party would never break up.

On the way home in the car, Fairlie turned to Joe and said, "Oh, you *are* wonderful! You kick and you kick and you go out to dinner and then you shine there!"

"What do you mean, shine?"

"You know what Mr. Medford said to me about you?"

"No," said Joe.

"He said, 'That's an unusual husband you have, Mrs. Wilson. I like him. I hope he'll come and fish with me soon.' What did I tell you, darling?"

"The old bastard."

"Why, *Joe!*" she cried. "How can you say that?"

"He doesn't give a god damn for the other fellow," said Joe, "that's why."

"What are you talking about?" said Fairlie.

"Nothing," he said. "It's O.K. Medford is O.K. Deer River is O.K. Trout are double O.K. But little Joe is hot in the neck." He patted her knee. "Forget it. It's just a matter of pride, it don't mean a damn thing."

LOVE IN THE SNOW

❧

JOEL SAYRE

PETER AND JANEY were both thirteen, although Janey's birthday was in October, and she was two months and eight days older. They had been in love nine days now, ever since that time they had ridden back with the other kids in the station wagon from the skating races. It was a good hour's ride back to the hotel, and, to pass the time away, Bill Preston, who was a fresh kid from Atlanta, said that everybody should tell the name of the person he was in love with.

He said he wasn't afraid to start it off, and he mentioned some girl, a Julia somebody, "down home," that nobody ever heard of. Betty Edwards was sitting next to him and he asked her. She said she was in love with Gary Cooper, and when everybody laughed she got sore and said, no, seriously, she *was* in love with him, and if she didn't see a new picture of his pretty soon she would just die. She said she had written to him and he had sent her a photograph of himself which she had framed. She carried it wherever she went, she said, and used to put it under her pillow at night and dream about him. Nobody paid any attention to her, though: she was just a kid. George Bush got very embarrassed, and, although they teased and coaxed him a long time, he kept insisting that he didn't have any girl and finally got sore and told Bill Preston to shut up before he got a rap on the jaw. Arthur Friend said he was crazy about a girl, a Rosemary that nobody ever heard of, and Peter suspected that he had made up the name. Everybody was laughing pretty hysterically by this time and yelling a lot. Once or twice the driver turned around and looked at them.

Peter felt the same funny, excited feeling in the pit of his stomach he had felt when he first became conscious of ladies' legs at a matinée of "Smiles" he had attended with his mother during the previous Thanksgiving vacation. It would be his turn to answer in a minute, and although he couldn't think of anybody he was in love with, he felt his heart pounding and a strange, swallowy feeling in his throat.

They were all asking Janey. Janey's father was the manager of the hotel. She had yellow hair and green eyes and white eyelashes.

She sat for a long time with her elbows on her knees and her chin in her hands and looked at the canvas curtain on the side of the station wagon before she answered. Finally, she said, "I guess I love Peter." Her face was very serious and she lowered her eyes to the floor.

Peter was surprised, although not so surprised when he thought about it later. That Christmas vacation was the first time he and his father and mother had spent in the Adirondacks. He met Janey the day they arrived, and she asked him if he played ping-pong. When he told her he did, she said there was a senior and junior tournament every year and they gave silver cups for the championship. He asked her who won the junior championship last year, and she said she had. A couple of days later he played her in the Casino and beat her three straight sets. After he took the last set point he said: "Sorry." He didn't know why he said it, but it seemed kind of a shame to trim a girl the first time you played her, especially as she had won the junior championship last year. Janey's older sister was standing by watching them, and while Peter was chasing a ball that Janey had knocked under a chair for one set point, he heard Janey's sister say to her friends, "I think they're just the cutest things together. When he beat her he apologized." Peter felt like a fool when he heard Janey's sister talking that way, and he went right to his room and got his skates and practiced racing starts all by himself until dinner time.

All the other kids were yelling at him to tell who his girl was, so he said Janey was. She was sitting across from him, and when he said it she stretched out her hand and he took it and they shook hands. Janey was still looking down at the floor and trying to keep a straight face. Peter felt very silly, and when the station wagon pulled up at the hotel a few minutes later, he jumped out and started firing snowballs at Bill Preston and Arthur Friend until he drove them indoors. But after that he prowled around the huge barn of a hotel, full of the delicious expectancy of suddenly encountering her.

Every week night there was a dance at the Casino, and he danced most of the dances with her: she was just about his height and he couldn't dance with little girls so well. He liked one-steps particularly, as he could take long strides and step out, and she was the only girl who could step out with him. One afternoon in the Casino, when they were all alone, she put "The Peanut Vendor" on the little portable Victrola that was there and taught him the rumba; and that night when the orchestra played "The Peanut Vendor" they did the rumba on the floor right before everybody. Peter insisted on waiting until some other couples started first, but after he and Janey got going the few other couples dropped out and it became practically an exhibition dance. When Peter noticed they were all alone he wanted to stop too, but Janey squeezed his hand and held him tighter around the neck and made him finish it out. She kept whispering to him what to do next whenever he got panicky. When the music stopped, everybody applauded, and Peter felt very embarrassed, but he couldn't help shaking all over with silent laughter, just like the time he saw his sister going up the aisle to get married.

For Christmas he gave Janey a thermometer mounted on a varnished board. On each side of the thermometer were painted fir trees and underneath it said, "Souvenir of Lake Placid." He bought it at the hotel cigarstand for a dollar. Janey gave him a blue muffler which she had knitted secretly in four days. When she gave it to him she said she wished she had had more time to work on it.

Janey invented a whistle so they could call to each other when they were wandering around the hotel, or whenever one wanted to draw the other away from a crowd to say something. The whistle was the same as the beginning of "The Star-Spangled Banner," the part that goes, "Oh, say, can you see," only in fast time. Nearly every morning Janey, who was an early riser, used to whistle it under Peter's window, and he would get out of bed and go to the window in his pajamas and whistle it back and wave to her. One morning the whistling woke his father, who wanted to know who the hell was making that god-damned noise, and Peter said it was just one of the kids. After that he got up earlier and whistled under Janey's window. She wore pajamas, too.

As soon as she was dressed they would go down to the lake with their skates. Peter dug up a couple of hockey sticks, one a goalie's, and a puck; and they set up two bricks for a goal and practiced shots. Janey got to be a pretty good goalie for a girl, although Peter never sent them in at her with any real steam as she didn't have any belly protector or shin guards or even gloves, only her mittens, to stop his shots with. But she was a good skater, and actually learned to poke-check a little. When they had practiced about an hour they would go in to breakfast.

Peter was leaving for New York on New Year's Day, as his father had to be at his office on the second, and Peter himself had a dentist appointment.

On the last day of the year he rose early and whistled under Janey's window, and she came down with her skates. When they got to the lake she started to walk over to the place under the Casino where they cached their sticks and puck and the two bricks, but Peter said, "Let's just skate this morning."

"All right," said Janey, "let's skate way out. Let's skate over to the island."

So they skated over to the island, which was about half a mile out in the lake. There was plenty of sun and almost no wind, and the ice was just the least bit soft. They held hands and skated together for a while, and then Peter let go and started to sprint. Janey tried to keep up with him, but he soon left her behind, and then he turned around and started to sprint back to her. He put on the brakes when he was about five yards away and drew up to her with his body on an angle. His skates left a long, wide slash on the beautiful clear ice. He came to a stop with a neat turn and a pirouette.

"You're a regular Charlie Jewtraw, aren't you?" laughed Janey.

They were within a hundred yards of the island.

"Come on," said Peter, "I'll give you a head start and beat you to the island."

"All right," said Janey, starting off, "but give me a decent start, now."

He watched her blue skirt wagging and her gray stockings twinkle until she was about twenty yards ahead of him. Then he dug in and started after her. They finished in a dead heat at the island's edge and fell at full length in the snow, laughing and panting.

After a while, Janey got up on her knees. Peter was still lying prone with his face in his folded arms. Janey picked up a twig and began to tickle his ear with it. "Hey, cut that out!" he shouted, laughing and twisting his head from side to side to dodge the twig. He peeked up at Janey. Her face was shining and she was grinning as she teased and tickled him. Peter could feel his heart pounding as he lay there, and there was that strange swallowy feeling in his throat.

Suddenly he arose to his knees and looked at his wristwatch.

"Gosh," he said, "it's ten after eight. We ought to be starting back."

Janey rose and they skated back to the hotel without saying anything. Peter's mother was standing on the front porch with her fur coat drawn around her when they reached the hotel. Peter could tell right off that she was mad. They took off their skates as fast as they could and put on their shoes.

"Your mother's looking for you, Janey," Peter's mother said. Janey said thank you and went into the hotel.

"Peter, I don't want you to go around with Janey any more," said Peter's mother when Janey had gone. She drew her coat more closely around her. "People are beginning to talk about it. She's the manager's daughter, you know, and they're Catholics. Her mother used to be the linen-woman here before she was married, I understand. Besides, Janey's funny-looking. There are plenty of nice children here for you to play with."

Peter looked down at the floor. "Aw, heck," was all he said. His mother led the way in to breakfast. His father was already eating buckwheat cakes and little pig sausages when they got to the table. He looked at Peter's face.

"Whassamatta wif 'ittle Petah?" he said. "Izzum sad becozzum's donna leave his 'ittle Janeywaney tomowwow? Izzum?"

"Stop it, George," said Peter's mother. She turned to the

waitress. "I'd like grapefruit. Will you have a grapefruit, Peter darling?"

Peter spent the rest of the day in his room reading. Several times he heard the "Oh, say, can you see" whistle under his window, but he didn't answer. That night at the New Year's Eve party in the Casino he avoided Janey and danced with all the other girls. When the orchestra played the "Peanut" rumba he went out on the balcony. He looked at the lake shining through the dark. He saw somebody walking in the snow on the dock. It was Janey in her white dress, walking with her head bent down. She had a shawl around her shoulders. She walked to the end of the dock, and then turned around and walked back. Peter watched her a while. He felt very badly and wanted to whistle, but didn't. The "Peanut" rumba ended, and he went back inside.

A week later while he was packing to go back to school, his mother came into his room and handed him a post card. She handed it to him without saying anything and then walked out of the room. The post card had a picture of several very big and very red roses on it. On the back it said:

DEAR PETER:
I don't know why you are mad at me. Did I do something to make you mad? If I did I am very sorry. You know I like you very much. I dreamed about you last night.
Your friend always,
JANE GEOGHEHAN

P. S. Address after next week St. Mary of the Springs Convent, St. Mary's, Ohio.

Peter heard someone coming. He tore up the post card and put the pieces in his pocket.

PROFESSION: HOUSEWIFE

❦

SALLY BENSON

ALTHOUGH THE WINDOW by the breakfast nook was open, it was
very warm. The yellow-and-white gingham curtains hung
still and the blue oilcoth tiebacks showed beads of moisture. Even
the painted table top felt damp and sticky, and Joe Grannis was
conscious of the discomfort of the hard bench on which he sat. He
heard Dorothy tear open the letter and, leaning back as far as he
could, he shook out his paper and held it before his face.

In a few minutes she slapped the letter down on the table so
hard that the coffee in her cup spilled over into the saucer. "I
might have known," she said. "They can't come. At least, she *says*
they can't come."

Although it was what he had expected, Joe Grannis lowered his
paper and managed to looked surprised. "That's funny," he answered. "Maybe some other time."

"Some other time," his wife repeated. "Don't be dumb. The
point is they don't want to come, now or any other time."

"I wouldn't say that," he said. "There's no reason why they
shouldn't want to come."

Dorothy Grannis lifted her saucer and poured the coffee that had
spilled back into the cup. Her face, normally a solid pink, had
turned a bright cerise and her hair lay against her forehead with
the metallic fixity of a doll's wig. "I'm sorry I asked them in the
first place," she told him.

Joe Grannis made a mistake. "Well, you can't say I didn't warn
you," he said. "You can't expect to make friends with people who
were friends of Louise's. Those things never work out. People feel
funny, sort of."

She pushed the sleeves of her chintz house coat further up on her arms with a hard, deliberate gesture and rested her elbows on the table. "Why?" she asked. "From the way you used to talk, I got the impression they were friends of yours. I got the impression that they didn't think so much of *Louise*, that you were the fair-haired boy with them. I got the impression that they couldn't wait until the divorce and everything was over so they could come here again."

She looked around the bright, shiny kitchen and laughed. "My God!" she went on. "If they saw this place now it might be too much for them. They might drop dead. Digging this place out was like excavating. It might be too much for them to see it clean for a change."

Joe Grannis took his watch from his pocket and looked at it. He edged from behind the table and stood up. "Time to go," he said.

"I suppose so," she told him. "You never know the answers to anything. Well, what are we going to do tonight? Sit here and listen to the radio?"

"Now, don't be sarcastic," he answered. "You've got friends of your own. Why don't you call Ruth and Van up and ask them out?"

"And have them wondering why nobody else ever drops in?" she asked indignantly. "That was all right at first. They didn't think anything of it the first few times. But the last time she acted plenty funny about it. Wanting to know if I didn't get lonesome here all day and everything. I'd rather rot."

He looked at her and his face grew set. "Suit yourself," he said. "And since you're speaking of impressions, I got some myself. I got the impression that all you needed to make you happy was a home of your own and to be able to quit work. God knows you sang that tune long enough. Three years, wasn't it? Well, you got what you wanted. You've spent money like a drunken sailor on this place and if you can't make friends for yourself, I can't help you."

"Well, really!" she exclaimed, her voice politely formal. "Really!"

She remained seated at the table until she heard the front door slam behind him, and then she got up and with brisk, efficient movements carried the breakfast dishes to the sink. The sink was of glaring yellow porcelain and the faucets were shiny and new.

The hot water on her hands made her feel warmer and she pulled down the zipper of her house coat. Her grasp on the dishes was rough, but she arranged them almost gently in the wire rack to drain.

Pretty soon now the girls would come straggling into the office where she used to work, cool and neat in their new summer dresses. Because the day was warm, the atmosphere about the place would relax and Mannie, the office boy, would be sent to the drug-store for double cokes. There would be gossip and cigarettes in the washroom and speculation as to whether Mr. Ackerman would leave early for a round of golf.

She opened the drawer of the kitchen cabinet and took out a towel, yellow, with blue featherstitching, and dried the dishes hurriedly. Glancing at the clock and seeing that it was not yet nine, she tried to slow her movements. She wiped the breakfast table with a damp cloth and put away the oilcloth doilies.

The dining room was cool and bare. In the centre of the shiny mahogany table was placed an etched silver bowl around which huddled four thin silver candlesticks. Going to the sideboard, she opened the drawers one by one, looking with satisfaction at the rows of silver-plated knives, forks, and spoons lying on their squares of felt. In each drawer was a lump of camphor to prevent tarnishing.

The stairs led out of the dining room and she walked up them to the upstairs hall. Four doors opened out into the hall, but only two of them stood ajar—the door to the bathroom and the one to their bedroom. She liked to keep the extra bedrooms shut off until she felt she could do them over decently. There was little disorder in their own room. Joe's striped silk pajamas lay folded on his bed and her pale-green satin nightgown lay on a chair by the window. She hung these in the closet and then spread the beds, fitting their lavender taffeta covers smoothly.

As she finished, the front-door bell rang briefly, and looking out the window, she saw a man standing there, a leather briefcase un-der his arm. She loosened her hair slightly about her face and pulled the zipper up on her house coat.

The man who stood at the door was very young and very thin. His light-gray suit was shabby and the coat hung limply from his shoulders. He wore no hat and his fine, light hair was too long and fell untidily over his forehead. He had been looking down when she opened the door, his whole figure drooping, but hearing the sound of the latch, he straightened up to face her, jerking his head up alertly, smiling pleasantly.

"Good morning, Madam," he said.

She stood looking at him for so long without speaking that he shifted his feet in embarrassment, the smile growing fixed on his face.

"Yes?" she asked finally. "Yes?"

He took the briefcase from under his arm, and after struggling with the catch, opened it and drew forth a book, which he held toward her. Its bright, flowered cover looked worn and dirty, as though it had been often handled. She made no motion to take it from him, but he stood bravely facing her, the book in his hand.

"I'm not interested in buying any books," she told him. "Nor anything else."

The young man laughed brightly. "This book, Madam," he said, "is not for sale. It is a gift to you from the company I represent."

"Yes, I know," she answered. "A gift if I subscribed to what?"

The young man lowered his arm, slightly abashed.

"Well?" she asked, raising her eyebrows and putting her head to one side. "Am I right?"

The young man gave another slight laugh. "I can see that you've learned, Madam, that we don't get anything in this world for nothing. A lot of people haven't learned that, and I guess you must be cleverer than average." For a minute he combed his mind to gather up the first rules of salesmanship, which lay scattered there. Then he went on with more assurance. "No, this book is not exactly free, and yet it is free in the sense that you will not actually be paying for this book. What you will be paying for is a three-year subscription to *Good Homes Magazine*. And you will be paying the exact price you would pay if you went to your local dealer. But by taking a subscription now from me, you also will receive this book of five hundred tested recipes, how to set your table for any occasion, and other helpful household hints. So, you see, in a manner of speaking, this book *is* absolutely free. And what is more, Madam, you are permitted to take it now, look it over, and return it to me if you decide you do not care to take a subscription to *Good Homes*."

He smiled triumphantly at her. "Could anything be fairer than that?"

Mrs. Grannis had heard his speech coldly, but now suddenly she opened the door wider and extended her hand for the book. "How long can I keep it before I decide?" she asked.

"For five days, Madam," he told her. Then he dropped his professional manner, and his voice changed. "To tell you the truth, we are supposed to leave them five days. And that's all right for guys that have a car and can come back for them. But I got to figure differently. It's like this—I go to one of these suburbs and spend a day there. I leave a book, if that's what the lady of the house wants, and then I stop by later in the day and pick it up. You see, we're responsible for the books we hand out, and if you don't take a subscription you can't keep the book. The company couldn't afford it. Why, those books cost three dollars to buy."

She stepped back and laid the book on the hall table. "I see," she said. "Well, I'll let you know."

There was something in her gesture that caused the young man to clear his throat anxiously before he spoke again. "May I ask what time will be most convenient for you?"

"Oh, any time," she answered. "I'll be in, all right."

His face cleared. "Well, let's see," he said. "It isn't ten yet and I'll come back about three. That'll give me plenty of time to cover this neighborhood, come back and write out your subscription, and grab a train back to New York. Now, don't think I am too confident, Madam, but I can safely say it will be worth your while to retain the book *plus* receiving *Good Homes* for three entire years."

He refastened the catch of his briefcase and tucked it under his arm. There was a dark spot where the moisture from his hand had stained the leather. He felt very thirsty and wondered if he dared ask for a drink of water. But the lady acted strange. To be sure, she had taken the book, but you never could tell how people were going to act if you asked for a favor. She might think he was trying to get fresh.

So with the sun beating on his head, he stepped back from the door, smiling. "Good day, Madam," he said. "I will be back later."

Halfway down the path, he turned and called to her. "You're the first lady that's taken a book today. It must be good luck or something."

Mrs. Grannis closed the door and walked into the living room. The glare of the sun hurt her eyes and she lowered the shades. Even then, because of the newness of the light, shiny maple furniture, the room had a sort of glint. She lay down on the couch and closed her eyes, trying to decide whether or not to put on her things and run in to see the girls at the office. She could tell them about the house, she thought, and might even ask them out to see it sometime, although she had almost decided to drop them gradually. Still, you had to see somebody, and with Joe's friends acting the way they did, there didn't seem to be much to look forward to in that direction. The dimness of the room soothed her and she fell asleep.

It was after twelve when she woke up, and her head felt stuffy. She made herself a glass of iced tea, heavily sugared, and toasted a cheese sandwich on the electric grill. Then she dressed leisurely and started for the centre of the village. It was almost three when she arrived back home, her hair freshly washed and waved, her face flushed from sitting under the drier. Remembering the young man, she glanced anxiously up and down the street, but he was not in sight. Upstairs, she took off her street things and slipped once more into her house coat. Then, carefully turning back the taffeta spread from her bed, she lay down and lit a cigarette. She heard the bell ring in the kitchen and, propping herself up on one elbow, she peered cautiously out the window. On the steps below stood the young man, who had come for his book. His clothes were even limper than they had been in the morning and he leaned against the side of the door ready to spring into alert attention at the sound of footsteps. She let the curtain drop and lay back on the bed, smoking and staring at the ceiling. The bell rang again, and then, after a few minutes, more urgently.

For a long while she lay there listening to the bell and then she got up and walked silently down the stairs. She picked up the book from the hall table and carried it back to her room. In a few minutes she heard steps once more on the outside walk and the bell began, persistently now. She sat up on the edge of the bed and, taking the book, deliberately and slowly ripped the pages out. When they all lay scattered on the bed beside her, she began tearing them across. With some difficulty she bent the cover. Then, gathering the pieces together, she went to the window and opened it.

The young man looked up at her and the expression on his face changed. He began to smile. "Wake you up?" he asked pleasantly.

She fumbled with the screen and slowly let the torn pages of the book fall to the grass below.

For a minute the young man stared at them, dazed. Without a word he stooped to pick them up, but realizing the hopelessness of his task, he straightened and stood staring up at the window. For a dreadful moment they looked at one another. Then he turned and walked away.

She fastened the screen, lit a cigarette, and lay down again on the bed, smoking and staring at the ceiling.

THE GREAT MANTA

❧

EDWIN CORLE

M R. GAGUS HAD A JOB. It was a good job, too. He said so and his wife said so. They were both very happy. Mr. and Mrs. Gagus lived in Brooklyn, almost as far out as New Lots, but not quite. They used the Van Sicklen Avenue subway station.

One of the best things about the job was that Mr. Gagus didn't have to be at work until ten o'clock in the morning. Of course that meant he got home late at night, but even so, it was pretty nice to be able to start the business day at ten. There was something aristocratic about it. It gave him an air.

But in spite of that fact, Mr. Gagus had to get up at 7:30 every morning. It took him an hour to shave and dress and eat his breakfast. While he did these things, Mrs. Gagus packed his lunch. Occasionally in this interval he had time to glance at a newspaper, but usually he reserved that for his subway ride.

At 8:30, he left his tiny flat and walked along Livonia Avenue to the subway entrance. At 8:38, he boarded a Broadway-Seventh Avenue express. Then occurred his customary perusal of the affairs of the world at large, which lasted until 9:27, when he arrived at the Times Square subway station. Here he changed to a Broadway-Seventh Avenue local, and at 9:30 he left it at the Fiftieth Street subway station, where he ascended to the street. Eastward on Fiftieth Street he walked to Sixth Avenue and his establishment of business, arriving there more often than not (provided, of course, that the weather was fair) at 9:35. In bad weather, he might be as late as 9:38, but certainly never any later than that.

The first thing he did when he reached his place of business was to take off his suit and shirt and collar, tie, and shoes. These he placed in a locker. Then he put on a pair of trousers that resem-

bled riding pants, but were not. They were marvellous trousers—
a nice light blue with red stripes running down the sides. On his
feet, he put a pair of black leather boots, and into the tops of the
boots he tucked the legs of the trousers. Over his head he slipped
a plain shirt of the type usually known as a sweatshirt. Over this
he placed a white waistcoat with gold braid adorning its visible
parts. Adjusting these garments with the skill of familiarity, he
then took from a hanger a heavy coat with a cutaway tail. This
coat was blue with red-and-white decorations, and the entire lining was a brilliant red. There were golden epaulets on the shoulders and several medals on the breast and a stiff brocade collar that
fitted tightly under the chin. With the coat resting correctly on his
back and shoulders and showing just the proper amount of waistcoat and none of the sweatshirt, he placed on his head a hat. This
hat was all of a foot in height and was faced with black fur,
adorned with a red plume and a gold band and a gold tassel. It
was held in place by a strap under the chin and gave him an appearance of tremendous height and imperious dignity. He took a
last look of self-inspection as he pulled a pair of white gloves onto
his hands. It was 9:57. And, dressed as a captain of the Grenadier
Guards of the First Empire, Mr. Gagus of Brooklyn, and doorman
of the Greatest Picture Palace in the World, was ready to go to
work. He would close the locker containing his own clothes, walk
out of the building, and appear before it on the street at ten
o'clock, on the job.

There wasn't much for him to do the first hour but look important and impressive and keep beggars away from the foyer. An occasional taxicab or private car would drive up and he would open
the door, and close it after the occupant or occupants had got out.
But by eleven o'clock the automobiles arrived with more fre-
quency, and from then until two o'clock he was kept pretty well
concentrated on the business of opening and closing automobile
doors.

At two o'clock, after four hours on duty, he was relieved by Mr.
Parkinson, whom he addressed below in the locker room as Otto,
but who, in public, was a captain of the Grenadier Guards, like
himself. Mr. Gagus, turning over his duties to Mr. Parkinson,
then retired to the locker room preparatory to eating his lunch—

sandwiches, an apple, cheese, sweet chocolate, and coffee kept hot in a small thermos bottle. Before he could eat, he had first to remove his white gloves, his high fur hat, his dignified and decorated coat, and his gold-braided waistcoat. The trousers and the boots he was allowed to leave on if he were careful not to soil or scuff them, but if he wished to appear on the street, he had to change completely back to his own clothes. As this was a great nuisance and as he had no desire to walk anywhere after four hours on his feet, he almost invariably spent his relief period in his undress uniform. He ate and read and dozed, and sometimes he just sat.

At 6 P.M. Mr. Gagus, again attired in full regalia, relieved Mr. Parkinson. By 9 P.M. things began to get a little easier. Fewer and fewer automobiles arrived, though he was occasionally obliged to summon taxicabs for departing patrons. At 10 P.M., he had reached the end of his day's work.

Again he descended to the locker room, and again he took off the white gloves, the high fur hat, the dignified and decorated coat, the gold-braided waistcoat, and this time the plain sweatshirt, the black leather boots, and the red-striped trousers. All of these he placed in the locker in exchange for his own unimpressive clothes, and by 10:22 he was ready to walk west on Fiftieth Street. At 10:28, he entered the Fiftieth Street subway station. At 10:31, he transferred to an express at Times Square. At 11:20, he arrived at the Van Sicklen Avenue subway station in Brooklyn. At 11:28, he unlocked the front door of his apartment building. At 11:29, he entered his tiny flat. At 11:35, he drank a cup of coffee and followed it with a supper of stew or vegetables or cold meat, or perhaps a bit of chicken and a piece of pie, and finished off with another cup of coffee. Mrs. Gagus might inquire as to whom he had this week, and he would laconically reply with a mouth full of meat, "John Barrymore," or "Katharine Hepburn," or "Will Rogers," or "Claudette Colbert," or some other name. Mrs. Gagus saw all of the big pictures at a neighborhood theatre in Brooklyn, but Mr. Gagus, being in the business, never went to the movies at all.

Between 12 and 12:15, they went to bed. Then, at 7:30 the next morning, Mr. Gagus arose once more in order to get to work on time. It was good to have a job that began at ten o'clock in the morning, and that required him to wear such impressive garments and that made him an integral part of the greatest theatre playing the greatest pictures in the greatest city for the greatest audiences in all this great world. He said so and his wife said so.

Then came The Great Manta.

At first Mr. Gagus wasn't concerned with it, didn't even notice it, and hadn't the remotest idea of what a manta was. But across Sixth Avenue from the Greatest Picture Palace in the World came this Great Manta and Mr. Gagus spent eight hours a day standing before it. The Great Manta—the largest devilfish ever exhibited, the most terrifying of marine monsters, and a barker with a line of wisecracks, who invited the public to come in and see it for ten cents, a thin dime, the tenth part of a dollar—was not at all out of place on Sixth Avenue, even directly across from the great cinema palace that provided a captain of the Grenadier Guards of the First Empire simply to open your carriage door. Sixth Avenue is an ambiguous street.

At first the attachés of the Greatest Picture Palace in the World were moved to smile and even laugh at this cheap Coney Island sideshow attraction. Its price was enough to belittle it. Ten cents to see a big devilfish. Why, they were charging a top price of a dollar sixty-five to see Katharine Hepburn. The Great Manta was beneath them. But Sixth Avenue, a street of heterogeneous shops, has also a heterogeneity of people. Men stood before the flashy advertisements of The Great Manta and read them. Of course at the beginning only a few men did so, but when four or five men stand still in New York and look at something, there is a crowd doing the same thing in a very few minutes. Then a few of the men went in, and before long most of the crowd managed to find a mere ten cents, and went in also. The Great Manta became a hit.

In time, the super-film with Katharine Hepburn left the Greatest Picture Palace in the World, and Anna Sten took her place in a super-super-production, but The Great Manta across the street stayed on. Four colossal, staggering, sensational super- and sometimes super-super-films went by, and still across the street The Great Manta stayed on.

Mr. Gagus, though he had no interest whatsoever in the fate of The Great Manta, could not help noticing this. A taxi-driver who had his stand near the entrance of the Greatest Picture Palace in the World once spoke to Mr. Gagus about it.

"Many people go see that damn thing?" he asked.

"Well, yes," admitted Mr. Gagus. "Quite a few."

And even as they looked over at this oddity, people were offering dimes to the ticket-seller and the barker was barking about The Great Manta, the largest devilfish ever exhibited, taken at the risk of a dozen lives. Usually he said it was the largest devilfish, but sometimes he made it the oldest, sometimes the meanest, occasionally the ugliest, and once in a while the heaviest. But always he came back to the point that it was the largest.

After some weeks of this, the thought, ever so casual, but nevertheless a thought, flickered through Mr. Gagus's mind to the effect that he had no idea what a great manta really looked like. The livid pictures outside the place were stirring but unsatisfying. He almost felt that he would like to see it. But the thought was so silly that he slammed a taxicab door a little harder than usual just to assert himself. Then one day, in his relief period in the locker-room, Mr. Gagus learned that Fritz, the assistant superintendent, and Joe, the first engineer, had both paid ten cents apiece to see The Great Manta.

"What's it like?" asked Mr. Gagus.

"Hell of a lookin' thing," said Joe.

"It is a great pig t'ing vot they got out of the ocean," said Fritz.

Mr. Gagus nodded, but experienced no feeling of satisfaction.

A few days later, Mr. Gagus learned that his alternate, Mr. Parkinson, had, during his rest period, paid ten cents and visited The Great Manta. Mr. Gagus did not deign to discuss the subject at the time, but some hours later, when Captain of the Grenadier Guards Gagus replaced Captain of the Grenadier Guards Parkinson, Captain Gagus caught Captain Parkinson's eye and, nodding his head toward the opposite side of the street, Captain Gagus said quietly out of the corner of his mouth, "What's it like?" Captain Parkinson did not reply. His face grew serious, he shook his head ever so slightly, winked one eye and raised his eyebrows, and then, without a word, marched off to the locker room.

And with the suspense at this high pitch, Mr. Gagus had to go to work for four hours, while across the street, when the roar of the "L" did not drown it out, came the rasping voice of the barker: "Here y' are, folks—step right up, one and all—the sensation of the age . . ."

At 10:22 that night, when Mr. Gagus walked west on Fiftieth Street to the Fiftieth Street subway station, he could still hear ringing in his ears "Step right up, folks—the sensation of the age," but he put it out of his mind and wondered what Mrs. Gagus would have ready for his supper.

At 11:35, he drank his first cup of coffee, and followed that with some pigs' knuckles and sauerkraut. And while he was eating with his mind on other things, Mrs. Gagus said, "Who do you have next week?"

"Oh, we got George Arliss."

"Oh, I like him," said Mrs. Gagus.

"And a Silly Symphony, too," added Mr. Gagus.

"My, my!" said Mrs. Gagus.

And at 12:15 they went to bed.

The days went by and Mr. Gagus continued his work. More and more of his casual acquaintances who worked at the Greatest Picture Palace in the World had succumbed to their instincts for romance and adventure and had gone to see The Great Manta. George Arliss and the Silly Symphony came and went. A musical talking-picture review with a blackface star and one hundred of the most beautiful girls in the world came to the Greatest Picture Palace in the World. In time it passed away and a foreign film, the greatest, naturally, that had ever been produced in Europe, took its place. The Great Manta stayed on. Every day, for four hours in the morning and four hours in the evening, Mr. Gagus heard the adjurations of the barker across the street and saw the crowds entering to see The Great Manta.

And as regularly as the earth turned, he stopped work at 10 P.M. And as regularly, at 10:22 he was ready to walk west on Fiftieth Street to the Fiftieth Street subway station. But hand in hand with regularity goes inevitability. Something had been going on in the environment of Mr. Gagus that made a reaction on his part inevitable. Through no really conscious control of his whatsoever, there came the inevitable night when, for the first time, he failed to walk west on Fiftieth Street at 10:22 P.M. Instead, without thinking much about it, and acting as if it were perfectly normal, he walked across Sixth Avenue and stopped at the ticket-seller of the attraction ballyhooed as The Great Manta. He paid ten cents and walked inside. Fifteen minutes later, he walked out. He had seen The Great Manta. He knew what it looked like. He was completely satisfied and he walked west on Fiftieth Street to the Fiftieth Street subway station.

That night it was 10:46 instead of 10:31 when he transferred to an express at Times Square. And it was 11:35 when he arrived at the Van Sicklen Avenue station, instead of 11:20. It was 11:43 when he unlocked his front door, and 11:44 when he entered his tiny flat, and 11:50 when he drank his first cup of coffee. Over the supper of corned-beef hash, Mrs. Gagus commented that he was fifteen minutes late, and she wondered why.

"Stopped to see The Great Manta," he explained.

That meant nothing to Mrs. Gagus. Naturally, she inquired what it was. Mr. Gagus swallowed more coffee, and she asked again, "What is The Great Manta?"

Mr. Gagus paused and looked at his empty plate.

"It's a devilfish," he said finally.

"What's it look like?" asked Mrs. Gagus.

"Oh, funny-lookin' thing," he answered. "Kind of a big fish that they got out of the ocean."

"Huh," sniffed Mrs. Gagus, which meant she couldn't possibly see why anybody should ever want to waste time to go see a big fish that somebody had pulled out of the ocean.

And that night they went to bed at 12:30 instead of 12:15—all on account of a big fish. But Mrs. Gagus used her self-control and said nothing more about it. Next morning Mr. Gagus got up at 7:30 on schedule, so everything was back in order again. He shaved and dressed and ate his breakfast. While he did this, Mrs. Gagus packed his lunch. At 8:30, he left his tiny flat. At 8:38, he boarded a Broadway-Seventh Avenue express. . . .

MY SISTER FRANCES

❦

Emily Hahn

A SOUND TRICKLED INTO the empty room. There was a scratching at the lock, and then the door opened and two people came in. The girl snapped on a light and the man hesitated an instant, glancing about with a quick, alert eye. There were no people. He saw only furniture, and plain wallpaper behind the overstuffed "suite" and the upright piano. Still, he hesitated shyly, dangling his hat.

"Oh, put it anywhere!" she cried gaily. "Just make yourself at home."

"Nice place here," said the young man.

"You think so? Well, thanks, only it's in an awful mess tonight. My sister Frances promised to clean it up before she went out, but I guess she was in too much of a hurry at the last minute."

"It looks fine to me," said the young man. "You'd ought to see how my place is."

She became solemn. "Oh, no, I don't believe you. Men are always a lot more neat and careful than girls are, don't you think so? I always notice it. Well—smoke?"

She held out a cigarette box with her arm stiff, leaning forward from her chair. She was a little breathless, very much excited at having him here, all to herself, in her own house. Like a little girl playing at housekeeping, she made an obvious effort to remember her duties.

"Have something to drink," she suggested. "You can have applejack or you can have gin. Frances—that's my sister—she brought the applejack home last week. It's awfully good. Ever tasted applejack?"

"Well," said the young man, "I guess we've got time for a little something. If you're going to have one anyway. Only I don't want to be any trouble."

"Oh, it's no trouble at all!" she said. "You just sit right here and wait a minute."

"Well now, say!" The young man stood up. "Why don't you let me help? Just tell me what you want me to do. I know my way around a kitchen!"

Together they walked down a tiny hallway to the kitchen, arguing amiably. The girl began to bustle about, collecting glasses and a tray. She leaned down to inspect the inside of the icebox. "Here you are, Mr. Kitchen Mechanic. Here's something for you to do," she said before her, into the cool white cave. "See? This little tray where the ice is   It always sticks If you pull very hard That's it, there she comes. My, what it is to be a big strong man!"

"Aw, lay off that." They laughed together and went back to the living room, carrying their tinkling glasses. She settled back in her chair with a sigh, her feet stuck out before her like a child's.

He gulped at his glass. "This is nice," he said. "This is mighty nice, I want to tell you."

"Hmm? I thought you'd like it."

"Yes, sir. It's smooth. Where do you get it? Do you know?"

"Oh, I guess you can get it lots of places, but Frances got this on her vacation up in the country. She brought back a jugful of it. She says they drink it all the time in the country. Just the way you drink beer, I mean. I mean, I don't think *she* drank it all the time, because it's pretty strong, but you never can be sure what Frances has been doing. She's a caution. I wish she'd come home right now so you could meet her. She said she'd be here."

The young man, still holding his half-full glass, extracted a watch from his pocket and looked at it. "I guess we better make this snappy if we're going to the last show," he said. "Just about ten minutes is all we've got."

"Oh." She was noncommittal.

"What do you say?" he persisted. "Is there anything special you'd like to see? What's on, anyway? Got a paper?"

"There isn't anything special. I guess I've seen just about everything, as a matter of fact."

"Me too."

She suggested timidly, "Do we have to go to the movies?"

"Why, don't you want to?"

"If you don't think you'd get tired of me," she murmured, "I'd just as soon we stayed right here like this."

"Tired of you?" he cried with enthusiasm. "It's just exactly what I'd like to do, only I didn't want to say so. You *sure* you don't want to go somewhere?"

"Oh, yes, I hate all this running around. I know people laugh at me sometimes, but I like to stay home, myself. That is to say, of course, if I'm with somebody I like to *talk* to."

"That's swell," said the young man. "I would of sworn there wasn't a girl like you in this town. I would of, honestly. Let me tell you, there aren't many like you."

She smiled, looking at him with placid, sweet eyes. "Oh, you just don't happen to know any quiet people. There are lots of girls like me, really. Why, there's some people who say Frances is like me, but she isn't really. She's so much prettier, for one thing, and then besides we're just different types."

"If she looks like you, she'll do."

"Oh, you think so?" She was demurely astonished. "Well, I guess there's a family resemblance, but Frances is much better looking. She's *really* attractive. Everybody falls for Frances. You'll see. She's the prettiest girl in the family."

"No, she's not," said the young man with conviction.

"You just wait till you see her. I expected you'd see her tonight. I kind of thought I'd get it over with. I mean, I had a kind of feeling we wouldn't be going to a movie or anything, and I want you to meet her. I want anybody I think I'm going to know very well —I mean—anybody who sort of gets along with me—I like Frances to know them, too."

"Say, is that straight? You mean I made an impression?" His face brightened pleasantly. "That's a coincidence. The first second I saw you, I had a feeling we would get along. You made an impression on *me*, all right."

"Oh, you're just saying that."

"No, I'm not, either. There was something about you. The minute I set eyes on you, I said to myself, 'She's different. That kid's different.' Listen, how long have you been living in New York?"

"A year," she said, and stood up purposefully. "Here, let me fix your glass."

When she came back, he was standing before the piano gazing at its open lid, his hands clasped behind his back as he mused.

"Why did you ask that?" she demanded.

"Ask what?"

"How long I've been living in New York."

"Well, I'll tell you why. You know, being unmarried and so on and so forth, I meet a lot of girls. And I've noticed something about these women who've been living a long time in this town. You see, they get spoiled. They meet a lot of fellows who make a fuss over them, and they begin to expect the world. A fellow gets fed up with these spoiled queens. Take me, for instance. I've got my job, but I like a good time, too. Only it costs a hell of a lot— excuse my plain speech, but I mean it costs a lot of money to satisfy one of these women."

"It certainly must. I've often thought about that."

"What these dames don't seem to realize is you can't keep going around night after night. You can't do it. And what's more, nobody can make whoopee all the time and then get to the office in the morning."

"Maybe I don't know that!"

"I've seen it a hundred times. A girl when she gets here might be the most natural kid in the world, but after a while she gets a swelled head. See what I mean? Then nobody's good enough for her any more."

"Isn't that terrible?"

"So that's why I say I had the idea you haven't been here very long. You aren't like the others. You aren't spoiled."

She got up and made a curtsy. "Thank you, kind sir."

"And that's on the level," he insisted.

She thought it over gravely, her brows wrinkled with the effort she was making to be impartial. "Maybe it's because I'm still kind of a home girl," she suggested. "I mean, I can't imagine living in a boarding house and all like that. My sister Frances, she says she'd rather not bother keeping house like we do, but I couldn't stand living any other way."

"Well, you just keep on the way you're doing. You're all right, let me tell you. I don't know when I've enjoyed anything so much as just sitting here, talking to you."

"It *is* nice," she admitted. "So quiet. I don't often get the chance to be as quiet as this. When Frances is home, there's always the gang dropping in, and all that. Frances is so popular."

"Well, their loss is my gain tonight, anyway," said the young man flatly. "Say, who plays the piano around here? Don't tell me you can do that, too! I certainly like a piano."

"Oh, I can't. It's Frances who plays. I wish I could. She's perfectly wonderful at the piano."

"Listen," said the young man fondly, "you stop trying to palm off your sister on me."

"I didn't try to palm anybody off on you. I just said—"

"Never mind, never mind," said the young man indulgently.

"I just said," she insisted, with a strange stubbornness, "that you'll fall for Frances. Everybody does. Just wait and you'll see."

"Well, I'll have to think it over," he said. "I tell you what, I promise to like her for your sake. How's that?"

She smiled at him slowly.

"And now," he said, "come over here and be friendly."

Again the lock rattled. The two on the sofa started apart, and the girl patted her hair hastily as the door opened.

"Yoohoo?" Another girl entered, her eyes widened with caution as she saw the dim lights. She tiptoed over to the couch, saw the people there, and smiled mischievously.

The young man scrambled to his feet and stood waiting. "Well, here she is—my sister Frances," said the girl. "Frances, I want you to meet Mr. Miller that I told you about. Say, what kept you so long? We waited and waited. We didn't go out at all."

"I'm awfully sorry," said Frances to Mr. Miller, charmingly. "I didn't think I was so important as all that." She smiled at him, looking straight into his eyes, and the girl on the sofa watched the smile and turned to see what answer it would call forth on Mr. Miller's face. He was blinking slightly.

"Why, sure you're important," said Mr. Miller. "I've been hearing quite a lot about what an important young lady you are. Vi says you even play the piano like a professional. Let's hear you. How about it?"

"Oh," said Frances, confidently, "I'm no good!"

"I bet you are. Let's hear you and I'll tell."

"Well, you brought it on yourself. Don't say I didn't warn you." With mock resignation she sat down at the piano and played for a while, her thin body swaying, her fingers nimble. Mr. Miller stood by and gravely watched her hands. Vi did not move from the couch.

"Well?" asked Frances at last, smiling with her direct stare up into his face.

"Swell!" said Mr. Miller.

Frances glowed, mysteriously satisfied. "And that's that." She thrust her fingers into her hair and stood up. "I'm off for a little beauty sleep. You children better not stay up too late. Pleased to have met you, Mr. Miller."

With a wave of her fingers and another special smile, she was gone. Vi turned and faced the young man, her shoulders squared. There was nothing really marked about the manner in which he had looked after Frances, but she smiled determinedly.

"Well?" she demanded.

"Well, what?" asked Mr. Miller, genuinely puzzled.

"Wasn't I right?"

"Right? What about?"

She stamped her foot, and breathed loudly. "About her, of course! You don't have to pretend."

"Oh, you mean Frances."

"Yes," she said with sarcasm, "I mean Frances."

"Well," he said noncommittally, "she's all right. She's a nice kid. She certainly can play the piano. But—"

"I thought so," said Vi, doom weighting her voice. "I thought that's what would happen. Well, you run along home now. You can call her up in the morning."

"You're goofy," said Mr. Miller, genuinely alarmed. "Look here—" He advanced toward her timidly. She sprang back.

"Don't you touch me!" she cried.

"I don't get you, Vi. I just don't get you. What's the matter with you? I was just trying to be polite. What's the trouble?"

"Nothing," she said, and the tears ran down her cheeks. "Nothing, nothing, nothing! Go on home!"

"But say—"

"Oh, get out!" she cried.

The door slammed behind him, and he stood in the hall staring at it. He could still hear her crying, and he hesitated for a moment. Then he shrugged his shoulders helplessly and walked away.

ACCIDENT NEAR CHARLOTTESBURG

❧

WILLIAM A. KRAUSS

THE AIRPLANE FELL into the lower meadow, killing four persons, shortly before five o'clock in the morning. The sun was coming over the eastern ridge then, and everyone was awake in the farmhouse. Pearl was in the summer kitchen making batter for pancakes when the crash jarred the early stillness. She had not heard the sound of the approaching motors. She could not imagine what the awful noise was.

The men, Charles pulling on overalls, Clarence stuffing his shirt into his pants, raced from the house and down to the meadow, with the boys at their heels, running hard. From the porch Pearl called after them, but they did not answer. She returned to her breakfast preparations, slicing the thick, spongy bread and counting the eggs that would, at the proper time, be broken into the frying pan. As she worked she told herself that her eye was worse this morning; she was afraid of the admission, but she knew it was true. It was more swollen, and more runny. Charles would have to recognize that. The witch hazel she had put on it all through the night had plainly done no good. More, her stomach was uneasy now; worry was the cause of that, she knew. Her mind returned to the rending, splitting noise—a loud noise, as though the roof of the barn had caved in. But she could see the barn roof through the dusty kitchen window; it had not been that. She could not guess.

Half an hour later the men came back. Charles, her husband, was wildly excited, his eyes blazing with amazement at the thing that had happened on his land. The boys were stunned, but they were not silent. They jabbered details of their observation, seeking corroboration of something they knew but could not believe.

"It's a passenger airplane," John said, confronted by the question in his mother's face. "It fell in the meadow next to the run and turned upside down. Three fellows in it, and a girl. They're all dead."

"Where are they?" Pearl asked.

"They're in the meadow," John said. "Pa and us pulled them out." The boy lifted his arm and indicated a red smear on his shirtsleeve. "They're all busted up. Clarence is running down to Price's to telephone town."

Pearl had not noticed that Clarence was not there. All the others were—five. She turned to the summer-kitchen door. "You want your eggs fried?" she asked. Although she had spoken to no one of them in particular, her husband answered. "Yes," he said. "Fried. Hurry them up."

They ate rapidly, scraping their heavy plates. When Charles pushed back his chair and rose, the others clattered to their feet and went out onto the porch. Pearl called to her husband from the summer kitchen. "My eye feels worse today, Charles," she said.

"Does it?"

He put a hand on her shoulder, stooping until his head was level with her. "It don't look so good," he admitted. "Why don't you put a hot salt-bag on it?"

"I used a lot of witch hazel last night but it didn't ease it."

"You should try a hot salt-bag," her husband said. "You got a cold in your eye. You want to bake it out."

Pearl found some assurance in the certainty with which Charles offered his diagnosis. She did not mention a doctor, because she knew how he felt about doctors. "Charging you three dollars or five dollars and guessing at what's wrong with you," he would say. She'd heard him before.

From the porch John shouted, "Are we going to milk now?" Charles went out. "Not now," he said. "Later." Then they saw Clarence running down the lane.

He arrived panting, and from the dining room Pearl heard him say he had got the chief of police in Charlottesburg. The chief was on his way in an auto, with doctors, Clarence said. "Do you want your breakfast?" Charles asked him. "No, Pa," he said. Together they walked—the boys trotting out in front—toward the meadow.

Pearl went upstairs and climbed the narrow steps to the attic.

The front window commanded a partial view of the lower meadow, but the line of willows along the run concealed the airplane wreckage. She watched the men until they walked behind the trees, and then went downstairs and cleared the dining-room table. Later she washed the dishes and made the beds. Later still, she fed the chickens behind the summer kitchen. She had thought to have turnips and pork and potatoes for the noonday meal, but wondered now if the men would be back to eat. Perhaps they would go to town. After she had considered a while, she decided it would be better to prepare the food. At half past ten o'clock the men came up the lane. Harry Price and Ed Brooke were with them. They sat on the edge of the porch a few minutes, talking, and then Charles entered the summer kitchen.

"Harry and Ed will be eating with us," he said. "I asked Chief Buell and Doc Horgan, but they had to go back to town."

"What happened?" Pearl asked.

"It was like I thought," her husband said. "They were all dead. Doc and the chief took the bodies to town about half an hour ago."

"Where'd they come from—this airplane?"

"I don't know."

"You can eat in twenty minutes," Pearl said.

She attended the pots that steamed upon the wood stove, adding salt to the contents of one. Then, delicately, with a hand that trembled slightly, she touched her right eye, tenderly fingering the swollen, moist lid. She wished Charles had not asked Ed Brooke and Harry Price up to eat, with her eye like it was. It looked so very bad—red, and wet. But Charles would be angry if she spoke about it, and besides they were here now and could not be sent away. It occurred to her that if Doc Horgan had come to eat he might have looked at the eye and suggested something to do, without charging because he had been invited as a guest. With a resolution she did not half believe, she told herself that unless it got better soon she would go see Doc Horgan anyway and let him charge.

When she called to the men that the food was on the table, they knocked out their pipes on the porch railing and entered the room without the usual scuffling delay. Ed Brooke and Harry Price were put at the upper end, one on either side of Charles. Pearl saw that her husband had taken on new importance because of the airplane in his meadow.

"People be coming out from town soon to see the wreck," Harry said.

"Wonder they're not here now," Ed added. "News travels."

Charles said, "It's lucky the danged thing didn't fall in the wheat."

"They'd trample it down for you," Ed said.

"I could charge admission."

Harry Price changed the course of a forkful of potatoes, dropping it back to his plate. With his left hand he slapped the table. "I'll be dog if you couldn't," he said. "You could charge 'em right now in the meadow. It's your land."

Charles shook his head.

"I ain't in the circus business. Let them look if they want to."

Not much later the first car came down the lane. It was Maxey Swan, the feed man from Charlottesburg, and his wife was with him. The men left their coffee and a lot of food untouched, going outside to tell Mr. Swan what they knew of the accident. Jack Wyllie of the Charlottesburg *Sentinel* drove up and wanted everything repeated so he could write a story for the paper. "This is a hell of a thing," he said. "They just can't make these air buggies safe."

"Give me a Ford," Charles agreed.

They all hurried down to the meadow. After she had cleared the table and stacked the dishes in the summer kitchen, Pearl went upstairs and looked at her eye in the dresser mirror. With a piece of cotton she wiped the heavy film of moisture from the lid. There was no white part any more; the whole eye was red as blood. It *was* more swollen than yesterday, she thought. And it hurt worse.

Kicking off her shoes, she lay crosswise on the bed, consciously relaxed. She cupped one hand over her eye; the slight pressure made it feel better, somehow. It was well to keep it closed, too. Light hurt it, and maybe did it serious harm, in its condition. She wondered about pads, hot applications; but in spite of what

Charles said, there would have to be something more than just heat. There would have to be some sort of ointment, a healing salve.

She heard shouting in the meadow.

It struck her, suddenly, that Doc Horgan would probably come back this afternoon. After he had laid out the bodies or signed the death certificates, or whatever he had to do, surely he would come back to talk to everyone about the accident, explaining in medical detail exactly what injuries had killed the fliers. From her window Pearl could see a line of cars parked along the fence on the upper road near the head of the lane, and people were climbing the fence and running down the slope of the meadow to the place behind the willows. She turned to the closet and took down the hanger that held her brown dress.

There must have been a hundred people in the meadow, she thought as she crossed the plank over the run. They were gathered in a tight circle about the wrecked airplane, waving their arms and calling to one another. She was surprised by the length of wing that jutted, crumpled at its tip, high into the air, and she stopped and looked, keeping her bad eye closed against the bright sunlight. In a minute Mrs. Swan, pushing her way to the rim of the crowd, saw her and ran awkwardly through the long grass to her side.

"Tell me," Pearl said loudly, "is Doc Horgan here?"

Mrs. Swan panted. "Land, what a crashup! Doc Horgan? Yes. I saw him a bit ago." She stared, dropping her head a little to one side, like a parrot. "What's the matter with your eye?" she asked.

"I don't know," Pearl said. It made her stomach sick to be so conspicuous, but there was no other way. "I want Doc Horgan to look at it. Will you find him for me?"

"Find him?"

"Yes. Please. I don't want to go over there with everyone. I'll wait by the willows."

"Sure," Mrs. Swan said. "I'll find him."

He saw her standing by the plank over the run, and hurried up to her, puzzled by the summons. "It's my eye, Doctor," she said. She took her hand away.

In the sunlight, under the willow, he tilted her head back and peered intently into her face. He was breathing hard.

"Pretty nasty," he said. She waited. "Have you got any vaseline up at the house?" he asked.

"Yes."

"Keep a little of it rubbed on your eyelid, and use hot applications. A hot-water bottle, if you have one, or a hot salt-bag. That'll ease the pain. There's not much else you can do but let it take its course. Cold settled in your eye. The inflammation should go down in a day or two. If it doesn't, call me."

"Yes," Pearl said. "Thank you, Doctor. How much is—"

"Forget it," Doc Horgan said. He looked across the meadow, at the crumpled wing tip lifting into the air. "I had to be out here anyway, with this accident. Quite a shock to you, this airplane falling on your doorstep, as you might say."

"It fell down just before five o'clock," Pearl said. "Where are the aviators from?"

"From Baltimore. Wealthy people. One of them owned the plane."

"It's a pity," Pearl said. "My God, falling like that."

IN HONOR OF THEIR DAUGHTER

John Mosher

BOTH THE GIRLS saw him at the same time, and they had to laugh. They put their pretty heads together and gave really quite a squawk into each other's ears. "Wouldn't you know!" they cried, and "The old baboon!" Then the younger one, who was in pink and didn't have to bother about other people, ran like a sandpiper through the crowd in the big drawing room and up the stairs and straight to the ballroom, where the boys were waiting. The older sister, so old, eighteen, who had to bother about everyone, especially these old wrecks on parade before her, braced herself with a long whiff of the white orchids, the white camellias, the white violets, the narcissuses, the white buds of roses that made the bouquet she held—braced herself with a whiff, smiled like an angel, and let the old baboon, Father's old friend, give her a kiss on the cheek. "So sweet of you, and good of you, Ezra, to come."

Never, it seemed to her as she stood in that line with her father and her mother, had she seen so many old people. The boys and the girls were there too, of course, but they would fly and sidle by, grab her hand, give her a smack in the curls, and run, bolt, for the swing band above. The old things, though, just hung around. Right out of the grave they came and made small talk. How they went on! Was she never again to see anything more of youth? Just perhaps a little, fleeting glimpse? All at once she thought how old she was herself, old as the hills, all her life lived, her own grave agape at the very foot of her Chanel. She was even glad and thought she had been sensible to take the practical advice given and wear her bedroom slippers.

"Soon I won't care," she thought, "if my toes do stick out from underneath my dress and everyone sees my fuzzy snuggies. These old parties will be coming all night. I suppose at daybreak old codgers and crones will be lining up in front of me. Tonight of all nights, I shall never dance. Not one dance shall I have tonight. Or any night? Perhaps I'll never dance again. Anyhow, any minute now I shall be too old to dance or even to think of dancing."

"The most beautiful party ever given on the face of the earth," people were saying. She could hear the murmur all about her: "The house is so beautiful, it's a freak, and the way the lace of the curtain spreads out a good yard over the Aubusson would make one sick with delight." Old eyes glittered with praise and appraisal; now that she was no longer a child, no more a little girl, she understood those eyes. "My own must have the same shine," she thought as she fixed them on the startling star rubies of Penelope Asia.

"Dear child," said Miss Asia, "you're the prettiest thing I have seen in all my days."

"Thank you, Miss Asia. And thank you, too, for the beautiful Victorian bouquet."

"An exact copy, you know, my dear, of one the Queen carried."

"I know, I know," she said, but she didn't feel back in her schoolroom with her history books and her Godey prints. Not in the least. She was part of history. Exhumed! "I just feel plain exhumed," she thought. And she had a kindly old person's condescension for the excitement she saw in Miss Asia and Ezra as they met. How they grabbed at each other and squealed and ran to squat right before her on a love seat, near enough for their ancient cackle to strike on her ears through the waltz strains from the musicians in the next drawing room, above the occasional rival flutings that drifted down from the dance music above.

"It's the last. There won't be any more parties like this," went the cackle, Ezra's cackle, above the dance music, through the shimmer of small talk.

"The last?" said Miss Asia, as though she had never heard the word in spite of what life had done to her.

"Houses like this. They won't exist. Give us a year or two and this will be—what? A community centre, a hospital for the aged and the decrepit, a home for delinquent mothers."

"I believe every word of it!" Asia screamed. "This is the end.

The end of a regime. The dying gasp of the grand epoch. And these beautiful young people—"

"Cannon fodder" came straight from Ezra to the ears of the girl with all her white flowers.

She just smiled. She smiled shyly because a figure who wrote plays of an important sociological character was bowing before her like an undertaker, and he would have stood there forever, measuring her with his eye, had not a crazy witch in black lace made a grab at him.

Asia saw this. "Black Lace loves literary celebrities," she said to Ezra. "Never so happy, holding pinkies with Ibsen!"

Past the orchids, camellias, rosebuds, and all filed a bishop, a senator, two Morgan partners, executives from Price, Waterhouse and J. Walter Thompson, six college professors, a governor of a Western state, twenty vice-presidents of successful enterprises, a radio magnate, the most eligible bachelor in Cleveland (vintage 1910), patriarchs out of the Union League, out of the Brook, out of the Knickerbocker, out of their tombs.

"A representative gathering," went the chant on the love seat. "Everyone is here. Everybody who counts is certainly here. They are doing their daughter well."

"Why not? Why not? With that exquisite girl—"

"Oh, I thought she was dead."

"Dead?"

"Oh, the one in puce—how sweet the girl is to her!" Ezra turned back to Miss Asia. "That one's never been so alive. They say she will marry again. At seventy. It was her sister you're thinking of. Caught a pleurisy. All over in a jiffy. She had no business trying Placid at her time of life."

"Nowadays the common cold has the perils of cholera."

"It's the nervous condition of the period. With everything crumbling all around us, why shouldn't we be nervous? How terrible to be young these days. That girl, just beginning—my heart bleeds for her."

She could hear them all the time. She felt quite sure this was the talk she would be always hearing now that she was a young lady and out in the world. Perhaps with practice she could have as good a time as they did, with the spots in front of their eyes and the creak in their joints. She could see them grab for the champagne and spruce themselves when the bulbs flashed and the cameras clicked.

Only the young people were grave and quick and deadly earnest as they went by her, but she knew well enough that once they had left the big drawing room they raced up the stairs to the ballroom with never a thought again for the crones and the codgers all dressed up and agiggle down below. She hoped they were having a good time, these young people who were so far away, whom she would never see again. She wanted them to dance and dance and drink the champagne until their eyes were brighter than young people's should ever be. And she thought of her sister, all in pink, dancing away with the cannon fodder and never dreaming that tomorrow the house would be turned into a refuge for the homeless and the aged.

"She was in an oxygen tent for days on end. And, oh, the expense!"

"They lost everything, sold the Long Island place, and the house in town, of course. It's been made into small furnished apartments for unmarried businesswomen of moderate means."

"That reminds me. Such a nice widow! If you know of a position! I thought as a receptionist. A hard life. She was thirty-five when she married, and he developed a bilious trouble. She was magnificent through it all. Mental troubles too—oh, he was more than eccentric. And didn't leave her a cent. I can quite see her setting off any office. A lady through and through."

Yes, it would go on like this the rest of her life. The hours had been years, and she was an old thing, a relic, Father's little relic, and the house was crumbling and was an institution already. "I wonder if I can't just sneak up to bed," she thought, "and have a glass of hot milk and dream about the years long ago, when I was almost young. And anyhow, isn't this whole night a dream, a nightmare, and am I not just dreaming that I'm tired to death and can't stand it any longer?"

Then, just as she was sure that it was all dream, she began to feel that she was waking up. Someone quite real, and alive, and alert and awake himself was right there in the line, where he had no business to be because he had been there before, and was saying something to her, and her mother was whispering to her too, and the trance was all over. There was something real in the world at last, something important to be done. "Bring me my slippers. I'm going to dance."

THE TEST

❧

Angelica Gibbs

O N THE AFTERNOON Marian took her second driver's test, Mrs.
Ericson went with her. "It's probably better to have someone a little older with you," Mrs. Ericson said as Marian slipped
into the driver's seat beside her. "Perhaps last time your Cousin
Bill made you nervous, talking too much on the way."

"Yes, Ma'am," Marian said in her soft, unaccented voice. "They
probably do like it better if a white person shows up with you."

"Oh, I don't think it's *that*," Mrs. Ericson began, and subsided
after a glance at the girl's set profile. Marian drove the car slowly
through the shady suburban streets. It was one of the first hot days
of June, and when they reached the boulevard they found it
crowded with cars headed for the beaches.

"Do you want me to drive?" Mrs. Ericson asked. "I'll be glad
to if you're feeling jumpy." Marian shook her head. Mrs. Ericson
watched her dark, competent hands and wondered for the thou-
sandth time how the house had ever managed to get along without
her, or how she had lived through those earlier years when her
household had been presided over by a series of slatternly white
girls who had considered housework demeaning and the care of
children an added insult. "You drive beautifully, Marian," she
said. "Now, don't think of the last time. Anybody would slide on a
steep hill on a wet day like that."

"It takes four mistakes to flunk you," Marian said. "I don't remember doing all the things the inspector marked down on my
blank."

"People say that they only want you to slip them a little something," Mrs. Ericson said doubtfully.

"No," Marian said. "That would only make it worse, Mrs. Ericson. I know."

The car turned right, at a traffic signal, into a side road and slid up to the curb at the rear of a short line of parked cars. The inspectors had not arrived yet.

"You have the papers?" Mrs. Ericson asked. Marian took them out of her bag: her learner's permit, the car registration, and her birth certificate. They settled down to the dreary business of waiting.

"It will be marvellous to have someone dependable to drive the children to school every day," Mrs. Ericson said.

Marian looked up from the list of driving requirements she had been studying. "It'll make things simpler at the house, won't it?" she said.

"Oh, Marian," Mrs. Ericson exclaimed, "if I could only pay you half of what you're worth!"

"Now, Mrs. Ericson," Marian said firmly. They looked at each other and smiled with affection.

Two cars with official insignia on their doors stopped across the street. The inspectors leaped out, very brisk and military in their neat uniforms. Marian's hands tightened on the wheel. "There's the one who flunked me last time," she whispered, pointing to a stocky, self-important man who had begun to shout directions at the driver at the head of the line. "Oh, Mrs. Ericson."

"Now, Marian," Mrs. Ericson said. They smiled at each other again, rather weakly.

The inspector who finally reached their car was not the stocky one but a genial, middle-aged man who grinned broadly as he thumbed over their papers. Mrs. Ericson started to get out of the car. "Don't you want to come along?" the inspector asked. "Mandy and I don't mind company."

Mrs. Ericson was bewildered for a moment. "No," she said, and stepped to the curb. "I might make Marian self-conscious. She's a fine driver, Inspector."

"Sure thing," the inspector said, winking at Mrs. Ericson. He slid into the seat beside Marian. "Turn right at the corner, Mandy-Lou."

From the curb, Mrs. Ericson watched the car move smoothly up the street.

The inspector made notations in a small black book. "Age?" he inquired presently, as they drove along.

"Twenty-seven."

He looked at Marian out of the corner of his eye. "Old enough to have quite a flock of pickaninnies, eh?"

Marian did not answer.

"Left at this corner," the inspector said, "and park between that truck and the green Buick."

The two cars were very close together, but Marian squeezed in between them without too much maneuvering. "Driven before, Mandy-Lou?" the inspector asked.

"Yes, sir. I had a licence for three years in Pennsylvania."

"Why do you want to drive a car?"

"My employer needs me to take her children to and from school."

"Sure you don't really want to sneak out nights to meet some young blood?" the inspector asked. He laughed as Marian shook her head.

"Let's see you take a left at the corner and then turn around in the middle of the next block," the inspector said. He began to whistle "Swanee River." "Make you homesick?" he asked.

Marian put out her hand, swung around neatly in the street, and headed back in the direction from which they had come. "No," she said. "I was born in Scranton, Pennsylvania."

The inspector feigned astonishment. "You-all ain't Southern?" he said. "Well, dog my cats if I didn't think you-all came from down yondah."

"No, sir," Marian said.

"Turn onto Main Street here and let's see how you-all does in heavier traffic."

They followed a line of cars along Main Street for several blocks until they came in sight of a concrete bridge which arched high over the railroad tracks.

"Read that sign at the end of the bridge," the inspector said.

" 'Proceed with caution. Dangerous in slippery weather,' " Marian said.

"You-all sho can read fine," the inspector exclaimed. "Where d'you learn to do that, Mandy?"

"I got my college degree last year," Marian said. Her voice was not quite steady.

As the car crept up the slope of the bridge the inspector burst out laughing. He laughed so hard he could scarcely give his next direction. "Stop here," he said, wiping his eyes, "then start 'er up again. Mandy got her degree, did she? Dog my cats!"

Marian pulled up beside the curb. She put the car in neutral, pulled on the emergency, waited a moment, and then put the car into gear again. Her face was set. As she released the brake her foot slipped off the clutch pedal and the engine stalled.

"Now, Mistress Mandy," the inspector said, "remember your degree."

"*Damn* you!" Marian cried. She started the car with a jerk.

The inspector lost his joviality in an instant. "Return to the starting place, please," he said, and made four very black crosses at random in the squares on Marian's application blank.

Mrs. Ericson was waiting at the curb where they had left her. As Marian stopped the car the inspector jumped out and brushed past her, his face purple. "What happened?" Mrs. Ericson asked, looking after him with alarm.

Marian stared down at the wheel and her lip trembled.

"Oh, Marian, *again?*" Mrs. Ericson said.

Marian nodded. "In a sort of different way," she said, and slid over to the right-hand side of the car.

GOODBYE, SHIRLEY TEMPLE

❦

JOSEPH MITCHELL

I HAVE BEEN GOING to Madame Visaggi's restaurant off and on since speakeasy days, and I know all the old customers. Madame Visaggi calls them "the regulars." Peggy is one. She is an Irish girl who works in the office of a wholesale butcher on First Avenue. She is around thirty-five. She is in Madame Visaggi's practically every night. Most often she is full of brandy when she leaves, but her apartment is only five or six blocks away, in Tudor City, and she always gets home all right. The butcher is her uncle and does not say anything if she shows up late for work. Peggy is an attractive girl despite a large birthmark on her left cheek, which makes her self-conscious. When she comes in, usually between five-thirty and six, she is always tense. She says, "I got the inside shakes." Then she sits in one of the booths across from the bar, orders a brandy, and opens an afternoon newspaper. By the time she has finished with the newspaper, she has had four or five drinks and has lost most of her self-consciousness. Then she doesn't mind if one of the other regulars comes over and sits in the booth with her. She knows many bitter, profane Irish stories, and people like to listen to her talk. The regulars know that Eddie, the bartender, has been in love with her for several years. He is a big, cheerful, dumb guy. He has an interest in the restaurant. He is always begging Peggy to slow down on her drinking and asking her to go out with him. Once Madame Visaggi sat down with Peggy and said, "Say, Peggy, sweetheart, what's the matter you don't like Eddie? He's such a nice boy, Eddie." Peggy said, "The back of my hand to Eddie." Then she laughed and said, "Oh, Eddie's O.K."

Another one of the regulars is Mike Hill. He works in an office around the corner, on Lexington, and usually drops in for a couple of drinks before going down to Grand Central to get his train.

Each Wednesday night his wife comes into town, and they have dinner in Madame Visaggi's and go to the theatre. Last Wednesday night they brought their little girl in to show her to Madame Visaggi. Mrs. Hill said she had been shopping most of the afternoon, and she looked tired, but the little girl was full of life. She appeared to be about five and she had curls. Madame Visaggi lifted her up, kissed her on both cheeks, and sat her on the bar. "Hello, Shirley Temple," she said. Eddie took a little white horse off the neck of a whiskey bottle and gave it to the child. Then Madame Visaggi told Eddie to chill a bottle of champagne. "On the house," she said. She turned to Mrs. Hill and said, "We'll have dinner together tonight. Special. On the house." They had Martinis at the bar and then they went into the dining room in the rear. At the door, Madame Visaggi turned and said, "Send in a bottle of ginger ale for Shirley Temple, Eddie."

In a little while the child came back into the bar. "Hello, young lady," said an old man standing at the bar. "Hello," said the child. The old man said, "How do you like this place?" The child said, "I like it," and the people along the bar laughed. This pleased the child. She said, "I have a riddle. Do you know Boo?" The old man thought a moment, and then asked, "Boo who?" "Please don't cry," the child said. Then she laughed and shook a finger at the old man and ran back into the dining room. In a minute or two she was back again. This time she walked along the row of booths, looking into each. I was sitting in one of the middle booths with Peggy and a girl named Estelle, a friend of Peggy's. The child looked at us and smiled. Peggy said, "Hello there." "Hello," said the child. "What's your name?" Peggy asked. The child said, "My name is Margaret." "Why, that's my name, too," Peggy said. Estelle lifted the child into the booth and put an arm around her. The child stared across the table at Peggy and said, "What's that on your face?"

Peggy hesitated a moment. Then she said, "It's something God put there, Margaret."

"Won't it come off?" the child asked.

Estelle interrupted. "Do you go to school?" she asked.

"No," said the child. She looked at Peggy again and said, "Why did God put it there?"

"Because I was a bad girl," Peggy said.

"What did you do?"

Peggy asked Estelle for a cigarette. While Peggy was lighting it, the child gazed at her.

"What did you do?" she asked again.

"I shot off my father's head and cut out my mother's heart and ate it," Peggy said.

"When?"

Estelle interrupted again.

"How old are you, sweetheart?" she asked.

"Five and a half," said the child.

She looked at Peggy and said, "Can I touch it?"

Peggy said, "Sure." She bent over and the child touched her left cheek. Then Madame Visaggi came out of the dining room, looking for the child. She picked her up. "You've got to come eat your soup, so you'll be a big girl," she said.

"Goodbye," the child said to Peggy.

"Goodbye, Shirley Temple," Peggy said.

Everything was quiet in the booth for a few minutes. I was afraid to say anything. Then Estelle asked Peggy to go with her to a movie at Loew's Lexington.

"It'll do you a world of good," Estelle said.

"The hell with it," Peggy said.

A game of Indian dice started at the bar, and Estelle and I went over and got in it. Peggy said she wasn't interested. There were six in the game, playing for drinks. The second time the dice went down the bar, I glanced over at Peggy, thinking I would ask her if she wanted a drink; Mike Hill's little girl was back again. She was standing just outside Peggy's booth. I saw Peggy lean over and speak to her. The child stared at Peggy, fascinated. When Peggy stopped talking, the child walked backward a few steps, retreating. Then she turned and ran headlong into the dining room. It was a long dice game with two ties, and we played one-tie-all-tie. I got stuck. I paid for the round, and Estelle and I went back and sat down with Peggy.

"I see the kid came back to see you," I said.

Peggy laughed.

"I sent Shirley Temple back to her mamma," she said.

Every twenty minutes or so, Estelle and I would go over to the bar and shake for drinks with the others. Every time we came back to the booth, we brought Peggy a brandy. We tried to get her to talk, but she wouldn't pay any attention to us. She was morose and silent.

At ten o'clock, Mrs. Hill came out of the dining room with Madame Visaggi. "Thanks for everything," Mrs. Hill said. "It was a wonderful dinner, and thank you so much for the champagne." "No, no, no," said Madame Visaggi. "It was nothing." Then Mike came out. He had the little girl in his arms. She looked sleepy now. They said good night to Eddie and started for the door. When they approached the booth in which we were sitting, the little girl began to kick and scream hysterically. Mike sat her down on a bar stool and said, "What in the world is the matter, baby doll?" The child continued to scream. "She's all tired out and nervous," Mrs. Hill said. "The day was too much for her. Here, let me take her." Suddenly Peggy said, "Damn it to hell." She got up abruptly and hurried toward the door. We thought she was going out of the restaurant and I got up to follow her, but at the front end of the bar she turned left and went into the ladies' room. As soon as Peggy was out of sight, the child calmed down. "She should've been in bed hours ago," Mrs. Hill said. Then they said thanks and goodbye to Madame Visaggi all over again, and left.

After a while another dice game began. While we were shaking, Peggy returned. She didn't go back to the booth. She came and stood next to me and put her elbows on the bar. I could see that she had been crying. Eddie automatically poured her a brandy.

"How's it, Peggy?" he asked.

Peggy didn't answer. She drank the brandy. Then she said, "You want to take me home, Eddie?"

"You kidding?" Eddie asked.

"No," Peggy said.

"You drunk?"

"I certainly am not," Peggy said.

"Look," Eddie said, "I'm not supposed to knock off until midnight, but I'll ask Madame to put one of the waiters behind the bar."

"O.K., Eddie," Peggy said.

HONORS AND AWARDS

❦

JAMES REID PARKER

IF FUR OCCASIONALLY FLEW at the meetings of the various faculty
committees, there was a notable exception in the case of the
Committee on Honors and Awards, which met twice a year, immediately after the mid-year and final examination weeks. These
conclaves were exceedingly dignified, with the President himself
occupying the chair. Perhaps the reason nothing ever gingered up
the proceedings was that the business on the agenda had the effect,
primarily, of reminding the members that they were persons of
consequence, who had gathered together to act in a judicial capacity on matters of high academic moment. They benignly awarded
scholarships and voted on the recipients of medals and small cash
prizes provided by various trust funds. Since the names of students
to be honored had invariably been endorsed by department chair-
men, the Committee met chiefly to approve these recommenda-
tions, which required their unanimous sanction, as a matter of
form.

In addition to President Galbraith, the Committee was composed of Dr. Guthrie of Chemistry; Dr. Kronenberg of Fine Arts;
Dr. Satterlee, whom the members of the faculty usually described
to outsiders as "our Chaucer man" and regarded in matters of academic policy as something of a dark horse; Dr. Overton of Math-
ematics; and two Professors Emeritus, Dr. Bowles and Dr. Mabbott. The Emeritus members had been placed on the Committee
chiefly because it was felt that their many years of service in the
college made them impressive ornaments for a body of this sort.

Assembled in the committee room of the Gryce Library for the
last meeting of the year, these gentlemen had already spent several
hours approving, without fireworks but with a good deal of lordly

discussion, the distribution of the Henry F. Rossiter Prize, the Richard Cortelyou Memorial Scholarship, the Adelaide Slaton Pinchot Prize, the Norton Talbot Debating Medals, the Class of 1891 Scholarship and the endowed scholarships established by each graduating class since that time, the Ainslee Fyfe Journalism Award, the Cyrus Swift Magrue Prize, the Paul S. Younkman Good Citizenship Cup, and so on. At the beginning of the third hour, the Committee came to an award over which it had sole juris-diction—the designation of one of the five highest-ranking seniors as Faculty Scholar. Although this honor went almost automatically to the student who had the highest average, the Committee was empowered to select one of the remaining four if it deemed this advisable. In the words of the catalogue, the members were to choose the student "best calculated to serve as a representative of the rich cultural life and the high degree of personal attainment for which this institution so proudly stands."

President Galbraith opened the discussion. "Will the secretary be good enough to read the names, together with the averages, of the five students whose academic status renders them eligible for the title of Faculty Scholar?" he requested.

"The list is as follows," said Dr. Overton, consulting a slip of paper. "Rabinowitz, Max, 4.9860; Hodenpyl, Clarence, 4.9731; Howells, Leonard F., 4.9422; Todd, William Mitchell, 4.8974; Randall, Harvey B., 4.8951."

There was a moment's silence.

"It would seem that the list is headed by Mr.—er—Rabinowitz," murmured the President. "Is anyone well acquainted with him?"

After a minute or two, several professors announced without conspicuous enthusiasm that they knew Mr. Rabinowitz.

"I am acquainted with the candidate's record, but I am not *inti-mately* acquainted with the candidate himself," observed the Presi-dent. His tone suggested that for some reason he wanted to absolve himself of any further responsibility in the matter. "Perhaps some-one will enlighten me as to whether he possesses the—um—the nec-essary qualifications for the designation of Faculty Scholar, apart from his scholastic standing."

No one accepted this invitation.

"Mr. Hodenpyl's average is excellent also," Dr. Overton reminded the Committee in general. "In fact, it is almost as high as Mr. Rabinowitz's. In order to be sure of this, I figured out the averages to four decimal places this year, instead of the customary three."

Dr. Galbraith asked whether anyone was acquainted with Mr. Hodenpyl, and quite a few professors assented promptly. It was pointed out that Mr. Hodenpyl, while not an athlete, was nevertheless what the college called "an activity man," and that he had been a prominent member of the varsity debating team. Much to the general satisfaction, it turned out that Mr. Rabinowitz had not been an "activity man" in any sense of the word.

"The award need not necessarily be made on the basis of scholarship alone," said Dr. Overton, still anxious to be helpful, "although this has always been the paramount consideration. I think we may interpret Mr. Hodenpyl's extracurricular prominence as meeting the 'high degree of personal attainment' stipulation just a little further than Mr. Rabinowitz's purely academic record meets it."

Dr. Bowles triumphantly pointed out that not only was Mr. Hodenpyl's academic record commendably high, but that the candidate possessed the quality of "all-aroundness." Concluding the little series of tributes, Dr. Guthrie gave a dramatic account of the young man's prowess in mastering Chemical Microscopy and Crystallography, seemingly one of the knottier items in the curriculum.

"Mr. Hodenpyl appears to be the general favorite," commented the President softly.

"I've never met the young man, but I gather that he's a capital student," said Dr. Mabbott.

"Capital," agreed Dr. Overton. "A very superior type."

"Will someone move that we designate Mr. Hodenpyl as the Faculty Scholar?" asked Dr. Galbraith.

"Er—Mr. President," interposed Dr. Kronenberg. "If I may be permitted to raise a point, I should like to suggest that Mr. Rabinowitz's average is higher than Mr. Hodenpyl's, and that as yet it has not been clarified that Mr. Rabinowitz is undeserving of the honor. Indeed, he still seems to be our chief candidate."

Most of the Committee members suddenly began to examine

their documents and notes, leaving Dr. Galbraith to clarify why Mr. Rabinowitz was undeserving of the honor. The President inquired whether Dr. Kronenberg was acquainted with the student in question, and the Professor admitted that he was not. "While none of the members have felt it advisable to speak in favor of Mr. Rabinowitz," Dr. Galbraith went on, "and since I take it that all of us are especially impressed with the qualifications of Mr. Hodenpyl, I should welcome any contribution to the symposium which would enable us to confer the award on the student most worthy of it. I believe we are all sincerely desirous of selecting the best man."

Several professors were now busily engaged in drawing elaborate geometric designs on their memorandum pads.

"In certain colleges, I regret to say, intolerance frequently characterizes the distribution of the annual awards," said Dr. Galbraith evenly. "Much as we may regret the fact, we—er—can hardly close our eyes to it. I should like to go on record at this time, Dr. Kronenberg, as protesting officially against these un-American practices in other institutions. We, on the other hand, as a liberal community devoted to the propagation of learning, are proud to disassociate ourselves from such grossly unacademic bias. It is our ambition to be motivated solely by an interest in merit, and to render decisions that are unassailably fair."

Having voiced these sentiments, the President promptly became more cheerful. The physician had healed himself.

"And now," he said, sounding as if he were about to put the whole disagreeable matter aside, "I have an idea whereby we can solve the problem of designating the Faculty Scholar and at the same time attend to the remaining items on the agenda before the afternoon is over. May I suggest that I be permitted to depute three of our number to adjourn to another room, where they can take up the Faculty Scholar question in detail? If we assign them our power of vote, and if they will be good enough to assign theirs to us, we can continue with the business of the day here in the committee room."

This proposal found favor at once. Dr. Kronenberg muttered something to himself in Latin. It was scarcely audible, and sounded like *"Pontius Pilatus."* He was resigned, however, and in a tired voice said that he would consent to turn over his power of vote to the subcommittee. Dr. Galbraith glanced around the table. He delegated Dr. Mabbott, the venerable Emeritus; Dr. Satterlee, the Boston patrician; and Dr. Overton, who had considerately figured out the averages to four decimal places, to retire to another part of the Gryce Library and settle in a discreet manner the rather trying business of choosing the Faculty Scholar.

"I have before me," he said, when the subcommittee had departed, "the data relating to the Tolerton Medals for Stage Design. The names of the first, second, and third prizewinners, all of whom have been endorsed by the Department of Drama, require your approval."

The meeting progressed uneventfully, save for the fact that the gentlemen who were attempting to choose justly between Rabinowitz, Max, and Hodenpyl, Clarence, remained out of the room for a singularly long time. Although the members who were busy with the Tolerton Medals tacitly assumed that the absence was intended to indicate a protracted discussion, with every phase of the case carefully weighed, it really seemed as if Dr. Mabbott and his associates might have returned sooner.

"I fear our colleagues are playing truant and have gone for a stroll on the campus," said Dr. Bowles jocosely.

Dr. Guthrie, who had a mildly roguish disposition, observed, "Ah, well, one can hardly blame them for wishing to avoid the tedium of our society."

Ever a tactful mediator, the President suggested that the subcommittee was no doubt having a difficult time arriving at a unanimous decision—a remark which evoked a dry smile from Dr. Kronenberg. Presently the deputies filed into the committee room. It was evident from their expressions that the Long Parliament had been a matter of necessity rather than a diplomatic gesture.

"May we know the subcommittee's decision?" asked Dr. Galbraith.

"After a very lengthy debate, we have agreed on Mr. Rabinowitz," said Dr. Mabbott, with sour dissatisfaction. Grunting, he lowered himself into a chair.

The professors who had not left the room were too astonished to say anything; they sat upright, wholly stupefied, watching Dr.

Mabbott. Dr. Kronenberg lost control of himself and sneezed out of sheer excitement.

"Gesundheit!" said Dr. Satterlee, with a cheerfulness in strong contrast to the gloom to be observed in Dr. Mabbott and Dr. Overton. It was clear that it had been his vote which had delayed the committee so long in arriving at a unanimous decision, and it was equally clear that in the end he had managed to break down the resistance of two notably obstinate gentlemen. Dr. Satterlee, the darkest of dark horses, had apparently honored scholarship for scholarship's sake.

"Thank you," said Dr. Kronenberg.

The Chaucerian bowed. Although the Committee on Honors and Awards had been badly shaken, it managed to rally and display a certain amount of its old composure.

"And now we come to the Cornelia Rhett Porterfield Award," said Dr. Galbraith hastily. "The Cornelia Rhett Porterfield Award for Distinction in Latin Composition . . ."

PASTORAL AT MR. PIPER'S

❧

MOLLIE PANTER-DOWNES

THE PLACE WAS ENGLAND, the time was half past nine on a summer evening. Light was deepening on the green meadows over which jolly monks used to amble home after a day's fishing. Willows edged the stream and threw a stunted cordon round the shapeless gray huddle of village and church. In the kitchen at Stoke Sheba Manor, Mrs. Swaddle picked up a tray and started off again for the dining room. Her employer, Mr. Piper, had provided her with a full-skirted dress of black alpaca and a dotted-swiss muslin apron; on her head was a starched Charlotte russe tied with long streamers of purple velvet ribbon. When she appeared, she created a mild stir among Mr. Piper's guests.

"My dear," said one of them as she passed, "who is the darling old trout? She looks a perfect pet—really too feudal for words, my dear. You're always so clever about things like that."

As Mrs. Swaddle crossed the hall, Mr. Piper shot past her. He was on his way to the front door. His hair was gilded and large red roses were sewn liberally over his eighteenth-century coat. His legs were encased in what seemed to be long pink silk gloves and gartered with bats.

"Beg pardon, sir," said Mrs. Swaddle, stepping back and avoiding a nasty collision. But Mr. Piper was already greeting the newly arrived guests.

"Benita, my sweet, this is grand!" cried Mr. Piper. "Dodie, darling, you look too marvellous! Come along in, my dears—it's all being the greatest fun. Cynthie Scroop is here and the Mallards, and Vi is going to sing for us afterward. Wait till you see her! I really can't *describe* to you how superb she looks."

He swept the guests into the dining room, where Mrs. Swaddle was steering a wary course with her tray through the crowd. People were arriving every few minutes, roaring up the lane from Stoke Sheba in large, shining cars that were driven off afterward by the chauffeurs to the stable yard, where Mr. Piper kept his pretty doves and a wicker wheelbarrow full of potted marguerites.

Mrs. Swaddle was used to quality that arrived at a quarter to eight sharp for eight-o'clock dinner, but this quality trickled in by degrees, smelling of grease paint and Chanel scents, dressed as nymphs in Woolworth tinsel or as Lily Langtry, with stuffed humming birds and an ostrich egg poised in their hair. Mrs. Swaddle found herself handing no fish with a white sauce, entrée with a brown, such as she had learned to expect at the quality's dinner parties. Mr. Piper's guests gobbled corned-beef hash and creamed haddock while champagne corks popped and flashlights went off.

Picking up the empty tray, Mrs. Swaddle prepared for another trip to the kitchen. She stood still for a minute in the hall, a little confused, for Mr. Piper had been very busy all day with some cans of whitewash and a quantity of coarse fishing nets, papier-mâché lobsters, and pampas grass dyed pink and green. Even the Misses Lorimer, the late owners of the Manor, would have been properly put to it to find their way about, Mrs. Swaddle considered. After a brief encounter with a lobster, she found the right aperture in the nets and pushed open the baize door that led to the kitchen.

Here Mr. Piper and his pampas grass had not penetrated. The kitchen was dank and cool, with the underwater smell of stone floors. A clock ticked, and the cook stood crossly filling an enormous white shell with peaches and figs that Mr. Piper had brought down the day before from London.

"Some of them will be wanting their coffee by now," she said to Mrs. Swaddle.

The door was pushed open and Crosby came in, carrying a tray. He set it down, brought out a handkerchief, and mopped his forehead.

" 'Er old ladyship's out there dressed like a dog's dinner with a ship on 'er 'ead," he said.

"Fancy!" said the cook sourly.

Crosby carried the heavy silver coffee service and Mrs. Swaddle followed with a tray of liqueurs. Sconces of candles guttered nastily, Mrs. Swaddle noted, with a cautious eye on the fishnets. The guests were outside, screaming among the herbaceous borders, and Mr. Piper was photographing them posed against the dovecot, clasping sheaves of whitened corn ears or perched on the edge of the wicker wheelbarrow.

"This ought to be too amusing for words," cried Mr. Piper. "Hold it just a minute longer, darling, while I pin up that naughty little fold of cheesecloth."

"Brandy, my lady?" said Mrs. Swaddle.

The sky was a beautiful deep green; frogs croaked in the reeds. Some of the Russian Ballet turned up in a Bentley and leaped about by the lake where Mr. Piper's little skiff floated, its oars garlanded with artificial honeysuckle. Mr. Piper's gardener, waiting among the bushes, applied a light to the first rocket and clouds of rose and blue stars unfolded softly over sleeping Stoke Sheba.

"Fireworks excite me *too* deliriously," shrilled Mr. Piper.

He had changed his dress and Mrs. Swaddle had to look carefully before she recognized him as a shepherd with sequin eyelids and buskins of leopard skin. She and Crosby carried trays of champagne among the guests.

A gentleman whose body was covered with ribbons and tiny skulls stopped her. "What a marvellous fanc' dress," he said.

"Thank you, sir," said Mrs. Swaddle.

She knew that the gentleman had been a little unwise over his wine. Her feet were beginning to hurt. She put out a smoldering papier-mâché lobster and went to the kitchen. The cook was taking a snack with Crosby.

"If you want to pop home, there's no call for you to stay, Mrs. Swaddle," she said.

Mrs. Swaddle took off the starched Charlotte russe and untied her apron. Then she put on her coat and hat and went round to the stable yard for her bicycle. A figure was sleeping in the wheelbarrow among the broken marguerites.

"Beg pardon, sir," said Mrs. Swaddle, carefully stepping over his legs.

She got on her bicycle and wobbled off down the lane to Stoke Sheba. The village was dark and still, huddled in the fold of the downs much as it had huddled for the last five hundred years. The tobacco flowers in Mrs. Swaddle's garden smelled very sweet as she wheeled her bicycle up the path and propped it against the hen house. Her feet were hurting much worse now, but she had enjoyed her evening. Oh yes, she always enjoyed going to help out at a party with the quality. Whenever they wanted her, she was always at their service. Like Stoke Sheba, Mrs. Swaddle had not altered in the last five hundred years.

Mr. Swaddle was snoring in the hot little room under the thatch.

"That you, Annie?" he mumbled as she climbed into bed beside him.

"Yes," said Mrs. Swaddle.

She fell asleep quickly, without thinking at all about the party.

Mr. Piper was speeding the last of the drooping nymphs and shepherds.

"My dear, what an evening!" they cried. "And how too clever of you, darling, to find this place. It's so completely *you*, isn't it?"

Mr. Piper's sequin eyelids winked as he nodded.

"I really think it is," he said happily.

MAN AND WOMAN

❦

Erskine Caldwell

THEY CAME SLOWLY up the road through the colorless dawn like shadows left behind by the night. There was no motion in their bodies, and yet their feet scuffed up dust that settled behind them as quickly as it was raised. They lifted their eyes with each step they took, peering toward the horizon for the first red rays of the sun.

The woman held her lower lip clamped tightly between her teeth. It hurt her to do that, but it was the only way she could urge herself forward step after step. There was no other way to force herself to drag her feet one behind the other, mile after mile. She whimpered occasionally, but she did not cry out.

"It's time to stop and rest again," Ring said.

She did not answer him.

They kept on.

At the top of the hill, they came face to face with the sun. It was a quarter of the way up, cut like a knife by the treeless horizon. Down below them was a valley lying under a cover of mist that was rising slowly from the earth. They could see several houses and farms, but most of them were so far away they were almost indistinguishable in the mist. There was smoke rising from the chimney of the first house.

Ruth looked at the man beside her. The red rays of the sun had begun to color his pale face like blood. But still his eyes were tired and lifeless. He looked as if he were balancing himself on his two feet with great effort, and as if the next moment he might lose his balance and fall to the ground.

"We'll be able to get a little something to eat at that first house," she said, waiting minute after minute for him to reply.

"We'll get something there," she said, answering for him. "We will."

The sun came up above the horizon, fast and red. Streaks of gray clouds, like layers of wood smoke, swam across the face of it. Almost as quickly as it had risen, the sun shrank into a small fiery button that seared the eyes until it was impossible to look at it any longer.

"Let's try, anyway," Ruth said.

Ring looked at her in the clear daylight, seeing her for the first time since the sun had set the night before. Her face was paler, her cheeks more sunken.

Without words, he started forward down the hill. He did not turn his head to see if she were following him, but went down the road drawing one foot from behind and hurling it in front of him with all his might. There was no other way he could move himself over the ground.

He had stopped at the front of the house, looking at the smoke that floated overhead, when she caught up with him at last.

"I'll go in and try," she said. "You sit down and rest, Ring."

He opened his mouth to say something, but his throat became choked and no words came. He looked at the house, with its worn doorstep and curtain-filled windows and its smoke-filled chimney, and he did not feel like a stranger in a strange country as long as he kept his eyes upon those things.

Ruth went through the gate, and around the side of the house, and stopped at the kitchen door. She looked behind her and saw Ring coming across the yard from the road.

Someone was watching them behind a curtain at the window.

"Knock," Ring said.

She placed the knuckles of her right hand against the side of the house and rapped on the clapboards until her hand began to hurt.

She turned around and glanced quickly at Ring, and he nodded his head.

Presently the kitchen door opened a few inches and a woman's head could be seen through the crack. She was middle-aged and brown-faced and had a long, thick scar on her forehead that looked as if it might have been made by a bursting fruit jar.

"Go away," she told them.

"We won't bother you," Ruth said as quickly as she could. "All we wanted was to ask you if you could give us a little something to eat. Just a potato, if you have any, or bread, or something."

"I don't know what you are doing here," the woman said. "I don't like to have strange people around my house."

She almost closed the door, but in a moment the crack widened, and her face could be seen once more.

"I'll feed the girl," she said finally, "but I can't let the man have anything. I don't have enough for both of you, anyway."

Ruth turned quickly around, her heels digging into the sandy earth. She looked at Ring. He nodded his head eagerly.

He could see the word forming on her lips even though he could not hear it. She shook her head.

Ring went several steps toward her.

"We'll try somewhere else," she said.

"No," he said. "You go in and eat what she'll give you. I'll try at the next house we come to."

She still did not wish to go into the house without him. The woman opened the door a foot or more, and waited for her to come up the steps.

Ring sat down on a bench under a tree.

"I'm going to sit here and wait until you go in and get something to eat for yourself," he said.

Ruth went up the steps slowly to the porch and entered the door. When she was inside, the woman pointed out a chair to her by a table, and she sat down.

There were potatoes, warmed over from the night before, and cold biscuits. These were put on the table in front of her, and then the woman poured a cup of hot coffee and set it beside the plate.

Ruth began to eat as quickly as she could, sipping the hot black coffee and chewing the potatoes and bread while the brown-faced woman stood behind her at the door, where she could watch Ring and her by turns.

Twice Ruth managed to slip pieces of bread into her blouse, and finally she got half a potato into the pocket of her skirt. The woman eyed her suspiciously when she was not watching Ring in the yard outside.

"Going far?" the woman asked.

"Yes," Ruth answered.

"Come far?"

"Yes," Ruth said.

"Who is that man with you?"

"He's my husband," Ruth told her.

The woman looked out into the yard again, then back at Ruth. She did not say anything more for a while.

Ruth tried to put another piece of potato into her skirt pocket, but by then the woman was watching her more closely than ever.

"I don't believe he is your husband," the woman said.

"Well," Ruth answered, "he is."

"I wouldn't call him much of a husband to let you walk through the country begging food like you did just a little while ago."

"He's been sick," Ruth said quickly, turning in the chair to face the woman. "He was sick in bed for five weeks before we started out."

"Why didn't you stay where you were, instead of making tramps out of yourselves? Can't he hold a job, or don't he want to work?"

Ruth got up, dropping the bread in her hand.

"Thank you for the breakfast," she said. "I am going now."

"If you take my advice," the woman said, "you'll leave that man the first chance you get. If he won't work at a job, you'll be a fool—"

"He had a job, but he got sick with a kind of fever."

"I don't believe you. I'd put you down for lying about him."

Ruth went to the door, opened it herself, and went outside. She turned around on the porch and looked at the woman who had given her something to eat.

"If he was sick in bed, like you said," the woman asked, following her past the door, "why did he get up and start tramping like this with nothing for you and him to eat?"

Ruth saw Ring sitting on the bench under the tree, and she was not going to answer the woman, but she could not keep from saying something.

"The reason we started out walking like this was because my sister wrote and told me that our baby had died. When my husband first got sick, I sent the baby to my sister's. Now we're going to see the grave where she's buried."

She ran down the steps and walked across the yard as rapidly as she could. When she reached the corner of the house, Ring got up and followed her to the road. Neither of them said anything, but she could not keep from looking back at the house, where the woman was watching them through the crack in the door.

After they had gone a hundred feet or more, Ruth unfastened her blouse and pulled out the pieces of bread she had carried there. Ring took them from her without a word. When he had eaten all there was, she gave him the potato. He ate it hungrily, talking to her with his eyes while he chewed and swallowed.

They had walked for nearly half an hour before either of them spoke again.

"She was a mean old woman," Ruth said. "If it hadn't been for the food, I'd have got up and left before I ate what she gave me."

Ring did not say anything for a long time. They had reached the bottom of the valley and were beginning to go up the grade on the other side before he spoke again.

"Maybe if she had known where we were going, she might not have been so mean to you," Ring said.

Ruth choked back a sob.

"How much farther is it, Ring?"

"About thirty or forty miles."

"Will we get there tomorrow?"

He shook his head.

"The day after?"

"I don't know."

"Maybe if we get a ride, we might get there tonight?" she asked, unable to hold back any longer the sobs that choked her throat and breast.

"Yes," he said. "If we could get a ride, we would get there a lot sooner."

He turned his head and glanced down the road behind them, but there was nothing in sight. Then he looked down at the ground he was walking on, counting the steps he took with his right foot, and then his left.

MAIN CURRENTS OF AMERICAN THOUGHT

❦

IRWIN SHAW

"FLACKER: ALL RIGHT NOW, KID, now you'd better talk," Andrew Draper dictated. "Business: sound of the door closing, the slow turning of the key in the lock. Buddy: You're never going to get me to talk, Flacker. Business: sound of a slap. Flacker: Maybe that'll make you think different, Kid. Where is Jerry Carmichael? Buddy (laughing): Wouldn't you like to know, Flacker? Flacker: Yeah. (Slowly, with great threatening in his voice) And I'm going to find out. One way or another. See? Business: siren fades in, louder, then fades out. Announcer: Will Buddy talk? Will Flacker force him to disclose the whereabouts of the rescued son of the Railroad King? Will Dusty Blades reach him in time? Tune in Monday at the same time etcetera etcetera—"

Andrew dropped onto the couch and put his feet up. He stretched and sighed as he watched his secretary finish scratching the dictation down in her shorthand notebook. "There's another thirty bucks," he said. "Is it the right length?"

"Uh huh," she said. "Eleven and a half pages. This is a very good one, Andy."

"Yeah," Andrew said, closing his eyes. "Put it next to 'Moby Dick' on your library shelf."

"It's very exciting," she said, standing up. "I don't know what they're complaining about."

"You're a lovely girl, Lenore." Andrew put his hands over his eyes and rubbed around and around.

"Tomorrow? At ten o'clock?"

"At ten o'clock. Dig me out of the arms of sleep. We shall leave Dusty Blades to his fate for this week and go on with the further adventures of Ronnie Cook and his friends, forty dollars a script.

I always enjoy writing 'Ronnie Cook' much better than 'Dusty Blades.' See what ten dollars does to a man." He opened his eyes and watched Lenore putting her hat on in the mirror. When he squinted, she was not so plain-looking. He felt very sorry for Lenore, plain as sand, with her flat-colored face and her hair pulled down like a rope, and never a man to her name. She was putting on a red hat with a kind of ladder arrangement up one side. It looked very funny and sad on her. Andrew realized that it was a new hat. "That's a mighty fine hat," he said.

"I thought a long time before I bought this hat," Lenore said, flushing because he'd noticed it.

"Har*riet!*" the French governess next door screamed, in the alley outside, at the next door's little girl. "Harriet, get away from there this minute."

Andrew turned over on his stomach on the couch and put a pillow over his head. "Have you got any ideas for 'Ronnie Cook and His Friends' for tomorrow?" he asked.

"No. Have you?"

"No."

"You'll get them by tomorrow," she said. "You always do."

"Yeah," said Andrew. "God-damn Ronnie Cook and his god-damn friends."

"You need a vacation," Lenore said. "Goodbye. Get a good night's sleep."

"Anything you say."

Andrew watched her with one eye as she went off the porch on which he worked and through the living room and dining room toward the stairs. Then he closed his eyes and tried to sleep. The sun came in through the open windows, and the curtains blew softly over his head, and the sun was warm and comforting on his closed eyes. Across the street, on the public athletic field, four boys were shagging flies. There would be the neat, pleasant crack of the bat and a long time later the smack of the ball in the fielder's glove. The tall trees outside, as old as Brooklyn, rustled from time to time as little spurts of wind swept across the baseball field.

"Har*riet!*" the governess called. "Stop that or I will make you stand by yourself in the corner all afternoon! Harriet! I demand you to stop!"

The little girl cried, "Mamma! Mamma! Mamma, she's going to hit me!"

The little girl hated the governess and the governess hated the little girl and they continually reported each other to the little girl's mother.

"You are a little liar!" the governess screamed. "You will grow up and you will be a liar all your life. There is no hope for you."

"Mamma!" wailed the little girl.

They went inside the house and it was quiet again.

"Charlie," one of the boys yelled, "hit it to me, Charlie!"

The telephone rang four times, and then Andrew heard his mother talking into it.

"It's a man from the bank," she called to him. "He wants to talk to you."

"You should've told him I wasn't home," Andrew said.

"But you are home," his mother said. "How was I to know that—"

"You're right." Andrew swung his legs over the side of the couch and sat up. "You're perfectly right." He went into the dining room to the telephone.

"You're a hundred and eleven dollars overdrawn," said the man at the bank.

Andrew squinted at his mother, sitting across the room on a straight chair with her arms folded in her lap, her head turned just a little, so as not to miss anything.

"I thought I had about four hundred dollars in the bank," Andrew said into the phone.

"You're a hundred and eleven dollars overdrawn."

Andrew sighed. "I'll check it." He hung up.

"What's the matter?" his mother asked.

"I'm a hundred and eleven dollars overdrawn," he said.

"That's shameful," his mother said. "You ought to be more methodical."

Andrew started back to the porch.

"You're awfully careless," his mother said, following him. "You really ought to keep track of your money."

"Yes." Andrew sat down on the couch.

"Give me a kiss," his mother said.

"Why?"

"No particular reason." She laughed.

"O.K." He kissed her and she held him for a moment. He lay back on the couch. She ran her finger under his eye.

"You've got rings under your eyes," she said.

"That's right."

She kissed him again and went away.

He closed his eyes. From the rear of the house came the sound of the vacuum cleaner. He got up and went to his mother's bedroom. She was down on one knee and bent over, running the machine back and forth under the bed.

"Hey!" Andrew yelled. "Hey, Mom!"

She turned off the machine and looked up at him. "What's the matter?"

"I'm trying to sleep," he said.

"Well, why don't you sleep?"

"The vacuum cleaner. It's shaking the house."

His mother stood up, her face setting into stern lines. "I can't use it while you're working. I can't use it while you're reading. I can't use it until ten o'clock in the morning because you're sleeping." She started the machine. "When am I supposed to clean the house?" she called over the noise of the cleaner. "Why don't you sleep at night, like everybody else?" And she put her head down low and vigorously ran the machine back and forth.

Andrew watched her for a moment. Then he went out of the room, closing the door behind him.

The telephone was ringing again, and he picked it up and said "Hello."

"Ahndrew?" his agent's voice asked. His agent was from Brooklyn, too, but he had a very broad "a," with which he impressed actors and sponsors.

"Yes, this is Ahndrew." Andrew always made this straight-faced little joke with his agent, but the agent never seemed to catch on. "The 'Dusty Blades' scripts are all through. You'll get them tomorrow."

"I called about something else, Ahndrew. The complaints're piling up on the 'Blades' scripts. They're as slow as gum. Nothing ever happens. Ahndrew, you're not writing for the *Atlantic Monthly*."

"I know I'm not writing for the *Atlantic Monthly*."

"I think you've rather ran out of material," his agent said lightly, soothingly. "I think perhaps you ought to take a little vacation from the 'Blades' scripts."

"Go to hell, Herman!" Andrew said, knowing that his agent had found somebody to do the scripts more cheaply for him.

"That's hardly the way to talk, Ahndrew," Herman said. "After all, I have to stand in the studio and listen to the complaints."

"Sad, Herman," Andrew said. "That's a sad picture," and hung up.

He rubbed the back of his neck reflectively, feeling the little lump behind his ear. Then he went into his own room and sat at his desk, looking blankly at the notes for his play, which lay to one side, neatly piled, growing older. He took out his checkbook and his last month's vouchers and arranged them in front of him.

"One hundred and eleven dollars," he murmured as he checked back and added and subtracted, his eyes smarting from the strain, his hands shaking a little because the vacuum cleaner was still going in his mother's room. Out on the athletic field more boys had arrived and formed an infield and were throwing the ball around the bases and yelling at each other.

Dr. Chalmers, seventy-five dollars. That was for his mother and her stomach.

Eighty dollars rent. The roof over his head equalled two "Ronnie Cook and His Friends." Five thousand words for rent.

Buddy was in the hands of Flacker. Flacker could torture him for six pages. Then Dusty Blades could be speeding to the rescue with Sam, by boat, and the boat could spring a leak, because the driver was in Flacker's pay, and there could be a fight for the next six pages. The driver could have a gun. It could be used, Andrew decided, but it wouldn't be liked, because he'd written at least four like it already.

Furniture, a hundred and thirty-seven dollars. His mother had always wanted a good dining-room table. She didn't have a maid, she said, so he ought to get her a dining-room table. How many words for a dining-room table?

"Come on, baby, make it two!" the second baseman out on the field was yelling. "Double 'em up!"

When Andrew was still in college he used to go out on a Saturday at ten o'clock in the morning and shag flies and jump around the infield and run and run all day, playing in pickup games until it got too dark to see. He was always tired now, and even when he played tennis he didn't move his feet right, because he was tired, and hit flatfooted and wild.

Spain, one hundred dollars. Oh, Lord!

A hundred and fifty to his father, to make up the deficit in his payroll. His father had nine people on his payroll, making little tin gadgets that he tried to sell to the dime stores, and at the end of every month Andrew had to meet the payroll. His father always gravely made out a note to him.

Flacker is about to kill Buddy out of anger and desperation. In bursts Dusty, alone. Sam is hurt. On the way to the hospital. Buddy is spirited away a moment before Dusty arrives. Flacker very smooth and oily. Confrontation. "Where is Buddy, Flacker?" "You mean the little lad?" "I mean the little lad, Flacker!" . . .

Fifty dollars to Dorothy's piano teacher. His sister, Dorothy. Another plain girl. She might as well learn how to play the piano. Then one day they'd come to him and say, "Dorothy is ready for her début. All we're asking you to do is rent Town Hall for a Wednesday evening. Just advance the money." She'd never get married. She was too smart for the men who would want her and too plain for the men she'd want herself. She bought her dresses in Saks. He would have to support, for life, a sister who would only buy her dresses in Saks and paid her piano teacher fifty dollars a month every month. She was only twenty-four. She would have a normal life expectancy of at least forty years. Twelve times forty, plus dresses at Saks and Town Hall from time to time . . .

His father's teeth, ninety dollars. The money it cost to keep a man going in his losing fight against age.

The automobile, nine hundred dollars. A nine-hundred-dollar check looked very austere and impressive, like a penal institution. He was going to go off in the automobile, find a place in the mountains, write a play. Only he could never get himself far enough ahead on "Dusty Blades" and "Ronnie Cook and His Friends." Twenty thousand words a week, each week, recurring like Sunday on the calendar. How many words was "Hamlet"? Thirty, thirty-five thousand?

Twenty-three dollars to Best's. That was Martha's sweater for her birthday. "Either you say yes or no," Martha had said last Saturday night. "I want to get married and I've waited long enough." If he got married, he would pay rent in two places, light, gas, telephone.

Flacker played with something in his pocket. Dusty's hand shoots out, grabs Flacker's wrist, pulls his hand out. Buddy's little penknife, which Dusty had given him for a birthday present, is in Flacker's hand. "Flacker, tell me where Buddy Jones is or I'll kill you with my bare hands." A gong rings. Flacker has stepped on an alarm. Doors open and the room fills with his henchmen. . . .

Twenty dollars to Macy's for books. Parrington's "Main Currents of American Thought." How does Dusty Blades fit into the "Main Currents of American Thought"?

Ten dollars to Dr. Faber. "I don't sleep at night, Doctor. Can you help me?"

"Do you drink coffee, Mr. Draper?"

"I drink one cup of coffee in the morning. That's all."

Pills, to be taken before retiring. Ten dollars.

If he married, he would take an apartment downtown, because it would be silly to live in Brooklyn this way, and he would buy furniture, four rooms full of furniture, beds, chairs, dishrags, relatives. Martha's family was poor and getting no younger and finally there would be three families, with rent and clothes and doctors and funerals.

Andrew got up and opened the closet door. Inside, stacked in files, were the scripts he had written in the last four years. They stretched from one wall of the wide closet across to the other—a million words. Four years.

Next script. The henchmen close in on Dusty. He hears Buddy screaming in the next room . . .

How many years more?

The vacuum cleaner roared.

Martha was Jewish. That meant he'd have to lie his way into some hotels if he took her to them at all and he never could escape from one particular meanness of the world around him.

He sat down at his desk. One hundred dollars again to Spain. Barcelona had fallen and the long, dusty lines had beaten their way to the French border with the planes over them. And out of a sense of guilt at not being on a dusty road himself, bloody-footed and in fear of death, he had given a second hundred dollars, feeling at the same time that it was too much and nothing he ever gave could be enough. Three and a third "The Adventures of Dusty Blades" to the dead and dying of Spain.

The world loads you day by day with new burdens that increase on your shoulders. Lift a pound and you find you're carrying a ton. "Marry me," she says, "marry me." Then what does Dusty do? What the hell can he do that he hasn't done before? For five afternoons a week now, for a year, Dusty has been in Flacker's hands, or the hands of somebody else who is Flacker but has another name, and each time he has escaped, but now how?

The vacuum cleaner roared in the hallway outside his room.

"Mom!" he yelled. "Please turn that thing off!"

"What did you say?" his mother called.

"Nothing."

He added up the bank balances. His figures showed that he was four hundred and twelve dollars overdrawn instead of one hundred and eleven dollars, as the bank said. He didn't feel like adding the figures over. He put the vouchers and the bank's sheet into an envelope for his income-tax returns.

"Hit it out, Charlie!" a boy called on the field. "Make it a fast one!"

Andrew felt suddenly like going out and playing with them. He changed his clothes and put on a pair of old spiked shoes that were lying in back of the closet. His old pants were tight on him. Fat. If he ever let go, if anything happened and he couldn't exercise, he'd get as big as a house. Maybe Dusty has a knife in a holster up his sleeve. How plant that? The rent, the food, the piano teacher, the people at Saks who sold his sister dresses, the nimble girls who painted the tin gadgets in his father's shop, the teeth in his father's mouth, the doctors, the doctors, all living on

the words that would have to come out of his head. . . . See here,
Flacker, I know what you're up to. Business: Sound of a shot. A
groan. Hurry, before the train gets to the crossing! Look! He's
gaining on us! Hurry! Will he make it? Will Dusty Blades head
off the desperate gang of counterfeiters and murderers in the race
for the yacht? Will I be able to keep it up? Andrew asked himself.
The years, the years ahead. . . . He would grow fat and the lines
would become permanent under his eyes and he'd drink too much
and pay more to the doctors because death was nearer and there
was no stop, no vacation from life, because in no year could he say,
"I want to sit this one out. Kindly excuse me."

His mother opened the door. "Martha's on the phone."

Andrew clattered out in his spiked shoes, holding the old, torn
fielder's glove. He closed the door to the dining room to show his
mother this was going to be a private conversation.

"Hello," he said. "Yes." He listened gravely. "No," he said. "I
guess not. Goodbye. Good luck, Martha." He stood looking at the
phone after he had put it down. His mother came in and he
picked up his glove and started down the steps.

"Andrew," she said, "could you spare fifty dollars?"

"Oh, God!"

"It's for Dorothy. She's going to a party, a very important
party—"

"Do the invitations cost fifty dollars apiece?" Andrew kicked the
top step and a little piece of dried mud fell off one of the spiked
shoes.

"No, Andrew. It's for a dress. She can't go without a new dress,
she says. There's a man there she's after."

"She won't get him, dress or no dress," Andrew said. "Your
daughter's a very plain girl."

"I know," his mother said. Her hands waved a little, helpless
and sad. "But it's better if she at least does the best she can. I feel
so sorry for her, Andrew."

"Everybody comes to me!" Andrew yelled, his voice suddenly
high. "Nobody leaves me alone! Not for a minute!"

He was crying now and he turned to hide it from his mother.
She looked at him, surprised, shaking her head. She put her arms

around him. "Just do what you want to do, Andrew, that's all. Don't do anything you don't want to do."

"Yeah," Andrew said. "Yeah. I'm sorry. I'll give you the money. I'm sorry I yelled at you."

"Don't give it to me if you don't want to, Andrew."

He laughed a little. "I want to, Mom, I want to."

He patted her shoulder and went down toward the baseball field, leaving her standing there, puzzled, at the top of the steps.

The sun and the breeze felt good to him on the baseball field and he forgot for an hour, but he moved slowly. His arm hurt at the shoulder when he threw, and the boy playing second base called him "Mister," which he wouldn't have done even last year, when Andrew was twenty-four.

THE KNIFE

※

Brendan Gill

Michael threw himself down, locked his hands over one of his father's knees, and began, in a loud whisper, " 'Our Father, who art in heaven, hallowed be thy name, kingdom come, will be done, earth as it is in heaven, give us this day—' "

Carroll folded his newspaper. Michael should have been in bed an hour ago. "Take it easy, kid," he said. "Let's try it again, slow."

Michael repeated distinctly, " 'Our Father, who art in heaven, hallowed . . .' " The boy's pajamas, Carroll saw, were dirty at the cuffs; probably he had not brushed his teeth. " '. . . as we forgive them, who trespass against us'—what does 'trespass' mean, Dad?"

"Why, hurting anybody."

"Do I trespass anybody?"

"Not much, I guess. Finish it up."

Michael drew a breath. " 'And lead us not into temptation, but deliver us from evil. Amen.' "

"Now," his father said, brushing back Michael's tangled hair, "what about a good 'Hail, Mary'?"

"All right," Michael said. " 'Hail, Mary, full of grace, the Lord is with thee, blessed art thou among women, and blessed is the fruit of thy womb, Jesus.' " Michael lifted his head to ask if a womb got fruit like a tree, but thought better of it. His father never answered questions seriously, the way his mother used to. Michael decided to wait and ask Mrs. Nolan. "Is Mrs. Nolan coming tomorrow?" he asked.

"She'll be here, all right," Carroll said. "I give you ten seconds to finish the prayer."

Michael grinned at the ultimatum. "I thought you wanted me to go slow. 'Holy Mary, Mother of God, pray for us sinners, now and at the hour of our death. Amen.' " He unlocked his fingers. "Will she?"

"Will she what?"

"Will she now and at the hour of our death, A-men?"

The words of Michael's prayer caught in Carroll's mind and stayed there, a long way beyond his smiling face. "Yes," he said, and set his pipe in the broken dish on the table beside him. He had not emptied the dish of ashes in two days. Mrs. Nolan would give him a piece of her mind tomorrow morning, as she did each week when she came in to give the apartment a general cleaning and to do the laundry.

"What good can she do?" Michael asked.

"Climb into bed, young ragamuffin," Carroll said sternly. "It's past nine."

"What *good* can she do?"

"She'll help you get anything you want. I suppose she'll help you climb up into heaven when the time comes. You know all about heaven, don't you?"

Michael felt himself on the defensive. "Of course."

"Well, then, get along with you."

But Michael had something difficult to say. "You mean she'll ask God for anything I want and He'll give it to her for me?"

"She's His mother."

Michael stood up and kissed his father carefully on the cheek. Then he walked from the room, and Carroll could hear his bare feet crossing the hall. The bed creaked as Michael lay down on it. Carroll opened the newspaper, read a paragraph, then dropped it in a white heap on the rug. He felt tired; perhaps tonight he might be able to get some sleep. He got up, slipped his suspenders from his shoulders, unknotted his tie, kicked off his shoes. He had learned to undress quickly in the last six months, since his wife had died.

His pajamas were hanging inside out in the bathroom, where he had left them that morning. When he had undressed he felt Michael's toothbrush with his thumb; it was dry. He should have explained to the child what happened to a person's teeth when he forgot to clean them every night and morning.

Carroll stared at his face in the mirror above the basin. He tried smiling. No one could honestly tell what a man was thinking by the way he smiled. Even Michael, who was like a puppy about sensing moods, could not tell. He entered the bedroom on tiptoe. Feeling the sheets bunched at the foot of the mattress, he remembered that he had made the beds in a hurry. The sheets felt fresh and cool only on Saturdays, when Mrs. Nolan changed them.

Michael was not asleep. "Dad?" he whispered.

"Go to sleep."

"I been asking Hail Mary for something."

"Tomorrow."

"No, I been asking her right now."

Carroll lay on his back with his hands over his eyes. "What've you been asking her for, Mickey?"

Michael hesitated. "I thought I'd better make it something easy first. To see what happened." He sat up in bed. "A jackknife."

A few blocks away the clock in the Metropolitan Life tower was striking ten. Michael was deep in the noisy middle of a dream. Carroll listened to his breathing. He tried matching his own breath to Michael's, to make sleep come, but it was no use. Every night Carroll pretended to himself he was just at the brink of falling off to sleep, but his eyes always widened with wakefulness in the dark. Now, as the clock stopped striking, Carroll got up and walked into the bathroom and dressed. Then he went into the living room, unlocked the outside door of the apartment, and then locked it again before he walked down the two flights of stairs to the sidewalk. Shops reached out of sight down both sides of Lexington Avenue. Carroll walked uptown as he always did. He stopped in front of each bright shop window, studying its contents for the fifth or sixth time. He knew by now the day on which each window was changed and by whom. Certain plaster models, certain fringed crêpe papers were old friends.

At the top of a long slope Carroll waited for the lights to change. On his left was a bar; on his right, across the street, a drugstore. Carroll waited a moment outside the bar. Between the slats of its cheap orange Venetian blinds he could see the gleaming mahogany counter, the stacked glasses, the barman slicing foam from a mug of beer. A man and a girl were sitting at a table by the window, a foot under Carroll's eyes. They did not seem to be speaking. The man's hands lay halfway across the table and the girl's black dress made her throat look soft and white. Carroll turned away and crossed the street to the drugstore. The owner, Sam Ramatsky, stood sniffing the night air under the painted sign bearing his name.

"Well, Mr. Carroll, nice night for March."

"Yes." Carroll wanted only to hear a voice. "How's business?" he asked.

"Can't complain." Sam grinned, shaking his head. "I take that back. It's *lousy*. I got to break myself of this old 'Can't complain.' I got to remember how serious it is. Business is lousy."

Carroll leaned back against Sam's window, which was crammed with hot-water bottles, perfumes, toys, and two cardboard girls in shorts and sandals. The girls had been there for two months. There was dust on their teeth and on their smooth brown legs. "You ought to brush their teeth, Sam," Carroll said, "and run your hand down their legs now and then."

"You walk a lot," Sam said. "I figure on you, ten or eleven, every night."

"I guess I do," Carroll said.

Sam patted his hard belly. "Nothing like exercise keep a man in shape."

Carroll nodded impatiently. It was not Sam's voice he wanted to hear, after all. "Give me a milk shake, Sam."

They walked into the store. Carroll sat down on one of the round stools at the fountain and watched Sam pouring milk into the shaker. "Nothing like milk," Sam said, "keep a man's system clean." Carroll watched the hands of the electric clock above the door. Ten-forty-five. He could not go to bed before twelve. He glanced at the packed counters behind him. "Sell any jackknives, Sam?"

"Sure. I sell everything. That's what keeps me broke. Nothing like keeping a thing in stock to kill demand." Sam lifted a tray of jackknives from a counter, brought it over, and set it down on the fountain. "Beauties," Sam said. "Fifty cents up."

Carroll looked at several of them and finally picked up the biggest and shiniest one. "I'll take this one," he said.

"Such expensive taste! One buck."

Carroll paid for the milk shake and the knife, said "Good night, Sam," and walked out into the street. In another hour and a half he should have walked six miles. By that time his body would be tired enough so that he could sleep. By that time, he hoped, no voice could rouse him.

It was morning when Carroll awoke. He lay with his face on his hands, listening to the sound of the March rain against the windows. He remembered suddenly the absurd song that everyone used to sing: "Though April showers may come your way, they bring the flowers that bloom in May." March rains brought you nothing. March rains only shut you in your room without any hope of escape.

Michael and Mrs. Nolan were talking together in the kitchen. Michael's voice was high with excitement. "Look at it, Mrs. Nolan, look at it! Isn't it beautiful?"

"It is that," Mrs. Nolan said in her deep voice. Carroll sat up in bed. It was too late to give Mrs. Nolan warning.

"Do you ask for things when you say your prayers, Mrs. Nolan?" Michael demanded.

"I do." A pan clattered to the floor. "I've seen many a nice clean sty I'd swap for this dirty kitchen," Mrs. Nolan said. "You live like a couple of savages from week to week. God love you."

"Do you always get what you ask for?" Michael said.

"It all depends. I sort of try to guess what the good Lord wants to give me, and I ask for that."

"That's how I got this knife," Michael said. "It's got a big blade and a little blade and a screwdriver and a thing to punch holes in leather with and a file."

"You must have said yourself a fine prayer," Mrs. Nolan said, There was no hint of surprise in her voice.

"It was only a 'Hail, Mary,'" Michael said, "but I did it very slow, the way Dad told me to." Michael was silent for a moment.

"But I'm asking for the real thing tonight. The knife was just to see. Someone's going to be here when you come next week."

Mrs. Nolan made a clucking sound in her mouth. "Someone instead of me?"

"She was here with Dad and me before you came," Michael said, his voice thin with its burden, "and she's coming back."

"Michael!" Carroll shouted.

Michael ran to the doorway. The knife gleamed in his fist. "Look what I got," he said. "I was showing Mrs. Nolan."

"Come here," Carroll said. When Michael reached the edge of the bed Carroll bent over and fastened his arms behind the child's back. There was only one thing to say, and one way to say it, and that was fast. "I'm glad you like it," he said. "I bought it for you at Ramatsky's last night. The biggest and shiniest one he had."

THE PELICAN'S SHADOW

❧

MARJORIE KINNAN RAWLINGS

THE LEMON-COLORED AWNING over the terrace swelled in the southeasterly breeze from the ocean. Dr. Tifton had chosen lemon so that when the hungry Florida sun had fed on the canvas the color would still be approximately the same.

"Being practical on one's honeymoon," he had said to Elsa, "stabilizes one's future."

At the moment she had thought it would have been nicer to say "our" honeymoon and "our" future, but she had dismissed it as another indication of her gift for critical analysis, which her husband considered unfortunate.

"I am the scientist of the family, my mouse," he said often. "Let me do the analyzing. I want you to develop all your latent femininity."

Being called "my mouse" was probably part of the development. It had seemed quite sweet at the beginning, but repetition had made the mouse feel somehow as though the fur were being worn off in patches.

Elsa leaned back in the long beach chair and let the magazine containing her husband's new article drop to the rough coquina paving of the terrace. Howard did express himself with an exquisite precision. The article was a gem, just scientific enough, just humorous, just human enough to give the impression of a choice mind back of it. It was his semi-scientific writings that had brought them together.

Fresh from college, she had tumbled, butter side up, into a job as assistant to the feature editor of *Home Life*. Because of her enthusiasm for the Tifton series of articles, she had been allowed to handle the magazine's correspondence with him. He had written her, on her letter of acceptance of "Algae and Their Human Brothers":

My DEAR MISS WHITTINGTON:

Fancy a woman's editor being appealed to by my algae! Will you have tea with me, so that my eyes, accustomed to the microscope, may feast themselves on a *femme du monde* who recognizes not only that science is important but that in the proper hands it may be made important even to those little fire-lit circles of domesticity for which your publication is the *raison d'être!*

She had had tea with him, and he had proved as distinguished as his articles. He was not handsome. He was, in fact, definitely tubby. His hair was steel-gray and he wore gray tweed suits, so that, for all his squattiness, the effect was smoothly sharp. His age, forty-odd, was a part of his distinction. He had marriage, it appeared, in the back of his mind. He informed her with engaging frankness that his wife must be young and therefore malleable. His charm, his prestige, were irresistible. The "union," as he called it, had followed quickly, and of course she had dropped her meaningless career to give a feminine backing to his endeavors, scientific and literary.

"It is not enough," he said, "to be a scientist. One must also be articulate."

He was immensely articulate. No problem, from the simple ones of a fresh matrimony to the involved matters of his studies and his writings, found him without an expression.

"Howard intellectualizes about everything," she wrote her former editor, May Morrow, from her honeymoon. She felt a vague disloyalty as she wrote it, for it did not convey his terrific humanity.

"A man is a man first," he said, "and *then* a scientist."

His science took care of itself, in his capable hands. It was his manhood that occupied her energies. Not his male potency—which again took care of itself, with no particular concern for her own needs—but all the elaborate mechanism that, to him, made up the substance of a man's life. Hollandaise sauce, for instance. He had a passion for hollandaise, and like his microscopic studies, like his essays, it must be perfect. She looked at her wristwatch. It was his wedding gift. She would have liked something delicate and diamond-studded and feminine, something suitable for "the mouse," but he had chosen a large, plain-faced gold Hamilton of railroad accuracy. It was six o'clock. It was not time for the hollandaise, but it was time to check up on Jones, the manservant and cook. Jones had a trick of boiling the vegetables too early, so that they lay limply under the hollandaise instead of standing up firm and decisive. She stirred in the beach chair and picked up the magazine. It would seem as though she were careless, indifferent to his achievements, if he found it sprawled on the coquina instead of arranged on top of the copies of *Fortune* on the red velvet fire seat.

She gave a start. A shadow passed between the terrace and the ocean. It flapped along on the sand with a reality greater than whatever cast the shadow. She looked out from under the awning. One of those obnoxious pelicans was flapping slowly down the coast. She felt an unreasonable irritation at sight of the thick, hunched shoulders, the out-of-proportion wings, the peculiar contour of the head, lifting at the back to something of a peak. She could not understand why she so disliked the birds. They were hungry, they searched out their food, they moved and mated like every living thing. They were basically drab, like most human beings, but all that was no reason for giving a slight shudder when one passed over the lemon-colored awning and winged itself-satisfied way down the Florida coastline.

She rose from the beach chair, controlling her annoyance. Howard was not sensitive to her moods, for which she was grateful, but she had found that the inexplicable crossness which sometimes seized her made her unduly sensitive to his. As she feared, Jones had started the cauliflower ahead of time. It was only just in the boiling water, so she snatched it out and plunged it in ice water.

"Put the cauliflower in the boiling water at exactly six-thirty," she said to Jones.

As Howard so wisely pointed out, most of the trouble with servants lay in not giving exact orders.

"If servants knew as much as you do," he said, "they would not be working for you. Their minds are vague. That is why they are servants."

Whenever she caught herself being vague, she had a moment's unhappy feeling that she should probably have been a lady's maid. It would at least have been a preparation for matrimony. Turning now from the cauliflower, she wondered if marriage always laid these necessities for exactness on a woman. Perhaps all men were not concerned with domestic precision. She shook off the thought, with the sense of disloyalty that always stabbed her when she was critical. As Howard said, a household either ran smoothly, with the mechanism hidden, or it clanked and jangled. No one wanted clanking and jangling.

She went to her room to comb her hair and powder her face and freshen her lipstick. Howard liked her careful grooming. He was himself immaculate. His gray hair smoothed back over his scientist's head that lifted to a little peak in the back, his gray suits, even his gray pajamas were incredibly neat, as smooth and trim as feathers.

She heard the car on the shell drive and went to meet him. He had brought the mail from the adjacent city, where he had the use of a laboratory.

"A ghost from the past," he said sententiously, and handed her a letter from *Home Life*.

He kissed her with a longer clinging than usual, so that she checked the date in her mind. Two weeks ago—yes, this was his evening to make love to her. Their months of marriage were marked off into two-week periods as definitely as though the / line on the typewriter cut through them. He drew off from her with disapproval if she showed fondness between a / and a /. She went to the living room to read her letter from May Morrow.

DEAR ELSA:
Your beach house sounds altogether too idyllic. What previous incarnated suffering has licenced you to drop into an idyll? And so young in life. Well, maybe I'll get mine next time.

As you can imagine, there have been a hundred people after your job. The Collins girl that I rushed into it temporarily didn't work out at all, and I was beginning to despair when Jane Maxe, from *Woman's Outlook*, gave me a ring and said she was fed up with their politics and would come to us if the job was permanent. I assured her that it was hers until she had to be carried out on her shield. You see, I know your young type. You've burned your bridges and set out to be A Good Wife, and hell will freeze before you quit anything you tackle.

Glad the Distinguished Spouse proves as clever in daily conversation as in print. Have you had time to notice that trick writers have of saying something neat, recognizing it at once as a precious nut to be stored, then bringing it out later in the long hard winter of literary composition? You will. Drop me a line. I wonder about things sometimes.

MAY

She wanted to sit down at the portable at once, but Dr. Tifton came into the room.

"I'll have my shower later," he said, and rolled his round gray eyes with meaning.

His mouth, she noticed, made a long, thin line that gave the impression of a perpetual half-smile. She mixed the Martinis and he sipped his with appreciation. He had a smug expectancy that she recognized from her brief dealings with established authors. He was waiting for her favorable comment on his article.

"Your article was grand," she said. "If I were still an editor, I'd have grabbed it."

He lifted his eyebrows. "Of course," he said, "editors were grabbing my articles before I knew you." He added complacently, "And after."

"I mean," she said uncomfortably, "that an editor can only judge things by her own acceptance."

"An editor?" He looked sideways at her. His eye seemed to have the ability to focus backward. "And what does a wife think of my article?"

She laughed. "Oh, a wife thinks that anything you do is perfect." She added, "Isn't that what wives are for?"

She regretted the comment immediately, but he was bland.

"I really think I gave the effect I wanted," he said. "Science is of no use to the layman unless it's humanized."

They sipped the Martinis.

"I'd like to have you read it aloud," he said, studying his glass casually. "One learns things from another's reading."

She picked up the magazine gratefully. The reading would fill nicely the time between cocktails and dinner.

"It really gives the effect, doesn't it?" he said when she had finished. "I think anyone would get the connection, of which I am always conscious, between the lower forms of life and the human."

"It's a swell job," she said.

Dinner began successfully. The donac broth was strong enough. She had gone out in her bathing suit to gather the tiny clams just before high tide. The broiled pompano was delicately brown and flaky. The cauliflower was all right, after all. The hollandaise, unfortunately, was thin. She had so frightened Jones about the heinousness of cooking it too long that he had taken it off the fire before it had quite thickened.

"My dear," Dr. Tifton said, laying down his fork, "surely it is not too much to ask of an intelligent woman to teach a servant to make a simple sauce."

She felt a little hysterical. "Maybe I'm not intelligent," she said.

"Of course you are," he said soothingly. "Don't misunderstand me. I am not questioning your intelligence. You just do not realize the importance of being exact with an inferior."

He took a large mouthful of the cauliflower and hollandaise. The flavor was beyond reproach, and he weakened.

"I know," he said, swallowing and scooping generously again, "I know that I am a perfectionist. It's a bit of a bother sometimes, but of course it is the quality that makes me a scientist. A literary —shall I say literate?—no, articulate scientist."

He helped himself to a large pat of curled butter for his roll. The salad, the pineapple mousse, the after-dinner coffee and liqueur went off acceptably. He smacked his lips ever so faintly.

"Excuse me a moment, my mouse," he said. His digestion was rapid and perfect.

Now that he was in the bathroom, it had evidently occurred to him to take his shower and get into his dressing gown. She heard the water running and the satisfied humming he emitted when all was well. She would have time, for he was meticulous with his fortnightly special toilet, to begin a letter to May Morrow. She took the portable typewriter out to a glass-covered table on the terrace. The setting sun reached benignly under the awning. She drew a deep breath. It was a little difficult to begin. May had almost sounded as though she did not put full credence in the idyll. She wanted to write enthusiastically but judiciously, so May would understand that she, Elsa, was indeed a fortunate young woman, wed irrevocably, by her own deliberate, intelligent choice, to a brilliant man—a real man, second only in scientific and literary rating to Dr. Beebe.

DEAR MAY:

It was grand to hear from you. I'm thrilled about Jane Maxe. What a scoop! I could almost be jealous of both of you if my lines hadn't fallen into such gloriously pleasant places.

I am, of course, supremely happy—

She leaned back. She was writing gushily. Married women had the damnedest way, she had always noticed, of gushing. Perhaps the true feminine nature was sloppy, after all. She deleted "gloriously," crossed out "supremely," and inserted "tremendously." She would have to copy the letter.

A shadow passed between the terrace and the ocean. She looked up. One of those beastly pelicans was flapping down the coast over the sand dunes. He had already fed, or he would be flapping, in that same sure way of finding what he wanted, over the surf. It was ridiculous to be disturbed by him. Yet somewhere she suspected there must be an association of thoughts that had its base in an unrecognized antipathy. Something about the pelican's shadow, darkening her heart and mind with that absurd desperation, must be connected with some profound and secret dread, but she could not seem to put her finger on it.

She looked out from under the lemon-colored awning. The pelican had turned and was flapping back again. She had a good look at him. He was neatly gray, objectionably neat for a creature with such greedy habits. His round head, lifted to a peak, was sunk against his heavy shoulders. His round gray eye looked down below him, a little behind him, with a cold, pleased, superior expression. His long, thin mouth was unbearably smug, with the expression of a partial smile.

"Oh, go on about your business!" she shouted at him.

INCIDENT ON A STREET CORNER

❧

ALBERT MALTZ

I T WAS A SUNDAY AFTERNOON in November, and a wet mist hung heavy on the dark street. Although there seemed to be few passers-by, a small crowd gathered quickly. The young man was very drunk. His face was set in a dull, thick mold with his eyes almost shut, as though he were asleep. And his movements were sleepy, slow, but strangely stubborn, persistent, with the steady, stubborn purpose of a drunken man set upon doing something. He wanted to get away. But the two policemen wouldn't let him.

The policemen were strong, thick-boned men. One was young; he was handsome, with a white, bony face that had a small scar over the lip. The other looked more seasoned; his face was meaty and red, as though he had been out in the wind for many years.

Each held onto one arm, and as the drunken man tugged heavily, persistently, from side to side, they swung with him. The policemen wore dark oilskins. These bore them down and seemed to restrict their arms. Occasionally they tugged at one of the clips in an effort to free themselves. But each time the drunken man pulled, and then they had to hold onto him again.

The men in the crowd watched in silence. Some had a look of vague fear about them; others held their lips in the curve of a smile, but all of them watched intently, waiting.

Suddenly the drunken man fell backward. The policemen had caught him off balance. He was not hurt when he fell; they had held onto him, and so his fall was broken.

The red-faced one stood up. "Hold him a minute," he said to the other. He began to undo his raincoat.

The drunk would not stay still. With his eyes shut and his

blond hair falling over his young face so that he looked like a sleepwalker, he kept up his stubborn, aimless struggle.

The red-faced one got his coat off. He turned to one of the bystanders, a little man in a derby. "Hold this, will you?" he asked. The man took the coat and folded it over his arm. The policeman stepped back. And as he stepped back, the drunk twisted his body, curled his legs under him, and got to his knees. It seemed as though the whole contest was to begin over again.

With a sudden, explosive movement the red-faced policeman crooked his leg and brought it up. "Awright!" he said.

The bone of his knee clumped against the man's face. It broke his nose, and the blood spurted out in a thick, red stream.

From the spectators there came an instantaneous, muffled cry. It was low, a sucking-in of breath. Then there was silence. The policemen straightened up.

The drunk was leaning forward on both hands, no longer making any attempt to get away. His head drooped down, too heavy for him to carry. Beneath the white skin of his neck the muscles were limp and trembling.

There was a ripple of quick movement in the crowd and a young man pushed forward, his face flushed. "Do something," he said. "You can't leave him like that. Do something."

The policemen looked up quickly, their faces vacant, bewildered. The red-faced one made a half-gesture with his hand. "We been arguin' with him half an hour," he said.

The drunken man moaned, his cry full of pain and shock. His head sagged back and the blood dripped down to his worn coat.

A man called out from the crowd, "Lay him down. Put somethin' under his lip."

The one who had stepped forward bent over and put a handkerchief to the drunk's nose. He pressed him back until he was lying full length on the sidewalk. The policemen watched awkwardly, their brows furrowed.

For a moment again there was silence.

A woman turned the corner and came up to the crowd. She was about thirty-five, with a shrivelled, hungry little body, and ugly teeth that pressed out beyond her lips. She pushed through the wall of bodies, and looked at the man on the sidewalk. Then, as though a shock of electricity had passed through her body, she began to scream. "I know you," she said. "I know you cops! You beat a poor man up. I know you."

The young policeman swung around. His face was flushed with rage.

"Go home," he said to her. His voice was ugly. "Go home. You better go home."

The woman kept on, her shrill voice rising higher and higher, her body trembling. "You brutes, you dirty brutes! Two dirty brutes arrested me once, too."

"Go home," the cop said. "I know your kind. Go home, go home." His face was ugly. He was crouching, with his head pulled in against his shoulders.

The woman spoke evenly, with sudden calm. "Just wait. You'll get yours some day, too." Then, as quickly as she had come, she was gone.

The red-faced cop pushed into the crowd. His voice took on the familiar tone. "Break it up," he growled. "C'mon, you're blocking the street. Break it up there."

The crowd opened before him. He cleared a lane and walked back. The curved wall closed again. The ring was solid once more.

The cop stared. He gestured with his hand. "We been arguin' with him half an hour," he said.

No one answered. The crowd was mostly composed of men. They looked like workingmen of one sort or another—Irish, all of them dressed in their Sunday clothes. They stood locked together, thickset, heavy-featured, with a sullen look to their faces. One of them took a piece of paper and a pencil out of his pocket. Looking at the cops, he started to write.

The young cop stepped over to him. "What are you doin'?"

The man didn't answer. He kept on with his writing.

"What are you doin'?" the cop asked again. "You want me to run you in?"

"You can run me in if you want to," the man replied. "I'm takin' down your number."

He put the paper in his pocket. The cop was silent. He remained where he was.

A passer-by came up and asked in a loud voice what had happened. A man in the back row answered him. "Some poor guy got drunk, so these cops went an' smeared him." The answer was loud, challenging.

"What about it?" the red-faced policeman said. He stuttered a little. "We've got to keep order, don't we? We're guardians of the law, ain't we?"

"Like hell you are!"

"Who said that? Who said that?" The older cop looked around belligerently.

"I did." A stocky, middle-aged man with a big head and a powerful set to his body stepped forward. He stood with his feet wide apart and his hands behind his back. "I did."

"Oh, you did?" the cop repeated. He stuttered. "You want me to run you in?"

"I don't give a damn what you do."

"You don't, eh? You don't?" the cop repeated. "What's the matter with you?" There was a pause. "What do you come around here for, tryin' to make trouble?" He turned to the others. "Why the hell don't you all clear out of here?"

"We ain't gonna make trouble, Officer," the stocky man answered softly. "We're just gonna see you don't beat him up no more."

"That's right," someone else said.

"You talk like we was apes or somethin'," the older cop said bitterly. "I'm an Irishman 'n' a Catholic. I've got my dooty 'n' I do it."

"I'll tell you somethin', brother," the middle-aged man replied, "as one Irishman to another. It was a good Irish Catholic like you who cracked my skull in the dock strike of nineteen-fifteen. When an Irish Catholic puts on a cop's uniform, he's a cop. He's no Irishman or Catholic any longer."

"I oughta run you in, you mick," the older cop burst out, swearing. "I oughta book you right now."

"Get an ambulance, you upstanding Irish Catholic," the middle-aged man said. "You're leavin' a hurt man lie on the ground."

The policeman glared at him.

"Go on, get an ambulance," several men repeated.

"I'm gettin' it, I'm gettin' it," the cop said. "Take your god-dam time. I don't need you to tell me my business." He moved toward the crowd.

"Get it before you need one yourself," someone said.

The cop stopped. He put his hand to his gun.

"Take it easy," the middle-aged man said.

The ring opened. The cop walked through to the telephone box on the corner. The ring closed again. The little man in the derby who had been holding the cop's raincoat on his arm stepped forward and put it on the ground.

"What's the idea?" the young cop asked. "What are you puttin' it on the ground for?"

The man didn't answer. The crowd opened for him. He walked away quickly. The solid ring closed again. It began to rain, but no one moved. It was quite dark now. They stood there, waiting for the ambulance.

"What's the matter with you?" the young cop burst out suddenly. "What the hell's the matter with you?"

No one answered him.

SUCH A PRETTY DAY

❧

DAWN POWELL

A
S SOON AS Dave had put the pen in the yard and waved goodbye to the baby, Sylvia got on the phone.

"Hello, Barbs. Scotty gone yet? . . . Listen, Barbs, Dave says
they're working overtime this noon, so he won't be home for
lunch. . . . Scotty, too, eh? Listen, Barbs, it's such a pretty day,
I thought we might go to the city. You bring the kids over and I'll
get Frieda. . . . Yes, I know she's a brat and she'll tell the whole
neighborhood, but she's good with the kids. Listen, don't say anything. My God, Dave'd kill me. You heard what he said last Sunday
—if he caught me thumbing again he'd get a divorce? Listen, he
means it. You come on over, Barbs. . . . O.K., Barbs. . . . Oh, I'm
goin' to wear my play suit. . . . Your linen? Why don't you wear
your play suit? It looks kinda cute on you. . . . Oh, come on, Barbs,
I'm going to. . . . O.K., Barbs. The baby's yelling. 'Bye."

Sylvia ran into the bedroom and whisked up the beds. She
snatched up newspapers, toys, Dave's pajamas, a ten-cent double
boiler with some petrified oatmeal in it, and tossed them all in the
closet. That was one thing about having your own house; your
mother couldn't be nagging at you to do things her way all the
time. Sylvia couldn't get over the thrill of her own house. Five
whole rooms, just for her and Dave and the baby. Never had even
one room to herself before she was married. Darn it all, she was
happy. Let 'em talk. Her own mother was married at sixteen, too,
wasn't she? Supposing she'd sat around and finished school, what
then? She could have a job in the factory and get up every
morning at six-thirty like Gladys Chalk, instead of lying around
her own house all day in a nightgown. She could sit around waiting
for some guy to call her up, and God knows there weren't enough

boys in town to go around, instead of having a nice fellow like Dave all sewed up permanently. So maybe Sylvia wasn't so dumb as her folks said. So what?

Mrs. Peters was in the back yard fooling with the baby when Sylvia went out, and that was all right, because she could ask her about Frieda.

"You look about ten years old in those overalls," said Mrs. Peters. "I should think youda put on more weight being married two years already. I wouldn't take you for more'n twelve at the most."

"No cracks," said Sylvia coldly. "I was nineteen last Tuesday. Did you see the toaster Dave got me? We don't eat much toast, but I have to make a lot 'cause it makes the baby laugh so the way the toast jumps out."

"I don't think that installment plan is good for young folks," said Mrs. Peters, as if it was any of her business, but Sylvia took it because she wanted Frieda.

"How else you going to get anything on eighteen a week, Mrs. Peters?" she merely asked. "Look, Mrs. Peters, could Frieda come over today and look after Davie? I got a chance to go to the city— there's a picture I want to see at the Majestic."

Mrs. Peters blew out her cheeks, and Davie laughed and squealed with joy. He was a good baby. Even Mrs. Peters had to say so.

"I couldn't run around the way you do when I was raising a family," said Mrs. Peters. "If it wasn't washing, it was canning or berrying or helping in Mr. Peters' store."

All right, we'll go into that, then. The trouble with those old married women was they thought they had a racket all to themselves and they didn't like pretty young girls breaking into it.

"Tell Frieda she can make a cake if she wants, too," Sylvia conceded. "There's flour and chocolate, and she can run the radio for a while."

"If it's that Barbara friend of yours you're going with," said Mrs. Peters, "I wouldn't let any daughter of mine run around with her. Her folks are nothing but trash. There hasn't ever been a Moller that amounted to a stick in this town. Frieda says she saw six beer bottles in the sink there one morning."

"Barbs and Scotty are Dave's and my best friends," said Sylvia in her best missus voice, and was that a lie, with Dave half the time saying just what Mrs. Peters was saying! "Tell Frieda to come about eleven. We want to get a good start."

Barbs walked in, wheeling the twins. They were not quite a year old but were big babies, like Davie, and made Barbs look like a school kid, which she probably should have been, but keeping house was a lot more fun. You could say what you liked about Barbs, maybe she did run wild until Scotty and the twins kinda settled her, but you had to hand it to her—she kept that dinky apartment of hers spick-and-span. "Maybe," Sylvia always said, looking around the trim little suite over the butcher shop, "if I only had three rooms instead of a whole house I could get interested, too."

Frieda came over at ten minutes to eleven. She wore thick glasses over her slightly crossed eyes and her former pigtails had been miraculously transformed into a kinky, tangled mass.

"I got a permanent," she said proudly.

Both Barbs and Sylvia were crazy for permanents, so they were silent for a moment in envious awe.

"I don't like permanents on kids," said Barbs haughtily.

"Everybody in my Sunday-school class has one," said Frieda, unperturbed. "My mother says it's a hundred-per-cent improvement. My mother's making me a play suit too. Where you going? To the city? I thought Dave told you not to thumb any more, Sylvia."

"Listen to the brat," said Barbs. "Do you run this town, Miss Wisie?"

"You better be careful or I won't take care of your old twins," said Frieda. "Can I really make a cake, Sylvia?"

Sylvia motioned Barbs into the house, and they went in to whisper ways of getting out to the turnpike without Frieda's being able to tell. Scotty didn't like Barbs' hitching any more than Dave liked Sylvia's, because everybody in the town talked enough anyway, and she was a married woman now and ought to know better.

At first Sylvia thought it was because Scotty was older—he was twenty-seven—and more settled—he'd worked in the factory since he was twelve—but then Dave, who was just twenty, got to talking that way, too. They didn't want their wives hiking around the

state like a couple of tramps, they both said. You didn't see the
Hull girls doing it, did you? Or Dody Crane?

"The Hull girls and Dody Crane! Can you imagine?" Sylvia repeated in indignation. "Why should they? They got their own
cars, and Dody's dad is rich."

At that, Sylvia had nothing against Dody. The Hull girls were
snobs because they'd gone away to boarding school while Sylvia
and Barbs were plugging through public school, but Dody was all
right; she always spoke to Sylvia, and once Dave had taken her to
a dance. She wouldn't let him kiss her, so he married Sylvia instead
and promoted Dody to be his ideal. Sylvia got kind of sick always
being pecked at to do things the way Dody would do them. That
was the only thing. But Dody was all right. She sent the baby a
cute blanket once.

Barbs stuck the twins' bottles in the icebox and Frieda put all
the babies in the pen. She was a fat little girl, but that wasn't the
only reason nobody loved her. She pulled out a campstool from behind the tool shed and sat down on it on the grass with a book.

"I'll read to them for a while," she said, "from the Bible."

The three fat little babies, clad in nothing but their G-strings,
stared at Frieda, rather pleased with her glasses.

"They'll love that," said Sylvia, and she and Barbs sneaked out
the front way, past the garage, to the pike.

They walked sedately enough past the straggling houses, and
tried not to look up at tempting cars shooting past, because you
couldn't tell yet; it might be somebody from the factory, who
would tell the boys. A roadster with two men in it slowed up and
one of them yelled, "Hi, Crawford," but the girls dared not look
up yet.

"You know, Sylvia, you do look kinda like Joan Crawford,"
said Barbs, studying Sylvia critically. "Somebody else, I forget who,
said so. Me, I'm more the Merle Oberon type."

"You got freckles, too, if that's what you mean," said Sylvia.

A blue sedan drove slowly past, and Barbs nudged Sylvia. It
was the Hull sisters on their way to the country club. They stared
at the two girls and Barbs and Sylvia stared insolently back. Then
Dody Crane's car came along, Dody driving with her mother, two

golf bags sticking out of the side. Dody nodded and Sylvia nodded back.

"Imagine a girl that old running around all the time with her old lady," said Barbs, who after all had been ignored by Dody.

Now they were past the club road and on the main highway. They stopped and began working. It never took them long, because they were a couple of good-looking girls, as they well knew, and even women weren't afraid of being held up by such a nice little pair. This time it was a woman in a big Cadillac. She was a thin, browned woman with iron-gray hair, and she drove like a house afire. Some fun! They were in the heart of the city in less than an hour.

"Let's go to the show right away," suggested Sylvia.

Everybody looked at the two bareheaded girls, in their red play suits, wandering through the business section. Barbs stopped short suddenly.

"Listen, Sylvia, I only got fifteen cents."

"But I told you we would go to the Majestic," said Sylvia, annoyed. "You know it's twenty."

"Well, I just don't have it," said Barbs, doggedly. "I guess you wouldn't have it, either, if you had two kids instead of one and your husband had to fork over two bucks a week to his mother."

"Why don't she get on relief?" complained Sylvia. "Dave's mother did."

"Dave's mother is in another town," said Barbs. "And anyway Scotty don't like the idea. So I only got fifteen cents."

Sylvia was furious.

"I go to work and get Frieda for us and let her mess up my kitchen baking a cake, and now you don't have twenty cents for a show. Barbs, honestly, you're a lousy sport. Why didn't you tell me?"

Barbs was sullen.

"I wanted to get outa town for five minutes, show or no show."

Sylvia counted her money. Thirty-seven cents.

"You go alone, and I'll look around the stores," said Barbs.

It ended with their each buying a Frojoy at a corner stand for lunch and then going on a shopping tour. They went through

Schwab's because Barbs dared Sylvia to go in. This was a large, cool, dark, swanky store, and so snooty that Barbs and Sylvia clutched each other's hand to keep up their courage before the hostile clerks.

"This is where Dody gets all her clothes," said Sylvia. "Except the ones she gets in New York."

"A lot of good it does her," said Barbs. "I'll bet she'd give her eyeteeth to be married and have kids like we have. She played with dolls longer than any of us. She had the first mamma doll in town."

"I wish I had a little girl," said Sylvia. "I'd get her a mamma doll."

"I'd get her a Quint Set doll," said Barbs, and that reminded her they must go to the Variety store next.

Schwab's doors swung thankfully behind them.

"Even if I had money, I wouldn't buy clothes in that lousy store," said Barbs. "Their styles are all hick. They've got braid on everything. Look!"

A window display of garden furniture, complete with sand, pool, unbrellas, and mint juleps, held them spellbound. Life-size velvety-lashed ladies in garden frocks sat in swings and deck chairs in attitudes of rigid enjoyment. A rosy, walleyed athlete in shorts relaxed on a tennis roller. Two beaming little boys in bathing suits sat stiffly on a rubber dolphin in the pool.

"I could get the twins bathing suits and one of those false fish," said Barbs. "I'd fill the old tank on the roof with water."

"Like a penthouse," said Sylvia.

They walked on silently to the big Variety store, Sylvia busy putting the fish and Davie in a bathing suit somewhere around her own premises, and Barbs thinking about the tank. The Variety store was more hospitable than Schwab's. A radio was on, and a girl at the piano counter, in a pink sharkskin sports dress, was playing and singing "I Never Knew Heaven Could Speak."

"Say, if I couldn't sing better than that," muttered Barbs.

"It's my favorite song, too," said Sylvia. "But don't she ruin it?"

They hummed it softly, looking over the counters.

"I'll bet we could sing over the radio if we practiced more," said Sylvia. "Honestly, Barbs, even Dave thinks we're good."

"Ah, nuts!" said Barbs. "Nobody's going to let us do anything ever. Wish I had my hands on that two bucks we sent off to Scotty's Mom right now.

"I could let you have ten cents, maybe," said Sylvia, relenting, but just then her eye caught something and she added, "Still, you got ten of your own, haven't you?"

Barbs saw what Sylvia saw. It was a baby's bathing suit for twenty-nine cents. Probably it was only fair. After all, Sylvia did have thirty-two cents and only one baby.

"Now, you only got three cents," was all Barbs said when the girl gave Sylvia the package. Sylvia unwrapped it right away and held it up. It was bright red, with a little white belt. It was the cutest thing.

"I'd rather have had the striped ones like the ones in the window," said Barbs, but Sylvia read the envy in her voice and grinned.

At the next counter were spades and beach pails, and here Barbs was as lost as Sylvia, because she had to buy two or nothing, so ten cents was no good. At the foot of the counter were rubber floats, and one was a dolphin almost like the one in the window. It was a dollar ninety-eight and it came in a box; you blew it up. Sylvia and Barbs stared at it.

"Kids don't need bathing suits on a roof," said Barbs. "I can fill that old tank anyway."

"Sure," said Sylvia.

"You can bring Davie up to play in it, too," said Barbs, generously. "But he won't need that suit."

"That'll be fun," said Sylvia. Twenty-nine cents wasted.

They could not take their eyes off the sample dolphin.

"He'd hold two, wouldn't he?" said Barbs.

"Sure—three, even," giggled Sylvia.

She almost knew what Barbs was going to do, and yet in a way you could have knocked her down with a feather. The minute the clerk walked off to the next counter, Barbs had snitched one of the rubber things out of its box and stuffed it down her front. Nothing happened. Nobody screamed. Nobody grabbed them. Barbs looked at Sylvia, and Sylvia's mouth moved helplessly.

"W-w-w-well," said Barbs, "I g-g-g-uess we'd b-b-etter be g-g-g-going to the M-m-m-ajestic."

They walked slowly out of the store. A man in a Panama hat watched them from the radio counter, but he couldn't be anything but a customer. The girl at the bathing-suit counter watched them.

"She saw," gasped Barbs. "Just as I popped it in, I saw her looking, but it was too late to yank it out then. Look—I'm afraid to—is anybody following?"

Sylvia was afraid, too. They walked in slow agony down the street. Someone was behind them. Out of the corner of her eye Sylvia saw it was the man in the Panama hat. He grinned. Sylvia grew red. Barbs clutched her arm frantically.

"Let's get a hitch, quick," she whispered. "We got to go home now."

"But it's only two o'clock," said Sylvia. "Anyway, if somebody's watching from the store, they'll see us."

"Oh—oh, what'll we do," whispered Barbs. "Does it show?"

Sylvia giggled.

"No, you only look like Aunt Jemima, that's all."

Barbs was looking up and down the street for a possible hitch. The man in the Panama hat was getting into a Chevrolet coupé. He grinned again, and imperceptibly winked. Barbs and Sylvia walked up to him. Before they spoke, two men in shirtsleeves from the Variety came out on the sidewalk, and with one accord the girls climbed into his car. He slammed the door and drove quickly around the corner.

"Oh, gee!" breathed Barbs. "Oh, thanks!"

The man was a swarthy, foreign-looking fellow, with a candy-striped shirt and a diamond ring.

"I got the idea," he said.

Nobody said anything more till they were outside the city limits, and then Sylvia noticed they were not going in the direction of home.

"Albany's my next stop," said the driver. He turned to Barbs. "That wasn't your first job there in the store, was it, sugar?"

Barbs looked blank.

"Don't act so innocent," he said, laughing. "I knew what you girls were up to as soon as I saw those red outfits. But you'd better not work that store again. They've got you down now. For that matter, you'd better leave that town alone a while."

"I don't know what you're talking about," said Sylvia, with dignity, "and anyway we're not going in this direction."

"What do you say going to Albany with me and then on to New York? A couple of girls like you could clean up a thousand dollars a week—just the big stores, understand, nice merchandise, not ordinary snatching. I could send you straight up to a friend of mine on 135th Street and you'd be treated right. A couple of nice kids like you could get away with murder. What do you want to waste your time stealing bathing suits and rubber gadgets?"

"I bought this bathing suit," said Sylvia angrily.

"Why," gasped Barbs, "you don't think we're thieves?"

The girls looked at each other in growing horror at his sardonic laugh.

"Of course you're not thieves, honey," he chuckled. "You was just taking what you liked, that was all. Don't kid me, sister, you're a smart girl—both of you, for that matter. You got talent; you could do big stuff, I'm telling you. I did you a favor today. Why don't you do me a favor now and try out the big time? You could wire your folks."

"We're married women," said Sylvia. "Our husbands would come after us."

"Think it over," said the driver, good-humoredly. "You might give me your names and I'll drop you a card, reminding you where to get in touch if you change your mind." He pulled a silver pencil out of his pocket and a card.

"Dody Crane," said Sylvia.

"Teresa Hull," quavered Barbs.

"Well, Dody and Terry, you'll hear from me," he said, and slowed up near a filling station. "You're the best talent I've seen in these parts. All you need is training and a little protection."

At the filling station, he got out and went inside. Without a word Sylvia and Barbs slipped out and ran to the road, hiding in the bushes along the way. They saw him come back out, look for them briefly, and question the mechanic. Then, with a shake of his head, he got in and drove off. Barbs and Sylvia looked at each other and drew a great breath of relief.

"I never was so scared," said Barbs. "Believe me, I'll never swipe anything again."

"I should hope not," said Sylvia.

Barbs pulled the rubber out of her dress and began to blow it up. Sylvia watched. Barbs' face grew redder and redder, and the fish grew bigger and bigger. It was bigger than the one in the window. It would easily seat the twins and Davie, all three. Then Barbs' face grew worried; she took the fish away from her mouth.

"I forgot to take the darned stopper," she panted, and tears stood in her eyes. "Oh, darn! Oh, Sylvia!"

"Maybe a piece of paper," suggested Sylvia, but the fish collapsed, dwindled to nothing. Barbs looked down at it in the middle of the ditch in disgust.

"I *would* forget the stopper," she said. "I'd *have* to forget the most important thing."

"Honestly, Barbs, you may keep your house better than I do, but you're dumb about lots of things," said Sylvia. "This is the last I go with her," she thought. "I didn't even get to see 'Dark Victory.'"

An empty ice truck drove along, and Sylvia and Barbs jerked their thumbs. The car slowed down and they climbed in among the burlap bags in the back, where a young man in a bathing suit and dirty white slacks sat, fiddling with a harmonica. The girls settled themselves in the corner opposite him.

"I still got ten cents," Barbs said.

The car jolted them along the country roads, past cornfields and waving wheat.

"Hi, Crawford!" the boy said to Sylvia.

The girls looked at each other and laughed.

"What's that you're chewing?" he asked.

"Bubble gum," said Sylvia, and snapped it.

He said nothing more, but stared at them as he played his harmonica. Barbs and Sylvia sang while he played their favorite piece, "I Never Knew Heaven Could Speak." They sang all the way home. The boy and the truck-driver both said they ought to be on the radio or, at the very least, the stage.

PORTRAIT OF LADIES

❧

MARK SCHORER

IT WAS TWO O'CLOCK in the morning and the still brilliantly illuminated living room of Lotta Gordon's country house had a cold air of emptiness, which the three people in it did nothing to relieve. All the other guests had gone upstairs to bed, and the ladies, having a last drink together, had turned their backs on Mr. Payson, who, unaware of the affront, was resting stuporously with his chin fallen forward on the bulge of his shirt front, his eyes closed.

Mrs. Payson leaned forward. "I must warn you, Lotta," she said. "In a moment he'll begin to snore. We'll try not to hear."

"Our conversation is not stimulating, I should say."

"Pay no attention to him," Mrs. Payson said as she turned to look at her husband with glassy-eyed distaste.

Lotta sipped at her highball before she said, "He drinks rather too much, doesn't he?"

Mrs. Payson nodded. "Every time we're asked out to the country for the weekend."

"I see," said Lotta.

"It *is* a delight to find someone who will sit up after everyone else had gone to bed and be lucid with one."

"Lucid?" Lotta repeated doubtfully.

"You *are* lucid, Lotta, you know."

"Am I?"

"Oh, definitely!"

Lotta looked down into her glass and said, "It was amusingly evident, just before he—went to sleep?—that a struggle was going on. His back so erect, eyes fixed on one small, stationary object or another, almost desperately."

313

Mrs. Payson laughed. "My dear, I know! He always loses." She smiled and put her head back, arched her spine, and lifted her arms in a long stretch. "Drinking, Lotta, is a refinement that should be reserved for the appreciative. Now I—I get the most delicious sensations. Sometimes almost of a submarine world. All movement becomes luxurious. Sometimes I seem to myself almost like a strange plant on the ocean floor."

A sound broke from Mr. Payson, at first almost like a purr, but in a few moments stronger and louder until presently it had developed into an obvious and disturbing snore. Mrs. Payson did not turn to look at him, but Lotta's eyes moved ever so slightly until her cold glance fixed itself upon him.

"Do be still," Mrs. Payson said sharply, without turning, and then, "You see, he destroys all loveliness."

"Yes."

"And now," she said, "now I must get him to bed!"

"We'll wake him—"

"*Wake* him? My dear, you don't know! You can't wake him. He's as good as dead now. Really. Wake him, indeed! That isn't sleep, Lotta. That is a drunken stupor."

"Yes," said Lotta, "so it is. What shall we do with him?"

Mrs. Payson put her head back and emptied her glass. Then she came to her feet, swaying slightly, and said, "There's only one technique."

"Let me call one of the servants," Lotta said, rising too, and standing beside Mrs. Payson. In their long gowns they looked very tall, fragile, and very slim.

"We must not take advantage of him," Mrs. Payson pointed out, and, glancing at him again, added, "Unattractive jelly that he is!" A speculative silence followed upon her words as they regarded him together. Finally Mrs. Payson said, "No, there's only one technique. If urged, his feet will more or less work, so we shall not have to carry him, at any rate. We'll push him up the stairs. From the rear."

"Oh."

"To begin," she went on crisply, "we must each take hold of an arm and pull."

They leaned over the figure in the chair and wrapped their long, sinuous arms round Mr. Payson's heavy ones, and, when Mrs. Payson signalled "All right," pulled. With a grunt which interrupted the snoring—indeed, ended it—Mr. Payson's ample body came to its feet.

"Walk!" Mrs. Payson ordered.

A kind of shudder passed through the sagging form, and then, feebly coöperative, the dragging feet moved along between the ladies' into the foyer and to the foot of the stairs.

"Now we rest," said Mrs. Payson breathlessly.

Mr. Payson was let slowly down on his face, his head on the fourth step, his feet on the floor. Mrs. Payson stood against his shoes so that he would not slip down. Lotta, dishevelled but hardly panting, leaned against the wall. Her hand, it seemed to Mrs. Payson, rose dreamily to her face as she said, "Such a burden to you, dear."

"I can't tell you, really."

"Poor dumb thing," Lotta said wearily.

"No pity!" Mrs. Payson warned her almost sharply. "I haven't a shred of it, you know, not a shred! It's a sad admission, but"—and her arm went out in a languid arc until her hand pointed at him with limp accusation—"I ask you, in all fairness, has he deserved it?"

"Poor dumb thing!"

"We'll have another highball," Mrs. Payson said, "once we've got him tucked away." And more briskly, more brightly than she had yet spoken, "Well, then, to work!"

With the efficiency of experience she bent swiftly to her task. "I get him up this way," she said, encircling his torso with her arms, and, panting, pulled him up. "Onto the banister, thus!"

With his chest flat against the broad marble banister, one arm flung over it, Mr. Payson seemed to rest comfortably. "Now I'll need you, Lotta. He's really quite heavy, isn't he? We push now."

She moved her arms until her hands were firmly planted against Mr. Payson's bottom, and Lotta arranged her hands similarly.

"Now!" cried Mrs. Payson.

Slowly Mr. Payson began to move up the stairs. Inch by inch his chest slid along the banister and his limp feet, reluctantly, with the ladies' feet just behind them so that they could not slip back, dragged themselves up, step by step.

"Save your strength for what's ahead," Mrs. Payson admonished. "A slow, steady pressure does wonders at this stage."

Lotta, laughing a little, said, "No one can know how much this has done for your figure."

"No one," Mrs. Payson said, "can know the discipline to my spirit!"

The unsteady progress continued until, with a note of imminent triumph in her voice, Mrs. Payson called out, "Gently, now! Gently! Just one more step!" And, "There!"

With a quick movement she braced herself against the body. "Up!" she commanded harshly as the feet threatened to slip. "Up, now!" The feet obeyed and Mr. Payson, doubled over the top of the broad banister, became stationary. Lotta moved to a mirror and pushed her hair back from her face with languorous hands.

"Lotta, with your head raised that way, your neck—really, it's lovely."

Lotta smiled and said, "Let's finish. Your room, fortunately, is just there."

"From here to that table, then on to the door," Mrs. Payson said. "Will you open it?"

Once more, with their arms wrapped round his, the ladies pulled Mr. Payson along between them, until, at the table, they let him down again. But the movement was too abrupt or Mr. Payson too heavy for the table, for instantly, without a warning creak, the table crashed under him and he fell headlong among the ruins of it, his head, after one thud, resting gently against the opened door of his own room, his body half across the threshold.

Mrs. Payson groaned, and Lotta, after one brief, unwilling glance at the spectacle, said, "It's quite all right."

"How too exasperating!"

"Look," said Lotta then, "don't you really think that one's always spending much too much time on drunkards, always trying to get them from where they are to where one thinks they should be? Why not leave him there? He's perfectly comfortable, you know."

Mrs. Payson's face broke into smiles of pleasure. "Lotta," she said, "you *are* lucid, you see! Just one moment."

Stepping cautiously around Mr. Payson's head, she disappeared into their room for a moment and returned with a comforter. "Or I'll be having to nurse him with a cold," she explained, spreading it over the still form. The gentle introduction to his snoring had begun again, and Mrs. Payson listened to it for a moment before she straightened up and said, "Now for our reward, our highball!"

Lotta started down the stairs, moving slowly, with infinite grace, her gown molded about her long legs and trailing behind her in exquisite folds. It seemed to Mrs. Payson that she moved like a figure in a slow dance or like vegetation in a submarine world.

Then Mr. Payson's purring broke again into the harsher snore, and suddenly Mrs. Payson swung around with repressed fury and stamped her long, narrow foot at him. "Oh, *you!*" she cried.

PAROCHIAL SCHOOL

❦

PAUL HORGAN

WHEN MATINS RANG, Sister Frances Agnes was already awake, though it was chilly and her teaching exhausted her every day. The night noises were still confusing the streets when she arose, and she closed the window, saying her early-morning prayers silently as she moved about her little room. There was, she thought in that half-devotional consciousness which she had learned as a novice, only one thing left to be arranged. Dawn came into her pale window; she felt a sudden limited joy at such a fine day in early spring, with the children waiting, and next week her birthday, and today, at St. Vincent de Paul's, the visit of the Bishop of Frumenta. Going down the hollow-ringing, sarcophagal corridor toward the chapel, she squeezed her white hands together upon her breast and then, ashamed of her exuberance, she settled her silver-rimmed glasses straighter on her arched nose and cracked the starch of her wimple.

At breakfast she observed total silence in penance for her exhilaration, but the tumult under her brown and black robes would not lessen. Some ecstasy that she related to her girlhood made the Bishop's visit heavy with meaning. Oh, she couldn't know why, or what! The children in her schoolroom were as excited as she was. They had talked of nothing else for weeks. How many times had they rehearsed the ceremonial etiquette: the ringing of the great brass bell in the hallway of St. Vincent de Paul's Parochial School, the momentary wonder whether it might be a fire instead of "Attention," the murmurs down the hall, with prelatic feet walking in settled state; the open door; the hand bell on the desk, which must be rung to bring the children to their feet; the wise eyes of the visitors, smiling; the greeting, and at last the children's chorus, "Good morning, Right Reverend Father!"

She must get away early, Sister Frances Agnes said; the ferns needed trimming, and as for the blackboards . . . Mother Mary Joseph said she should go on, cautioning her to expect the Bishop between ten and eleven. Monsignor was bringing him. "Was the whole class instructed?

"Instructed!"

"Well?"

"Oh, Mother, we've done nothing else for weeks!"

Mother Mary Joseph nodded her majestic head; her hood eclipsed the thought she held of how great a goose that Frances Agnes was.

When Sister Frances Agnes reached her classroom in the red-brick and white-stone schoolhouse and found Tony there ahead of her, her joy was almost too much. In his arms Tony was hugging the package. Sister Frances Agnes actually ran to him, her habit and rosary swinging wantonly.

"Oh, Tony!" she cried, in a voice like a low bell.

Tony stood up.

"*Si, si,* O.K., we'll fix it now," he said.

He was a small Italian with an impudent smile. He served the altar at six-o'clock mass. Sister Frances Agnes was certain he would have a vocation. They had talked of it often, and often they had stood before the tremendous photograph of the Cardinal that hung in the reception room at St. Vincent de Paul's, admiring it and pitying themselves for the splendor of the ermine and moire, the cross of jewels, the benignity written upon those eminent features, the glory of a destiny rooted in Divine Good. Tony had no trouble picturing himself in such a pose, fifty years hence.

Sister Frances Agnes took Tony's package, opening it, and before looking at what he had brought, carefully folded the brown paper of its wrapping. Then she looked. She covered her mouth with her hands, her eyes consulted Tony in a brimming happiness. On the desk, revealed, was a holy-water basin made of an abalone shell to which was wired a wreath of artificial flowers.

"Eh?" said Tony.

"Oh, Tony, it's beautiful. We'll offer it to Monsignor to hand the Bishop."

"You hand it."

"Oh, I couldn't. Come, pour the water into it from this bottle."

She brought a small bottle from the drawer. Its water looked whiter than city water; Tony knew it was because it had been blessed. While he worked Sister Frances Agnes went to the window boxes with her shears. She trimmed some brown edges from the ferns, settled the curtains beyond them straight, examined the blackboard, where the hymn, "Holy Lord, We Praise Thy Name," was exhibited with sheaves of roses done in colored chalks. Beside it was the list of gold stars. Perhaps the Bishop would step to the board, after congratulating her with a smile, and read some of the names.

The bell broke intemperate upon her last-minute inspection, and the children came. Always, at their coming, Sister Frances Agnes had a small sinking of the heart, at so much energy, so much ignorance, so much sinfulness, and so little time and strength to right these things. But Tony was a little tower of strength. He placed the abalone shell on the brightest corner of her desk and took his seat in the front row. Graziella Paceco laid a clutched geranium on the desk, a city flower, wan at best, now mangled by childish intensity. Sister Frances Agnes thanked her and put the geranium into a glass. Her spirit fell again; this sad flower would be a flaw in the day.

The second bell rang. She tapped the hand bell on her desk; they all sank to the floor for morning prayers, during which a kicking contest developed in the last row and was quelled by a fierce gleam from Sister Frances Agnes.

Some time after nine o'clock, there was a portentous step in the hallway. Sister Frances Agnes put down her speller and listened. She almost nodded to Tony to open the door, but before anything could happen the door was flung open and Mother Mary Joseph stood there, bland, pink, staring at Graziella, and reducing the room to a terrible hush simply by not changing her gaze. Graziella began to blush, though everyone knew it was only the Mother Superior's way of "looking in." This morning the inspecting gaze shifted to Sister Frances Agnes, then to the abalone shell with the

valiant flowers. Tony bridled in virtue. Sister Frances Agnes dared
to smile.

"Merciful heaven!" whispered Mother Mary Joseph, and then,
with a moue of distaste, changed the direction of her glance. "He's
over at the Rectory with Father now. Be sure, children," she said,
turning her pink anger upon the class, "be sure you know what to
do if Monsignor brings the Bishop in here!"

She nodded, closed her eyes for a second in the sight of them all,
as if she had more than she could be expected to bear, and vanished, closing the door.

Sister Frances Agnes felt Tony's eyes, afraid, upon her own.
Good heaven, could there be any doubt that the Bishop would
come in here? Mother had said "if."

An insurrection in the back row again.

"Sssst!"

It was Sister Frances Agnes who made the noise; it quite startled
everybody, there was such venom and hatred in it. Tony dropped
his book from excitement, in sympathy, and she turned to him,
crying: "Pick it up! Ask God to forgive you for being a lazy idle
boy!"

It was another excitement that possessed the classroom when the
brass bell crashed again, at ten minutes to eleven. The children
were afraid they might forget something when the Bishop came
and Sister Frances Agnes was embarrassed now for the abalone
shell as well as the geranium, and Tony, whom she had imagined
in vestments so many times, was as black as a heathen in his scowl.
But there was no time for last-minute plans. They all heard the
great front door swing open, a portly laugh down the hall (that
would be Monsignor MacMurphy), and then a faint rustle and
breeze, with clicks from Mother Mary Joseph's great heavy rosary,
footfalls on the old wooden floors, as the procession came nearer.
The children saw Sister Frances Agnes grow whiter, her eyes im-
plored them to remember: not to forget to kneel for the blessing,
to rise and answer, not to stammer and cry, to cast the eyes modestly down.

The steps in the hall stopped. There was a confusion of words,
then a booming laugh, a fragment of conversation: ". . . and the
Cartinal sait to me, 'You nefer ent your joking,' " and a strange

voice, very low and pleasant, saying, "Indeed, indeed, indeed."
Then the steps resumed, they were coming, they were closer, there
was Mother Mary Joseph in the doorway! For a brief second! Then
her robes whirled, she turned away and graciously led the Bishop
and Monsignor to the next room. The children had a glimpse of
white hair and black cassock with purple sash. They could hear
the scuffle and the chorus rise in the next room, "Good morning,
Right Reverend Father;" they knew emptiness and ache in their
bellies from suspense and relief and disappointment. Sister Frances
Agnes was now a curious, bluish pink. She lifted her speller,
listening and refusing to listen to the next room.

"Tony," she said, "spell 'apostolic.' "

I AM WAITING

❦

CHRISTOPHER ISHERWOOD

THE INCIDENTS which I am about to describe are true, but I can offer you no proof—at least not for the next five years. By that time you will probably have forgotten that you ever read this story. So please believe it or disbelieve it, just as you wish.

Today, October 17, 1939, is my birthday. At the age of sixty-seven I am what you, or anybody else, would call a failure. I have no career, no outstanding achievements behind me. I have never married and I cannot truthfully say that I have ever been loved, though half a dozen people are, perhaps, mildly fond of me. I live in a pleasant house on the outskirts of a town not far from Hartford, Connecticut. The house belongs to my younger brother, a successful and energetic lawyer. Mabel, my brother's wife, is very kind to me on the whole—as long as I am careful to be tidy and not unnecessarily visible. There are three sons, all grown up and married; they frequently visit us with their wives. All these people are well disposed toward me, I think. Why shouldn't they be? I am no sponger; I pay for my board and lodging from a small inherited income. I do try not to be a nuisance, though I know I am sometimes rather a bore. With reference to the story which follows, I need only add that I have never at any time had reason to believe that I possessed psychic powers. I have never been particularly interested in spiritualism, astrology, or the occult. And I know no more of the works of Professor Einstein than does the ordinary semieducated man in the street.

On the evening of Friday, January 6th, of this year—I can be exact, for this was the day after the anniversary of my brother's marriage—I was sitting in the drawing room of our house, alone. The others had all driven into town to go to a movie, so I could enjoy the luxury of drawing my armchair into the very middle of the hearthrug, facing and monopolizing the fire. The time was about twenty minutes to nine. I remember this because I kept glancing at the clock on the mantelpiece in order to be ready to turn on the radio and listen to the news bulletin.

This clock is a wedding present given to my brother by the members of his firm. It is made of china and vaguely supposed to be valuable. A boy and a girl in peasant costume are supporting the clock itself, contained in a basket of purple and green fruits. It would probably have joined several of the other wedding presents in the trunk room years ago, but my sister-in-law likes it and so it remains.

I may have dozed off, as I so often do. At any rate, I had closed my eyes. When I reopened them it was with a violent start, as though somebody had called my name. Perhaps the others had returned unexpectedly early. Some such thought passed through my mind, but I didn't turn my head. I don't know why. All my drowsy attention was focussed upon the clock. And what I immediately noticed was that the left hand was missing from the china figure of the peasant boy.

It is very difficult for me to describe my precise sensations at that moment. In order to do so I have to think back to a time when this discovery had no particular significance. I saw only that the hand had been broken off, wondered how long it had been broken, and was surprised that I had never noticed it before. Mabel would be cross, I thought, and this led me to a fear that I might somehow have done the damage myself while I was asleep. I rubbed my eyes and sat up suddenly in my chair. I blinked several times. How absurd! I must have been dreaming. For now, as I examined the clock, fully awake, I saw that I had made a mistake. The clock wasn't damaged, after all; the china hand was still intact.

One morning about a week later, when I was walking in the garden, Mabel came out of the house with an expression of extreme annoyance on her face. "Wilfred," she said, "I'm afraid I shall have to fire Annie after all." Annie was our new maid, and she wasn't being a success.

"Why?" I asked. "What's she done now?"

"Can you imagine!" Mabel exclaimed. "She's managed to break

the drawing-room clock. She was dusting it, she says. She must have used a sledge hammer."

But already I was pushing past her toward the French windows which open into the drawing room. Entering the room, I saw what in my excitement I had dimly expected to see: the china boy's left hand was broken off at the wrist.

Half an hour after Mabel had shown me the damaged clock, I had forgotten all about my dream. That evening I sat alone in front of the fire and regarded the mutilated boy without a flicker of recollection. Next day the hand was mended, almost without a trace; there was nothing left to remind anybody of the accident. And yet, when the time came to remember, I remembered everything, down to the smallest details.

The second occurrence took place at 11:25 A.M. on Monday, February 20th. I was in my bedroom, standing near a bookcase which occupies the corner behind my bed. Mabel, as far as I know, was in the kitchen with the cook. The maid was cleaning the bathroom. My brother was at his office. None of my nephews were staying at the house.

It was a gray morning. Although, from where I stood, I could not see out of the window, I knew by the pattering noise on the glass that it had begun to rain. I had just decided to look up some passages in "The Ring and the Book." I am very fond of reading Browning.

As I reached out my hand for the volume, I experienced an extraordinary sensation, which swept over me, leaving my body tingling and trembling and the sweat breaking out on my forehead. I stood there as if frozen, with my hand outstretched. What followed cannot have taken more than a minute. Perhaps it occupied only a few seconds.

At first I was aware only of a change of mood, very difficult to describe. I felt lighter, happier, as though some oppression had been lifted from my mind. Lighter; yes, that was the exact word, for my room was actually full of light, of bright sunshine. The sun was casting shadows on the wall above the bookcase. I could feel its warmth on my hands and the back of my neck.

As I stood, I began not only to feel and see but to hear also. Sounds were coming up through the window from the garden below. I heard laughter, voices, and the noise of a tennis ball being hit back and forth across the net. Then one voice, much more distinct than the others, called out, "Come on, Joyce! Give them hell! They're beginning to crack!" It was my youngest nephew. Joyce is the name of his sister-in-law, my eldest nephew's wife.

No words of mine can describe the strangeness of those familiar words and sounds. I listened to them as a dead man might listen to the voices of the living. They were so near to me, and yet so immeasurably remote. "Oh, tricky! Very tricky!" I heard Joyce exclaim. And Bob, my eldest nephew, retorted, "What do you think you're playing—ping-pong?"

That was all. The next moment, the contact—or whatever you like to call it—was broken. My fingers had touched the book, and there I was, back in the gray, clear continuity of normal consciousness, with the rain pattering fast on the pane behind me and the light of a February morning all around. I heard the maid come out of the bathroom and begin to descend the stairs.

I forget exactly what I did next. I think I must have paced the room several times, backward and forward, pausing to look down through the window at the wet tennis court and the empty garden beyond. I was deeply excited and disturbed. Although it still wasn't entirely clear what had happened to me, I was aware that something *had* happened, something so dimly tremendous that it dwarfed every other experience of my whole life. I carefully wrote down what I had heard and seen, as I have described it here. When I had finished, I felt very tired. I lay down on my bed and slept soundly till lunch.

Thereafter I was like a reader who searches for some half-remembered passage in a book. I had a kind of assignation with a certain moment in time. Could I find that moment or would it find me? Obviously, if I had really travelled into the future and not back into the past, I should have several months to wait. It was very difficult to be patient.

Toward the end of May, Jack, my youngest nephew, came to visit us. He was to stay a fortnight. The fine weather had started and the tennis court was already put in order. Whenever anybody spoke of tennis, I, who have never taken any interest in the game, felt my pulse throb with suppressed excitement. But where were the other actors in the strange, meaningless little drama I hoped to witness? I repeatedly asked Mabel and my brother if Bob and Joyce were expected. No, they said, not yet. Bob, who is a certified public accountant, had an auditing job in Boston. He wouldn't be likely to visit us before August.

On the afternoon of Saturday, June 3rd, I returned by bus from shopping in town. It was about a quarter to three. Hearing a confused sound of voices from the garden, I decided to slip into the house by the back door, not wishing to meet the visitors, whoever they were, while I was hot, dusty, and laden with parcels. Encountering nobody, I climbed the stairs to my room. I had bought several books at the local stationery store and my first thought was to unwrap them. As I moved toward the bookcase I heard Jack's voice on the lawn below, calling the score, "Fifteen all!"

A girl's voice, which I didn't recognize, cried, "You skunk, you're cheating!"

"Oh, good shot!"

"Lousy!"

"Don't try that Forest Hills stuff here!"

"Damn!"

"Come on, Joyce! Give them hell! They're beginning to crack!"

It was there, my moment. And even as, with a gasp, I recognized it, it was past—it flashed by me and was gone. Long before I recovered my wits sufficiently to hurry to the window, the actors had spoken their familiar lines. The drama was over. Looking down into the garden, I saw Jack, Bob, Joyce, and a strange girl chatting and joking across the net at the end of their game. The girl was a friend of Joyce's. She had been brought over in the car from Providence, I later discovered, when Bob planned this surprise visit. He had come to stay for the weekend.

Almost exactly two weeks later, on the afternoon of Sunday, June 18th, I had gone into the trunk room to hunt for some old photographs. The trunk room is at the top of the house; it has no windows, only a skylight let into the roof. It is crowded with bits of damaged furniture, cardboard boxes, and old trunks. Mabel, who was sitting in the drawing room, had made me promise to put everything back exactly as I found it. She also suggested that I should wear one of her aprons.

Wondering where to begin my search, I decided upon a scarred
and much-labelled Gladstone bag, which looked large enough and
ancient enough to contain the entire family archives. Blowing off
some of the dust, I knelt down beside it and undid the fastenings
and straps. No sooner had I done so than the contents began to
spill out over the floor. It was packed full, almost to bursting, with
papers, bills, copies of old magazines, theatre programs, newspaper
clippings, dance cards, autographed menus, and all kinds of fascinating relics, many of them dating back to the end of the last
century. I was delighted and began examining these treasures,
quite forgetting what it was that I had set out to look for. In this
way I must have passed about a quarter of an hour.

Then, as I still bent over the papers, the attack seized me.

This time the sensations were different and incomparably more
violent. My ears began to sing, my limbs stiffened, and a convul-
sion like an electric shock seemed to take place at the base of my
spine. Half fainting, breathless, dizzy, I had barely time to think,
"It's going to happen again!" Then I closed my eyes.

How long the fit lasted I don't know. Probably it was very brief.
Gradually my arms and legs relaxed, my head cleared, I began to
inhale deeply and easily. The sense of relief was exquisite. Very
cautiously I opened my eyes and looked about me.

At first I hardly recognized the room in which I found myself.
It was the same room, but the papers, the trunks, and the furniture
had all disappeared. The floor on which I knelt seemed to have
been recently scrubbed, for it was quite clean, and the cobwebs
had been dusted away from the corners. Looking up at the skylight, I saw a patch of clear sky above my head. Its brightness suggested an early summer morning.

For several minutes I didn't move. I was scared, of course, but
much more excited than scared. Rising to my feet, I performed
what was unquestionably the bravest action of my life. I walked
over and turned the handle of the door.

It was locked.

For some moments I stood stupidly twisting the knob in my
hand. Then I began to rattle it, to beat the panel with my fist.
Finally I shouted aloud, "Let me out! Let me out!"

There was no answer, and after a while I stopped. It was no good. The house must be empty.

Slowly I returned to the middle of the room. My heart was beating so fast now that it almost choked me. My brain was racing like an engine. "I've got to get out!" I kept telling myself. I looked at the skylight, but it was too high above me and I had nothing upon which to climb.

From boyhood I have admired, though somewhat grudgingly, the extreme lucidity of my brother's intelligence. Now, as I stood there baffled, I asked myself what would he, who was never at a loss, have done in my place. He would have applied himself, as he always did, to the available data, no matter how scanty. Well, that must be my method also. Wouldn't this bare room yield up some small clue? I started to examine it, foot by foot, with the eyes of an amateur detective.

It was then that I made my great discovery. In the shadows of the far corner, crumpled against the baseboard, lay some dirty sheets of paper. Sitting down upon the floor, I smoothed them out with trembling hands. They were the inside pages of a magazine. I read its name, the *Cage Bird Fancier*. And the date, July, 1944.

Only an archeologist can imagine the intensity of my excitement at that moment. Here was an actual tiny fragment of the future itself, palpable to my present-day fingers. It had been manufactured by men who could answer, offhand, many of those burning questions which still perplex the wisest mortals of 1939. Shaking with eagerness, I began to read.

I suppose I was very silly. I suppose I ought to have realized from the start the utter futility of my search. But I was too perturbed to be capable of reasoning. My mind shouted questions: "Had the United States jumped into the war? Had there been a revolution? What is happening in Europe? In China? In the Near East?" And the men of the future, as if teasing my impatience, would only answer, "It is rather difficult to give exact dimensions for stock cages as they often have to be built to suit the individual breeder's accommodation. Generally speaking, however, they should not be less than 36 inches long, 12 to 15 inches high, and 12 inches wide. . . ."

For all the information it gave me, the *Cage Bird Fancier* might equally well have been written in Turkish or Japanese.

Yet I read on, with the obstinacy of desperation: "We have a hen siskin which was very fussy about feeding her young, and it was quite by chance that my father squeezed a meal worm (after breaking its head off) and gave it to her when she was sitting on the nest. . . . If anyone can make chaffinches feed their young solely on a suitable soft food consisting of a really scientific formula, most of our troubles would be at an end. ["Most of our troubles," indeed! I cursed the single-mindedness of the mono-maniac.] . . . Owing to present conditions ["At last!" I thought. "Now we're getting on the track of something!"], the June meeting of the Winchester Audubon Society had to be postponed." I read on avidly, only to discover that the Society was in a state of temporary suspension because three of its most prominent members had lately died.

I read on and on, learning all manner of highly relevant and unfruitful facts—that the legs of a canary will sometimes denote its approximate age, that narrow perches are best for birds which have slip claw, that baldness is not unusual among greenfinches. These tiresome details are imprinted upon my memory forever. But nowhere, nowhere could I find a trace of any wider implication. And even as my eyes hurried along the last lines of the print, I knew, in the deepest marrow of my bones, that I had outstayed my welcome. "Come along, now," something seemed to mutter in my ear. "It's time. You must be getting back."

"No, no!" I protested. "Wait! Give me one more moment!" But the singing noise was growing louder inside my head, my sight was dimming fast. Painfully, I spelled out the concluding sentences: "Time, unfortunately, prevented my visiting any more Waterbury fanciers, but I hope to pay them a return visit at some future date. In the meanwhile, I should just like to add—"

Everything went black. Clenching the paper in my two fists like a fraying life line, I pitched forward into oblivion.

When I recovered consciousness I found myself in bed, in my own room, with Mabel hovering anxiously around me. It was she who had discovered me, when she came upstairs to call me down to tea, lying senseless on the trunk-room floor. "Was there anything in my hand?" I asked her; and she replied, "Yes. You found them all right. Don't you remember?" "Found them?" I echoed stupidly. "Why, yes. The photographs. One of them is rather crumpled, but I'll iron it out. And now you're not to talk any more. The doctor will be here any moment."

The doctor, when he arrived, could find nothing much the matter. He advised a thorough rest, a little trip to the Cape later on. Both he and Mabel were curious to know the exact circumstances under which my fainting fit took place. I answered their questions as vaguely as possible. I had decided, of course, to tell them nothing. I have no wish to end my days in a mental home.

And now here I am, waiting for whatever may come next. Sometimes I feel frightened, but in general I manage to regard the whole business quite philosophically. I am well aware that the next adventure—if there ever is another—may be my last. The conditions of time travel may prove too violent for my elderly frame. Perhaps I shan't survive the journey. But I wouldn't refuse to make it on that account, even if I could. What other experience can be comparable to this? What else have I to live for now? So let the moment call for me when it will—at whatever time, in whatever place. I shall be ready.

A LETTER FROM THE BRONX

ARTHUR KOBER

BELLA GROSS RIFFLED THE PAGES of the dictionary, paused at a leaf headed "dike," ran her finger down a column of words and, when she came to "dilatory," wrote "tardy and inactive" on a slip of paper. She thumbed the book again, hunted for "epistle," and snagged it after a little difficulty owing to her uncertainty over its spelling. She made the notation, "a formal letter."

Fortified by these two items, Bella was ready to plunge into the writing of the grave and important letter she had long planned. Whenever she engaged in such elaborate preliminaries—unearthing the coverless dictionary and bringing it into the dining room, placing pen, ink, and paper on the oilcloth table cover, using her "good" stationery, bought at a sale at Macy's—it was an indication that she was going to compose something of momentous importance.

And this letter to Monroe Rosenblatt, written in her mind time and time again, was of importance. Bella was finally going to do what she had so very often told her friends Jennie and Sarah she would do: "Give Monroe back to the Indians." It was one thing to make fine promises under a romantic summer moon at Kamp Kill Kare. It was another thing, she thought with burning indignation, to fulfill those pretty promises under the harsh and prosaic moon over the Bronx.

Bella reached for a sheet of her good stationery, so impressively monogrammed with the letter "G." No, she thought, no use wasting the paper. This letter needed careful construction. It would be better to make a rough draft first and then rewrite it. She disappeared into her bedroom for a moment and returned with several sheets of business stationery which she had filched from her office.

She dipped her pen in the ink, corrugated her forehead in deep reflection, and then, under several printed lines which read "Solomon Silk Mills, Harry I. Solomon, Pres., Silks, Acetates—Plain and Novelty, 'A Satisfied Customer Is Our Best Recommendation,' " she wrote, "Dear Monroe."

She studied this a moment. "Dear Monroe." No, that sounded too warm, too inviting, too intimate. That was hardly her present attitude toward him. Dear Monroe, indeed! She suddenly had it! All that was necessary was to add "Rosenblatt" to the salutation. "Dear Monroe Rosenblatt." That was it—formal, severe, cold, implacable. "I should have written"—she stopped to consult her notes, and then went on, slowly and painstakingly, employing an almost childish chirography—"this epistle before the present inst. but the reason"—again there was a visual consultation with the notes—"I was so dilatory was because I wanted to carefully weigh what was on my chest. Now that I have weighed same I am going to get it off my chest irregardless of whom it affects even though it be—" There was only a moment's pause to consider grammar, and then she wrote, "I."

"First of all," she went on, "I don't want to throw up anything to your face but I feel this matter must be thrown up. Namely you might of forgotten about the fact that when I left 'Kamp Kill Kare' you declared yourself with all sorts of promises galore. I took you at your word in connection with the matter and gave up some 'contacts' which to me I didn't want to give up, at the same time I thought inasmuch as you declared yourself the fair and square thing to do was not to go 'galvinating' around, not that I am the 'galvinating' type girl inasmuch as I wouldn't stoop to be that common. But still in all I wanted to be fair and square with you. In fact one 'contact' I had was very serious inasmuch as the certain party was 'matrimonyally-inclined' along the lines of marriage, only I thought he should have his two feet on the ground first because too many marriages end up on the rocks due to circumstances over which the girl in the matter has no controll. He's a professional person with a college degree."

Bella allowed her mind to dwell on Max Fine for a moment. Poor Mac! A fine fellow—intelligent, well educated—a Certified Public Accountant. If only he had a substantial income. Well, what's done is done. It's silly to regret. Still in all, Mac's a fine boy, she thought, one whose friendship was certainly well worth keeping. Perhaps she ought to attend the regular meetings of the Excelsior Social Club. She had avoided these because of the embarrassment that would follow upon seeing and talking with Mac, the club's president. Oh, well. She sighed deeply, picked up the pen, and continued writing.

"For some time now we've been going out regularly with each other like clock-work. In fact, so regularly have we been going out with each other that one of my girl friend's (Jennie) commented on same and said, 'We're beginning to look like two peas in a pot' and everybody was taking matters for granted. To be crudly blunt about the matter, I too thought that the issue was understood. I hope you won't think me 'mercinarilly-inclined' if I mention the fact that I didn't bring up the matter of a ring but the matter was brought up by you, yourself. Well all you did was to bring up the matter without bringing up the ring. We been seeing each other regularly like clock-work and not once did you lift a little finger to get same but all you did was to talk 'a poor mouth' about how business was bad and the responsibilities you got and gee whiz, people are not buying merchandise like they used to and this, that and the other thing.

"In other words, Monroe, I suddenly came to the realization that I had no protection whatsoever in giving up my 'contacts' for what? So that you can keep me on tender hooks. So that you can come to my house for supper again and again, compliment my Mother on saying the food is very lucious, and then suddenly we wake up and find we got a boarder with us, only boarders at least pay the rent.

"Well I think that in view of this attitude on your part, in view of the fact that all the time you are saying that business conditions are bad so that we got to assume it don't warrant any serious step on your part, not even to the extent of a ring, in view of the fact that I am giving up chances which to me may prove valuable as I am not growing any younger each day and opportunities don't hang on trees, all a girl has to do is to go out and pick it off the tree just like if it was an apple or some piece fruit, in view of all this, Monroe, suppose we better call it just 'quits.'

"Now please don't get the idea I am calling you 'A Cheap Skate' just because I haven't got a ring to show on my finger. I am not placing you in that catagory whatsoever inasmuch as you have on several occassions shown me a very good time. Still in all if you had merely said to me 'O.K. Billie. String along with me for another couple months till business conditions gets on its feet and then everything will be O.K.' I would of been only too pleased and happy to have strung along with you. But you didn't even have this common courtesy to the girl to who you apparently seemed so crazy about at camp last summer when you swore to me that this here was no typical summer romance you write down on ice it's quickly forgotten, but would culminate to a mutual union. Oh, no, not you! After all promises are cheap and cost nothing. What have you got to loose? Say, it's a wonder to me I'm openning my eyes now. God knows they were closed long enough before.

"So you see, Monroe, why it's better for me to get this matter off my chest once and for all rather than I should waste my time brooding about it because I just can't dismiss things with a snap of the fingers. Perhaps if I was the type girl who could dismiss things with a snap of the finger I would be better off today, believe me. So, Monroe, leave us call it 'quits' and just say it all comes under the heading of 'Experience.' I'm afraid that even if you should dig up a ring, and judgeing from the way your business is at the moment I can just imagine what type ring you would dig up, I'm afraid I'd still have to say 'I'm sorry, I'm not interested.' You had your chances and too bad, you didn't make the most of them. Better luck with some other girl next time. As for me, don't worry. I got along very nicely without you a long time before I met you, and I'll still get along without you inasmuch as I have some very worth-while 'contacts,' friends who don't talk a 'poor mouth' whenever they have to dig in their pockets, be it a ticket for a movie or just a chocolate ice-cream Sunday.

"This letter means 'finis' so please don't reply nor communicate with me via the phone inasmuch as I will be out. I am not 'sore-headed' the least bit about the matter but I merely want to drop it once and for all.

"Assuring you of my sincerest feelings about the matter, and trusting that you meet a girl who appreciates you a little more than I do in view of the whole situation, I am—"

Bella wondered if "Very truly yours" wasn't just a bit too businesslike and formal. But that was exactly what she wanted to be. She wrote, "Very truly yours, Bella Gross." There! Signing "Bella" instead of "Billie" would make him realize that their relationship was completely over.

She picked up the scribbled pages and read them carefully. Once or twice she stopped to make a correction and to consult the dictionary about spelling. When she had finished reading what she had written, she added, "P.S. Please excuse the handwriting." She then reached for a sheet of her good paper, inked her pen, glanced at the rough draft, and started to write, "Dear Monroe Rosenblatt."

LITTLE WOMAN

❧

SALLY BENSON

PENNY LOOMIS LIKED TO LOOK back to the day when Ralph had first seen her. It was the day she had first seen Ralph, too, but she didn't think of that. She remembered only the delighted, incredulous look in Ralph's eyes when he caught sight of her sitting in the large wing chair in the Matsons' living room. In the short skirts and long waists of ten years ago, she had seemed just like a doll. Later in the evening he had told her so. "I can't get over you!" he exclaimed. "You're so tiny!"

"Oh, I know! And I hate it!" she answered. "It's dreadful, really! About clothes, I mean. Why, I wear size eleven!"

"You could look taller," Louise Matson said. "Naturally, those flat-heeled shoes make you look awfully little. If you *wanted* to look taller, you could wear high heels."

Penny Loomis had surveyed her strapped, patent-leather shoes thoughtfully and then her eyes had rested for a rather long instant on Louise's substantial Size 7 brocade slippers. "It's all very well for you to talk," she replied ruefully. "Your feet are a decent size, not disgraceful little Chinese feet like mine. You have nice, *big* feet."

Taking her home that night, Ralph had commented on Louise's attitude. "She was just trying to be catty," he said. "And you were swell about it. You may be little, but you aren't *small!*"

There was nothing to it after that first evening. It was as though Ralph never knew what hit him. There were three months of being engaged, of dancing night after night, attracting attention because Ralph was so tall—over six feet—and she was so tiny. He was enchanted with her daintiness and made jokes about it. "Now where," he would ask, looking over her head and pretending he couldn't see her, "did I put that woman I had with me?"

Everybody would laugh, especially Penny. "Big silly!" she would say. "Take me home!"

Everything she did pleased and amazed him. When, the Christmas before they were married, she presented him with a scarf she had knitted, he was genuinely overwhelmed. "I don't believe it," he said, smoothing it over and over with his hands. "You're not big enough to hold the needles."

He made so much fuss about the scarf at home that his mother, who had knitted scarves, sweaters, and socks for him all his life, was inclined to be bitter. "You act as though she'd knitted that scarf with her feet," she said acidly. "And, by the way, I put those golf stockings I just finished for you in your bottom bureau drawer."

His enchantment lasted long after they were married. It amused him to see her childish, round-toed shoes lying on the floor, to see her diminutive dresses hanging in the closet. Their house was full of company, too, those first months, men mostly, who marvelled with Ralph at the sight of Penny in an apron actually being able to get dinner, carrying platters of food almost bigger than she was.

They had no children, which was a pity, as Penny had fancied the idea of herself surrounded by tall, stalwart sons, but she had Ralph to flutter over and take care of. She made few friends and was content in their small apartment. Once Ralph asked her why she didn't go out more. "Do you good," he said, "to get out and play bridge or something in the afternoon. Why don't you look up Louise? You and she used to be pretty good friends."

Penny replied scornfully. Women were all right, she supposed. But she hated bridge, really. It was such a silly game. And she felt so funny going out with Louise, who was so tall. They looked ridiculous walking together.

Ralph had laughed at that. "Say, listen," he said, "I'm taller than Louise."

"You are a man," she answered. "Men are supposed to be big."

She looked so little and so pretty that Ralph agreed with her. "Louise is kind of a horse," he said.

They spent their vacations in Canada, where Ralph liked to fish.

And Penny, dressed enchantingly in boy's denim trousers, checked shirt, and felt hat, lounged against cushions in the canoe while he paddled. She would scream a little, hiding her head, as he took the fish off the hooks. When they walked, Ralph carried her over the rough spots and took her arm up the hills, so that finally, although he insisted she was no trouble, he took to fishing nearer the Lodge.

Sometimes he was surprised at the number of things a man who was married to a little thing like Penny had to think of. There was the question of theatre tickets, for instance; he had to make an effort to get seats in the first row so that Penny wouldn't have to crane her neck or sit on her coat to see the stage; he must also remember to shorten his steps when they walked together or Penny got tired and out of breath; things must be left where Penny could reach them without having to stand on a chair.

Once he had spoken to her about it. "Gosh," he said, "it is kind of tough to be as little as you are! I never thought how it must be for you, not being able to do things that other people do."

The instant the words were out of his mouth, he knew he had said the wrong thing. "I'd like to know what I can't do that other women can!" she told him indignantly. "I think I manage to keep busy!"

He had to admit she did keep busy. In fact, she was never still. She was as busy, he thought, as a canary in a cage, fluttering, picking, keeping up an incessant chirping. "Sure you keep busy," he said. "Busy as a bird."

When they had been married almost ten years, he went on a business trip to Chicago. The thought of being left all alone frightened Penny and she made a great deal of it. He must put a chain lock on the front door and write down where he would be every night so that she could call him in case anything happened. Her anxious fluttering depressed him, and his depression lasted until he was safely on the train and seated in the warm, noisy dining car.

His second night in Chicago, the man he had come to see, a Mr. Merrick, asked him out for dinner. Mrs. Merrick went with them. She was a plain-looking woman, a little too stout, but there was something pleasing in the monotony of her solid brown hair that had no disturbing highlights, in her soft, friendly brown eyes, and her uninteresting brown felt hat. She had the appearance of a woman who had contemplatively set aside all personal vanity and turned to other things.

Ralph was surprised to find himself having a rather hilarious evening with them, and delighted to learn that Mr. Merrick had about decided to go back to New York with him and wind up their business for good and all. "And take me," Mrs. Merrick said.

"Oh, sure, take you," Mr. Merrick agreed.

And Ralph had added, "You bet!"

That night at the hotel, he wrote to Penny. It was a long, enthusiastic letter, and he wrote everything he could think of to please her. "They asked all about you," he wrote. "And I told them you were no bigger than a minute and as pretty as a picture. So we'll take them to dinner, when I get back, which should be about Friday. I'll wire exactly when. I miss you."

As he wrote "I miss you," he stopped and put his pen down on the desk. It struck him that he hadn't missed Penny at all, while she—well, he supposed that she was rattling around in the apartment not knowing what to do with herself. It occurred to him that she ought to have something to do, something better than fussing around with things at home. Not that he wanted her to work, he thought. Penny was far too helpless and little to be able to cope with a job. His heart softened when he remembered their evenings together with Penny curled up on his lap as he sat in the big chair, talking to him a mile a minute in her rather high, clear voice. He was ashamed of the many times he had wished she would read more, and recalled one dreadful evening when he had looked up from his paper at the sound of her nervous wandering about the room to say, "For the love of Pete, *light*, can't you?"

Thinking of these things and of the fine evening he had had with the Merricks, he picked up his pen again and underlined "I miss you."

The trip back to New York with the Merricks was great, but Penny was not at the station to meet him. "Unless we've missed her," he said gaily. "She's so darned little, she's easy to miss."

He assured the Merricks that he would just dash home, change his clothes, pick up Penny, and meet them at their hotel.

Penny was waiting for him at home. She was almost hysterically glad to see him, and he noticed that the house was shining and spotless, with fresh flowers in the vases and a wood fire burning in the grate. She was already dressed for the evening in a pale-pink taffeta dress with many ruffles, and stubby satin shoes tied with large bows. She wore a ribbon around her hair, and in the shaded lights of the living room she looked very young. It was only when she followed him to the bathroom to talk to him while he shaved that he noticed her more closely; the line of her mouth, always too thin, looked set and unhappy; the skin on her face looked drawn; and there was more than a sprinkling of gray in her black hair. The pink taffeta dress looked suddenly absurd on her, and he wished that she had worn something more suitable, something more her age. Why, Penny must be thirty-five!

She was curious about the Merricks, she said. "I never heard you make so much fuss over any two people in my life. What's she like?"

"Mrs. Merrick?" he asked, struggling with his stiff white shirt. "Oh, she's darned nice."

"Oh, I *know* that," Penny answered impatiently. "I know you think she's nice. What does she look like? Is she pretty?"

"No," he told her. "You couldn't call her pretty."

"Well, is she big, little, fat, thin?"

"She's not little," he said. "Why, she'd make two of you."

This seemed to satisfy her and she asked no more about the Merricks.

At the hotel they were told that Mr. and Mrs. Merrick were waiting for them in the main dining room. Walking through the lobby and down the long corridor, Penny was pleasantly conscious of the stir they created. She even shortened her steps a little, so that she appeared to be keeping up with Ralph by tripping at his side.

Mrs. Merrick's first words to her were what she expected. "Why, you're tiny!"

Penny laughed sweetly and looked up at Ralph. "Yes, isn't it silly?" she said. "I must look perfectly absurd beside Ralph, who is so enormous."

Mrs. Merrick's eyes took in every detail of Penny, her dress, her shoes, and the ribbon around her hair, and then she said, in almost the exact words that Louise had used so many years ago, "Do you know, with heels you'd look much taller. Why, you must be five feet one or so, and with good, high heels you'd look three inches taller! That would make you five feet four, which is a nice height. A great many movie actresses are five feet four."

Penny laughed again, but she flushed slightly.

"Now, Nellie," Mr. Merrick said, "don't go to making people over the first minute you see them. Maybe Mrs. Loomis *likes* to look small."

"Nonsense!" Mrs. Merrick exclaimed heartily. "No one wants to look like a midget! That is, no one wants to look *too* different. I know I was awfully tall for my age when I was about fifteen and I felt terribly about it. I was a sight, I can tell you."

And you're a sight now, Penny thought furiously. She chose a seat next to Mrs. Merrick and during dinner she rested her small, thin hand next to Mrs. Merrick's large, square one. She picked at her food daintily and exclaimed pleasantly when the other woman ordered ice cream with chocolate sauce for dessert. "Not that I wouldn't love it, but I just haven't *room*," she said.

Later, when the music started, she was surprised to see Ralph spring eagerly to his feet and ask Mrs. Merrick to dance.

"I haven't danced much lately," he said. "But let's go!"

He put one arm around Mrs. Merrick's waist and they started off. It was pleasant to have her face so near his own, to feel her soft, straight hair brush his forehead. She wore a dark-brown velvet dress, not very new and not very smart, but she had dignity and she moved smoothly with him across the dance floor. Over her shoulder he saw Penny dancing with Mr. Merrick. She was looking up into his face and talking brightly and animatedly. Mr. Merrick was bending down to catch what she was saying, smiling a frozen sort of smile, but he didn't look very happy.

The rest of the evening was not especially successful. Ralph tried in vain to recapture the spirit of hilarity he had felt with the Merricks in Chicago. But there was a sort of uneasiness in the air, even though Penny showed them several match tricks.

He was a little relieved, as they said good night, to learn that the Merricks had bought theatre tickets for the following evening and were leaving the day after for Chicago.

All the way home, Ralph sat in one corner of the taxi watching

Penny as she talked. Her head was bent slightly to one side in the birdlike way she affected, and the white street lights flashing through the window were not kind to her. As he looked at her, she seemed to grow smaller and smaller until there was nothing much left of her but a pink taffeta dress and a pink ribbon. It had started to rain and the drops on the glass cast black dots on the pink taffeta dress, and he had the impression that it, too, might eventually disappear.

He did not notice that the cab had stopped in front of their apartment until Penny's voice gaily brought him back to earth. It was habit that made him pick her up and carry her across the wet, slippery pavement. And for such a little woman, she felt surprisingly heavy in his arms.

THE APOSTATE

❧

George Milburn

HARRY, YOU BEEN JACKING ME UP about how I been neglecting Rotary here lately, so I'm just going to break down and tell you something. Now I don't want you to take this personal, Harry, because it's not meant personal at all. No siree! Not a-tall! But, just between you and I, Harry, I'm not going to be coming out to Rotary lunches any more. I mean I'm quitting Rotary! . . .

Now whoa there! Whoa! Whoa just a minute and let me get in a word edgeways. Just let me finish my little say.

Don't you never take it into your head that I haven't been wrestling with this thing plenty. I mean I've argued it all out with myself. Now I'm going to tell you the whyfor and the whereof and the howcome about this, Harry, but kindly don't let what I say go no further. Please keep it strictly on the Q.T. Because I guess the rest of the boys would suspicion that I was turning highbrow on them. But you've always been a buddy to me, Harry, you mangy old son of a hoss thief, you, so what I'm telling you is the straight dope.

Harry, like you no doubt remember, up till a few months ago Rotary was about "the most fondest thing I is of," as the nigger says. There wasn't nothing that stood higher for me than Rotary.

Well, here, about a year ago last fall I took a trip down to the university to visit my son and go to a football game. You know Hubert Junior, my boy. Sure. Well, this is his second year down at the university. Yes sir, that boy is getting a college education. I mean, I'm all for youth having a college education.

Of course I think there is such a thing as too much education working a detriment. Take, for instance, some of these longhairs running around knocking the country right now. But what I mean is, a good, sound, substantial college education. I don't mean a string of letters a yard long for a man to write after his John Henry. I just mean that I want my boy to have his sheepskin, they call it, before he starts out in the world. Like the fellow says, I want him to get his A.B. degree, and then he can go out and get his J.O.B.

Now, Harry, I always felt like a father has got certain responsibilities to his son. That's just good Rotary. That's all that is. You know that that's just good Rotary yourself, Harry. Well, I always wanted Hubert to think about me just like I was a pal to him, or say an older brother, maybe. Hubert always knew that all he had to do was come to me, and I would act like a big buddy to him, irregardless.

Well, like I was telling you, Harry, I started Hubert in to the university two years ago, and after he had been there about two months, I thought I would run down and see how he was getting along and go to a football game. So I and Mrs. T. drove over one Friday. We didn't know the town very well, so we stopped at a filling station, and I give Hubert a ring, and he come right on down to where we was to show us the way. Just as soon as he come up, I could see right then that he had something on his mind bothering him.

He called me aside and took me into the filling-station restroom, and says: "For the love of God, Dad, take that Rotary button out of your coat lapel," he says to me.

Harry, that come as a big surprise to me, and I don't mind telling you that it just about took the wind out of my sails. But I wasn't going to let on to him, so I rared back on my dignity, and says, "Why, what do you mean, take that Rotary button out of my lapel, young man?" I says to him.

"Dad," Hubert says to me, serious, "any frat house has always got a few cynics in it. If you was to wear that Rotary button in your lapel out to the frat house, just as soon as you got out of sight, some of those boys at the house would razz the life out of me," he says.

"Hubert," I says, "there's not a thing that this lapel badge represents that any decent, moral person could afford to make fun of. If that's the kind of Reds you got out at your fraternity, the kind that would razz a what you might call sacred thing—yes sir, a sacred thing—like Rotary, well I and your mamma can just go somewheres else and put up. I don't guess the hotels have quit running," I says to him.

By now I was on my high horse right, see?

"Now, Dad," Hubert says, "it's not that. I mean, person'ly I'm awful proud of you. It's just that I haven't been pledged to this fraternity long, see, and when some of those older members found out you was a Rotarian they would deal me a lot of misery, and I couldn't say nothing. Person'ly I think Rotary is all right," he says to me.

"Well, you better, son," I says, "or I'm going to begin to think that you're sick in the head."

The way he explained it, though, Harry, that made it a horse of a different tail, as the saying goes, so I give in and took off my Rotary button right there. Stuck it in my pocket, see? So we went on out and visited at Hubert's fraternity house, and do you know that those boys just got around there and treated we folks like we was princes of the blood. I mean you would of thought that I was an old ex-graduate of that university. And we saw the big pig-skin tussle the next day, fourteen to aught, favor us, and we had such a scrumptious time all around I forgot all about what Hubert had said.

Ever'thing would of been all right, except for what happened later. I guess some of those older boys at the frat house begin using their form of psychology on Hubert. I mean they finely got his mind set against Rotary, because when he come home for the summer vacation that was about the size of things.

I mean all last summer I thought Hubert never would let up. He just kept it up, making sarcastic remarks about Rotary, see? Even when we was on our vacation trip. You know we drove out to California and back last summer, Harry. Come back with the same air in the tires we started out with. Well, I thought it would be kind of nice to drop in and eat with the Hollywood Rotary— you know, just to be able to say I had. Well, do you know that that boy Hubert made so much fun of the idea I just had to give it up? That was the way it was the whole trip. He got his mother around on his side, too. Just to be frank with you, I never got so sick and tired of anything in all my born days.

Well, Harry, I had my dander up there for a while, and all the bickering in the world couldn't of shook me from my stand. But finely Hubert went back to college in September, and I thought I would have a little peace. Then I just got to thinking about it, and it all come over me. "Look here, Mister Man," I says to myself, "your faith and loyalty to Rotary may be a fine thing, and all that, but it's just costing you the fellowship of your own son." Now a man can't practice Rotary in the higher sense, and yet at the same time be letting his own son's fellowship get loose from him. So there it was. Blood's thicker than water, Harry. You'll have to admit that.

Right along in there, Harry, was the first time I begin to attending meetings irregular. I'll tell you—you might not think so—but it was a pretty tough struggle for me. I remember one Monday noon, Rotary-meeting day, I happened to walk past the Hotel Beckman just at lunchtime. The windows of the Venetian Room was open, and I could hear you boys singing a Rotary song. You know that one we sing set to the tune of "Last Night on the Back Porch." It goes:

> I love the Lions in the morning,
>   The Exchange Club at night,
> I love the Y's men in the evening,
>   And Kiwanis are all right . . .

Well, I couldn't carry a tune if I had it in a sack, but anyway that's the way it goes. So I just stopped in my tracks and stood there listening to that song coming out of the Hotel Beckman dining room. And when the boys come to the last verse,

> I love the Optimists in the springtime,
>   The Ad Club in the fall,
> But each day—and in every way—
>   I love Rotary best of all. . . .

I tell you, Harry, that just got me. I had a lump in my throat big enough to choke a cow. The tears begin coming up in my eyes,

and it might sound ridiculous to hear me tell it now, but I could
of broke down and bawled right there on the street. I got a grip
on myself and walked on off, but right then I says to myself, "The
hell with Hubert and his highbrow college-fraternity ideas; I'm
going back to Rotary next week."

Well, I did go back the next week, and what happened decided
me on taking the step I decided on. Here's what decided me. You
know, I never got very well acquainted with Gay Harrison, the
new secretary. I mean, of course, I know him all right, but he
hasn't been in Rotary only but about a year. Well, on that particular day, I just happened to let my tongue slip and called him
Mister Harrison, instead of by his nickname. Well, of course, the
boys slapped a dollar fine on me right then and there. I haven't
got no kick to make about that, but the point is, I had a letter
from Hubert in my pocket right then, telling me that he had
run short of money. So I just couldn't help but be struck by the
idea "I wish I was giving Hubert this dollar." So that's what decided me on devoting my time and finances to another kind of
fellowship, Harry.

I get down to the university to see Hubert more frequent now.
I make it a point to. And the boys come to me, and I been helping them a little on their frat building fund. There's a fine spirit
of fellowship in an organization like that. Some boys from the
best families of the State are members, too. You might think
from what I said that they'd be uppish, but they're not. No siree.
Not a bit of it. I been down there enough for them to know me,
now, and they all pound me on the back and call me H.T., just
like I was one of them. And I do them, too. And I notice that
when they sit down to a meal, they have some songs they sing just
as lively and jolly as any we had at Rotary. Of course, like Hubert
said, a few of them might have some wild-haired ideas about
Rotary, but they're young yet. And as far as I can see there's not a
knocker nor a sourbelly among them. Absolutely democratic.

It puts me in mind of a little incidence that happened last
month when the frat threw a big Dad's Day banquet for us down
there. All the fathers of the boys from all over the State was
there. Well, to promote the spirit of fellowship between dad and
son, the fraternity boys all agreed to call their dads by their first

name, just treating the dads like big buddies. So at the table
Hubert happened to forget for a minute, and says to me "Dad"
something. Well sir, the president of the frat flashed right out,
"All right, Hubie, we heard you call H.T. 'Dad.' So that'll just
cost you a dollar for the ice-cream fund." Ever'body had a good
laugh at Hubert getting caught like that, but do you know, that
boy of mine just forked right over without making a kick. That
shows the stuff, don't it, Harry? Nothing wrong with a boy like
that.

And the whole bunch is like that, ever' one of them. I'll tell
you, Harry, the boys at that frat of Hubert's are the builders in
the coming generation. Any man of vision can see that.

Well, that's that. Now what was you going to say?

SAILOR OFF THE BREMEN

❧

IRWIN SHAW

THEY SAT IN THE SMALL white kitchen, Ernest and his brother Charlie and Preminger and Dr. Slater, all bunched around the porcelain-topped table, so that the kitchen seemed to be overflowing with men. Sally stood at the stove turning griddlecakes over thoughtfully, listening to what Preminger was saying.

"So everything was excellent. The Comrades arrived, dressed in evening gowns and—what do you call them?"

"Tuxedos," Charlie said.

"Tuxedos." Preminger nodded. "Very handsome people," he said, his English precise and educated, but with a definite German accent. "Mixing with all the other handsome people who came to say goodbye to their friends on the boat, everybody very gay, everybody with a little whiskey on the breath, nobody would suspect they were Party members, they were so clean and upperclass." He laughed at his own joke. With his crew-cut hair and his straight nose and blue eyes, he looked like a young boy from a Middle-Western college. His laugh was a little high and short and he talked fast, as though he wanted to get a great many words out to beat a certain deadline, but otherwise being a Communist in Germany and a deck officer on the Bremen had not left any mark on him. "It is a wonderful thing," he said, "how many pretty girls there are in the Party in the United States."

They all laughed, even Ernest, who put his hand up to cover the empty spaces in his front teeth. His hand covered his mouth and the fingers cupped around the neat black patch over his eye, and he smiled at his wife behind that concealment, getting his merriment over with swiftly so he could take his hand down and compose his face. Sally watched him from the stove. "Here," she said, dumping three griddlecakes onto a plate and putting them before Preminger. "Better than Childs restaurant."

"Wonderful," Preminger said, dousing the cakes with syrup. "Each time I come to America, I feast on these. There is nothing like it in the whole continent of Europe."

"All right," Charlie said. He leaned across the kitchen table, practically covering it because he was so big. "Finish the story."

"So I gave the signal," Preminger said, waving his fork, "when everything was nice and ready, everybody having a good time, stewards running this way, that way, with champagne, and we had a very nice little demonstration. Nice signs, good, loud yelling, the Nazi flag cut down one, two, three from the pole, the girls standing together singing like angels, everybody running there from all parts of the ship." He smeared butter methodically on the top cake. "So then the rough business. Expected. Naturally. After all, we all know it is no cocktail party for Lady Astor." He squinted at his plate. "A little pushing, expected. Maybe a little crack over the head here and there, expected. Justice comes with a headache these days, we all know that. But my people, the Germans, you must always expect the worst from them. They organize like lightning. Method. How to treat a riot on a ship. Every steward, every oiler, every sailor was there in a minute and a half. Two men would hold a Comrade, another would beat him. Nothing left to accident."

"What's the sense in going over the whole thing again?" Ernest said. "It's all over."

"Shut up," Charlie said.

"Two stewards got hold of Ernest," Preminger said softly, "and another one did the beating. Stewards are worse than sailors. All day long they take orders, they hate the world. Ernest was unlucky. The steward who beat him up is a member of the Nazi party. He is an Austrian. He is not a normal man."

"Sally," Ernest said, "give Mr. Preminger some more milk."

"He kept hitting Ernest," Preminger said, tapping on the porcelain top with his fork. "And he kept laughing and laughing."

"You're sure you know who he is?" Charlie asked.

"I know who he is. He is twenty-five years old, very dark and good-looking, and he sleeps with at least two ladies a voyage."

Preminger slopped his milk around in the bottom of his glass. "His name is Lueger. He spies on the crew for the Nazis. He has sent two men already to concentration camps. He knew what he was doing when he kept hitting Ernest in the eye. I tried to get to him, but I was in the middle of a thousand people screaming and running. If something happens to that Lueger, it will be a very good thing."

"Have a cigar," Ernest said, pulling two out of his pocket.

"Something'll happen to him," Charlie said. He took a deep breath and leaned back from the table.

"What do you prove if you beat up one stupid sailor?" Ernest said.

"I don't prove anything," Charlie said. "I'm just going to have a good time with the boy that knocked my brother's eye out. That's all."

"It's not a personal thing," Ernest said in a tired voice. "It's the movement of Fascism. You don't stop Fascism with a personal crusade against one German. If I thought it would do some good, I'd say sure, go ahead."

"My brother, the Communist," Charlie said bitterly. "He goes out and gets ruined and still he talks dialectics. The Red saint with the long view. The long view gives me a pain. I'm taking a very short view of Mr. Lueger."

"Speaking as a Party member," Preminger said, "I approve of your brother's attitude, Charlie. Speaking as a man, please put Lueger on his back for at least six months. Where is that cigar, Ernest?"

Dr. Slater spoke up in his polite, dentist's voice. "As you know," he said, "I'm not the type for violence." Dr. Slater weighed a hundred and thirty-three pounds and it was almost possible to see through his wrists, he was so frail. "But as Ernest's friend, I think there'd be a definite satisfaction for all of us, including Ernest, if this Lueger was taken care of. You may count on me for anything within my powers." His voice was even drier than usual, and he spoke as if he had reasoned the whole thing out slowly and carefully and had decided to disregard the fear, the worry, the possible great damage. "That's my opinion," he said.

"Sally," Ernest said, "talk to these damn fools."

"I think," Sally said, looking at her husband's face, which was stiffly composed now, like a corpse's face, "I think they know what they're talking about."

Ernest shrugged. "Emotionalism. A large, useless gesture. You're all tainted by Charlie's philosophy. He's a football player, he has a football player's philosophy. Somebody knocks you down, you knock him down, everything is fine."

"Please shut up, Ernest." Charlie stood up and banged on the table. "I've got my stomach full of Communist tactics. I'm acting strictly in the capacity of your brother. If you'd had any brains, you'd have stayed away from that lousy boat. You're a painter, an artist, you make water colors. What the hell is it your business if lunatics're running Germany? But you go and get your eye beat out. O.K. Now I step in. Purely personal. None of your business. Please go and lie down in the bedroom. We have arrangements to make here."

Ernest stood up, hiding his mouth, which was twitching, and walked into the bedroom, closed the door, and lay down on the bed in the dark, with his eye open.

The next day, Charlie and Dr. Slater and Sally went down to the Bremen an hour before sailing time and boarded the ship on different gangplanks. They stood separately on the A deck, up forward, waiting for Preminger. Eventually he appeared, very boyish and crisp in his blue uniform. He walked past them, touched a steward on the arm—a dark, good-looking young steward—said something to him, and went aft. Charlie and Dr. Slater examined the steward closely, so that when the time came, on a dark street, there would be no mistake. Then they went home, leaving Sally there, smiling at Lueger.

"Yes," Sally said two weeks later, "it is very clear. I'll have dinner with him, and I'll go to a movie with him and get him to take at least two drinks, and I'll tell him I live on West Twelfth Street, near West Street. There's a whole block of apartment houses there. I'll get him down to West Twelfth Street between a quarter to one and one in the morning, and you'll be waiting— you and Slater—on Greenwich Street, at the corner, under the

Ninth Avenue 'L.' And you'll say, 'Pardon me, can you direct me to Sheridan Square?' and I'll start running."

"That's right," Charlie said. "That's fine." He blew reflectively on his huge hands. "That's the whole story for Mr. Lueger. You'll go through with it now, Sally? You're sure you can manage it?"

"I'll go through with it," Sally said. "I had a long talk with him today when the boat came in. He's very—anxious. He likes small girls like me, he says, with black hair."

"What's Ernest going to do tonight?" Dr. Slater asked. In the two weeks of waiting his throat had become so dry he had to swallow desperately every five or six words. "Somebody ought to take care of Ernest tonight."

"He's going to Carnegie Hall," Sally said. "They're playing Brahms and Debussy."

"That's a good way to spend an evening," Charlie said. He opened his collar and pulled down his tie. "The only place I can go with Ernest these days is the movies. It's dark, so I don't have to look at him."

"He'll pull through," Dr. Slater said professionally. "I'm making him new teeth. He won't be so self-conscious. He'll adjust himself."

"He hardly paints any more," Sally said. "He just sits around the house and looks at his old pictures."

"He used to be a very merry man," Slater said. "Always laughing. Always sure of what he was saying. Before he was married we used to go out together all the time and all the time the girls—my girl and his girl, no matter who they were—would give all their attention to him. All the time. I didn't mind. I love your brother Ernest as if he was my younger brother. I could cry when I see him sitting now, covering his eye and his teeth, not saying anything, just listening to what other people have to say."

"Mr. Lueger," Charlie said. "Our pal, Mr. Lueger."

"He carries a picture of Hitler," Sally said. "In his watch. He showed me. He says he's lonely."

"I have a theory," Slater said. "My theory is that when Ernest finds out what happens to this Lueger, he'll pick up. It'll be a kind of springboard to him. It's my private notion of the psychology of the situation." He swallowed nervously. "How big is this Lueger?"

"He's a large, strong man," Sally said.

"I think you ought to have an instrument of some kind, Charlie," Slater said. "Really I do."

Charlie laughed. He extended his two hands, palms up, the fingers curved a little, broad and muscular. "I want to take care of Mr. Lueger with my bare fists."

"There is no telling what—"

"Don't worry, Slater," Charlie said. "Don't worry one bit."

At twelve that night, Sally and Lueger walked down Eighth Avenue from the Fourteenth Street subway station. Lueger held Sally's arm as they walked, his fingers moving up and down, occasionally grasping the loose cloth of her coat.

"I like you," he said, walking very close to her. "You are a good girl. You are made excellent. I am happy to accompany you home. You are sure you live alone?"

"Don't worry," Sally said. "I'd like a drink."

"Aaah," Lueger said. "Waste time."

"I'll pay for it," Sally said. She had learned a lot about him in the evening. "My own money. Drinks for you and me."

"If you say so," Lueger said, steering her into a bar. "One drink, because we have something to do tonight." He pinched her playfully and laughed, looking obliquely into her eyes with a kind of technical suggestiveness.

Under the Ninth Avenue "L" at Twelfth Street, Charlie and Dr. Slater leaned against an Elevated pillar, in deep shadow.

"I wonder if they're coming," Slater said finally, in a flat, high whisper.

"They'll come," Charlie said, keeping his eyes on the little triangular park up Twelfth Street where it joins Eighth Avenue. "That Sally has guts. That Sally loves my dumb brother like he was the President of the United States. As if he was a combination of Lenin and Michelangelo. And he had to go and get his eye batted out."

"He's a very fine man," Slater said, "your brother Ernest. A man with true ideals. I am very sorry to see what has happened to his character since—is that them?"

"No," Charlie said. "It's two girls from the Y.W.C.A. on the corner."

"He used to be a very happy man," Slater said. "Always laughing."

"Yeah," Charlie said. "Yeah. Why don't you keep quiet, Slater?"

"Excuse me," Slater said. "I don't like to bother you. But I must talk. Otherwise, if I just stand here keeping still, I will suddenly start running and I'll run right up to Forty-second Street. I can't keep quiet at the moment, excuse me."

"Go ahead and talk then," Charlie said, patting him on the shoulder. "Shoot your mouth right off, all you want."

"I am only doing this because I think it will help Ernest," Slater said, leaning hard against the pillar, in the shadow, to keep his knees straight. The Elevated was like a dark roof stretching all the way across from building line to building line. "We should have brought an instrument with us, though. A club, a knife, brass knuckles." Slater put his hands in his pockets, holding them tight against the cloth to keep them from trembling. "It will be very bad if we mess this up. Won't it be very bad, Charlie?"

"Sh-h-h," Charlie said.

Slater looked up the street. "That's them. That's Sally, that's her coat."

"Sh-h-h, Slater. Sh-h-h."

"I feel very cold, Charlie. Do you feel cold? It's a warm night but I—"

"For Christ's sake, shut up!"

"We'll fix him," Slater whispered. "Yes, Charlie, I'll shut up. Sure, I'll shut up, depend on me, Charlie."

Sally and Lueger walked slowly down Twelfth Street. Lueger had his arm around Sally's waist. "That was a very fine film tonight," he was saying. "I enjoy Deanna Durbin. Very young, fresh, sweet. Like you." He grinned at Sally in the dark and held tighter to her waist. "A small young maid. You are just the kind I like." When he tried to kiss her, Sally turned her head away.

"Let's walk fast," she said, watching Charlie and Slater move out from the "L" shadow. "Let's not waste time."

Lueger laughed happily. "That's it. That's the way a girl should talk."

They walked swiftly toward the Elevated, Lueger laughing, his hand on her hip in certainty and possession.

"Pardon me," Slater said. "Could you direct me to Sheridan Square?"

"Well," said Sally, stopping, "it's—"

Charlie swung, and Sally started running as soon as she heard the wooden little noise a fist makes on a man's face. Charlie held Lueger up with one hand and chopped the lolling head with the other. Then he carried Lueger back into the shadows against a high iron fence. He hung Lueger by his overcoat against one of the iron points, so he could use both hands on him. Slater watched for a moment, then turned and looked up at Eighth Avenue.

Charlie worked very methodically, getting his two hundred pounds behind short, accurate, smashing blows that made Lueger's head jump and loll and roll against the iron pikes. Charlie hit him in the nose three times, squarely, using his fist the way a carpenter uses a hammer. Each time Slater heard the sound of bone breaking, cartilage tearing. When Charlie got through with the nose, he went after the mouth, hooking along the side of the jaws with both hands until teeth fell out and the jaw hung open, smashed, loose with the queer looseness of flesh that is no longer moored to solid bone. Charlie started crying, the tears running down into his mouth, the sobs shaking him as he swung his fists. Even then Slater didn't turn around. He just put his hands to his ears and looked steadfastly at Eighth Avenue.

Charlie was talking. "You bastard!" he was saying. "Oh you dumb, mean, skirt-chasing, sonofabitch bastard!" And he kept hitting with fury and deliberation at the shattered face.

A car came up Twelfth Street from the waterfront and slowed down at the corner. Slater jumped on the running board. "Keep moving," he said, very tough, "if you know what's good for you." Then he jumped off the running board and watched the car speed away.

Charlie, still sobbing, pounded Lueger in the chest and belly. With each blow, Lueger slammed against the iron fence with a noise like a carpet being beaten until his coat ripped off the pike and he slid to the sidewalk. Charlie stood back then, his fists swaying, the sweat running down his face inside his collar, his clothes stained with blood. "O.K.," he said. "O.K., you bastard." He walked swiftly uptown under the "L" in the shadows, and Slater hurried after him.

Much later, in the hospital, Preminger stood over the bed in which Lueger lay unconscious, in splints and bandages.

"Yes," he said to the detective and the doctor, "that's our man. Lueger. A steward. The papers on him are correct."

"Who do you think done it?" the detective asked in a routine voice. "Did he have any enemies?"

"Not that I know of," Preminger said. "He was a very popular boy. Especially with the ladies."

The detective started out of the ward. "Well," he said, "he won't be a very popular boy when he gets out of here."

Preminger shook his head. "You must be very careful in a strange city," he said to the interne, and went back to his ship.

BARMECIDE'S FEAST

❦

MARC CONNELLY

THE EVENING OF DECEMBER 24th, Morton came home about
seven.

"The crowds held me up," he said. "I had to get something for
Aunt Helen. I forgot to tell you to put her on your list."

"What did you get her?" his wife asked.

"A handbag."

"They won't deliver it tonight."

"I took it to a telegraph office. There's a boy on his way to
New Rochelle with it now. It's funny I never thought of her for
your list."

"I asked you again yesterday if you were all set."

"I know. I just never thought of it till I was coming uptown."

"Well, you hardly ever see her. Don't turn the radio on now.
Dinner is ready."

They went in to dinner. She told him about the three-handed
bridge game in the afternoon. Edna hadn't shown up until half
past three and Eleanor didn't come at all. 'Phoned at five o'clock
that she was still shopping.

"There's more fish if you'd like it."

"This is plenty."

He told her he hadn't got out of the office until almost two.
He'd gone to the club and had lunch all alone. Some fellows came
in and they'd played kelly pool a while. Then he and Dr. Harvey,
one of the fellows he'd been playing with, went to the barber's.
Then he'd walked up town, and all of a sudden remembered Aunt
Helen. It was a nice-looking bag. The boy had lots of time to catch
the 6:45 train. He took a little more of the soufflé. This new cook
was much better than the last one. Yes, he was fine so far. He was
a Jap. She hoped he was going to be all right.

"Will you hurry a bit, dear? Clara wants to get home early."

"Oh, I don't have to get there awful early, Mrs. Durant. Don't hurry, Mr. Durant."

"Do you live with your family, Clara?"

"Yes, sir."

"Clara has to go to 145th Street."

"You having a party?"

"No, sir. We're just going to fix up a tree for my sister's children."

They told her not to bother with the coffee things. Mrs. Durant would put them away.

"I'll be in early in the morning, Mrs. Durant."

"All right, Clara. Good night."

"Good night, Mrs. Durant. Good night, Mr. Durant."

"Good night, Clara. Have a good time."

"Yes, ma'am. I mean sir. Good night."

The Jap made good coffee. Yes, didn't he? That Jap they'd had last year made rotten coffee. She said she thought maybe the coffee itself was a little better.

"Here's the paper. Oh, dear, it's just the front part. Do you want the other part? It's on my dressing table. I'll get it."

This part was enough. There wouldn't be anything in the sports section, anyway, and he'd seen the market reports at the club. My, they'd caught that murderer over in Jersey. Yes, and she didn't doubt for a minute he'd really done it. How do you suppose he thought he could ever get away with it? Oh, he was probably a crazy fool; just like that policeman. What policeman? That one last summer; the one that said he'd got an inheritance from an aunt in Albany. Oh, yes. Had they killed him yet? He wasn't sure. On the third page he looked at the pictures of the people who had got home from Europe that morning. Had she seen them? Did he mean the girl showing her knees? Yes. Imagine sitting on a boat deck on a cold day like this so the photographer could snap you with your legs crossed. She probably had sat there in the cold for five minutes giving him just the right pose. They'd found that little boy that was lost. Yes, wasn't it nice? Imagine how his mother and father must feel, getting him back the day before Christmas. All the poor kid thought was that he might get a spanking.

Wouldn't it have been terrible if it had been the wrong little boy?
Well, he'd have had a good time anyway as they had said they'd
look after him over Christmas even if he wasn't their boy, if the
police would let them. They must be nice people.

He put the paper down and looked at his watch. Did he want
some more coffee? No.

"Do you think we ought to go over to Arthur's?" he asked.

"I don't know."

"He invited us."

"I think that was just because we'd told him we didn't have any
definite plans. After all it is Christmas Eve and he and Marcia
probably would really like to be alone even if they didn't say so.
It isn't a party. They're just going to trim the tree for the kids."

"Did you get something for them?"

"I got them a couple of little painting sets. Like the one I got
for your secretary's little girl. They both draw, you know. Marcia
said the kids would love them."

He smiled.

"When I gave the package to Miss Kelsey," he said, "I'd for-
gotten what the hell it was. I didn't know it was a painting set.
I just said, 'I think it's something she'll like.' Miss Kelsey thought
I was getting roguish, I guess."

They both laughed.

"I'd told you what it was."

"I'd forgotten all about it. My God, there were eight packages
for people in the office."

"Did you forget what was in the others, too?"

"No, of course not. Gerald showed me the lighter. He thought
it was fine. I told him you'd picked it out."

"I'm glad he liked it."

"Yes, he thought it was fine."

"Did Miss Kelsey open the painting set?"

"No, she put it with some other packages on her desk. Everybody gave her something."

"I wish you'd admitted you'd forgotten what was in it."

"Why?"

"I don't know. It might have made it seem a little nicer. She
probably guessed you hadn't bought it yourself."

"Maybe she did. She knew you'd bought some of the other presents for me."

"I bet you didn't fool her. Want to hear the radio?"

"It'll be a lot of Christmas stuff. Let's go to a show."

"You can't get seats this late."

"On Christmas Eve? That's one of the worst nights in the year in the theatres."

She thought she'd like to see that play that opened last Monday. He telephoned an agency and was told the seats would be at the box office in his name.

They told the driver to go over to Ninth Avenue and then down to Forty-fourth so as to avoid the traffic jam around Times Square. Ninth Avenue was crowded, too. People buying presents at the last minute, poor things. Some of them probably were buying supplies for over the holiday, she guessed. Imagine what it must be like down on the East Side.

They found the curtain up when they entered the theatre. After the first act they went out into the lobby and lighted cigarettes. They met Joe Haldridge and his wife. They hadn't had anything particular to do, either. Nothing like getting your presents off a week ahead.

They'd got the Durants' card on Thursday. It was a peach. The Haldridges' card had come yesterday. It was slick, too. Had they got a card from Tony Franch? Yes, wasn't it funny? Yes, Tony always sent a funny card. How did they like the show? Pretty good so far. What were the Haldridges going to do tomorrow? Oh, stay at home until dinner time, then dinner with Joe's father and mother. They would go on to the Bakers' later. The Durants were going to the Bakers' too. Oh, were they? Fine! They'd see them there.

It was a pretty fair show. When it was over they waved goodbye to the Haldridges as the Haldridges started for Gramercy Park in their new car. It was a nice-looking car, wasn't it? Yes. He hoped their car would be repaired by next week. The shop had said they would have it back Tuesday at the latest. She hoped they would. She wanted to drive out to Coralie's in Stamford on Thursday. The colored carriage starter appeared on the running board of a taxi. Morton gave him a quarter. They got in. Did she want to go to a night club? No, she was rather tired.

The new Jap had left some sandwiches out for them. Wasn't that nice of him? She hadn't asked him to. What did she call him? Naka.

Naka? Yes. Wasn't Naka the name of the Harrisons' Jap? Well, he said his name was Naka. She supposed it was a common Japanese name.

Morton mixed two highballs, and they ate some of the sandwiches.

That light in the pantry needed fixing. Yes, she'd speak to the superintendent about it. The switch hadn't worked quite right when she tried it the other night, either. She said she was sleepy. He said he'd read a few minutes.

When she had gone to their bedroom he took a photograph of a new automobile from his pocket. He wrote on it, "Merry Christmas. Look out the window and see what's at the curb."

In the bedroom she unlocked her closet and took down the evening cane with the head which lighted so you could hail cabs, and the dressing gown that had come from Paris last week. She placed them carefully on the floor next to her bed, so that she could stealthily place them on the chair beside his bed before he wakened in the morning.

He came in. She had turned out her light. He put the photograph of the car on her dressing table as he walked past it.

He brushed his teeth and turned out the light in the bathroom. He got into bed and turned his light out.

"You didn't read long."

"No, I was tired, too."

There was a minute of silence. Their apartment was so high that the street noises did not reach them.

"Are you asleep?"

"No."

"I forgot to ask you. Did you stop at the bank on the way downtown?"

"Yes. You mean the gold pieces?"

"Yes."

"I got two twenties, three tens and two fives. Was that right?"

"Yes. I gave the laundress a five-dollar bill today. She won't be here again until Tuesday."

"You're giving Clara a little present, too, aren't you?"

"Yes. A little bracelet. She's an awfully nice girl."

"Yes."

"Good night, dear."

"Good night, dear."

They fell asleep. It was after midnight and bells began to ring somewhere.

FISH STORY

❧

DONALD MOFFAT

SPRING COMES EARLY and somewhat furtively to northern France. Warily, it settles down on the land, warning the stiff fields, lighting up the sour, wintry faces of the peasantry, and bringing a cheerful, optimistic clatter to the gray towns. It's like watching the tide come in, thought Mr. Mott, seated in the warm sun opposite the ramparts of Orne, where an old stone bridge arched above the little Baguette: it sneaks in when you're not looking.

But today, he decided, as his lazy glance followed the swift, grassy little stream to the point where it disappeared behind a jutting bastion further up, Spring was definitely laughing her almost too girlish laughter. Birds fluttered and cheeped among the budding fruit trees trained against the gray walls of the ramparts. Insects buzzed and tickled. A man's voice sang, off key, in an adjacent field. On the terrace of the little riverside restaurant beside Mr. Mott's green bench—a terrace of gravel, shaded by a spreading vine and terminating in the cressy border of the stream itself—Monsieur Pochin was setting out green iron tables and chairs. Spring brought more than warmth; it brought the customers that such a charming spot had every right to expect.

So sat Mr. Mott, a human vacuum, the sun warm on his back, the smell of fresh-turned earth in his nostrils, his soul at peace. He drowsed, and presently, when he looked up again, saw that he had company. A thin little middle-aged man in working clothes— corduroy trousers, blue flannel bellyband round his middle against the possible treachery of a lingering winter, purple *cache-nez* wound about his neck—flung a leg over the parapet of the bridge and seated himself on the flat top, his feet dangling toward the stream below. In his hand he held a long bamboo rod; beside him he set a can of worms. Mr. Mott watched him carefully bait his hook, drop it into the stream, light a cigarette, and settle to the patient (and, in Mr. Mott's experience with the rivers of France, hopeless) contemplation of the water.

A pretty scene, charming in its implication of laziness, of uselessness: man fishing, no fish, of course, but—man fishing. What was, then, Mr. Mott's surprise presently to see a miracle: man gently lifting rod, line swinging in toward bridge, fish dangling from end of line. Not more than four inches long, yet a veritable fish. Mr. Mott felt like rising and clapping his hands as the fisherman, smiling complacently, unhooked his capture and filed it in the pocket of his coat. *"Bravo, Monsieur!"* Mr. Mott called out across the intervening ten feet of water.

The fisherman returned his smile, and with a gesture indicated that he had been lucky, that the prize was small, *enfin*, that there were other fish in the pool below.

"What kind of fish is it?" Mr. Mott asked, after the line had been rebaited and dropped in the stream again.

The angler gave him the look reserved by the French for indicating surprise at the ignorance of foreigners about familiar matters of known importance. *"C'est l'goujon, Monsieur,"* he answered. "That is to say, *goujon* is the family name. My own little fish," he went on, patting his pocket, "is named Philippe. And if you will watch attentively, you will see the capture of his sister Célestin, his brother Raoul, and, I hope, other members of the family. *Hah!"* He lifted the rod gently. *"Et voilà: c'est Célestin."*

Then, as Mr. Mott continued lazily to watch, this wonder man proceeded to catch and pocket no fewer than eight more little fish, all identical with Philippe—surely, thought Mr. Mott, who had spent many a contented hour watching the fruitless avocation of the quai-side sportsmen of Paris, an all-time record for France.

For a time, there were no more bites, and, as the pause grew into a period, the fisherman examined his bait more and more often, then passed through the customary stages of perplexity, irritation, and low dudgeon, till finally he just sat there, slack, his rod stuck under one thigh, gazing dull-eyed into the glassy water.

Mr. Mott would have offered sympathy had he not felt that it would be tactless to intrude on such despair.

The sound of heavy footsteps crunching the gravel of the restaurant terrace caused Mr. Mott to look around, and he saw the innkeeper, Monsieur Pochin, his work done, come to the edge of the stream. He stood there a moment and regarded the springtime, his hands linked under his white apron, his mammoth belly protruding. Then he nodded to Mr. Mott, nodded to the fisherman.

"*Bonjour, Monsieur Dutoit. Ça va bien?*" And M. Dutoit was forced to admit, exhibiting a fistful of his trophies, that although the day had started well, it was ending badly.

Pochin laughed; he was from the Midi, and therefore prone to take life's tragedies less grimly than his Northern neighbors. He suggested knocking off till the fish still in the river grew old enough to eat worms. "Those you have there are hardly weaned yet," he declared, laughing heartily at his own fancy, and invited Dutoit in for a glass of wine. But M. Dutoit shook his head. No, he was there to fish. Pochin then suggested that he change his luck by letting him, Pochin, have a try; and without a word, but with the proper air of skepticism, Dutoit handed down the rod, butt first.

Immediately Mr. Mott noted the change in M. Pochin's character. He had been a jovial innkeeper, now he was a serious sportsman. Gravely he stood on the low bank and soberly lowered the baited hook into the water. Almost at once the line jerked sharply, depressing the tip of the rod. "*Holà!*" shouted Pochin, jerking back. "*Tiens fort!*" shouted Dutoit from the bridge above, almost falling into the water in his scramble to get down to the kill. "*Viens vite, Mathilde!*" called Pochin to his wife, who came out on the run, a woman as compact and gray as her husband was large and red. Even Mr. Mott felt the contagion, and jumped to his feet, for the fish which M. Pochin had miraculously jerked from the water, and which even now flopped about under one of the tables, was a good twelve inches long—the whale of the Baguette, necessarily.

M. Pochin unhooked the fish and proudly held it aloft, saying, "There is magic in your rod, Monsieur Dutoit."

By his side, Dutoit beamed with excitement and pleasure. "And in your skill, Monsieur Pochin," he added. "Madame Dutoit will be pleased indeed when I show it to her." He leaned over and picked up the rod, then held his hand out for the fish.

Pochin looked troubled. "But, my friend," he said gently, "it was I who caught the fish. That I am grateful for the use of your rod goes without saying, but—"

"One moment, Monsieur," Dutoit interrupted gravely; and Mr. Mott felt the atmosphere change again. "That it was actually you who caught the fish is incontestable. Yet, but for the accident of your holding the rod, it might as well have been I. But the rod itself, you see, is mine; and that which is caught by the rod belongs to the owner."

"*Aaah, çà alors!*" exclaimed M. Pochin, drawing himself up in stately dignity. "You accuse me, Monsieur, of taking what is not mine! I find your insinuation insupportable. Mathilde! Take the fish and put it safe indoors." He held the fish out to his wife, who hesitated, in an unwifely manner, long enough to enable Dutoit to make an angry snatch at it. Pochin put it quickly behind his back.

Dutoit abandoned diplomacy and shook his fist under Pochin's nose. "The fish is mine, I tell you!" he shouted. "It was caught with my rod!"

Pochin shook *his* fist. "The fish is mine; it yielded to my superior skill! *N'est-ce pas, Monsieur?*" he appealed to Mr. Mott, who quickly wiped the grin from his face, and said nothing. He might under certain circumstances, he decided, intervene between a man and his wife, or between a tiger and his kill; but between two fishermen, never.

Pochin, still clutching the fish, took a step toward the kitchen door.

"*Halte-là!*" shouted Dutoit, springing forward. Again he shook his fist. "You will give up my fish or I will appeal to the law! Pierre," he called to an urchin on the bridge above, one of three who, after their kind, had appeared by spontaneous generation at the first hint of excitement, "run quickly for the gendarme, and tell him that I am being robbed by a miserable assassin. Run!" The urchin stood fast.

"And add that I, Pochin, am in danger of assault by a madman who wishes to steal my property. Never fear, Monsieur, I can defend myself!" He dropped the fish on the ground behind him, and with a quick shrug slipped out of his apron. Then he raised his fists and advanced toward his diminutive enemy. Dutoit retreated and Mr. Mott settled down to enjoy himself, knowing well that whatever else might happen, no blow would be struck; a grave offence, that, in France.

Then began a long growling match. Face to face the two men tramped up and down across the terrace, and, as crises arose and dwindled, flung off their coats and put them on again. They shook their fists and snapped their fingers under each other's noses. They called each other horrid names culled from the garden and the zoo. But they did not touch each other. Finally M. Pochin, breathing hard, held up his hand.

"*Attendez, Monsieur Dutoit.* We are grown men, after all. Let us settle this affair amicably. The rod, I admit, is yours. But equity demands that I, who caught the fish, should be rewarded for my part. You find this just, Monsieur?" He returned again to Mr. Mott, who again refused to be drawn.

"I am a reasonable man," said Dutoit simply. "What do you propose?"

"*Eh bien,* I propose the payment of—"

"Payment!" shrieked Dutoit. "For my own fish? Hah! We shall see about that!"

"*Doucement, doucement, mon pauvr' ami.*" M. Pochin held up a great, red hand. "I was about to suggest that you give me half of the little fishes in your pocket in exchange for the big one. As to the latter, I am indifferent. Often I have caught larger from my terrace here."

"Pah!" remarked Dutoit, his pride stung. "However, to soothe your sense of justice, I willingly offer one of my fish, as a token as it were, of—"

It was Pochin's turn for outrage. "One!" he cried. He roared with sarcastic laughter.

"Two, then, for the *déjeuner* of yourself and Madame Pochin."

"Six at least I must have. Six!" He folded his arms.

Dutoit considered the matter. "Six fish, when you have, *enfin,* no right to even one, is of course out of the question. Three, in my generosity, I might consider. More than three, however, I—"

"*Alors, entendu*, four it is. And you shall have this monster for your table."

"I said three, Monsieur. You are deaf, perhaps?"

"And I four. But let us dispute no longer over such shrimps. Give me four and the big fish is yours."

Dutoit thought a moment. "Very well, Monsieur. I shall be generous out of respect for an old friend." They shook hands gravely, and then M. Pochin bent his great bulk and managed to pick up the big fish. Dutoit meanwhile retrieved his coat from the ground, put his hand in his pocket, and at that instant the big fish in M. Pochin's hand gave a final convulsive wriggle, fell to the ground, and with one flop was in the stream, where it lay belly uppermost on the water, then turned and feebly waggled down toward the depths. The two men watched it go, too stupefied to act.

Dutoit, his hand still in his coat pocket, withdrew it. It held the mangled remains of Philippe, Célestin, Raoul, and their little brothers and sisters, trodden into a scaly fish hash by the heedless feet of Battling Dutoit himself. Dutoit flung them into the stream with an oath. The two men turned to each other, their eyes met, and both smiled sheepishly. Pochin was the first to laugh.

"Since we are to have no fish after all," he roared, "we can at least have our drink. Come, my friend, let us forget our foolishness." He clapped Dutoit on the back.

"*Très volontiers, Monsieur*," Dutoit smiled. "*Passez, Monsieur, passez.*"

"*Non-non-non, après vous, mon cher.*" Arm in arm and side by side, the two crossed the terrace, Madame Pochin following them like a gray shadow, and entered the kitchen. The three urchins, grinning, drifted away. Mr. Mott got up from his sunny bench and went home, full of delight, to tell his wife all about it.

I'VE GOT AN ANCHOR ON MY CHEST

R. H. Newman

It was long past dark one evening last summer when I pulled up at the dog wagon, a regular roadside diner with tourist cabins in the rear. The counterman was reading a newspaper as I came in and he kept right on reading it while he went to get me a cup of coffee.

"We're going to fight for Canada," he said when he came back with the coffee. "You want anything to go with this?"

I shook my head. "What's that you say about Canada?"

He motioned toward the newspaper. "The President told Canada we're going to fight for 'em. Anybody makes funny with Canada, we got to go up there and fix things."

"When did he say that?"

"Yesterday," the counterman said. "Don't you read none?"

"I've been on the road since day before."

"Oh," he said. "I guess that accounts for you not knowing." He rested both elbows on the counter. "A guy should keep in touch," he said. "You never can tell what's going to be while you're not looking."

"I guess maybe you're right," I said.

"Brother, you're well informed I'm right. Take those guys in Washington. Every day they got a new law. Suppose they passed one while you was on the road. Suppose they passed one saying you couldn't drive Buicks. Then where'd you be?" He let that one soak in, and then he said, "What you driving?"

"A Ford."

"Well then, say they passed one about Fords. He don't like old Ford anyway, Roosevelt don't. Then where'd you be? In the soup, brother, in the soup." He rolled up the newspaper and reached out to swat a fly with it. "It's just like Russia," he said.

The coffee made me hungry and I ordered some eggs. The counterman started to fix them, but he also kept on talking about the President. From time to time he tipped the skillet so that the hot grease sizzled. The grease and his voice had much the same tone.

While he was talking the door opened and a man came in, a man I had passed about a mile back walking along the road. He was tall and thin. In the bright light his face was yellowish. He had deep, sad eyes and a slightly twisted mouth. Without nodding or saying anything, he sat down on the stool next to me.

"This spring," the counterman was saying, "them WPA guys was fixing the turnpike and they all of them ate right in here. And, by God, if them slobs didn't order the most expensive stuff I sell! Steaks they had to have, and liver with onions. The most expensive stuff!"

The tall man drummed on the counter with his fingertips, but the counterman went right on talking. Then the tall man cleared his throat a couple of times. "I've been here five minutes, friend," he said. "Five minutes. And if I'm not too bold, might I ask what the hell you're going to do about it?"

There was a loud hiss as the counterman gave the eggs a final basting. Then he turned and said, "Keep your shirt on. I got only two hands."

The tall man glanced at me, "Funny, isn't he? A regular two-a-day comic."

The counterman slid the eggs at me and waited while I took the first swallow.

"How are they?" he asked.

"They're O.K.," I said.

"Enough salt?"

"Plenty. Just right."

He turned to the other man. "What's yours?"

"One cup of coffee with cream."

"One cup of coffee with cream," the counterman said, "and I'm supposed to break my neck for a flyspeck order like that." He shook his head. "Look, Mac, on a steak or even a hamburg you could yell my ears off. All the beefing you want. But on coffee I don't even break even. I serve good coffee."

The other man didn't answer. He sat there looking up at the ceiling.

"Maybe you'd like some crullers? Or a piece of pie?" The counterman leaned way over. "How about a toothpick, sport?"

"This guy here now," the tall fellow said to me in a low, patient voice, "I don't even know he's in the joint."

Nobody said anything for a while, not even the counterman when he came back with the coffee. The tall fellow was the first one to speak. "These Republicans give me shooting pains," he said. "Always harping against Roosevelt."

"In the head," said the counterman.

The tall man looked at him slowly, up and down, then he turned back to me and made a great show of ignoring the counterman.

"No," he said. "Roosevelt's done plenty. Look what he's done for show business. Put it up on its feet again. He's some guy."

"Are you an actor?" I asked.

"In a way, friend. In a way."

The counterman motioned with his thumb. "Ain't you heard?" he said. "It's Clark Gable."

A patient look came into the tall man's eyes and he said, "I've got an anchor on my chest."

The counterman snorted.

"It's the truth," the tall man said. "I've got snakes on my arms and an anchor on my chest." He shoved one sleeve back and, sure enough, there was a long blue snake tattooed on his arm. The tail was at his wrist and the fangs must have reached up to his vaccination mark. The snake's scales were red. On either side of the snake he had all sorts of other things tattooed—hearts and arrows and flowers and scrollwork, and a nautch girl where his muscle was. He also had an American flag. There was hardly an inch of skin on his arm that wasn't inked. I looked at it all politely, and while I looked the tall man seemed very pleased. He softened up toward the counterman, too.

"Want to take a look?" he asked.

The counterman said no, but he looked just the same.

"In good times," the tattooed man said, "this would have cost you two bits. Fifteen cents on matinées."

"In good times maybe you would have ate a sandwich," said the counterman.

"Not in cheap dog wagons I wouldn't have."

They were all ready to start at each other again, so I asked the tattooed man if he was still with a circus. He shook his head. "Nowadays you got to be a gorilla to get anywhere—a gorilla in a white cage." He opened his coat and unbuttoned his shirt part way down. "Look at this," he said, and pointed to his chest.

There was the anchor, a bright-red one. It stretched from his collarbone to his navel, and behind it was a frigate under full sail. "Old Ironsides," he told us. "But you haven't seen nothing yet."

He pointed to a row of heads on his collarbone. "Lincoln, Washington, Theodore Roosevelt, Wilson. It took me twenty years to get this way and now they won't even look at it. You know what I started with? With this." He pointed to a little heart with a purple arrow through it. "I was goofed about a girl, so I got me this. Well, I liked the way it looked, so I got me more. All my money I spent on it. Finally I got with the circus, with the big time, and then I could have big jobs like the boat done on me." He shrugged. "Now nobody'll even look at it. But I figure it this way: Roosevelt fixes show business. Then when he gets around to it, he'll probably fix circuses."

He suddenly started to take off his shirt. He was in such a hurry to get the bottom buttons undone that he ripped one off. It popped onto the counter and the counterman picked it up and threw it away. He was very disgusted with the whole affair.

"Look," the tattooed man said as soon as he had his shirt off. The main feature of his back was a tiger's head. The mouth was open and there were tremendous fangs. "You can almost hear the bastard, can't you? At night I wake up and sometimes I think I hear roaring."

"Bells, too," said the counterman.

"And now"—the tattooed man shook his head—"now I can't get an engagement. No place can I show my stuff."

"You want anything else?" The counterman pointed to the empty coffee cup.

The tattooed man smiled at me and then at the counterman. "I've got a little proposition," he said.

"Yeah, I was waiting for that." The counterman gathered in the empty cup. "Five cents, please. I ain't having propositions this week."

"No? How much were his eggs?"

"Two bits." The counterman crossed his arms and began chewing on a toothpick.

"O.K. Two bits—two bits and five cents. That makes thirty cents. Well, you know what I got?"

"I can guess," said the counterman, without shifting the toothpick.

"I got Mae West on my leg. Down here." He tapped his right thigh. "I got Mae West and a lot more, and for thirty cents—for eggs, that is, y'understand, I'll—"

"The hell you will."

"Ah, c'm on." The tattooed man's voice was wheedling now. "Be a sport. She's got nothing on. Not a stitch. You'd like that, wouldn't you?"

"Five cents is all I'd like outa you."

The tattooed man turned to me. Way back in his eyes was something pitiful and not at all pretty. He didn't say a thing. I reached down in my pocket and his face lit up a little. He put his shirt on the counter and climbed off the stool. Then he began to unbutton his trousers.

The counterman spat the toothpick out.

"See that," he said, pointing up at a "Tables for Ladies" sign on the wall.

"Sure, sure, I see it," said the tattooed man.

"Well, that means no bums is taking their pants off in here. Not even if they got the whole New Testament typewrote on their legs in gold."

"I don't see any ladies," said the tattooed man. He let his trousers slip down a little more. His hips were very thin and I could see the beginnings of his tattoo marks. "The only lady is here," he explained. Down went the trousers until Mae West's head appeared over his belt. It was not a very good Mae West.

"Put your pants on," the counterman said, and came out from behind the counter with an iron skillet in his hand.

"Wait a minute," the tattooed man said. "Wait till I show this guy."

"You ain't showin' him nothing. Just your rear. Beat it. I ain't having nothing like this in here."

The tattooed man looked at the counterman and then at me. He started to say something, then he sighed instead, and pulled his trousers up and buckled his belt. I held a quarter out to him, but I suppose he didn't see it. He put his coat on over his bare skin and stuffed his shirt in his coat pocket. Then he threw a nickel on the counter.

"Christ," he said, "not even in a lousy dog wagon."

The door banged shut and bounced on its hinges a couple of times, and he was gone.

The counterman went back around the counter and hung up the skillet.

"Him!" he said. "Him and that Roosevelt. A pair of deuces. Over my dead body he'll do it."

"Do what?" I asked.

"Fight for Canada."

THE HAPPIEST DAYS

❦

John Cheever

"You're sure you haven't seen a football around?" Tom Baker asked his wife. "You're quite sure?"

"Positive," Carole said, and then, for no apparent reason, she added, "All we need is a balalaika."

Though her husband didn't understand either the origin or the exact meaning of her remark, he knew it expressed contentment. Her contentment was his and he looked happily about him at the stretch of lawn, at the Connecticut hills behind the hedge, and then at his three guests—Mrs. Morgan and Mrs. Townsend, the two widowed sisters from up the road, and Mike Borden, who was trying to sell the Bakers an automobile. Tom didn't care very much for him. He was a tall, restless man who talked a great deal about his past successes in business and about the intrigue and injustice that had reduced him to selling cars. And there was just something about him that you didn't like. Tom stretched out, feeling too big for his clothes, and turned to his wife. "I wish I knew where it was," he said.

"You may have left it over at the Burkes'," Carole said.

"No, I remember bringing it back last year." He felt somehow that he would recapture the happiest days of his life if he could only get up a game of touch football. "We were playing," he said, "and it began to snow. And we had to quit, the ground got so slippery. And I can remember bringing it home."

"Louis says that Detroit Edison is very good," Mrs. Morgan said.

"That guy!" Borden exclaimed. "Honestly!" He had been sprawled on the grass, staring into the sky, but now he sat up. "They've had guests for dinner every night since the war began. Just because he's an investment counsel, everybody wants his advice. Louise and I drove by there last night and the house was full of people. People sticking out of the windows." He raked the lawn with his fingers, pulling out a handful of dry grass.

"I can't understand how he gets ahead," Mrs. Townsend said. She was the younger of the sisters. Her husband had died quietly and left her enough to winter in Santa Barbara. "I'm sure he's stupid," she said, "really stupid. And he's president of Harcourt & Devereaux now. I went up to Squirrel Island to spend a week with them last summer and I wouldn't have stayed the week if I'd had any way of getting out. He was up at six in the morning, banging into furniture and singing 'Mr. Zip, Zip, Zip,' or whatever that song is, and hollering in the shower. He'd play badminton for a little while and then he'd get out the archery set and then the aquaplane and the water skis, his pistols, his sailboat, and then, if there was any time left, he'd go fishing. Just like a child, a two-hundred-pound child. Marie told me herself she doesn't see how he gets ahead. She's lived with him for fifteen years and she's sure he hasn't a brain in his head, and now they've made him president."

"You're sure you didn't give the football away?" Tom asked.

"No, darling," Carole said.

"I wonder what's happened to it. It was new last year. It was a good football."

"Oh, look at that cloud!" Mrs. Morgan exclaimed. Her husband had hanged himself from an apple tree on a suburban golf course in 1932, and since his suicide she had supported herself, first by teaching contract bridge and then by running a dress shop. "It looks just like a sofa. Like one of those horsehair sofas everyone used to have."

"It isn't in the attic," Tom said, looking at the sole of his shoe, "and it isn't in the hall closet." Carole attracted his attention by rattling the ice in her empty glass.

"Oh," he grunted. "Sorry."

He got to his feet, collected the glasses, and went into the house.

"Imagine what it would be like," Mrs. Townsend said, "if we should suddenly see a fleet of bombers."

"That cloud looks like an English sheep dog," Carole said.

"Which reminds me," Mrs. Townsend said. "I ran into Mrs.

Bemis. They're British subjects, you know, and they're worried because their son is of military age."

"Oh," Mrs. Morgan sighed.

"She's very worried," Mrs. Townsend went on, "but she wouldn't want her son to shirk his duty to the Empire—Empah," she corrected herself.

When Tom returned with the drinks, he stood on the stoop for a minute. The house had already cut the sunlight off from half the lawn, and Carole and Borden were sitting in the shade. "How about a demonstration tomorrow?" Borden asked, and Tom saw Carole's shoulders shake with laughter as she accepted the invitation. The intimacy between them startled him.

"The effect all this trouble has had on me," Mrs. Morgan was saying, "is that it has made me superstitious, quite superstitious." Borden sat up quickly when Tom approached with the drinks and Carole smiled, though there was no particular reason to. "I won't leave the house without my scarab," Mrs. Morgan said. "I avoid black cats, knock on wood, cross my fingers, and I wouldn't go under a ladder for anything."

"Black cats are considered lucky in France," Mrs. Townsend said.

"The awards," Mrs. Morgan went on, "the good things in life, seem to be distributed by a capricious sort of destiny. So many honest and conscientious people have failed that I can't think of it as anything but luck. It's all made me very superstitious."

"Yoo-hoo, yoo-hoo!"

They turned and saw Miss Coolidge coming through the break in the hedge. She was carrying asters and chrysanthemums in her arms. "I shan't stop, my dear," she said as she handed Carole the flowers. "I shan't stop—hello, Mrs. Morgan. I just wanted you to have some of these lovely flowers. Good afternoon, Mr. Borden." She turned to Tom and said mischievously, "You'd better watch Mr. Borden, Tommy. He's a very attentive admirer of Carole's." Then she faced the others again. "I hope you'll forgive this hideous smock I'm wearing, but the day when a lady could go into her garden in the morning and cut the roses with the dew on them is past. Isn't the news in the papers frightful? I do wish there was some way I could help. But I'm growing old, of course, and my brother always said that charity begins at home. You look lovely in that blue dress, Carole. . . . No thank you, my dear, I won't join you. I want to pick everything I can before the frost gets here. You won't have to split the stems. I've done that." She waved goodbye and then she started off toward the hedge.

"She's so lovely to us," Carole said, glancing down at the flowers. "I do wish we could do something for her."

"She's always bringing Carole flowers and vegetables," Tom said.

"Louise Beauchamp has some of those asters," Mrs. Townsend said. "Poor Jim." She laughed. "What with the garden and Charlie Lewis, he can hardly call Louise his own. Everybody knows about it. They talk about it in the A. & P. And Louise certainly doesn't make any effort to cover up her tracks. She comes up to the club with Charlie and leaves with Charlie and goes into New York with Charlie, and poor Jim doesn't even get an explanation."

Tom glanced at his wife and saw the color rising in her face.

"Of course, I may be old-fashioned," Mrs. Townsend said, "but I can't help it. I've always thought of a marriage as a marriage and I can't see that all this tolerance and running around is doing anyone any good. When a man and a woman stand up at the altar they assume a responsibility, and if that—"

"Oh, damn it!" Carole cried. She had spilled her drink, and she got up quickly, letting the whiskey-and-water run off her skirt.

"You poor dear," Mrs. Morgan said. "On that blue dress, too."

"It's lucky it wasn't coffee," Mrs. Townsend said cheerfully. "You can't get coffee stains out, I don't care what the advertisements say."

Carole blotted her skirt with a handkerchief and Tom picked up her glass. "I'll make another," he said, and when he spoke he looked for some recognition in her eyes, but she seemed completely absorbed in repairing her dress.

When he had returned with a fresh drink, he went back to his place on the grass and watched her. She was staring at the hedge or the sky.

"There were two penguins," Mrs. Townsend was saying, "a little boy penguin and a little girl penguin. They met at the equator and they played around with one another, and then the little boy penguin returned to the North Pole and the little girl penguin returned to the South Pole. Well, about a month later the boy penguin received a wire—a cable, I suppose—from the girl penguin at the South Pole. 'Come at once. Am with Byrd.' "

"The trouble with that story," Borden said when Mrs. Townsend had stopped laughing, "is that there aren't any penguins at the North Pole."

"Aren't there?" Mrs. Morgan said.

"No," Borden said.

"But why? The climate is the same, isn't it?"

"Climate doesn't make any difference."

"I guess it doesn't," Mrs. Townsend said. "In South America there aren't any songbirds."

"Really?"

"Nope."

"I feel sorry for the boy penguin," Borden said, "receiving cables, worrying, wondering what to do. I guess he could go aboard the Bremen now that the Bremen's in Murmansk."

"That's right," Mrs. Morgan said, "he could go aboard the Bremen. It must be fantastic, that ship up there in the Arctic, with the sailors all lounging around the social halls."

"I don't know about you people," Mrs. Townsend said suddenly, "but I'm going to follow the sun if I have to walk to Stamford. It's too cold for me in the shade." She dragged her chair fifteen feet down the lawn into the sunlight. The others followed, carrying chairs and rugs.

"I've been reading a novel about the pioneers," Mrs. Morgan said to no one in particular. "I don't see how the pioneers got along. I'm sure I'd never have the courage to do what they did —go out West in a covered wagon, with Indians, and the little they had to eat. I'd rather die. I'd rather stay in the East and die."

"I'm going to be a war profiteer," Borden said. He was lying with his face on the grass and his voice was indistinct. Each word added to the weight of the hatred Tom felt for him. "I'm going to make a fortune in leather and cocoa and buy a speedboat and shoot doves and cover my wife with emeralds."

There was no reply to such a remark, and for several minutes they all seemed absorbed in their own thoughts. Carole was the first to speak. "I'm freezing," she said. "Shall we go in?"

No part of the lawn or of the lawns and fields they saw beyond the hedge held any sun. They stood and stretched and moved toward the house. When Tom began to gather the empty glasses he found that he was unsteady on his feet. "Even if I did find the football," he said to himself, "it would be too dark to play." He stopped to pick up a glass and realized, as if it were the last detail in a bewildering circle of deceit, that anyhow he was too drunk to pass a ball.

BLACK BOY

❦

KAY BOYLE

AT THAT TIME, it was the forsaken part, it was the other end of the city, and on early spring mornings there was no one about. By soft words, you could woo the horse into the foam, and ride her with the sea knee-deep around her. The waves came in and out there, as indolent as ladies, gathered up their skirts in their hands and, with a murmur, came tiptoeing across the velvet sand.

The wooden promenade was high there, and when the wind was up the water came running under it like wild. On such days, you had to content yourself with riding the horse over the deep white drifts of dry sand on the other side of the walk; the horse's hoofs here made no sound and the sparks of sand stung your face in fury. It had no body to it, like the mile or two of sand packed hard that you could open out on once the tide was down.

My little grandfather, Puss, was alive then, with his delicate gait and ankles, and his belly pouting in his dove-gray clothes. When he saw from the window that the tide was sidling out, he put on his pearl fedora and came stepping down the street. For a minute, he put one foot on the sand, but he was not at ease there. On the boardwalk, over our heads, was some other kind of life in progress. If you looked up, you could see it in motion through the cracks in the timber: rolling-chairs, and women in high heels proceeding, if the weather were fair.

"You know," my grandfather said, "I think I might like to have a look at a shop or two along the boardwalk." Or, "I suppose you don't feel like leaving the beach for a minute," or, "If you would go with me, we might take a chair together, and look at the hats and the dresses and roll along in the sun."

He was alive then, taking his pick of the broad easy chairs and the black boys.

"There's a nice skinny boy," he'd say. "He looks as though he might put some action into it. Here you are, Sonny. Push me and the little girl down to the Million Dollar Pier and back."

The cushions were red with a sheen of dew over them. And Puss settled back on them and took my hand in his. In his mind there was no hesitation about whether he would look at the shops on one side, or out on the vacant side where there was nothing shining but the sea.

"What's your name, Charlie?" Puss would say without turning his head to the black boy pushing the chair behind our shoulders.

"Charlie's my name, sir," he'd answer with his face dripping down like tar in the sun.

"What's your name, Sonny?" Puss would say another time, and the black boy answered, "Sonny's my name, sir."

"What's your name, Big Boy?"

"Big Boy's my name."

He never wore a smile on his face, the black boy. He was thin as a shadow but darker, and he was pushing and sweating, getting the chair down to the Million Dollar Pier and back again, in and out through the people. If you turned towards the sea for a minute, you could see his face out of the corner of your eye, hanging black as a bat's wing, nodding and nodding like a dark heavy flower.

But in the early morning, he was the only one who came down onto the sand and sat under the beams of the boardwalk, sitting idle there, with a languor fallen on every limb. He had long bones. He sat idle there, with his clothes shrunk up from his wrists and his ankles, with his legs drawn up, looking out at the sea.

"I might be a king if I wanted to be" was what he said to me.

Maybe I was twelve years old, or maybe I was ten when we used to sit eating dog biscuits together. Sometimes, when you broke them in two, a worm fell out and the black boy lifted his sharp finger and flecked it carelessly from off his knee.

"I seen kings," he said, "with a kind of cloth over they heads, and kind of jewels-like around here and here. They weren't any

blacker than me, if as black," he said. "I could be almost anything
I made up my mind to be."

"King Nebuchadnezzar," I said. "He wasn't a white man."

The wind was off the ocean and was filled with alien smells. It
was early in the day, and no human sign was given. Overhead were
the green beams of the boardwalk and no wheel or step to sound it.

"If I was king," said the black boy with his biscuit in his fingers,
"I wouldn't put much stock in hanging around here."

Great crystal jelly-beasts were quivering in a hundred different
colors on the wastes of sand around us. The dogs came, jumping
them, and when they saw me still sitting still, they wheeled like
gulls and sped back to the sea.

"I'd be travelling around," he said, "here and there. Now here,
now there. I'd change most of my habits."

His hair grew all over the top of his head in tight dry rosettes.
His neck was longer and more shapely than a white man's neck,
and his fingers ran in and out of the sand like the blue feet of a
bird.

"I wouldn't have much to do with pushing chairs around under
them circumstances," he said. "I might even give up sleeping out
here on the sand."

Or if you came out when it was starlight, you could see him sitting there in the clear white darkness. I could go and come as I
liked, for whenever I went out the door, I had the dogs shoulder-
ing behind me. At night, they shook the taste of the house out of
their coats and came down across the sand. There he was, with his
knees up, sitting idle.

"They used to be all kinds of animals come down here to drink
in the dark," he said. "They was a kind of a mirage came along
and gave that impression. I seen tigers, lions, lambs, deer; I seen
ostriches drinking down there side by side with each other. They's
the Northern Lights gets crossed some way and switches the wrong
picture down."

It may be that the coast has changed there, for even then it was
changing. The lighthouse that had once stood far out on the wild
rocks near the outlet was standing then like a lighted torch in the
heart of the town. And the deep currents of the sea may have

altered so that the clearest water runs in another direction, and houses may have been built down as far as where the brink used to be. But the brink was so perilous then that every word the black boy spoke seemed to fall into a cavern of beauty.

"I seen camels; I seen zebras," he said. "I might have caught any one of them if I'd felt inclined."

And the street was so still and wide then that when Puss stepped out of the house, I could hear him clearing his throat of the sharp salty air. He had no intention of soiling the soles of his boots, but he came down the street to find me.

"If you feel like going with me," he said, "we'll take a chair and see the fifty-seven varieties changing on the electric sign."

And then he saw the black boy sitting quiet. His voice drew up short on his tongue and he touched his white mustache.

"I shouldn't think it a good idea," he said, and he put his arm through my arm. "I saw another little oak not three inches high in the Jap's window yesterday. We might roll down the boardwalk and have a look at it. You know," said Puss, and he put his kid gloves carefully on his fingers, "that black boy might do you some kind of harm."

"What kind of harm could he do me?" I said.

"Well," said Puss with the garlands of lights hanging around him, "he might steal some money from you. He might knock you down and take your money away."

"How could he do that?" I said. "We just sit and talk there."

Puss looked at me sharply.

"What do you find to sit and talk about?" he said.

"I don't know," I said. "I don't remember. It doesn't sound like much to tell it."

The burden of his words was lying there on my heart when I woke up in the morning. I went out by myself to the stable and led the horse to the door and put the saddle on her. If Puss were ill at ease for a day or two, he could look out the window in peace and see me riding high and mighty away. The day after tomorrow, I thought, or the next day, I'll sit down on the beach again and talk to the black boy. But when I rode out, I saw him seated idle there, under the boardwalk, heedless, looking away to the cool wide sea. He had been eating peanuts and the shells lay all around him. The dogs came running at the horse's heels, nipping the foam that lay along the tide.

The horse was as shy as a bird that morning, and when I drew her up beside the black boy, she tossed her head on high. Her mane went back and forth, from one side to the other, and a flight of joy in her limbs sent her forelegs like rockets into the air. The black boy stood up from the cold smooth sand, unsmiling, but a spark of wonder shone in his marble eyes. He put out his arm in the short tight sleeve of his coat and stroked her shivering shoulder.

"I was going to be a jockey once," he said, "but I changed my mind."

I slid down on one side while he climbed up the other.

"I don't know as I can guide him right," he said as I held her head. "The kind of saddle you have, it gives you nothing to grip your knees around. I ride them with their bare skin."

The black boy settled himself on the leather and put his feet in the stirrups. He was quiet and quick with delight, but he had no thought of smiling as he took the reins in his hand.

I stood on the beach with the dogs beside me, looking after the horse as she ambled down to the water. The black boy rode easily and straight, letting the horse stretch out and sneeze and canter. When they reached the jetty, he turned her casually and brought her loping back.

"Some folks licks hell out of their horses," he said. "I'd never raise a hand to one, unless he was to bite me or do something I didn't care for."

He sat in the saddle at ease, as though in a rocker, stroking her shoulder with his hand spread open, and turning in the stirrups to smooth her shining flank.

"Jockeys make a pile of money," I said.

"I wouldn't care for the life they have," said the black boy. "They have to watch their diet so careful."

His fingers ran delicately through her hair and laid her soft mane back on her neck.

When I was up on the horse again, I turned her towards the boardwalk.

"I'm going to take her over the jetty," I said. "You'll see how she clears it. I'll take her up under the boardwalk to give her a good start."

I struck her shoulder with the end of my crop, and she started towards the tough black beams. She was under it, galloping, when the dogs came down the beach like mad. They had chased a cat out of cover and were after it, screaming as they ran, with a wing of sand blowing wide behind them, and when the horse saw them under her legs, she jumped sideways in sprightliness and terror and flung herself against an iron arch.

For a long time I heard nothing at all in my head except the melody of someone crying, whether it was my dead mother holding me in comfort, or the soft wind grieving over me where I had fallen. I lay on the sand asleep; I could feel it running with my tears through my fingers. I was rocked in a cradle of love, cradled and rocked in sorrow.

"Oh, my little lamb, my little lamb pie!" Oh, sorrow, sorrow, wailed the wind, or the tide, or my own kin about me. "Oh, lamb, oh, lamb!"

I could feel the long swift fingers of love untying the terrible knot of pain that bound my head. And I put my arms around him and lay close to his heart in comfort.

Puss was alive then, and when he met the black boy carrying me up to the house, he struck him square across the mouth.

THE NICE JUDGE TROWBRIDGE

❦

RICHARD LOCKRIDGE

IT HAD BEEN an unusually serene evening, with the Norths reading comfortably under their respective lights, and Mr. North at first hardly noticed that Mrs. North had laid her book down. He turned a page and read to the bottom of it and went on to the top of the next before Mrs. North spoke.

"He was really a *nice* man," Mrs. North said.

Mr. North read down to the middle of the second page before the tantalizing obscurity of the remark caught up with him and pulled at his coattails. He read another sentence by sheer momentum and then looked over his book at Mrs. North.

"Did you say something?" he inquired politely, marking the place with his thumb. Mrs. North shook her head.

"No, dear," she said. "It wasn't anything. I didn't mean to interrupt. Just go on with your reading."

Mr. North looked at her skeptically and tried to, but it was no go. Her remark kept jerking at him.

"Who was so nice?" Mr. North said. "Who was this perfectly swell guy who was so damned nice?"

"What?" said Mrs. North, and then, as if coming back from a long distance, "Oh, that!"

"Well," said Mr. North, laying down his book.

Mrs. North looked at him thoughtfully, as if she were checking him over.

"It was just Judge Trowbridge," she said. "Somebody I used to know when I was a girl. I was just thinking how nice he was."

"Oh," said Mr. North.

"To his wife," Mrs. North said. There wasn't really anything in her tone. Nobody in the world except Mr. North would have heard anything in her tone. But Mr. North scrambled back through his conscience, turning things over. He didn't find anything, or at least not anything recent. One or two small matters, perhaps, but nothing anyone could call hot. He made inquiring sounds.

"I was just thinking about him," Mrs. North said. "Not in connection with anything. He was a federal judge."

"Was he?" Mr. North said, a little disapprovingly.

"He was a very important judge, and once when his wife had a cold he put off court for the whole day so he could stay home with her. Wasn't that nice of him?"

"Well," said Mr. North, taking the matter under consideration. "I mean, did she have a bad cold? Pneumonia, or something? I mean, it would all—"

"No," Mrs. North said. "Just an ordinary cold. That was what made it so nice. And he always had the bills sent to his office."

"Well," said Mr. North, "as for that—that isn't anything. Just routine, probably. It—"

Mrs. North shook her head, and said Judge Trowbridge had a special reason, of course.

"So Mrs. Trowbridge wouldn't see them and worry," she explained. "He was awfully nice to her."

"He sounds to me—" Mr. North began, and was surprised to hear a defensive note in his own voice.

"Of course," Mrs. North said, "men don't do that sort of thing nowadays. Nobody expects it." She paused. "No wife," she said.

Mr. North said, "Listen!"

"It's perfectly all right," Mrs. North went on. "Men were different in those days. Judge Trowbridge took care of his wife, sort of protected her. You know what I mean?"

"Of course I know what you mean," Mr. North said. "And it was very silly of them. Made their wives very silly too, I expect."

Mrs. North shook her head pityingly, and said that it made their wives lovely. "Mrs. Trowbridge was lovely," she said. "Sort of sweet and Southern. You could tell just by looking at her . . ." She let the sentence run off, softly. Mr. North waited. "She never had to worry about anything," Mrs. North said wistfully. "Judge Trowbridge thought she was perfect. When she wanted to wear something, because it was something she liked, he never raised any objections. He wouldn't have *dreamed* of it."

Mr. North began to remember something—something about something Mrs. North wanted to wear and he didn't want her to wear. He hurried back through his mind. There was something about a suit, he thought. There was usually something about a suit, because Mrs. North loved suits and he hated her to wear them. He didn't like suits on women, except perhaps on very tiny, fluffy women, but that was offset by the fact that he didn't much like very tiny, fluffy women.

"Was she a little, fluffy woman?" Mr. North suddenly demanded. Mrs. North looked at him and shook her head.

"She was no fluffier than anybody else," Mrs. North said. "Whatever that has to do with it. I'm just talking generally about Judge Trowbridge, and how nice he was. I just happened to remember how he was always doing things for her."

"Now," said Mr. North, "if you—"

"Once he took her measurements," Mrs. North said, rather quickly, "and bought some materials and had a tailor come to his office. He had the tailor make her—"

"All right," said Mr. North, "all right, a suit." He spoke more quickly even than Mrs. North had, and then he stopped because Mrs. North was looking at him, surprised and a little hurt.

"A suit?" Mrs. North said. "There wasn't anything about a suit. It was a coat, really, but it wasn't that. It was just his thinking about her, just the way he felt." There was something in her tone. "What made you think of a suit, dear?" she asked. "I thought you didn't want me to get a suit."

Mr. North looked at her and their eyes met and, unaccountably, he flushed.

"All right," he said. "O.K. But no tweeds. For God's sake, no tweeds!"

Mrs. North smiled contentedly. She said she hadn't even thought of anything in tweeds, not for a moment. She liked smooth materials much better anyway.

LOVE IN BROOKLYN

❧

Daniel Fuchs

I WAS SITTING in my usual seat at the lamppost in Owen D. Larkin Park, reading a newspaper while I waited for the Macy's Walking Club. This was the humorous name three girls I know gave themselves, because they all worked at Macy's department store. They were Ruth, Betty, and Gertrude. I always waited for Gertrude in the park, since I couldn't take her to a night club or some place like that, and it wouldn't do for me to spend too much time at her home when her parents knew I was unable to consider marriage because of financial circumstances. Most young couples, I think, will understand how it happened that the scene of my meetings with Gertrude was usually out of doors, and I chose Owen D. Larkin Park because there at least you could sit down.

While I waited that day, Mrs. Rand, who was the mother of young Dr. Rand, came along and took a seat near me. She was a tidy little woman, very proud and happy since she was, after all, the mother of a doctor of medicine. To her it was not only an honor but the satisfaction of a lifetime, and she came to the park regularly every evening to feel superior over the rest of us.

"Grass and trees and fresh air from the river," she sighed, looking about her. "The park is just like a wilderness."

"This is no park, Mrs. Rand," I said, killing time. Owen D. Larkin Park in Brooklyn is really a small plaza, an odd triangular area which the streets left when they intersected haphazardly. To fill up the space, the city had planted some greenery and so it was a park. "Were you ever in Central Park?" I asked Mrs. Rand. "Or Bronx Park? They're something. They're parks."

"No, Mr. Peru," the doctor's mother said to me. "I don't travel hardly nowhere. My son the doctor, he don't like me to go in the hot, congested subways."

"I can appreciate the point of view," I said. "But this place is really nothing. Those others are real parks."

Mrs. Rand refused, as always, to be impressed, having no further room for admiration. It was enough for her that her son was "the doctor," and other glories seemed to her irrelevant and trifling.

"My son the doctor," she said, "once he went to Bermuda. A cruise he took."

Then suddenly she stopped, all warmth left her voice, and she turned her back. That meant, I knew, that she saw the Macy's Walking Club arriving, for she had taken a sharp dislike to Ruth. I suppose she had her reasons, even then. Gertrude and the other two girls were coming up the path and I rose to greet them.

The girls stopped and Gertrude settled down on an empty bench for a little chat with me. Betty took up an impatient position a little distance away and started whimpering, "I should like to inquire whether we're going to stay here all night or did we start for a walk in the first place?"

"Just a minute," Gertrude told her. "Let's rest for a while."

"No one takes my inclinations into consideration," Betty said. "I was putting curlers in my hair after supper. Ruth comes along and says hurry up, we're going for a walk. So, if we're walking, then let's walk. It's only logical."

Ruth had gone over and seated herself next the doctor's mother. She took her knitting out of the bag she carried and started to work on it. Ruth was a well-developed girl, husky but not fat; a little coarse, Gertrude and I thought, but even so I didn't then understand why Mrs. Rand had to dislike her so intensely. When I think of it now, I suppose it must have been maternal instinct.

"How is the doctor?" Ruth asked Mrs. Rand. "I see him so seldom."

"The doctor is a busy man," Mrs. Rand replied. "He has to attend to his office hours, his clinic service, and the visits to the patients outside. He is occupied with serious things. He has no time for enjoyment or girls."

"Listen to her," Ruth said in her heavy, gross voice. "Somebody would imagine heavens knows what. Don't worry, Madam Doctor. I won't steal your baby and marry him."

"I assure you it don't worry me in the least," Mrs. Rand said. "Miracles don't happen every day in America."

"Does anybody listen to me?" Betty was wailing. "Does anyone consult my inclinations? Who am I?"

"My son the doctor," said Mrs. Rand, talking to nobody, "he isn't like all the other boys. He don't go running crazy the minute he sees a pair of silk stockings. He's a good boy. Big as he is, he minds what his mother says. He keeps his head on his practice."

By this time Ruth was ignoring the doctor's mother in a very elaborate way. She stood up with the knitting in her hands and measured it over her bust. "Three balls of wool I put into this sweater and it still isn't enough. My God, it's simply terrible. I'm getting fat as a horse." But the way she said it, it sounded like a direct insult to Mrs. Rand.

"I've been reading 'Ulysses,'" Gertrude said to me. Gertrude and I generally discussed literature, the new dance, modern art, and subjects like these. I liked Gertrude very dearly, I confess. She meant much to me, more than most girls do to their boy friends, for ours was a genuine intellectual companionship, and that, I believed then, was the soundest basis for a mixed relationship. A girl of Ruth's type, of course, could hardly understand this. She thought there was something peculiar about our friendship simply because it was maintained on a high level. We both tried to ignore her cynical comments.

"Oh, yes, 'Ulysses,'" I said. "By James Joyce."

"Don't you love his down-to-earth realism?" Gertrude asked. "Parts of the book are simply terrifying."

"There she sits talking James Joyce," Ruth said. "She's impossible. Listen, Gertrude, where does James Joyce get you?"

"I don't understand," Gertrude said to her. "Why do you feel it's necessary to say those things to me?"

"Don't mind her, Gertrude," I said.

"I don't like to see it," Ruth said. "It makes me feel bad to see one of my sex making a fool out of herself. Wake up, for pity's sakes, Gertrude, if it's only to do me a personal favor."

"There's enough trouble in the world as it is," Gertrude said. "Why should your own friends be nasty?"

"Don't pay attention to her," I said. "She just can't understand."

"Can I help it if I'm sensitive?" Gertrude asked. "All day I work at Macy's in ladies' unmentionables. Most of my day is spent in a cultural vacuum. I get so little out of life, why don't they let me enjoy an intellectual companionship in peace?"

"I'm only doing this for your benefit," Ruth said. "Don't think it's just to be nasty."

Gertrude and I moved down the row of benches for a little privacy, and I told her that she really should ignore Ruth, a girl who was of an altogether different type. There was no point in taking offence at her, since, to put it unkindly, she was ignorant.

"I know she's common and crude," Gertrude said. "I make the allowances. I tell myself not to let her make me worry. But I do!"

"Everybody does what they prefer," Betty wailed again. "Here Ruth sits knitting and now he goes off with Gertrude. But are my wishes ever taken into consideration? Oh, no!"

So we walked away some distance and talked of Proust and Joyce and the art of Mary Wigman. But not for long. Soon there was Ruth before us, insisting that they go on with their walk.

"Come," she said, "or Betty will break out in a rash. Besides, I don't like to see you wasting away your life on literature and philosophy."

"Oh, go away, Ruth," I said. "I didn't send for you."

"I don't want to seem just a little impatient," Betty whined. "But an hour ago did we start out on a walk, or was I mistaken?"

So Gertrude resigned herself and joined Ruth and Betty, and the three went on with their evening stroll.

Then it was that I first began to resent Ruth. She was a busybody, an interferer, an extrovert of an obnoxious sort, and I wished heartily she didn't take up so much of Gertrude's time.

Mrs. Rand was sitting quietly at her place near the lamppost, absorbed in her own thoughts. I sat down by her again. "Girls see a professional," she confided sadly, "they run like ants. Especially when it's a doctor of medicine."

"What have you got against Ruth?" I asked. I had my reasons for disliking the girl, that was true, but what offence had she given Mrs. Rand?

"You're a nice boy, Mr. Peru," she said to me. "I like you. But after all, what do you know about girls? What good will it do to talk to you?"

I remember I was somewhat offended then, but how right Mrs. Rand was.

It is, unfortunately, more understandable to me now than it was then, but from that evening which I have just described I had great difficulty in seeing Gertrude. She seldom came to the park and the Macy's Walking Club was broken up. One evening, about two weeks later, when I went to my usual seat at the lamppost I saw Betty alone, reading a book, her hair done up in curlers. I asked her whether she knew where Gertrude was, and she said she hadn't seen her or Ruth in ages, not even at Macy's, for they worked in different departments. I should have sensed then that something was in progress. It worried me and I missed Gertrude's company, but it hardly occurred to me that the situation was growing serious.

Soon the doctor's mother came into the park for her evening visit. It made her happy to see Betty reading a book.

"That's nice," Mrs. Rand said, a mournful note in her voice. "Most modern girls today don't bother with books. All they got on their minds, they got boys."

"You're right," Betty said. "My God, you're right, Mrs. Rand. Take me. I won't pet, I won't neck. What happens? I got no boy friends."

"You should worry, young lady. You go the right way. Books are better than wild times."

She drifted away into her sad thoughts and Betty went back to her book. "You slave for your children," Mrs. Rand said, almost talking to herself. "You go through sickness and fire for them. Every day you're at the dispensary with them. You bring them up, make all the sacrifices so they can go to college and medical school. You finally live to see the day they become a doctor of medicine. And then what happens? A young, ignorant girl who has no heart, she steals him away."

So I sat in the park, with Betty reading and Mrs. Rand moping. I read my paper, wondering where Gertrude was and why I hadn't been seeing her. The minutes passed and I thought this would be another day and no Gertrude.

About nine o'clock Ruth walked into the park. She was all dressed up and said she had an important appointment. Mrs. Rand had always disliked her, but tonight she positively hated her. The doctor's mother turned her back and muttered angrily so that Ruth would make no mistake about her attitude.

"My goodness," Ruth said. "Am I a bad draft or something? The temperature here resembles the North Pole."

"Insinuations," Mrs. Rand muttered.

"My goodness," Ruth said, "what did I ever do to you in my young life?"

"No law says I must speak to everybody," Mrs. Rand said, still addressing no one.

"All right," Ruth said. "So I saw the doctor. I admit it. So what? We went to an ice-cream parlor and had a soda. So what's the crime in that?"

"I'm not talking to anybody in particular," Mrs. Rand said. "But my understanding is that decent, respectable girls don't wait in the streets to catch a professional."

"It was an accident, Mrs. Rand!" Ruth cried. "I was walking home in the street, so I met the doctor. I didn't wait for him on purpose. And supposing I did, I didn't hurt him. I didn't eat him up."

"Please!" Betty said, looking up from her book. "Have a heart! A person can't even concentrate in the park. It's a shame."

"Oh, shut up, Betty," Ruth said. "Who's asking you?"

"Please!" Betty said. "Just because you're angry, don't take it out on me!"

The doctor's mother maintained her icy reserve, waiting with insulting obviousness for Ruth to leave the park so that she could breathe the air again.

"Ruth," I said. I realized this was a bad moment to approach her, but I was anxious to know. "Did you see Gertrude today?"

"Who needs you?" she shot at me. "Listen, Peru, when you grow up and become a man, then come around."

"Now, that's unnecessary," I said. "Did you see Gertrude?"

"Let me tell you something, Peru," she said. "No man has the right to bother a girl unless he's in a position to support a wife. That's a motto."

I swallowed my pride and ignored her insult, for there was no sense, I thought then, in paying attention to a person of Ruth's type.

"Did you see Gertrude?" I asked again.

"Yes, I saw her!" she said. "I had lunch with her today and I went home with her after work. All I hope is that someday she gets some sense in her head. She's at the beauty parlor."

Ruth took one more angry look at Mrs. Rand and swept away to her appointment. I didn't like what Ruth had told me about her motto for girls and especially I didn't relish her association with Gertrude. It affected me unpleasantly to think that they were spending so much time together.

Mrs. Rand still kept quiet, noble and proud in her silence, and yet, it was clear to see, unhappy.

What was I to do? By this time I hadn't seen Gertrude for more than two weeks and I realized her feelings toward me must have undergone a radical change. What was more, I learned that Gertrude and Ruth had grown inseparable. I couldn't understand this new fondness for Ruth and I somehow felt that this association could do me no good.

I could not buy Gertrude flowers. That wasn't customary among the people who lived near Owen D. Larkin Park in Brooklyn. Nor, as I mentioned in the beginning, did my financial circumstances make it possible for me to take Gertrude to a night club or the theatre. I did the best I could and bought two tickets for a lecture on "The American Revolution and Eighteenth-Century Poetry." I thought this would be an attractive subject, but when I went to Gertrude's home to invite her, her mother wouldn't even let me go inside the house. She kept me in the hall, told me Gertrude wasn't at home, and closed the door. I went to Owen D. Larkin Park, hoping that Gertrude might pass by. I fingered the two tickets in my pocket and bought a newspaper to help me while away the time.

At the park were Betty and Mrs. Rand. The doctor's mother was completely wrapped in some private grief and every time Betty offered to say something, Mrs. Rand said, "Not interested!" I opened the paper and read, waiting.

"Sacrifices we make for the children," Mrs. Rand said.

"The way of life," Betty agreed with her.

Mrs. Rand took to nodding her head as if in great grief, and there I sat, waiting for Gertrude with two tickets in my pocket. But she did not come.

A half-hour of waiting passed in this quiet way until suddenly the doctor's mother stood up as though she had been hit. The lines of her face became set in the classic, calm attitude of misery and she began to move out of the park slowly and tragically. I wondered what the matter was, and then I noticed Ruth had come along.

"Momma," said Ruth.

I could hardly recognize her. She was altogether changed in dress and in manner. She wore a simple black dress with a plain white collar and she seemed reserved. There was a strange air of dignity about her.

"Don't go away, Momma," she called to Mrs. Rand, and now, of course, I could understand the reason for that poor woman's sorrow. "I came for you. We're eating dinner, Momma. I haven't any spite. Come to dinner with me, please."

Mrs. Rand stopped. "Please don't call me Momma," she said in heartbroken tones. "You are not my child. You take my child away from me." And she moved away majestically.

"That's a fine way to treat an intended daughter-in-law," Ruth finally said to Betty and me.

"Well, under the circumstances," Betty said, "you must take her feelings into consideration. After all, she's his mother."

"I'm practically breaking my neck to be nice to her," Ruth cried. "I'm willing to go down on my hands and knees. What more can I do? I can't jump off the roof."

"Ruth," I said. I was impatient. I did not like to intrude at such a time but she was the only person who could help me. I had no choice. "Ruth, did you happen to see Gertrude?"

"Yes, I saw her," she snapped at me.

"I'd like to find her," I said. "I have two tickets for a lecture. Do you know where she is now?"

"Listen, Peru," she said, "am I an information booth? I can't be annoyed."

"Listen to her, listen to her," Betty said. "She can't be annoyed! All of a sudden she's very refined."

"Oh, I see. I'm not so popular now," Ruth said. "All you have to do to lose your popularity is to get engaged to a professional, especially a doctor of medicine."

Then Ruth and Betty scrapped around for a few minutes, the way girls do, until finally Ruth felt she had wasted enough time. She pulled on her black gloves and started to go out of the park.

"I'm late as it is," she said airly. "The doctor has to attend a professional function at nine-thirty. Believe me," she confided, "it's no bargain to be a doctor's wife. You've got to make up your mind to expect a crazy home existence."

She walked away, leaving Betty to stare helplessly and say, "Well! Well! Well!" Her sarcasm barely covered the burning envy in her, and after trying a few minutes to collect herself, she gave it up and said she was going to take in a movie. Her day had been ruined.

So I was all alone in the park now, sitting under the light of the lamppost, trying to read my newspaper. My head was full of premonitions. I could tell that Ruth knew where Gertrude was and that she just didn't want to tell me. Those two were fast friends and I didn't like it.

Later that night Gertrude did come into the park. She, too, was transformed, the general intention clearly being to avoid anything that might give her the appearance of one who had intellectual interests. It was a revelation. Her hair was waved and arranged in small curls over her neck; she had discarded her eyeglasses; and when she walked she had a new sort of swagger.

"Gertrude," I said, but I knew at once from the listless glance she gave me that our companionship was nearing its end. She had an engagement at the beauty parlor, she told me, and explained that she went now twice a week. I told her about the tickets and she said she was sorry, it was thoughtful of me, but a previous engagement prevented. That was peculiar, too, because I hadn't told her when the lecture would be given.

"What's the matter with you, Gertrude?" I asked. "You're so changed. Have I done anything to offend you?"

"Well, to be frank about it, I've decided to make a change," Ger-

trude said. "What was I getting out of life? All day I worked at
Macy's in ladies' unmentionables. At night I soaked my feet in Ep-
som salts and discussed Marcel Proust and Joyce with you. When
you stop to think about it from a certain viewpoint—from the
feminine angle—you can't blame me if I think it's time to make a
change."

"I still don't understand," I said. "It must be something Ruth's
been telling you."

"Don't pick on Ruth," she said, and it hurt me to see how ar-
dently she defended her new intimate. "She's not as bad as some
people think. Take me. I was sensitive and refined, interested in
intellectual matters. What happened? Nothing. Look at Ruth. You
think she's common and ignorant. And I agree she hasn't an ounce
of sensitivity. But what happens to her? She catches a doctor."

"Oh," I said. "I understand. I see."

"Don't think I'm hard and unfeeling about it," Gertrude said.
"But after all, when all's said and done it boils down to this: at
bottom every girl wants a husband. I can't continue fooling myself
indefinitely."

"All right, Gertrude," I said, and I picked up my newspaper.
"Naturally I can't blame you if that's the way you feel. I won't say
a single word."

"I'm sorry," she said. "I'm really very sorry."

I said it was all right again and started to read the paper, pretending I was very much absorbed in it. And finally Gertrude left.

It was all Ruth's fault. She had talked Gertrude into this new
philosophy on men and love, and also, I suppose, every normal
girl would have felt desperate and unhappy when she discovered
Ruth had caught the doctor. Betty had gone to the movies to forget
the pain, and as for Gertrude, all she could do was to make a change
in her life. That I was the person to be affected was only inciden-
tal. It was unfortunate for me that our companionship had come
to an end, but I knew there was no use moping about it. That
wouldn't help, and I applied myself conscientiously to the newspaper. Tomorrow, it said, would be fair, and I went on from that
point to read the news.

THE GREAT-GRANDMOTHER

❦

NANCY HALE

THE HOUSEHOLD was all split into separate parts that August before old Mrs. West, who was the great-grandmother of the little boy, died at last. All day—each yellow, melting day—the household was split into the sick part upstairs, where the old woman tossed and tried pitifully to get out of bed, and cried out for help to people who had been dead for fifty years; and the regular, necessary part downstairs—in the living rooms and the kitchens, with the servants and the cooking, and Mrs. West's daughter, Mrs. Cambridge; and the little boy's part, which was the garden full of red and blue flowers, and crickets singing, and the murmurous orchard full of long, sweet grass that he would run through, and the burning, pulpy swamp beyond the orchard, and the two toads that lived under the garden water faucet.

Only at night did they all go to sleep on the same floor, in the big, summery bedrooms that stayed stifling until midnight or later. In those hot, long nights the sick, confused old woman would cry out with her terror—feeble, piteous calls. Ever since her mind had begun to go, this house, where she had lived with her daughter for twenty years, had become something mysteriously frightful to her, and she could not rest for wanting to get out of it. In her perpetual fear, she tried and tried to get out of bed, dragging at the heavy plaster mass that held the hip she had broken months ago.

In the night, her small, old voice kept calling, "Father! Father! Come quick!"—and the boards that had been placed about her bed to keep her from throwing herself out would rattle; then, in the night, there would be the low voice of the night nurse trying to soothe her, droning dimly through the silent house. But the broken voice would keep calling, "Father! Come and take me

away, Father! I'm so afraid!"—and then the night nurse would tiptoe across the hall into the bathroom and fix something for her
patient to drink, and in a little while there would be quiet when
old Mrs. West slept. But the little boy never woke up at all in the
nights.

His grandmother would put his mattress on the floor near the
windows, when the nights were very hot, and he would sleep hard
all night with the tiny August breeze blowing in his damp hair.
His grandmother would go to look at him before she went to bed
herself, near midnight; he lay in his cotton pajamas on the white
sheet, close to the floor, his legs spread out and one of them drawn
up, as if he were running, and his arms thrown up above his head,
and his hot face turned sideways; he slept intensely. He still looked
like a baby when he was asleep, she thought. The August moon-
light came in through the windows and lay delicately along the
innocent curve of his forehead and his white eyelids. His hair had
grown long during the summer, and it curled up from the hot
creases in the back of his neck.

He always slept hard through the nights, from seven till seven.
His grandmother was afraid of his being frightened by the queer
callings in the dark house, but he never woke up. He had his
breakfast with the maids off the kitchen table in the morning, and
they turned him out into the garden early. His name was Robert
Cambridge, and he had never had any mother since he was born;
his grandmother took care of him. She buttoned his sun suits and
buckled his sandals before he went out to play in the mornings,
and she hoped that he would not hear his great-grandmother crying out so terribly all day long. She often felt frightened herself.

All day long Mrs. Cambridge moved about the big, dim house,
doing the accounts and seeing the cook and reading to herself, lying on the straw chaise longue in the hall. The sun came in in
stripes through the closed blinds and lay upon the dark floors; the
chairs were all in white linen cases; sweat stood on the silver vases,
and the flowers in them filled the rooms with heavy sweetness. A
bowl of cold water stood beside Mrs. Cambridge, and she would
squeeze a cloth out in it and lay it on her hot forehead as she read.
"Sister Louise! Where are you? Can't we go home soon? Oh, I'm so
frightened!" Upstairs the feeble voice called and called in despera-

tion. Mrs. Cambridge turned a page and changed the cloth on her forehead; her Aunt Louise had died long before she was born.

Mrs. Cambridge would have lunch with Robert off the round, green table under the lilac trees in the garden; he was very red in the face and his hair stuck to his head in curls, and he swung his bare legs back and forth under the table while they ate cool salads and lemon ice. Then he would go and have his nap on the reed sofa in the summerhouse, and Mrs. Cambridge would go back into the house; it gave her a headache to sit long in the sun.

Later she would go upstairs to see her mother, but she never stayed very long, because her mother thought she was a stranger, and cried out louder in her fear and homesickness.

The old woman was tiny under the sheet except for the great hump of plaster cast around her left hip and leg. Her face had shrunken and fallen far back to its bony structure, and Mrs. Cambridge looked at her own mother, who had brought her up and taken care of her for so long, and thought, "This is what she really looked like all the time. This is really Mother . . ." She tried to hold the little, gray hand and smooth it, but the old woman snatched it away with the great energy of terror, and tried to shrink back, staring with those birdlike eyes that stood out, stripped of all flesh, the true, underlying eyes of Jane West—of Jane Gardiner, who was born eighty-four years ago.

One afternoon the day nurse brought Mrs. Cambridge a scrap of paper, shaking her head and smiling with professional pity.

"She wanted to write last night. She said she had to write a letter, and I saved it to show to you."

Mrs. Cambridge read the poor scrawl of a few desperate words:

Father dear, *please* come soon Louise and I are so afraid in this strange house we waited so long at the railway station . . .

Then she sighed and folded up the paper. She was devoted to her mother, but she felt helpless about her now. The names and the places that the sick woman cried out about Mrs. Cambridge remembered from the stories her mother used to tell her when she herself was a little girl, going to sleep in long-ago nights. It made her feel strange to hear these things brought back into immediacy so many years after by her mother's delirium, and she felt that there would be something wrong in the little boy's hearing those cries about long-dead things. She did not want him to be shocked or frightened.

He was out in the swamp that day under the red, August sun, trying to catch grasshoppers, very earnestly and clumsily. Streams of sweat ran down his bare little back; he squatted on his heels, a huge straw hat shading him like an umbrella. A green grasshopper would jerk onto a leaf near him, and he would lift one sunburned, fat hand from the ground, where it was keeping his balance, and make a deliberate grasp for the grasshopper. But it was always too fast for him; lifting his hand from the ground made him lose his balance, and he would sit down squashily on the wet ground. Finally he was disgusted, and climbed to his feet and began wandering up toward the house. The seat of his sun suit was black with damp and earth.

Through the edges of the swamp, alive with crickets at the roots of the long grasses; they tickled his bare shoulders as he plunged through them. Up the slope of the orchard, smelling of apples growing ripe; a small green one fell suddenly from a tree as he passed, hitting the ground with a hard thump. Robert jumped, and looked at it with surprise. Under the long pergola of grapevines, shady over him, with neat bunches of half-formed grapes, apple-green, hanging just out of reach; he had picked all the lower ones to play marbles with. He climbed the rough-stone steps that wound through the rambling garden to the upper grass terrace, and went to see the two toads that lived under the water faucet.

The toads were sitting facing each other, blinking their glittering eyes at intervals and looking very hot and dingy. Robert took hold of the larger one, which was his favorite, and dusted it off with the strap of his sun suit; then he put it down again. The other toad hopped away under the sweating stone foundation of the house.

Robert went round the corner of the house to the cellar bulkhead, and climbed up on all fours to the top. The paint had blistered under the sun. Robert tried to slide down, but the points of peeling paint caught his sun suit, and a splinter scratched his buttocks. He tried it again, and then he went and lay on his back in the damp grass under a lilac tree. The grass had not lately been cut, and the blades were soft and tickled his skin; ants walked up the blades and onto Robert. He scratched his ribs and left little, red scratches on his sunburned side.

He looked straight up above him at the mesh of leaves shifting against the hot blue sky. The sweat ran down the sides of his nose, and he wished somebody would come out and fix the circular attachment on the hose that made a tall, curving fountain for him to run through. He thought about the cool trickles of water running down all over him for a little while, and then he climbed to his feet and went to look for his grandmother.

She was asleep on the straw lounge in the hall, with the wet cloth fallen slanting across her eyes. Robert held his face close to hers and breathed on her cheek. But she did not wake up. Her hand had fallen limp to the floor, and now and then it twitched a little.

"Oh, Father! Father! Why don't you come?" a frightened voice called from upstairs. Robert tiptoed across the hall and began to climb the steps one by one.

He went into the room that the voice was calling from, and there was his great-grandmother lying in her bed, looking very little. There were boards put up like a fence all around the bed. Robert went over to the bed and held his head up straight to look over the edges of the boards. His great-grandmother was crying.

"What's the matter, Great-Granny?" he asked her in his high, clear voice. "Did you get hurt?"

She reached out frantically with her skeleton hand, tiny and trembling, and took hold of his hot, soft one.

"Oh, take care of me!" she cried. "You're a big boy. Where did you come from?"

"I came from down in the swamp," Robert said. "Don't be scared, Great-Granny."

"Oh! Take care of me! Oh, I'm so frightened here all alone!"

"I'll take care of you," Robert said. He breathed softly in his great-grandmother's face and stared at how little her face was.

"Don't go away. You won't let them come at night, will you? You're a boy."

"All right," Robert said, holding the shaking, bony hand.

"I want my father so! I can't find him!" She began to throw her poor body about, tethered to the plaster mass.

"Was he going to come?" Robert stood on tiptoe to look closer at the little face.

"Oh, yes! He was coming to get Louise and me long ago, and I can't find him anywhere."

"Do you want me to go and look for him?"

"Will you? Will you? Oh, you could find him, you're bigger. Oh, Father!"

Robert put her hand down carefully and started out of the room.

His grandmother, coming upstairs, met him at the top. It was very dim and large in the upper hall, and Robert was small and hot and red, with a golden head.

"Robert, have you been in Great-Granny's room? I told you you mustn't, dear. She is very, very ill."

Robert continued toward the stairs intently. He did not stop as he explained to his grandmother.

"She's just awfully scared," he said. "She wants her father. She and Louise have been waiting a long time for her father. I'm going to look for him."

He started downstairs vigorously, one step at a time. From the room at the end of the hall the broken, terrified voice began again, "Oh, Father! I'm all alone! Father, come quick!"

Robert twisted his body around as he climbed down the stairs, and called back.

"It's all right. I'm going to look for him."

The voice stopped crying.

CHUTZBAH

❧

JEROME WEIDMAN

THE PEOPLE on our block never had any doubts about Marcel Cohen's ultimate success in life.

Dr. Cohen's son was considered an unusual child. First, because he was "a doctor's son," and second because of his name—Marcel.

As far as all of us on Fourth Street, from Avenue D to the East River, were concerned, the name was a new one. It was considered bad taste to call children anything but Harry or Julius or Aaron. But a doctor was permitted a certain amount of freedom from convention. Doctors were different. They had gone to college and were, as a rule, American-born, and had telephones and, occasionally, automobiles.

Until he graduated from public school, Marcel was not permitted to play on the street with the other children. Mrs. Cohen explained to the women in Deutsch's Bakery or Greenberg's Butcher Shop that this was not because he was too good for the other boys. It was simply that Marcel was an unusual child. The mothers of the block thought the explanation adequate.

After the *bar mitzvah* ceremony that marked his thirteenth birthday, however, Marcel was allowed to mingle with the other boys, and he became better known.

He read a great deal, and in the years of his seclusion he had accumulated an unusual collection of Frank Merriwells and Nick Carters and other paper-covered books. Every boy on the block devoured books of this nature, and when news of Marcel's collection leaked out, he was besieged with requests for them. At first he said his mother would not allow him to lend them. Shortly afterward, however, he let it be known that she had granted him permission to sell them.

He charged three cents a copy, and bought them back for a penny after his customers finished reading them. A boy could read a Merriwell in one or, at most, two days. Marcel had enough to go around for six months, until every boy on the block had read the entire collection, at two cents a copy. Then he disposed of them all at two cents apiece.

The mothers of the block thought Marcel was a good influence on their sons. He kept them off the streets a little. He was the first one to start a stamp collection. He sent for stamps on approval and sold them to the boys, making a little commission on the side. Many times he would show his friends a stamp in his album, say what he had paid for it, and substantiate his statement by showing them the price in Scott's. Then someone would offer to buy it and Marcel would let it go reluctantly. Later, after they found that Scott's listed an ordinary U. S. two-cent stamp at five cents, it was felt that Marcel had been overcharging them by using catalogue prices, but nothing came of it. Marcel could talk very convincingly.

His face was clean-cut and honest-looking, more so than those of his companions, and his clothes were always new and neat, of the department-store type, which in itself was enough to set him apart. All the other clothes on the block came from the *storkes* on Avenue A and Stanton Street. Mrs. Cohen was the only woman on the block who shopped in department stores.

Among his friends, he soon established a reputation for nerve. He avoided fights and "raids," claiming that he had a weak heart, but he did things the other boys were afraid to do, or, rather, never thought of doing.

If a boy had a nickel and wanted to buy candy, Marcel would offer to do it for him, guaranteeing him more for his money. He would go into the candy store and wait until the woman's back was turned. Then, deft as lightning, he would snatch something from the counter and jam it into his coat pocket. When the proprietress turned around, he would be waiting quietly for change or to be served. He looked so honest and clean-cut and incapable of wrong-doing.

From his father's books, particularly from the pictures in them, he gleaned an early, if somewhat sketchy, knowledge of the facts of life. Resting on a stoop or in an empty hallway after a game of

Kick the Can and Hiding, or Leevio, he spread his information among his friends. Talking in his low, convincing voice, his handsome face set in seriousness, he repeated what he had read and seen, simplifying and enlarging. He taught them to sing bawdy songs, and even added occasional lyrics. But of all this the parents of the block knew nothing.

Every boy on the block was a practitioner of the art of hitching on the backs of wagons, but Marcel improved even on that. He introduced the practice of hitching on trucks. There was excitement in this. Getting off a moving truck was a difficult feat in our neighborhood, because there were no traffic lights then, but Marcel was adept at it.

Dr. Cohen pointed with pride to his son, and told patients to feed their children as he fed his. Regular meals, the Doctor insisted (and believed), were responsible for his son's rapid growth. No eating in between meals, no fancy foods, and, above all, no delicatessen. But Marcel was already leading expeditions as far west as Astor Place for long red weenies, with plenty of sauerkraut and mustard, at a nickel each. Frequently, one of his companions, unable to finish his hot dog because of a recent meal, would throw part of it away. Marcel soon stopped this. All leftovers and unfinished parts were turned over to him. He ate all day, even shamelessly asking for remains of lunches in school. The Doctor, watching him down his evening meal, and noting his ruddy cheeks, plump body, and close approach to six feet in height, complimented himself on the excellence of his theory about regular meals.

Marcel's self-assurance was amazing. He lied with an ease and grace that was disarming. While in high school, he was caught operating a "pick-board," a gambling device that cost fifteen cents and yielded three dollars in profit. The school disciplinarian sent for the Doctor. Marcel stared at them innocently for a while. Then he broke down and confessed: he didn't even know what he had been doing. A strange boy had approached him in the lunchroom and asked him to hold the "pick-board" while he got some lunch. He went into details about time and the color of the stranger's hair. He walked out of the disciplinarian's office, his name officially unblemished, pledged to aid in the discovery of the true culprit.

Shortly before he graduated from high school, the Doctor had a serious talk with him.

"Son," the Doctor said, being very American and modern, "what do you want to do when you grow up? What do you want to be?"

Marcel was probably the only boy in the neighborhood who had ever been thus spoken to.

"Anything at all, Pa. Anything you say." Marcel creaked into a more comfortable position on the most expensive sofa on the block.

The Doctor looked sternly down at his son. "Well, what do you like? What are you good at?" He couldn't help but sound a bit exasperated.

"Everything. Anything," Marcel said.

The Doctor suggested medicine, not very enthusiastically. "O.K.," Marcel said. Or maybe law? "O.K.," Marcel said. Teach? "Yeah, O.K." Well, *what?*

"Oh, anything, Pa. I can do anything." Marcel was getting tired of this.

"Well, *what?*"

"Oh—say medicine. No, wait." Marcel remembered his father's stories of the hard years he had spent in study. He felt so comfortable now. "How about pharmacy? That's like medicine, isn't it? It won't take me so long and I could be earning money soon."

"All right, son, if that's your decision. If you feel you'd be good at it."

"Yeah. I'm good at anything."

The Doctor went to give the news to his wife, feeling that he had stirred his son from his lethargy. Marcel went to sleep.

His pharmacy studies kept him busy only part of the day. He looked around for a job to fill the spare hours. An advertisement asking for young men to sell X-ray supplies to doctors and hospitals caught his fancy. He went around to see what he could do. They were not particular about the men they hired (it was on a commission basis), but they asked for a deposit on the samples they supplied to their salesmen. Marcel soon talked them out of this notion.

In a few weeks he was earning so much money that he begrudged the few hours he had to spend in school every day. His success as a salesman amazed everybody but himself.

"I knew I'd be good at it," he told his father.

X-ray materials were supposed to be difficult to sell. Marcel didn't think so. He bluffed his way into the offices of hospital purchasing agents and kidded nurses of private doctors into placing their orders with him. But he remained in school, paying his own tuition until he graduated.

A year after he passed his examinations, while working in a drugstore on Seventh Avenue, he talked his grandfather into a non-interest-bearing loan and bought his own store on the West Side. The store had been losing steadily for three years when he took it over, but within fifteen months he had repaid his grandfather, and he owned it free and clear.

One day a man came in and asked for a bottle of expensive perfume. Marcel didn't have it in stock, but he had a dummy bottle in the showcase. He wrapped the bottle neatly and sold it. As soon as the customer left, he telephoned his jobber for a bottle of the perfume and sent his porter to fetch it immediately. Shortly afterward the customer returned with the dummy bottle. Marcel apologized profusely for the "accident," gave the man the bottle just received from the jobber, and returned the dummy to the showcase.

One day he arrived at the conclusion that his fountain was not profitable enough. He was paying too much for the "makings." In a week he had organized a druggists' association. He had no difficulty because there were no membership fees or dues. It was merely a collective buying organization, with Marcel as its spokesman.

He spoke to his milkman. "What am I paying you for milk?"

"Ten cents."

"How many druggists on the West Side buy from you?"

"Twenty-three."

"Well, if you had a hundred, all buying from you, would you sell for eight cents?"

"Nope. Can't be done."

"O.K.," Marcel said, turning away. "Don't deliver here any more after today. And," he added, "that goes for twenty of your other twenty-two customers."

"Ah, gee, Doc, now listen, Don't be like that. I tell ya—"

After the two-cent reduction in milk, Marcel turned to the baker, the ice-cream company, and the syrup manufacturer. It wasn't long before his fountain was running at a profit more to his liking.

During the prohibition era, he wasn't supposed to sell liquor save on a doctor's prescription, but he carried several impressively labelled, although cheap, brands. As his customers disliked the bother and difficulty of securing a doctor's prescription, here was a source of revenue that insisted upon being tapped. For the privilege of printing his own name in one corner, Marcel supplied several of the neighboring doctors with all the prescription pads they needed, and as each order of pads came from the printer, he took one or two for himself, and sent the rest to the doctor. In this way he had quite a variety to choose from, and when one of his many steady customers came into the store for supplies, Marcel scribbled something illegible on one of the pads, passed the bottle across the counter, and filed the "prescription" away.

With repeal, the slot-machine racket began to receive considerable attention from City Hall, but it paid a split of fifty per cent on all takings, and Marcel was loath to let his machines go. So he moved them behind the prescription panel and catered to a discriminating clientele. He was one of the few who continued to defray expenses in this easy manner throughout the reform period.

The store was on the West Side, and it was a long trip home to his father's house, late at night, after closing. Very frequently, particularly on Saturdays, because his clerk was off on Sunday and he had to open the store early himself, he slept in the neighborhood. But hotels are expensive, and not very private. Marcel soon arranged with the superintendent of a neighboring apartment house for the use of a furnished apartment while its tenant was out of town. In return, Marcel supplied him with medical supplies and third-rate whiskey. It was a convenient arrangement, in more ways than one.

All his escapades, everything that happened to him, he related to his father. They would sit in the waiting room, smoking cigars that Marcel brought from the store.

"So when the real tenant, you know, when he came home unexpectedly and he found me there, in the apartment, what do you think I said?" Marcel would ask with a grin.

"That the superintendent let you in?" the Doctor would suggest gleefully.

"No-o-*oh!*" Marcel's voice would be tolerantly reproachful. "Naturally, I didn't want to get the *super* in Dutch. I told him, I said, I was a new tenant and I must've gone to the wrong apartment by mistake. Naturally, the super backed me up."

The Doctor never failed to laugh heartily. Some boy, this son of his. What a head! What brains! What nerve!

The stories were too good to be kept secret. The Doctor repeated them to the neighbors of the block, adopting his son's method of presentation, asking for a solution before overwhelming his listeners with the climax.

They laughed, too, sincerely and appreciatively. They remembered Marcel as a boy and were glad to hear that he had "turned out all right." A doctor was entitled to have an unusual son.

Even among themselves, when the Doctor was absent, they spoke highly of Marcel. They reminded each other of their prophecies, made years before, when he was a boy.

"A *finer jung!*" they would say. "He's all right, that boy. He's got *chutzbah!*"

MR. PALMER'S PARTY

❧

Tess Slesinger

"WELL, WE'RE all here then," said Mr. Palmer brightly. He rubbed his hands together genially and rocked from his toes to his heels. But his party went right on without looking up, Miss Field picking threads off handsome Mr. Sedley's coat, Mr. Palmer's own Agnes continuing disloyally to pass the cakes. Even in his own house, at his own parties, people were apt to forget that Mr. Palmer was in the room, and that would have been all right except that there were times when Mr. Palmer forgot it himself. He had only one way of reminding people (and himself) that he was there, and that was by clearing his throat. It was a grand, momentous process. It began with a low clucking in the back of his throat. Mrs. Palmer had once been able, at this point, to end it all merely by meeting his eyes with a clear and threatening gaze, but Mr. Palmer, after years of practice, had learned to combat Agnes by keeping his own eyes lowered throughout the preliminaries. By the time he arrived at the second stage, which was a series of crescendo staccatos like the rattle of movie machine-gun bullets, she was too late; he could even afford to lift his eyes and meet hers with a mild and righteous defiance. By this time, indeed, Mr. Palmer could stand back and watch how the increasing volume of his own voice went striking at corners of the room, like a billiard ball, knocking each of his guests skillfully into a pocket of silence. Now Miss Field sat brooding over Mr. Sedley's sleeve, Mr. Johnson paused in the middle of an anecdote, Agnes's hand bearing cakes was suspended in mid-air. Mr. Palmer's party sat respectfully at attention, as if it had been frozen in jelly. "So we might as well start," said Mr. Palmer merrily.

He suffered a moment of panic. Start what? Why had he said

that? You didn't "start" a party. Besides, it *had* started, without him, and now he had stopped it. He darted his hand under his vest and let it rove furtively over his chest while he avoided looking at his wife. If only he could clear his throat again! But the process had spent itself. "I was just going to say," Mr. Palmer finished lamely, "that he, that Mr. Sedley, *looks* like somebody," and brought his hand out to the public gaze again, examining it minutely.

"Mr. P.," said Agnes, the cakes shaking bitterly in her hands, "can never rest until he has found who people look like."

"But doesn't he," said Mr. Palmer, anxiously, "doesn't he remind you a little, Aggie—"

"Not at all," said Mrs. Palmer shortly. "Can't I give you some more cake, Miss Field? Mr. Johnson? Mr. Sedley?"

"Goodness," said Mr. Sedley lightly, "are my ears burning! Is my conscience worrying! Help me, Miss Field!"

Miss Field fell to twisting a button on Mr. Sedley's sleeve, Mr. Johnson stuffed his mouth with cake and started over on his anecdote, and Mr. Palmer's party went on again nicely, in spite of him.

Mr. Palmer retired modestly and watched his guests with pride. All of them, he felt, belonged to him for the evening, whether they listened to him or not. He had made a stage for them, and in the sense that their coming together made a pattern which had never exactly happened before, he had created them. He had gone to the telephone and called eight times, first this one, then that, Mrs. Palmer standing anxiously beside him. Eight times he had said quizzically, "I wonder, could you come to my house on Thursday evening? I'm having some interesting people." After he had got through telephoning, Mr. Palmer had wondered guiltily just which were the interesting people and which the guests who had been asked to meet the interesting people. He had also been a little concerned lest he might have said "Wednesday" to some of them, and "Friday" to others, but here it was Thursday, and he had gone to the door eight times, in blissful gratitude for the coincidence that brought all of his guests to his home on one and the same evening. *And* an extra. The inclusion at his party of Mr. Sedley, a stranger, an uninvited guest, made Mr. Palmer's party almost a "function."

"All the same," Mr. Palmer started happily, in a burst of gratitude toward Mr. Sedley, and not even bothering with his process
this time, "Mr. Sedley *does* put me in mind of someone."

"Aha," said Mr. Sedley, cowering melodramatically, "the blood-
hounds are on my trail! Will you protect me, Miss Field?" Miss
Field almost died laughing, falling into Mr. Sedley's arms.

"But doesn't he," said Mr. Palmer, addressing Agnes, "put you
in mind, just a little bit—I don't say he has the expression, mind
you—of that man on The Boat who made things out of wires?"

"As little as possible," said Mrs. Palmer coldly. "We are now
going to play a word game that I cut out of the papers," said Mrs.
Palmer hospitably, to her eager guests.

Mr. Palmer retired again and grew pensive. Mention of The
Boat—which meant, of course, their honeymoon, their one flyer
into the world one read about—always left Mrs. Palmer cold and
Mr. Palmer sad and frustrated. Perhaps he had hoped that marriage with Agnes would make him grow tall, plant hairs on his
chest, somehow improve his position in life. But the trip, The
Boat, had made it plain that no such miracle would happen. And
with the years, Agnes had merely grown discontentedly fat and Mr.
Palmer had simply grown seedy. Not Agnes's fault. Oh, not at all.
And not Mr. Palmer's, either. It was just life, somehow. He looked
pitifully at Agnes. Her face was large and round and full, and her
mouth was tragically small, like a fish's, a little, feeble hole of a
mouth. Poor old Agnes! But his disease was on him again, the longing to fit things and people into place. Mr. Palmer started his
coughing process again.

"Perhaps of the second mate, that time, Agnes," he said gently.
"You remember, when he came on deck—that time on The Boat,
Aggie? Doesn't he—"

"We are playing a word game," said Agnes. "You are interrupt-
ing. What was your second syllable, Mr. Johnson?"

"My goodness," said Mr. Sedley, laughing in his sophisticated
way, "he'll be taking my fingerprints next! Don't pay any attention to our host, Miss Field," he said, and Mr. Palmer saw him
touch her boldly on the knee. Now, there was a man, thought Mr.
Palmer, feebly. There was a man. And because they all turned
back to their game again, Mr. Sedley and Miss Field with their

shoulders lightly meeting, Mr. Palmer went back to thinking of
The Boat.

For an odd thing had happened on The Boat, and as the years
went by it had come to be the only incident of the trip which kept
reality. They had been lounging (just like the advertisements) over
their morning broth one day, halfway to England. Suddenly a
group of sailors closed in about a lifeboat, tore off the canvas covering, and dragged forth the gauntest figure of a man. His face
was black, literally black, with starvation. His eyes were the eyes
of a hunted dog. The second mate came leaping across the deck,
and Mr. Palmer never forgot the study in contrasts as the officer
stood questioning the ragged stowaway. The stowaway kept muttering through his blackened lips, "Where are we? How soon do
we land? Where are we?" At last they took him away.

The incident seemed like a concrete symbol of Mr. Palmer's
whole existence. In his mind, all people were forever afterward
catalogued accordingly: either they were stowaways or they were
lucky second mates. Dreamily he catalogued the people at his
party: Mr. Divine, who had held the same job for thirty years, was
a stowaway like Mr. Palmer himself; Mr. Johnson was on the
fence; Mr. Sedley and Miss Field were clearly second mates. All at
once, the remembered episode became plain as day to him—the
second mate standing in his handsome arrogance, his hand on the
stowaway's shoulder; Mr. Sedley now, touching Miss Field upon
the knee! Mr. Palmer coughed convincingly.

"By gad," he broke out recklessly, in the very teeth of Agnes's
anger, "he *does* remind me! You must remember, Aggie. Don't
you remember that morning on The Boat? We were drinking our
broth, and the second mate—"

"Well now, Miss Field," said Mr. Sedley smoothly. "What say
we trot? Speak up for me, Johnson," Mr. Sedley said gaily, "and
tell Miss Field I'm safe to go home with. Before our host," he said,
and turned and stared at Mr. Palmer with so clever a simulation
of anger that Mr. Palmer would have sworn he was that second
mate, "before our host accuses me of being a stowaway or something."

And Agnes darted at her husband a look of hate, for now all
their guests were rising, laughing, and protesting that they *must*

be trotting; it was late (though it was barely midnight), and any minute, they cried, struggling into their coats and hats, Mr. Palmer might remember who *they* looked like. Agnes held out the platter of cakes as if she were pleading for alms, Mr. Palmer pretended to refuse to give them their coats and threatened them with some of his California wine, but it was all over. Miss Field picked a last thread off Mr. Sedley's sleeve, Mr. Johnson said, "Age before beauty," ushering Mr. Divine out the door, and Mr. Palmer's party was definitely at an end.

A DIFFERENT WORLD

☙

ROBERT M. COATES

JIM BARNETT held the apartment door open with his foot while he took the key out of the lock and dropped it into his pocket. Then he stepped inside and let the door slam behind him. "Hi!" he said. "Anybody home?" There was no answer, and in a way he hadn't expected any; from where he stood in the little entrance hall he could see into the living room, with its white painted walls and carefully placed furniture and the chill end-of-the-afternoon light coming in from the two windows, and the very air of the place seemed empty. It was Della's day off, he remembered; probably Helen had Jamie out in the Park, or somewhere. Jim was a young man, under thirty, with a bony, brown, handsome face, dark eyes, and a wide mouth beneath a small black mustache. He had on a gray overcoat and a carelessly crumpled felt hat, and he had a brown paper parcel, wrapped tightly enough to define the shape of two bottles, under his arm.

He put the parcel down on the telephone table in the hall and walked into the living room. The doors of both bedrooms were standing open and—not that he expected to find any notes propped on dressing tables or anything; that would have been silly—he walked past each and looked in. His and Helen's was neat as usual, the bed made up, his pajamas put away, the counterpane drawn into place. Jamie's was the customary jumble: toys, picture books, games and fragments of games overflowing the big catchall box in the corner; a scooter propped against a chair; and, spread out on the play table, a half-dozen cardboard rectangles of the kind they use to keep shirts in shape, all of these now covered with scrawls of colored crayon. He stood looking at it a moment. "A different world," he said, for some reason aloud. "Well, the laundry came anyway, I see." He turned back to the living room.

With no one in it and no noise or voices stirring, it looked bare. The morning's *Times* lay folded on one end of the sofa, and bunched on the seat of the easy chair in the window corner were three or four pairs of silk stockings rolled up in balls. Helen's wooden workbasket, that was shaped like a Shaker cradle and that she'd had for God knows how many years—long before she'd had him, anyway—was standing on the floor beside the chair. He picked up one of the stocking balls and looked at it. It was rolled so that all you saw was the hem, doubled back in a kind of bag in which the rest of the stocking lay bunched, and the top of the bag was loose and wrinkly; he couldn't help thinking how humdrum and unattractive the thing looked compared to the way a stocking looked on a woman's leg.

If Helen ever really left, he thought, it wouldn't be without her workbasket. He tossed the ball back onto the chair, aiming for the others in the group and overshooting a little. He went to the hall and, taking off his overcoat and hat, hung them in the closet, then walked into the kitchen, picking up the parcel and unwrapping it as he went. It contained two bottles of rye. He opened one, got some ice from the refrigerator and the bottle of Italian vermouth from the liquor shelf, and mixed himself a Manhattan. Then he went into the living room and, pushing the stockings to one side, sat down in the easy chair. He had hardly settled himself there before he heard the scrape of a key in the lock. It was Helen and Jamie; he could hear Jamie's high, excited voice saying something and Helen replying, laughing, as she opened the door. Then they both came in.

They came in in a kind of tangle, Helen pulling at Jamie's toboggan cap and he squealing and trying to get past her, and at first they didn't notice the man in the chair. Then he said, "Well, what ho!" and they both turned around.

"Oh, look, Mummy, look! Daddy's home!" Jamie shouted, and ran over to him. He was about five, with his mother's pale skin and bright-blue eyes, and he was holding something small and red in his hand and waving it. "Daddy, look!" he said, but the man didn't pay much attention. He put his hand on the boy's head and rubbed it absently. He was looking at Helen. "Sure, kiddo," he said. "Sure, sure."

Helen hadn't moved. "Jamie!" she said sharply, and stopped, and then for a second she didn't say anything. She had on her black caracul jacket and the little black matching fur hat, and her cheeks were flushed and fresh-looking from the cold air outside. She wasn't laughing now. Her face had gone set and expressionless, and after that first quick glance of surprise she hadn't really looked at him at all. "Well," she said finally. "You're home early."

He took a sip from his glass, his eyes watching her over the rim. "You don't seem too pleased," he said.

"About what?"

Jamie was leaning over the side of the chair, pulling at his father's sleeve. "Daddy, look," he kept saying. Jim stiffened his arm and held him away. "Just a minute, kid. Don't spill my drink now," he said. "About my being home, of course."

"Should I be?" she said coolly. She hung her things in the closet and shut the door. "Jamie. Better take off your snow suit now. Before you get hot."

"But Daddy hasn't looked yet."

Helen sighed. "It's that little dump truck he lost the other day in the Park. Another boy found it and gave it to him. You might look at it."

Jim looked at it and then at the boy. Jamie was staring up at him with that clear, intent gaze a child's eyes can assume. "It was Stevie Albright that found it," he explained. He had captured his father's attention at last and he didn't want to relinquish it, but he felt the pull of his mother's command, too, and it made him talk faster and faster, his eyes wide and his voice excited. "He found it in the sand pile where I losted it and he took it home and his mummy told him it was mine, so he brought it right back and he gave it to me. Today."

"Well, well," the man said.

Helen was standing by the couch. "Jamie. Come," she said.

This time he obeyed. He went over to the couch and climbed on it, dangling his legs so she could pull off his galoshes. "It was Stevie Albright, Mummy," he repeated.

"I know," she said. He sat fingering the loose stuff of her dress at the shoulder and looking past her at his father. "Wasn't Stevie nice to find my truck for me, Daddy?" he demanded.

"He sure was, kid."

"I'll have to give *him* something next time, I guess."

"I suppose you will." The man got up and walked over to where Helen was kneeling in front of the couch. She didn't look around. "I got some rye," he said. "Would you like a drink?"

"Not just now, thanks."

He stood looking down at her. "You still sore about last night?" he asked.

"How did you think I would feel?"

A sort of stubborn look came over his face, but he kept his voice even. "Because that's why I came home. I thought maybe the way we were talking last night—I mean I got to thinking about it. I really do feel lousy about the whole business, Helen. I wanted you to know that."

"Look," she said. "Let's just not talk now, shall we? While someone's here?"

Jim glanced at Jamie, and Jamie smiled. But his father's glance went right back to his mother's head again. His mother had her head bent down. "I just wanted to say I was sorry, that's all," his father said. "There's no harm in anyone hearing that."

"I suppose not. There's no harm in anyone hearing anything, I guess."

Suddenly his father's face got dark red. "Well, you'd rather hear about things like that than not be told anything, wouldn't you?" he demanded. "God almighty! That's what we always agreed on anyway, isn't it? And then when I do tell you—"

"Please, for God's *sake!*" she cut in, "I said not *talk* about it." She pulled off Jamie's ski pants and then gave him a pat as he slid off the couch. "Jamie, run into your room and play there, will you?" she said. Then she turned to face his father. "And it's not what *I* hear that bothers me," she went on. Her face had got white and her lips tight. "It's what everybody else will hear. If you'd done it with some stranger, some woman you were never going to see again. But doing it with a woman we both know, and in such a way—so you'd disgrace me and her and everybody, as well as yourself. No. This time it's really too much. This is really the end."

Jamie stood watching them both. He could tell by his father's expression that he was really angry, and though he couldn't see his mother's face now, he could tell by her voice that something was wrong with her too; her voice was so high and uneven that it sounded almost as if she were crying, and at the thought of that, though he had no idea what could be troubling her, such a feeling of insecurity and dread went through him that for a moment he wanted to cry too. "Mummy," he started to say, but as soon as he spoke she turned on him, and he saw at least that she wasn't crying; her eyes were bright and hard. "Jamie," she said, in a strange, tense voice that he'd never heard her use before, "I told you to go into your room." His father didn't say anything; he just turned abruptly away and walked over to look out the window.

"Can I take my truck too?" Jamie said.

"Yes, of course you can," she said, and gave him a little push toward the door. As Jamie walked away he heard his father start back toward his mother. "Now, listen," his father said, but then they both went into the other bedroom, and when they got there they shut the door. He could still hear them talking, but he couldn't make out the words, and anyway he was forgetting about all that now; there was so much here that was interesting. He liked his room and everything in it, and the way things were scattered around represented no disorder to his mind; if you wanted something you picked it up, and if you tired of it you put it down, and if they all got mixed up, as they did in the box in the corner, it only meant more surprises later when you started digging among them. In that way every toy was almost a new toy every time you found it.

But now he wanted to do something with the dump truck, and after he had looked around for a moment he went over to the play table and pushed the shirt boards off onto the floor. This made the table a clean, level place where anything might happen, and he began pushing the dump truck tentatively around its edge. Gradually ideas occurred to him. It was a policeman's car that he was driving down a street past a great many stores, and at each store he had to stop and back the car into the curb and park it and buy things and load them in and then drive away again. There was a long scratch that had been made in the table top once long ago. Where it crossed the street it became a river, and that made it the river they had all crossed in the ferry, his mother and father and he, and he sitting on his mother's lap because the back was all loaded down with suitcases and bundles.

That was when they had gone to the beach last summer. He drove on and when he reached the beach the car became a dump truck again, because a dump truck goes where they have a lot of sand. He raised his head suddenly. He was wondering why it was that, all through last summer, he had never once seen a dump truck coming to the beach for sand, and he almost started into the other room to ask someone, his mother or his father, why that was.

But just as he was almost going to do so, the door of their bedroom slammed and his father walked rapidly across the living room, and then he heard him yank at the clothes closet and the outer door slammed too. He sat for a moment, thinking. It had struck him that maybe the trucks only came to the beach at night, when no people were there, and in that case he'd have to have headlights and this truck didn't have any headlights. But then he began to forget about the sand problem and he went back to pushing the toy around again. It could just as well not be the beach at all. It could be that place up the street where they had torn the building down and all the steam shovels were working. There were plenty of trucks around there.

ARE WE LEAVING TOMORROW?

❧

JOHN O'HARA

IT WAS COOL, quite cool, the way the weather is likely to be at an in-between resort when the Florida season is over but the Northern summer season has not yet begun. Every morning the tall young man and his young wife would come down the steps of the porch and go for their walk. They would go to the mounting block where the riders would start for the trails. The tall young man and his wife would stand not too close to the block, not speaking to anyone; just watching. But there might have been a little in his attitude, in his manner, of a man who felt that he was starting the riders, as though his presence there made their start official. He would stand there, hatless and tanned, chin down almost to his chest, his hands dug deep in the pockets of his handsome tweed topcoat. His wife would stand beside him with her arm in his, and when she would speak to him she would put her face in front of him and look up. Almost always his answer would be a smile and a nod, or perhaps a single word that expressed all he wanted to put into words. They would watch the riders for a while, and then they would stroll over to the first tee of the men's golf course to watch the golfers start off. There it would be the same: not much talk, and the slightly superior manner or attitude. After they had watched their quota of golfers they would go back to the porch and she would go up to their rooms and a Negro bellboy would bring him his papers, the Montreal *Star* and the New York *Times*. He would sit there lazily looking at the papers, never so interested in a news item that he would not look up at every person who came in or went out of the hotel, or passed his chair on the porch. He watched every car come up the short, winding drive, watched the people get in and out, watched the car drive away;

then when there was no human activity he would return to his paper, holding it rather far away, and on his face and in his eyes behind the gold-rimmed spectacles there was always the same suspicion of a smile.

He would go to his room before lunch, and they would come down together. After lunch, like most everyone else, they would retire, apparently for a nap, not to appear until the cocktail hour. They would be the first, usually, in the small, cheery bar, and until it was time to change for dinner he would have a highball glass, constantly refilled, in his hand. He drank slowly, sipping teaspoonfuls at a time. In that time she might drink two light highballs while he was drinking eight. She always seemed to have one of the magazines of large format in her lap, but at these times it was she who would look up, while he hardly turned his head.

Not long after they came she began to speak to people; to bow and pass the time of day. She was a pleasant, friendly little woman, not yet thirty. Her eyes were too pretty for the rest of her face; in sleep she must have been very plain indeed, and her skin was sensitive to the sun. She had good bones—lovely hands and feet—and when she was in sweater and skirt her figure always got a second look from the golfers and riders.

Their name was Campbell—Douglas Campbell, and Sheila. They were the youngest people over fifteen in the hotel. There were a few children, but most of the guests were forty or thereabouts. One afternoon the Campbells were in the bar and a woman came in and after hesitating at the entrance she said, "Good afternoon, Mrs. Campbell. You didn't happen to see my husband?"

"No, I didn't," said Mrs. Campbell.

The woman came closer slowly and put her hand on the back of a chair near them. "I was afraid I'd missed him," she said to no one; then suddenly she said, "Do you mind if I sit with you while he comes?"

"No, not at all," said Mrs. Campbell.

"Please do," said Campbell. He got to his feet and stood very erect. He set his glass on the little table and put his hands behind his back.

"I'm sorry I don't remember your name," said Mrs. Campbell.

"Mrs. Loomis."

Mrs. Campbell introduced her husband, who said, "Wouldn't you like a cocktail meanwhile?"

Mrs. Loomis thought a moment and said she would—a dry Daiquiri. Then Campbell sat down, picking up his drink and beginning to sip.

"I think we were the first here, as usual," said Mrs. Campbell, "so we couldn't have missed Mr. Loomis."

"Oh, it's all right. One of us is always late, but it isn't important. That's why I like it here. The general air of informality." She smiled. "I've never seen you here before. Is this your first year?"

"Our first year," said Mrs. Campbell.

"From New York?"

"Montreal," said Mrs. Campbell.

"Oh, Canadians. I met some awfully nice Canadians in Palm Beach this winter," said Mrs. Loomis. She named them off, and Mrs. Campbell said they knew them, and he smiled and nodded. Then Mrs. Loomis tried to remember the names of some other people she knew in Montreal (they turned out to have been Toronto people), and Mr. Loomis arrived.

A white-haired man, a trifle heavy and about fifty, Mr. Loomis wore young men's clothes. He was brown and heavy-lidded. He had good manners. It was he who corrected his wife about the people from Montreal who actually were from Toronto. That was the first time the Loomises and the Campbells had done more than speak in passing, and Mrs. Campbell was almost gay that afternoon.

The Campbells did not come down to dinner that evening, but they were out for their stroll the next morning. Mr. Loomis waved to them at the first tee, and they waved—*she* waved, Campbell nodded. They did not appear for cocktails that afternoon. For the next few days they took their stroll, but they had their meals in their room. The next time they came to the cocktail lounge they took a small table at the side of the bar, where there was room only for the table and two chairs. No one spoke to them, but that night was one of the nights when the hotel showed movies in the ballroom, and after the movie the Loomises fell in with them and insisted on buying them a drink, just a nightcap. That was the way it was.

Mr. Loomis brought out his cigar case and offered Mr. Campbell a cigar, which was declined, and gave the orders for drinks, "Scotch, Scotch, Scotch, and a Cuba Libre." Mrs. Loomis was having the Cuba Libre. As the waiter took the order Mr. Campbell said, "And bring the bottle."

There was a fraction of a second's incredulity in Mr. Loomis's face; incredulity, or more likely doubt that he had heard his own ears. But he said, "Yes, bring the bottle." Then they talked about the picture. It had been a terrible picture, they all agreed. The Loomises said it was too bad, too, because they had crossed with the star two years ago and she had seemed awfully nice, not at all what you'd expect a movie star to be like. They all agreed that the Mickey Mouse was good, although Mr. Loomis said he was getting a little tired of Mickey Mouse. Their drinks came, and Mrs. Loomis was somewhat apologetic about her drink, but ever since she had been in Cuba she'd developed a taste for rum, always rum. "And before that, gin," said Mr. Loomis. Mr. Campbell's glass was empty and he called the waiter to bring some more ice and another Cuba Libre, and he replenished the highball glasses from the bottle of Scotch on the table.

"Now this was my idea," said Mr. Loomis.

"Only the first one," said Mr. Campbell. They let it go at that, and the ladies returned to the subject of the star of the picture, and soon Mr. Loomis joined in. They got all mixed up in the star's matrimonial record, which inevitably brought up the names of other movie stars and *their* matrimonial records. Mr. and Mrs. Loomis provided the statistics, and Mrs. Campbell would say yes or no as the statement or opinion required. Mr. Campbell sipped his drink wordlessly until the Loomises, who had been married a long time, became simultaneously aware of Mr. Campbell's silence, and they began directing their remarks at him. The Loomises were not satisfied with Mrs. Campbell's ready assents. They would address the first few words of a remark to the young wife, because she had been such a polite listener, but then they would turn to Mr. Campbell and most of what they had to say was said to him.

For a while he would smile and murmur "Mm-hmm," more or less into his glass. Then it seemed after a few minutes that he could hardly wait for them to end an item or an anecdote. He began to nod before it was time to nod, and he would keep nodding, and he would say, "Yes, yes, yes," very rapidly. Presently, in the middle of an anecdote, his eyes, which had been growing brighter, became very bright. He put down his drink and leaned forward, one hand clasping and unclasping the other. "And—yes—and— yes," he kept saying, until Mrs. Loomis had finished her story. Then he leaned farther forward and stared at Mrs. Loomis, with that bright smile and with his breathing become short and fast.

"Can I tell you a story?" he said.

Mrs. Loomis beamed. "Why, of course."

Then Campbell told a story. It had in it a priest, female anatomy, improbable situations, a cuckold, unprintable words, and no point.

Long before Campbell finished his story Loomis was frowning, glancing at his wife and at Campbell's wife, seeming to listen to Campbell but always glancing at the two women. Mrs. Loomis could not look away; Campbell was telling her the story, and he looked at no one else. While Mrs. Campbell, the moment the story was begun, picked up her drink, took a sip, and put the glass on the table and kept her eyes on it until Campbell signalled by his chuckling that the story was at an end.

He kept chuckling and looking at Mrs. Loomis after he had finished, and then he smiled at Loomis. "Huh" came from Loomis, and on his face a muscular smile. "Well, dear," he said. "Think it's about time—"

"Yes," said Mrs. Loomis. "Thank you so much. Good night, Mrs. Campbell, and good night." Campbell stood up, erect, bowing.

When they were entirely out of the room he sat down and crossed his legs. He lit a cigarette and resumed his drinking and stared at the opposite wall. She watched him. His eyes did not even move when he raised his glass to his mouth.

"Oh," she said suddenly. "I wonder if the man is still there at the travel desk. I forgot all about the tickets for tomorrow."

"Tomorrow? Are we leaving tomorrow?"

"Yes."

He stood up and pulled the table out of her way, and when she had left he sat down to wait for her.

THE GETAWAY

❦

DOROTHY THOMAS

WHEN THE KITCHEN DOOR slammed to after her little daugh-
ters, Mrs. Clint Riggs wiped the children's kisses from her
mouth with a plump wrist and dropped into a chair to gulp a last
mouthful of coffee. "Gosh, I gotta hustle!" she said aloud, and
began noisily shoving the four chairs back from the kitchen table
against the walls. The table was a mess, but it could stay so. She
stuffed her apron, the dish towel, and little Evelyn's bib into the
large paper carton, in the kitchen corner, that served as a clothes
hamper.

She pulled her dress off over her head and in her slip, which was
split and frayed at the seams, went to the sink, took a washcloth
from its nail over the faucet, and rapidly washed the front of her
face, her neck, and her armpits. She took her husband's soap-
spattered mirror from its hook, shined it quickly against her thigh,
and rested it on the window ledge. Then she scrutinized her face,
stretching her thick neck to one side and the other. All her
make-up necessities were handy, lined up along the upper sashes
of the two kitchen windows. First she smeared her face with pink
cream, rubbing it in well with the heel of her hand and wiping it
off with the family towel. When she had powdered, she reached
down a bottle of toilet water and poured a good teaspoonful of the
liquid into the crack at the top of her brassière. Her hair at the
part, she discovered, was a darker yellow than the rest. She spatted
her grayed powder puff along it to even the color. She was remak-
ing her mouth, shaping a more definite Cupid's bow, when someone knocked at the door. She caught up her dress and draped it
around her across her bosom before she called "Come in!"

"Gosh, Myrtle, you scared me," she said when she saw it was a

431

friend who worked as a waitress in the Odeon Café. Her greeting was good-natured but not exactly cordial.

"You going downtown?" the visitor asked. "See you got your good shoes on. Well, hurry, kid, and I'll wait for you. You'll have to step on it, though. I got to get down there. Tony'll kill me; this is the third day I been late since he tried to fire me that time."

Mrs. Clint Riggs reached for her cup and took another swallow of cold coffee. "Let him wait!" she said, with a flap of her free hand. "Whata you care? Who's *he*? Whata you wanta take all you do off that old greaser for anyway? Myrt, why don't you get out? Why don't you tell him where to head in, and get out?"

Myrtle laughed shortly. "Ya," she said, "and then what? It ain't so bad." She looked around at the disorderly kitchen. "It's a nice café."

"Myrt, you want me to tell you something?" Mrs. Riggs leaned forward to ask the question. "Well, I'm getting out!"

"You! Why, where you goin', Gladys? What you gonna do? You goin' off with somebody?"

"Yep! I'm drivin' to Kansas City!"

"You goin' with that guy, that guy you was out to Firefly Inn with?"

"That's him!"

"Gee, Gladys, he's swell!"

"Yep," Gladys said, "he's class, that's what he is. Did you see his car, Myrt?"

"You leaving Clint?"

"You bet I am."

"Well, what about the kids? What about the little girls?"

"Clint can find someone to look after 'em, he thinks he's so darn smart. He says I don't know how to raise kids! He can see how good *he* is at it, the big cheese! Myrt, you'll excuse me, won't you? I gotta hurry. Wanta see my hat? I got a new hat."

"Clint's outa town, ain't he?"

"Ya, he's with the truck, but he'll get in tonight. Neighbor'll look after the little girls till he gets here. Junior'll fix 'em a piece if they get hungry. Junior—that kid'll look after himself!"

Myrtle got to her feet to go. "Well, I sure wish you luck," she said.

"Here, wait a minute, I want you to see my hat!" Mrs. Riggs said, and ran into her bedroom and snatched the hat from its paper sack on the dresser. Before the shaving mirror she put it on her head and turned, smiling, for her friend's approval. " 'Course you can't tell so much about it," she said, " 'thout a dress on, but don't you like it?"

"I sure do," Myrtle answered. "You got the shape to wear a big hat like that, kid. You got the class, too. I like a big hat, but you know I can't wear 'em. I look just like a toadstool in 'em. Listen, I gotta get down there. Tony'll fire me again. I sure wish you luck!"

"You keep this under your hat till tomorrow, anyhow," Mrs. Riggs said.

"Sure," Myrtle said. "Won't let out a peep. Goodbye. I'm a good half-hour late now. Tony'll kill me!"

When her friend's run-over heels had taken her down the back steps, Gladys ran into her bedroom, yanked a dusty suitcase from under the bed, tossed it onto the rumpled covers, and began to throw into it pink panties and gowns from the dresser drawers. Then she opened the closet door and felt in the semi-darkness for her plum-colored satin dress. Her hand touched something she thought at first was her husband's other pair of Union-alls, and when it moved under her fingers she screamed and staggered back. "Junior," she yelled, "you come outa there! What you doin', hiding in there? What you mean, playing hooky? Why ain't you up at school?"

The boy came stumblingly out of the closet, freeing his feet, as he came, from the clinging folds of the plum-colored satin dress.

"I'm going with you!" he said.

"You *are* not!" his mother said. "Where'd you get that notion? I ain't going anywhere. Mamma's not going anywhere, Junior! Junior, look what you're doing! Look what you done to my good dress!" She snatched the dress from the floor and held it out to see that it wasn't torn, and shook it. "You got it all so wrinkled it ain't hardly fit to wear!"

"I'm going with you," the boy said again. "I'm going to Kansas City!"

"Kansas City!" his mother cried. "Listen, Junior, Mamma's not going to Kansas City! Who told you such a thing? Junior, you get on to school!"

"You said you were," Junior said stoutly. "I heard you! I heard you and him, last night. I was right there by the car. I heard every word you said! I'm goin' along!"

His mother set her arms akimbo, her red-nailed hands on her hips, and looked at him from under the brim of her hat. She sighed, and her bosom heaved under the worn satin of her slip. "Junior," she said, "now listen to Mamma! Whata you wanta go for? Kansas City ain't any fun. Listen, you skin on up to school and Mamma'll give you fifty cents."

The boy shook his carroty head.

"A dollar!"

"No, I'm going along!"

"Two dollars, Junior!"

"I'm going!"

"Junior, you can't act like this! Don't you know it's almost time for the last bell? Now, you get on to school!"

"No!"

"Now, Junior, you're spoiling Mamma's trip! I'm just driving down there with a friend and I'll be back. I'll be right back! *Three* dollars, Junior—Mamma hasn't got but three dollars!"

"I'm going with you!"

Mrs. Riggs heard, and knew by the way her son turned his head and narrowed his eyes that he had heard, too, the sound of car wheels on the gravel beside the house. She came close and put her hands on her boy's shoulders. "Junior," she said almost tearfully, "I'll send you a bicycle!"

He shook his head and tried to back away from her. "With a horn, and lights, and everything!" she pleaded.

"I'm going with you!"

With a quick shove she sent him sprawling into the closet, leaped to shove the door to, and slipped the latch into its catch.

"There!" she puffed. "Now, Junior, you quit that pushing! It won't do you any good! The girls will let you out when they come home at noon. You fix 'em something to eat. You can open a can of sardines."

While he kicked and lunged at the door, she got into the rumpled purple dress and pulled on a pair of white gloves. "Gosh, I wish I'd have time to press this," she said, smoothing it over bust and hips with her hands. "It's a sight! Junior, you quit that kickin', now! You make me so jumpy I can't hurry!"

She snapped the suitcase shut and ran out through the kitchen with it.

"Hi!" the man in the car said. "Girlie, you had me scared here for a minute. I thought you mighta got cold feet." He leaned to swing open the car door for her.

"Hi!" Mrs. Riggs panted. "I had to hurry so, I don't know whether I'm all together and here or not. Will my suitcase sit up here, backa the seat? Oh gosh! I forgot my purse. I'll be just a minute!"

"Here's your purse, Mamma," Junior said at her elbow.

"Why, Junior, how'd you get—" His mother stopped abruptly. The latch on the closet door must have been weaker than she thought. "Junior, why ain't you at school?" she continued more calmly, and got into the car. "Junior, you get along now, you get along now to school! You'll be late!"

"Well, hello," the man said in surprise. "Who's this?"

"It—it's my boy. It's Junior," Gladys answered. "Run on now, Junior. Go on! Mamma'll bring—"

Junior climbed into the car, squeezing in between his mother and the driver. "I'll sit in the middle!" he cried triumphantly, and grinned up at the man with a missing-tooth grin. "I always ride in the middle in the truck."

"Well, see here, let's get this straight," the man said. "You didn't say you had a kid. You didn't—"

"I'm the oldest. I'm nine," Junior told him before his mother could speak, "and Lola Belle's next, and Evelyn's the baby. She's in first grade."

"Well, say!" the man said.

"Oh," Gladys said, "he's just actin' up, Junior is. . . . Junior, get out now. . . . I can explain it to you. I was gonna tell you last night, and we got talkin' about something else, and I forgot, I guess. Say, the neighbors are lookin' out the windows! Wouldn't you—won't you please just drive on out this street, out on the highway, outa town, out by the camp grounds, and I'll explain? Won't you just—"

"O.K.," the man said, with a glance toward the slightly lifted window curtain of the house on the right. "O.K., but is he—is this kid going along?"

"No, I should say not," Gladys said, "but he's got a notion he wants to go, and I got to get it through his head he ain't goin' to. Junior, you're going to get *out* when we get up here to Center Street and run on over to school. I'll write you an excuse when —when I get back. Mamma'll—"

"I'm goin' along," Junior said. "Ain't I? Can't I, Mister?"

"Junior, Mamma'll be back! She's just driving down to Kansas City with this gentleman to do a little shopping. I'll bring you . . . Turn here, and go out this way, out by the camp grounds, will you, please, and then we can cut over to the highway from there. . . . Junior, you got to mind Mamma now. I'll tell your—Junior, you're actin' awful!"

"How far is it? How far is it to Kansas City?" Junior asked, looking up at the man and ignoring his mother.

"Well, say," the man said, "what *is* this? I sure want you to go, girlie, but I don't think we oughta take this kid. Don't you know they could get us for that? They could make trouble for us. Don't you know that?"

"Dad won't care!" Junior said. "I go with him in the truck sometimes."

"Is this the camp grounds, up here ahead?" the man asked. "I don't see any cabins. Can't you do anything with this kid?" He turned to Junior. "See here, Captain, I'll give you a dollar!"

"It's not a cabin camp," Gladys explained. "It's a camp-meeting camp, where they have camp meetings. It's not used but in middle of the summer. If you'll just stop here, I'll talk to Junior."

"O.K.," the man said, and turned from the pavement onto the dirt lane that led up to the weathered pavilion.

"Junior," Gladys said, "you get out now. You get out and let Mamma talk to you a minute. Mamma wants to tell you something."

"No," Junior said.

"Come on," his mother urged. "Junior, you can stand by the road and thumb you a ride in easy. You don't have to go to school. You can go home and play jacks, 'n' listen to the radio, or just whatever you want till noon. There's some gum up in the kitchen cupboard in a teacup, Junior—two sticks!"

"I'm goin' with you 'n' him," Junior said.

Mrs. Riggs got out of the car. "Come on," she pleaded desperately. "Come on, Junior, come over here to the bench an' let Mamma talk to you!"

She took hold of his shoulders and pulled with all her might, but Junior grabbed the steering wheel and held on. "Please," she said to the man, smiling at him, a quick smile, from under the hat, "if you'll just take Junior's hands off'n the wheel and give him a little push, will you?"

"Sorry, Captain," the man said to Junior, and loosened Junior's hands.

The boy's hands let go so suddenly that Mrs. Riggs sat down on the ground, Junior clasped to her bosom. "Junior," she panted when she could get her breath, "listen to Mother! I'll bring you—"

"Look't, look't!" Junior yelled. "He's going! He's getting away!"

Mrs. Riggs struggled to her feet and stood waveringly, her high heels digging deep into the damp, leafy loam. "Maybe he's just turning round," she said. "Maybe—"

"Naw, he's headin' for the other gate," Junior said.

"Well, what a lowdown, lousy, mean trick!" Gladys cried. "Junior, now look what you did!" She stuck out her lip and swung her hand to box Junior on the ear. The boy dodged. She walked to the nearest bench and sat down. "Junior, how far out are we?" she asked. "How far is it to home?"

"I don't know," Junior answered. " 'Bout two miles, maybe two and a quarter." He came and sat down beside his mother.

"Well, however am I gonna walk in these shoes?" Mrs. Riggs asked. "I can't, that's all. They're killin' me now."

"Take 'em off," Junior suggested.

He looked ruefully after the disappearing car and leaned to pull a blade of grass and put it between his teeth. His mother took off one of her pumps and then the other. "Gosh, that's a relief!" she said. Then, "Ain't that the lowdowndest trick you ever heard of? Junior, what's that? What's that weed over there?"

"Huh?" Junior asked.

"That weed?" his mother said, pointing with her gloved hand. "Ain't that a greenweed, Junior? It is, sure as anything! That's a dandelion, for biled greens. My, and look what a lot there is of 'em! If I had anything to pick 'em in, I'd pick a mess for supper. They're so good!"

"You could pick 'em in your jacket," Junior suggested.

"This ain't a jacket, honey," Mrs. Riggs told him. "It looks like a jacket, but it ain't. It's part of my dress."

"Well, you could pick 'em in your hat then."

Mrs. Riggs took the hat from her head and turned it upside down on her lap. "Why, so I could," she said. "You got a head on you, Junior! We'll fill it up and then we'll get out to the road and thumb a ride in. There's trucks—there's trucks'll pick up Mrs. Clint Riggs and son! Your father's a good truck-driver, Junior, and is known by all of 'em. Yes sir, we'll pick 'em in my hat, a good big mess of 'em, and we'll have 'em biled for supper, with salt pork. Your dad's crazy about 'em."

INDEX